cett

was born and brought up in Preston, Lancashire and lived for several years in the Lake District. Married to a pharmaceutical scientist, she has three grown up children. She now lives in Barnard Castle, a small market town in the North Pennines, with her husband, daughter, dog and cat.

SCEPTRE

Patricia Fawcett

Set to Music

PATRICIA FAWCETT

SCEPTRE

Copyright © 1996 by Patricia Fawcett

First published in 1996 by Hodder and Stoughton
A division of Hodder Headline PLC
A Sceptre Paperback

The right of Patricia Fawcett to be identified as the Author of
the Work has been asserted by her in accordance with the
Copyright, Designs and Patents Act 1988.

10 9 8 7 6 5 4 3 2 1

All rights reserved. No part of this publication may be
reproduced, stored in a retrieval system or transmitted,
in any form or by any means without the prior written
permission of the publisher, nor be otherwise circulated
in any form of binding or cover other than that in which
it is published and without a similar condition being
imposed on the subsequent purchaser.

All characters in this publication are fictitious and any
resemblance to real persons, living or dead, is purely coincidental.

A CIP Catalogue record for this book is available
from the British Library.

ISBN 0-340-65804-5

Typeset by Hewer Text Composition Services, Edinburgh
Printed and bound in Great Britain by
Cox & Wyman Ltd, Reading, Berkshire

Hodder and Stoughton
A division of Hodder Headline PLC
338 Euston Road
London NW1 3BH

For my husband Ken

1

Barbara checked her watch as she left the house, knowing that, providing nothing unexpected happened, she would arrive at Bettys at precisely ten o'clock for her rendezvous with Meg.

Mixed emotions. Morning coffee, afternoon tea or whatever at Bettys Café was a joy but Meg herself was a damned nuisance, an acquaintance of long standing who had not yet and probably never would achieve the status of friend. However, Barbara had been avoiding her lately and this was an attempt to smooth things over.

She had slept badly and was feeling the effects. Fortunately Guy would sleep through an earthquake and her small-scale tossing and turning had not disturbed him in the slightest. She looked wretched when she looked at herself first thing but some careful make-up and the new pale green suit had worked wonders. At forty five, you couldn't afford to lose too much sleep.

She felt better for being in the fresh air and, although it was still cool, it was a touch warmer than of late. Spring was having a hard time getting itself together after a desperately long winter but there were signs of hope. Glad that she had chosen to wear a cashmere sweater under the jacket, Barbara walked briskly through Valley Gardens into town. She adored Harrogate. It was home and never for a second had they considered leaving it. Guy's business, the Shawcross empire as his mother would have you believe, was well and truly anchored here and they had a beautiful grand house almost in the heart of the town. Barbara had her own car, complete control of the purse strings, and was perfectly content. Well . . . almost.

She emerged from the gardens and started purposefully up Royal Parade. She really ought to pop into one or more of the antique shops as she and Guy were on the look-out for a particular desk but she could not divert just now. After coffee, when her conscience was soothed, she could indulge in shopping.

She was nearly there. Montpellier Hill was steep and she slowed deliberately, pausing to look in some of the more exclusive shops, not wanting to arrive pale and puffed out. Meg would notice. Meg noticed everything.

Bettys occupied a corner site and had to be one of her favourite cafés. It did not seem to change or, if it did, it did so with great care and consideration for its customers. To take tea here was an experience and she and Meg had experienced it often. Meg was waiting at the door, just arrived she said, exchanging a polite kiss with Barbara. "Are you all right?" she enquired, "You look peaky."

"I'm fine." Barbara smiled, noticing with amusement the glance Meg gave her suit. Meg was in black and orange like a bee. A queen bee of course.

"And Guy? How is he?" Meg beamed, not waiting for a reply, "And Daisy? Such a sweet girl."

"They're fine too," Barbara murmured. Sooner or later, she would have to break the news about Daisy.

Coffee and a cinnamon muffin for her and for Meg, tea and toast. They ate, chatted, or rather Meg did, about this and that. Barbara let it wash over her, absorbed in her own thoughts, wondering how soon she could decently ditch Meg. She did not want Meg taking over in antique shops.

There was a flurry of people leaving and a couple were being shown to a nearby table. Idly, Barbara watched, taking immediate stock of them. Twenties. Handsome couple in fact. As she often did, she found her professional eye taking over, wondering what they would be like on the dance floor. He would no doubt be a moderate dancer, maybe even a good one, but alas his partner . . . she was pretty, yes, but there was something about the way she moved. Something that told Barbara the poor child would be hopelessly uncoordinated. She had no rhythm, not a single ounce.

*   *   *

The girl had no rhythm, not a single ounce. After three lessons it was still like leading a lump of lead round the floor and she had no memory for the steps. However, she did have blonde hair and interesting green eyes and that almost made up for it.

"You're improving," David told her as he led her to the little table at the side where coffee was waiting. "You need to relax more though. Why are you so tense?"

"Am I tense?" she asked, with a shy glance his way. "I can't think why."

David could. He smiled as he lit an after-dance cigarette, taking in the splendour of the ballroom. The venue was partly the reason for her nervousness for after all the Tower Ballroom, Blackpool, had some reputation and she was naturally a touch overwhelmed by it. The other reason was him. She was nervous of him probably because she couldn't quite trust herself with him, and on the dancing front . . . well, he was something of a local celebrity . . .

For a girl who looked like she did, she was remarkably innocent, unless that was a ruse. He hadn't worked that one out yet and he had learned from bitter experience, from many years of charming the ladies, that you did not make a move until you got the green light.

He smiled again. "Tell me, how did you learn about me?" he asked, putting on his interested look. "About the dancing?"

"Oh . . . from someone at the Club, your Club," she said, returning his smile. She was pleasantly flushed after her exertions, the green eyes clear and bright. "They said you were a terrific dancer and that you occasionally did private lessons. I'm very impressed," she added, "All those trophies! I've seen those pictures of you and your wife. The Latin American ones."

"That's not my wife," he said sharply, wondering if she knew about Ruth. Probably not. Some things he kept quiet. He inhaled, not giving out any other information. It was none of her business.

"Would you teach me some Latin American dances?" she asked. "Once I've mastered the waltz."

He smiled at that. Who did she think he was? A miracle worker? She'd never master the waltz let alone them. You needed a helluva lot of rhythm for dances like the samba and the rumba, more rhythm than she'd ever have. "Of course I'll teach you." He let his hand drift across the table, trying to gauge her reaction. "Are you doing anything this evening?" he said abruptly, stubbing out his cigarette as the impulse hit him. "We could have a meal. I know this very discreet restaurant."

Her lips were red and shiny, the teeth perfect. "I'm getting married in June, Mr Ambrose," she said, and to his satisfaction he detected a measure of regret in the words.

"For God's sake, call me David." He glanced up irritably as someone yelled that there was a telephone call for him. Getting married eh? So what? All he was proposing was a bit of harmless fun. "I'll be back in a minute. I'll just field this call first." He smiled at her, not leaving until he got a little smile in return. He was aware that her eyes were on him as he moved across the floor. She was interested. She fancied him. The satisfaction buzzed as he realised he could still do it. He was still attractive to women, thank God. It was simply a question of not rushing things, particularly as she . . . What the hell was her name? . . . was just a mite cautious and riddled with loyalty to her fiancé.

He picked up the phone. "David Ambrose," he barked into it, annoyed to be interrupted. "Who is this?"

"David? At last . . ." Linda's tinny little–girl voice sounded strange, stranger than usual. "I've been trying to get you everywhere. Why don't you tell people where you are? Nobody knew."

"What do you want, sweetheart? I'm in the middle of a bloody lesson."

"Oh David . . ." her voice trembled as only Linda's could. "It's Ruth."

"What about her?" He knew at once, rocking on his feet, putting out a hand to steady himself on the wall. "I told you not to go to see her."

"I didn't. I rang, David. I rang the hospital. I told them I was your sister, family you see, and then they told me. She died this morning. Ten thirty-three. They've been trying to get hold of you so I said I'd tell you. Oh God . . ." she wailed, "I should have come to see you instead of telling you like this."

He gripped the phone and heard his heart thud. Ruthie!

Expected of course. Or rather, expected soon. Next week maybe or the week after. Not just now. Not today. Not this minute. Ten thirty-three Linda had said . . . why so precise? Ruth dead.

"Are you all right, darling?" Her voice was full of concern and she was obviously trying not to cry. "I'm sorry, David. I really am. I shouldn't have broken the news like this. I should be there with you . . ."

"Shut up, Linda." He hung up and rested his head against the wall. Just for a moment until he regained control. Then he took a deep breath and walked back to where he had left the green-eyed blonde. She was gone and all that remained was a hint of her perfume.

He sat down again and lit another cigarette. Bloody Ruth. She'd always had rotten timing.

2

Guy was terribly proud of his wife. Barbara was one of those rare things, a beautiful woman, one of those women whom people stole a second glance at. Even in the Harrogate circle they moved in, crammed as it was with elegant ladies, she stood out. Well dressed, superbly groomed and with a lovely smile, she was destined to stand out. He was well aware that people did not expect him to have a wife like Barbara. He always looked for that little hidden start of surprise when he introduced her to colleagues who had not met her before. It amused him that they expected an ordinary chap like him to be married to an equally ordinary woman, someone with permed hair, tweeds and twinsets maybe, brittle-voiced, horse-riding, dog-loving, one of the county set.

His gorgeous Barbara. As lovely now as she had been at seventeen. More so in a way because now there was a lifetime of experience mirrored in those amazing eyes, the first thing he had noticed about her, after the legs of course. He had watched her, dreamed about her, so very long before that first opportunity came to dance with her. She had been the only reason he'd tagged himself onto the group she went around with. Funny sort of crowd they'd been. They'd joined in with the modern stuff, damned good at it too, but they were all hooked on ballroom dancing, just why Guy couldn't fathom, and so he'd had to follow suit. She and David Ambrose had seemed a pair on and off the dance floor. How insanely jealous he had been, irritated too that she had not seen through that chap for what he was. David was a dodgy character. Already mixed up in odd sorts of deals by the time he was twenty, it didn't augur well for the future. Guy didn't like that in a man. He liked honesty. Integrity. He'd watched David slipping fivers into fiddly hands for favours rendered, refused to hand over his own money for equally dubious purposes and just waited for the bets to fail, for David to trip himself up. As far as he knew he hadn't. Those sort either ended up in jail or big business.

He was a bit more relaxed about it now. Bit of a prude and a prune in those far-off days, jealousy probably clouding his judgement. David was no worse than any of the crowd but he was one of those sort of men who attracted the girls, despite or maybe because of the ruthless streak. Barbara had been just as easily fooled as the rest of them, smiling into his face, clinging onto his arm, and there had been damn all he could do except grit his teeth and wait for something to happen. He had continued to stick around with them despite his mother's constant irritated murmurs that they weren't good enough for him. She approved of their ballroom dancing leanings but disapproved of their pedigree. He hated that sort of snobbish thing and it made him try the harder even though he knew that some of them didn't think much of him either. You couldn't damned well win.

Already loving Barbara to distraction, unable to think straight, dreaming about her, he had been patient, biding his time, waiting. They led a pretty pigeon-holed sort of life, the gang of them. During the week, they went to the cinema once or twice, or to some local dives where they heaved and jived like the rest of them, shrieking to the great tunes of the Beatles and the Hollies and all that other mid to late-sixties stuff. Weekends unfortunately they indulged in their favourite pastime and went ballroom dancing, the whole lot of them to various venues. A pretty hopeless dancer, himself, Guy nevertheless persevered.

It was at the Tower Ballroom, Blackpool, that she and David had an argument in the middle of the dance floor. The inclination to fight his way through the crowd and punch lover boy on the nose had been very strong but instead he waited. She walked off the floor and came to stand nearby, breathing deeply, looking as if she was working hard not to cry. She was wearing a green dress, a matching broad belt pulling in her slim waist, her dark hair softly fluffed on her shoulders, and she looked absolutely

stunning as only Barbara could look stunning. He caught one or
two other males eyeing up their chances but his concentration
and determination were such that he dismissed them. For once,
he felt supremely confident as he walked up to her, smiled at
her, asked her very politely if she would care to dance as the
band struck up a new tune. He pretended he knew nothing
of the argument for, although public, it had been sizzlingly
restrained and he held her tightly as David waltzed by, not
wasting any time, little Ruth Earnshaw in his arms. That first
dance had been a waltz and he had been horribly conscious of
trying to do it right, not stand on her feet, her dancing feet. He
had hummed the tune the band were playing in an attempt to
draw attention away from their feet. In the event, he thought
he managed tolerably well, allowing for his first-time nerves,
only having to apologise a few times as his feet landed on
hers. It was just as well the floor was crowded and he could
be forgiven. Sweating, heaving bodies. As he held Barbara, she
smelt, certainly not of sweat, but of a lovely flowery fragrance
that he later discovered was called Apple Blossom. He had tried
to get it for her a couple of years ago as a little surprise, but
it was discontinued the over made-up woman on the perfume
counter told him. Did he not fancy Chanel instead? Only if
Chanel smelled of apple blossom.

Smells were memories. He smiled at the memory of that first
dance. Dearest Barbara . . . she still had the power to entrance
him. He had no need to tell her. After twenty five years, what
was the point of flowery nonsense. Barbara knew he loved her,
although, physically, things had mellowed. In fact, sexually,
Barbara was a trifle cool, not frigid, God no, but not ecstatic
either. It was just one of those things and he was damned if
it was going to bother him. He loved her and he abhorred the
idea that she should ever feel he was forcing himself on her. If
she wanted him, she let it be known by her responses to him.
Quality not quantity he reminded himself and, occasionally, it
would be just wonderful. What the hell! He was content to have
her at his side, proud to introduce her as his wife.

"It's the next on the left, Mr Shawcross. You'd be best to
indicate as you pass the petrol station. It's quite a sharp turn."

"Oh . . . thank you, Gladys." He blinked and brought his

mind back to the matter in hand, the safe delivery home of his secretary. In the seven years she'd worked for him, he had never before driven her home, in a strange way never thought about her having a life outside the office. She had to live somewhere and he was about to discover that she lived not many miles out on the Knaresborough road. She called herself Mrs Ward but he knew she was separated, perhaps divorced by now, and he also knew there were no children. It was one of the reasons he had taken her on. Women without children were more reliable, although he kept that observation very much to himself.

"Third one along with the green door," she muttered, fiddling with her seat-belt and shopping bags as he pulled to a halt. The house was a neat semi with a trim garden, wooden gate and frilly nets. As expected. Exactly as expected somehow. He switched off the engine and raced round to help her out of the passenger door. She seemed unprepared for the small courtesy, already struggling out, bags on the pavement. "Thank you very much, Mr Shawcross," she said, as he picked up a couple of the heavier looking bags. "I don't know why I get so much food. Just for me." She stood there, quite still, as he slammed the passenger door shut and offered to carry the bags up the drive for her.

"I can manage thanks." She took them from him and he turned to go. "Would you like a coffee?" she blurted out, flushed with embarrassment. "It won't take a moment and the traffic might have eased off by the time you've had it."

Guy pretended to hesitate, although the sole purpose of giving her a lift in the first place was to have the opportunity of talking to her privately out of the office, and driving through busy traffic had not given him that opportunity. Personal matters ought not to be discussed in the office, particularly the plan he was hatching. He was a touch ashamed that he should never have thought of offering her a lift before. It was not far out of his way, and he knew she didn't own a car so the number of times she must have struggled on the bus through the rain and snow of this past winter. Poor woman.

"A coffee would be lovely." He locked the car, noticed a curtain dropping at a nearby window, felt instantly guilty, before following Gladys up the path. She dumped her bags in the kitchen, returning to the hall and indicating the phone. "Please feel free to use it," she said, "Mrs Shawcross might be wondering where you are. We've already worked late and now . . ." she glanced worriedly at the clock. "Is it really that time?"

"It is. Sorry to have kept you late again but I particularly wanted to finish off the Layfield correspondence. I don't need to use the phone, thank you," he added, not bothering to explain that Barbara did not worry about him. Thankfully, she had never been one to grumble about his long working hours.

Awkward now to be in Gladys's home like this, he let her take his coat away to an unseen room at the side before she led him through to a very tidy small sitting room.

"Do sit down, Mr Shawcross." She was as embarrassed as he. It was as if they were about to embark on an illicit affair which was ridiculous, although he had to own up to a certain feeling of flattery if that had crossed her mind. She was at least fifteen years younger than he was, a large lady, as smart as her size allowed, with a liking for working suits in bright colours. She was always carefully made up and her hair was a longish reddish blonde styled in a very curly style that was popular amongst the secretarial staff at the office. Her feet seemed to be perpetually squeezed into shoes one size too small, high-heeled black shoes as often as not. If she lost some weight, she would be a very glamorous woman.

"So this is where you hide away," he called out as she busied about in the kitchen. Stupid remark. Why he should feel so nervous he had no idea. Hadn't he gone over this again and again and hadn't Gladys seemed the obvious choice? He knew her better than the other ladies in the office for one thing and he trusted her. With what he had in mind, he had to trust her, for not an inkling of this must ever get back to Barbara or it would all be spoilt. With a sigh for what was to come, he moved a cushion from behind his back and waited, looking round the little room. Rich colours, deep emerald green for the walls, dark furniture, oddly masculine, the blatantly frilly floral curtains a strange contrast. Quite unlike his own home where soft pastels soothingly dominated. A curious lack of photographs or family paraphernalia. Not so curious, of course, as she had no family as far as he knew. A collection of CDs piled beside a player, a small portable television off to one side as if she didn't sit and watch it much. A pile of what must be library books sat on a little table. How little he knew about her. Funny that. He had worked with the woman for seven years, day in and day out, and he knew nothing about her, what made her tick, what music she liked, what she did in her leisure time, nothing.

"You have a lovely home, Gladys," he found himself calling out again, wishing he could shut up. Quiet people talked when they were nervous. It was a lovely home in the context of who she was and what she earned. At once, he frowned, despising the snobbery that sometimes viciously and unexpectedly attacked him. Just because Gladys did not possess any antiques or some original paintings as he and Barbara did . . .

He hated the thought that he was, in any way, like his mother Leila but some things sneaked through, squashed in the genes. His dear mother made a life's work of being a snob, quick to point out to whoever happened to be listening who she was. Quick to mention the vast numbers of properties she owned in Harrogate. Quick to show off the miniature jewellery shop she carried round on her person. A mugger's paradise. It was a miracle that her home in Skipton had never been burgled.

Guy smiled as, a little flustered, Gladys reappeared with a tray. "Thanks." He widened his smile, not wanting her to be nervous of him. "I'll take it black," he murmured as she questioned with her eyes. Gladys, he felt sure, would be agreeable to his plan but it was asking a lot of her and he couldn't expect her to give up her free time for nothing. On the other hand, overtime payments were not suitable so he would have to think of some other way of rewarding her when it was finished. He had racked his brains to think of someone else but he had decided he couldn't possibly ask any of their friends to oblige, not a woman with whom Barbara was acquainted. Meg Fairley, for instance, would probably have agreed to it, even if he could have imagined himself asking her, but she would surely have blurted it out to Barbara, ruining everything. And, if he was honest, the thought of holding Meg in his arms was faintly chilling. There wasn't an ounce of warmth in her entire designer clad body. There would be no such problems with Gladys, plump and homely, Marks & Spencer from top to tail, and he knew she would be the soul of discretion if she were ever to come into contact with his wife.

"I do the decorating myself," she said now, proudly, sitting opposite him. "When Will walked out on me, I made a decision that it would not be the end of the world. I've seen too many women go to pieces. So . . . I completely redecorated to rid myself of anything of him and here I am. I like living alone," she added, a shade defiantly.

"I'm sure it has its advantages," he soothed. He and Gladys had never had a private conversation and he had simply picked up the odd thing about her, as she no doubt had about him. Everyone unfortunately seemed to know about Daisy. "Do you regret not having children?" he asked, aware as he said it that it was impertinent. "Sorry," he said at once. "No business of mine."

"It's all right, Mr Shawcross." She smiled softly. "I used to want children when I was younger. Not any more. It's not something that worries me too much. I don't let it. But I think you're lucky to have a daughter. Such a lovely girl, isn't she? Like her mother of course. Mrs Shawcross is so elegant." Her smile was fixed. "Model shape. Tall and slim. It makes it easier to wear clothes. I like clothes but . . ." She stopped, reached out and poured herself more coffee.

"You know about Daisy . . . the little rebellion." He sipped his coffee, giving himself time to think. He hadn't talked about it to anyone other than Barbara and his mother and it helped to talk to someone outside the family. "Damn nuisance," he went on, "She's gone off with a young man. What's the word for eloping when you don't actually bother to get married?" His smile was slight, tight, and he felt sympathy waves drifting from her. "I know things are different these days, more relaxed, but we . . . her mother and I . . . we did want her to have a wonderful wedding, something that she would always remember. I realise that her mother and I had something of a whirlwind romance . . . once we decided . . . we knew each other quite a long time just as friends." He stopped, realising he was going on a bit. "So we can't really complain about the time factor . . . she only seems to have known him a few months but . . ." he shook his head and sighed, "I always dreamed of walking her down the aisle, being very proud of her." He paused, remembering suddenly how Barbara had looked as she walked towards him on their wedding day. He gulped, embarrassed at the emotion he was in acute danger of showing.

"It's the same for all fathers. And mothers," Gladys said comfortingly. "Children can be awfully ungrateful, can't they? With a bit of luck, it'll be just a passing phase and you'll still get the chance to have the wedding." Her brown eyes were large and soft, fringed with long black lashes. A doe's eyes. "If I can help in any way . . ." she offered, a blush staining her cheeks suddenly, "You only have to ask."

It was now or never, dammit. They had reached a point they had never been at before and he had to snatch the opportunity. "There *is* something I need your help with," he said, "It's not concerned with Daisy though. It's Barbara." He clattered his cup on the tray and refused more coffee with a wave of his hand. "You're going to think me damned cheeky and I will understand if you don't feel you can do it but . . ." he took a deep breath as he caught her puzzled look, "I'm asking a favour of you, Gladys. Out of hours work so, of course, we'll have to come to some arrangement about special payment. I shall need you for a couple of evenings a week straight after a five o'clock finish. I can have you back here for about . . . say, eleven to half past. Tuesdays and Thursdays. Starting, I'm afraid, next week. Sorry it's such short notice but I've been mulling this over for too long and if I don't take the plunge, I'll never do it."

"Tuesdays and Thursdays? Of course, that's perfectly all right, although I suppose I'd better hear what the favour is first," she added with the slightest of smiles.

"Those nights okay for you then," he said with relief. He had worried that she might go to evening classes, aerobics or weight watching. "That is lucky."

"I never go out during the week, Mr Shawcross," she said, crossing her legs so that her skirt slid up to reveal a glimpse of very white lace, dark-stockinged legs and ample thighs. "What is it you have in mind?"

He told her.

It was so hard trying to keep everyone happy. All the people who mattered to her. Daisy was racked with guilt but, as she saw it, she had no choice. When you had to choose between your parents and the man you loved, there was no choice.

It was fun at first living in the little flat. Playing at houses, she supposed, with Alan.

It took her about a week to realise she couldn't possibly live in the flat as it was. The landlord had a cheek to call it a furnished flat, for he had surely bought the furniture for a song at a saleroom. Old, tatty stuff. She slipped him a few extra pounds without telling Alan and asked if he could put it in store somewhere and would he mind if she bought some of her own. He shrugged, pocketed the cash, and said it was no skin off his nose. He also eyed her up and down in a way that made her feel most uncomfortable. She said nothing about that of course to Alan. When it came to men, she was a bit of a beginner. Before Alan, all her relationships had been so innocent, little youthful flings. That was part of the problem because her parents still treated her like a child. She couldn't forget the expression on their faces when it had finally dawned that she was going to live with Alan.

She chose good quality pine furniture. Golden and solid. Alan left it to her, rather irritatingly refusing to come shopping with her, claiming he never noticed his surroundings. Despite the excitement of getting the new furniture, it only took about a further week for the novelty of cooking and cleaning to wear off too. Let's face it, she wasn't used to it. At home, she only had to keep her own room reasonably tidy which she did and the lady who came to help mother did the rest. And mother loved cooking so much that Daisy never got a look-in in the kitchen. Not that she minded that. Cooking was a chore and a bore.

A double bore now that she worked as a waitress at a hotel and was looking rich creamy food in the face for hours at a stretch. The job was hard work, paid meagre wages, and even the tips didn't make up for it. The other girls were nice enough but she knew she did not quite fit in and that they regarded her as a bit odd. And, because of Alan, she did not have time to make any real friends. Pity that. She needed a female to confide in.

Tired at the end of her shift as she was tired at the end of every shift, she loaded the shopping into her little car and drove the short distance home to Alan. The car would have to go, she decided reluctantly, as it was a luxury they could do without, although just what they would do without transport she could not imagine. As long as she could remember, she went everywhere by car. Occasionally now, conscience twingeing, her mother would make a great thing of walking into town, but not often. The little car had been a present for her eighteenth birthday and she loved it and would miss it.

Alan helped her carry the shopping upstairs. It was mostly frozen dinners from Marks & Spencer and he laughed at her as he stacked them away. "You should be buying scrag end from the butchers, darling," he said, "And making your own stock from bones."

She laughed too, taking a swipe at him with a new glossy book she had bought. "Look at this then," she said, "It tells you how to prepare simple, cheap meals from the store cupboard."

"What store cupboard?" His smile was back again, "How much did it cost? It looks pricey."

Daisy giggled, ducking and weaving as he tried to grab it from her. They ended up in an embrace and what did it matter about a silly book that had torn a sizeable hole out of the last twenty-pound note she had in her purse? The twenty pounds that was supposed to last them the rest of the week.

All the same . . . Daisy pondered on the state of their bank balance as Alan pottered about making their meal. Or to be accurate, *her* bank balance. It had seemed so much a few weeks ago but it was disappearing faster than she was earning and she had not finished improving this place yet. She had seen a lovely desk she would like and she might as well have the matching chair. What was the use of a desk without a chair? It was all very well Alan going on about economizing but she had standards that she had to keep up for her own self-esteem. As soon as she could take a pride in the flat, she would start to pull in the purse strings. It couldn't be that difficult surely.

She tried to snap out of her slightly depressed state over dinner. She could only pick at the pasta concoction he had made and at last pushed it aside with an apology.

He reached instantly for her hand and squeezed it. "You poor darling," he said softly, "You shouldn't have to work your fingers to the bone. Don't worry," he added, as her tired tears started to flow. "I'll sell some of my paintings soon."

"I know you will." She brushed the tears aside and tried to smile. She had confidence in him, even though her parents had none. What did they know about painting? "I just hate scratching around for money, Alan. I've never done it before."

"Where's your sense of adventure?" he asked. "We've got to make a go of it, Daisy. We can't go running back to them, can we?"

"No." She was sure of that. She was not going back until they were on their feet, earning money of their own. She took a deep breath and stood up, starting to stack the dishes into a neat pile. "Give me a hand . . ."

"Stop behaving like a waitress. Leave the dishes, I'll wash them up later. You need cheering up," Alan told her, gently pulling her towards him, tilting her face and kissing her.

He thought *that* solved everything. However, snuggled not too unhappily beside him later, Daisy knew of another way to cheer herself up. When mum was miserable, she went shopping. And Daisy needed some new clothes, particularly some pretty underwear. She liked pretty underwear. It was, however, quite ridiculous to waste money on that when they needed to live. A square meal had to come before a flimsy negligée.

She would ask her grandmother for a sub. Dearest gran would understand.

Barbara was in bed. She tossed her book aside as Guy came in. She hadn't been able to sleep but could not stay awake sufficiently to take in the story. He slipped his tie off, leaned over to plant a kiss on top of her hair. "Sorry I'm so late, darling," he said, "Hellish busy."

"You work too hard. How many times must I tell you?" She sighed, offering to make him a hot chocolate which he declined. He looked exhausted and the worry hit her again that he might be overdoing things, sure to end up with a coronary. "We could do with a holiday," she said thoughtfully, "Can you take some time off? We needn't do anything particularly extravagant. Heavens, Guy, you of all people should be able to fix something up. One of your cottages will do, just a short break in the country. Why don't you book one out in your name?"

"Not at the moment but we'll fix something up soon."

Barbara sighed. Damn him. "I thought we might have a dinner party next week," she said, deciding it was wise to shelve the holiday suggestion for the moment. "It's our turn. Just the six of us. The usual crowd. Tuesday if that's all right with you. There's a new recipe I want to try for the main course. Trial tomorrow evening," she added with a smile.

"Not another poison testing?" He smiled too, undressing and leaving his clothes in a neat pile. "Tuesday's a bit awkward though at the moment. Tuesdays *and* Thursdays come to that for the foreseeable future."

"Why? That's a nuisance, Guy. Tuesday's usually pretty convenient for everyone."

"The thing is . . ." he gave a sigh, "It's the building side of the business, Barbara. I don't want to bore you with technical details but we're having a lot of problems at the St Andrew's site and the architect is proving difficult. He's only in this area those two days and he's going to be tied up during the day so he's asked me to keep the evenings free so that we can meet at his hotel for discussions. A working dinner. It's so complicated it's going to take weeks to sort out. Very unusual I know and damned inconvenient for us all but it's delicate and, frankly, it's better we do it out of hours, privately. It could be worth a lot to us."

"That's very odd," she said, glancing sharply at him. What was he talking about? He never met architects out of hours except socially. He was fussing more than usual with his clothes but it wasn't just that. Something in his voice told her he was lying. And why on earth should he lie? It hit her sharply, the only possible reason. She wasn't born yesterday. The only reason men of his age lied was if they were seeing another woman.

She tried not to show her misgivings, making no further comment, as, pyjama clad, he clambered into bed beside her, but she could not stop a little anxious frown. Guy seeing another woman? Extraordinary maybe but it wasn't as if he was repulsive. Far from it. He was a nice-looking man, not exactly handsome in the way David Ambrose for example had been but attractive for all that. He bought all his clothes from a traditional tailors' in Harrogate. He wore hand crafted suits, good shirts, dressed very well in other words, and it showed. Mostly he hid his shyness but not always and *that* women would find appealing.

"Mind if I read a moment?" He reached for the morning paper. "Haven't had a chance to read it yet? Anything interesting?"

"Just the usual." She kissed his cheek. "Goodnight, darling," she said quietly, turning her back on him. He would not disturb her. If only . . . well, frankly, if only he would reach for her sometimes in a flurry of passion. She had read in a magazine that she ought to take the initiative herself, to spice things up, but it was against her nature and she felt sure it would turn Guy completely off. Lukewarm love was sad.

If she had married David, it would not be lukewarm. David had fiery blood in his veins. David would be the sort of man who would make love in the kitchen, on the rug in front of the fire if it took his fancy, not just in the comfort and respectability of the marriage bed. David would be unpredictable for God's sake.

Beside her, the paper rustled. Uncomfortable, she heaved herself over and looked at him as he read. A little heavier than he had been but still firm muscled and definitely not overweight for his considerable height. He had kept his hair, fairish straight hair that, coupled with the pale blue of his eyes, and large frame gave him a Scandinavian appearance. He looked good for his age. When David dumped her, not quite but it felt like that, she had turned to Guy out of spite. At first she had deliberately strung him along before she had grown genuinely fond of him. She had, she supposed, been pushed into an engagement not least by her parents who were delighted at the thought of her marrying into such a fine Harrogate family. Guy was from good stock, good county stock, as Leila repeatedly reminded them. According to Leila, the Shawcross family name had to be protected at all costs. In spite of all the painstaking research she had done into the Shawcross family tree, Leila had regrettably not been able to discover a drop of blue blood and that was a constant irritation. However, according to her, the Shawcrosses of old were most definitely the next best thing to noblemen, a very prominent northern family with "connections". Barbara never bothered to enquire where on earth she got that from, content to let Leila have her little harmless pleasures.

When she and Guy first announced their engagement, Barbara was unsure quite how Leila would react. She had welcomed her, rather to her surprise, and it was some time before she understood why she had been so readily accepted. It made her realise how superficial Leila was, for it was apparently Barbara's looks that had swung it. Leila could not stand ugliness in any shape or form and, as Guy had seemed slow in entertaining the thought of marriage, Leila had been working relentlessly behind the scenes for some time trying to arrange a suitable match for him. All the girls of marriageable age of the right class were so ugly she later confessed to Barbara, big-boned, hefty girls who would not do justice to the lace wedding dress Leila had decided her daughter-in-law would wear. Barbara, however, his own choice at that, was so very lovely and quietly spoken, a quality dear raucous Leila approved of and she so liked the contrast the pair provided, Barbara's dark looks to her son's fair.

As Guy was the only son, everything would come to them and Daisy. The enormous old house in Skipton as well as the other properties here in Harrogate, the business interests Leila dabbled in, the shares, the jewels, the antiques, the paintings. Leila was rolling in it.

"Seen this?" Guy rustled a fraction more, spreading the paper out, pointing to something. "Surprised you didn't spot it?"

"What?" She craned to see, reluctant still to make use of her spectacles that were an aid to reading the small print. How often did you need to read the small print after all?

"Remember David Ambrose? Thought he was God's gift to women, didn't he?" He couldn't stop the bitterness edging in. "Haven't seen him for ages have we? Must be over twenty years? It must be the same chap surely, here . . . in the Deaths column."

"Deaths?" She felt her heart thud, leaning towards the paper, trying to focus. She snatched it from him and checked the notice. The first entry in the column and, yes, it was surprising she had not noticed herself. Ambrose. Yes, he had lived in Blackpool for years as he had always promised or rather threatened he would do although there had been a change of address on the last Christmas card to St Annes. She was surprised he had placed the announcement in the *Telegraph* but there it was. It would seem that his wife had died four days ago. The notice was brief.

"In hospital, after a short illness and a courageous fight, Ruth Grace, beloved wife of David Ambrose. Aged forty five years. Loving and loved mother of Annie." Funeral arrangements were mentioned. All friends were invited.

Barbara put the paper down. She had forgotten that Ruth's middle name was Grace. Not that it mattered now. "Well . . ." she said, stuck for words. All friends invited . . . she was not exactly a friend and she wasn't sure if she would be wise to see him again. She had been dreaming about him recently. Worryingly vivid dreams so that it was almost obscene to consider it. She said nothing to Guy, fluffed up her pillows and lay down, thinking.

Poor Ruth. God, it brought it home to you when someone of your own age died. To be honest, she had quite liked Ruth until she pinched David from her. Quiet Ruth who blushed easily, looked permanently worried even in her teens, was a neat if uninspiring dancer. She was shorter than Barbara, too short for David in ballroom dancing terms, the only kind of dancing that mattered to their crowd, but that had not stopped the explosion of anger as she watched the pair of them dance together especially as, at the time, Guy, red-faced, was standing on her feet and muttering apologies. The music, that first dance with Guy, had been a lovely slow number that she would always remember but she had been seething, the beauty of the words at odds with her feelings. Furious with David for arguing with her like that where everyone could see them. Her fury had caused her to shiver and Guy, mistaking the movement, had drawn her close with a sigh. Seeing David's eyes on them, she had leaned her head on his shoulder, realising as she did so that it was not that unpleasant. There was a certain sturdiness to Guy's shoulder.

Little things like that could change your life.

Pounding the pillow again, she snuggled under the duvet

and considered what she should do. She was older and wiser and she had no doubts that she would be able to handle the situation. There would be nothing unusual in her attending the funeral of an old friend, absolutely no reason why she should not. Perhaps Guy might come too but even as she thought that, she knew she did not want him to. The last time they had seen David and Ruth had been at their wedding. It had followed hot on the tail of her own marriage to Guy and she recalled the occasion with a shudder. Intent on hammering it home to David that she was blissfully happy with Guy, she had clung cloyingly to him throughout. To repeat the performance at a funeral was not permissible. Therefore, she would prefer, on this occasion, to keep the men separated.

Ruth's premature death was so sad for David, sad too for the daughter. She was younger than Daisy, the card one Christmas effectively announcing her arrival. David, Ruth *and* Annie with a little photograph enclosed of a baby. The baby looked like Ruth not David and that, for some odd reason, pleased her. Annie would be . . . let's see . . . about seventeen now, nearly three years younger than Daisy. Poor child. Barbara felt a sudden urge to offer her some comfort although just what you could say to a seventeen-year-old who had lost her mother she had no idea. After a short illness it had said, so that meant they must have had to help nurse her through a very difficult time. At seventeen, you should be enjoying life, not having to sit beside a dying parent.

It was too upsetting to contemplate. She wished she hadn't seen the wretched notice now as she would never sleep with that hanging over her. She would simply send flowers with a sympathy card. Attending the funeral, over in Blackpool, was not a serious option although it would be interesting to see David again even though he would, of course, not be at his best. On second thoughts, perhaps it would be *for* the best, a sort of cleansing, a getting him out of her system once and for all, for he would probably be changed out of all recognition.

Lying quietly, watching the curtains move a little in the slight breeze, Barbara tried to imagine how he might have changed. To him, she would certainly have changed. Her hair colour had changed for one thing and he had always admired her dark brown locks which were now tinted honey blonde. She was much the same shape, about half a stone heavier that's all. Money had brought her confidence in the way she dressed and she reckoned she might very well surprise him. Worryingly, he might very well surprise her. He might be bald and fat and wheezy although she was hard pushed to imagine that. It might be better though if he was. At least, she would then be able to laugh about her silly romantic dreams. One thing she felt sure of, however, was that he would not have lost his ability to dance. Timing and rhythm was something you never lost. A dancer was a dancer. There would be no opportunity to find out, although wouldn't it be just wonderful to dance with him again. Dancing at funerals was out of the question.

As she drifted into sleep, she heard music and saw David dancing by, confusingly first with herself and then with little Ruth. Steps faltered when he danced with Ruth. The mood changed, the drumbeat was stronger, the colour blazed and he was once more dancing with her. She saw the scarlet of her dress, the sensuous swish of the satin and David's eyes flashing at her as he closed in on her. And then the music changed once more. Funeral dirge. Black-coated figures. A coffin. She reached for him but he was gone. And so was Ruth.

Startled, she shot from her sleep, physically jumped, before she felt Guy's comfortingly solid presence beside her. Grumbling a bit in his sleep. "Guy . . .?" She shook his arm. "Are you awake?"

He grunted a reply and she took a deep breath, still seeing the dream although it was fading fast, "You wouldn't mind if I went to Ruth's funeral?" she said, sleepily searching for the right words. "It's the least I can do. After all, we kept in touch didn't we with the Christmas cards? I could just send a condolence card and flowers, I suppose but I feel that's getting us off the hook, don't you? We ought to go. Do you want to come too? You did say you were awfully busy just now."

"I am," he muttered flatly. "Go to sleep, Barbara. We'll talk about it in the morning."

She nodded, satisfied. "I know things were a bit awkward. I know you never liked him," she added, wishing she didn't feel the need to explain. "But that's all in the past and we can be adult about it. I want to tell David personally how sorry we both are and I'd quite like to meet their daughter. The poor child, losing her mother at such a young age. It's quite upset me. Guy . . .?"

He was asleep.

3 ∫

If she jumped in the sea now, where would her body be washed up? Drowning if you wanted, did not resist, was easy. Painless they said although how did anyone know that? The spray was cold on Annie's face, furious at meeting the grey stone of the sea wall, lashing against it, shooting up, spilling over. She could taste the salt, licking her lips, both loving and hating it. The wall was slimy, greenish with watery vegetation on it, smelly, but Annie did not notice. She was too intent on watching the waves as they battered in from afar. Grey, brown, dishwater colour, with cream froth, the wind whipping it, stirring it.

It was a dangerous place to be and she knew it. She hadn't been born and bred in Blackpool to be in ignorance of the occasional drownings. She would not survive more than minutes in that choppy churning tide, her limbs would stiffen with shock and cold within moments of entering and the fact that she was a more than decent swimmer would count for nothing, not with the weight of her clothes and the icy cold. She felt no fear, however, because she now knew, and it was a relief to know, that she would not do it. She would not deliberately throw herself in and there would be no accident either. Slowly, carefully, she moved away and with the vicious sea wind beating against her back, she climbed slippery wet steps to the upper level of the promenade walk, turning once more to look at the angry morning sea, at the dirty cloudy horizon so murky that she couldn't see the distant shipping lane.

The sun was nervous, peeping from the cloud, pale gold with no warmth. Jumping into the sea was the easy way out of the pain and grief she felt. Her mother would expect more of her than that and it wasn't fair on dad either, to lumber him with his daughter's suicide, although he didn't deserve a smudge of consideration.

He had been out all night, not even bothering to ask now if she would be all right on her own. Mum wasn't even buried yet and he was at Linda's. Mistress or whatever you liked to call her, he had given up all pretence lately. He was a wonderful actor, had truly missed his vocation. At the moment, he was playing the part of bereaved husband to perfection. A hint of a tear. A break in the voice. Underneath it all, he was glad, glad to be free of the hassle. It was not pretty watching someone die even if it had been so tragically quick, particularly someone you loved. It was horrifying to see the weight drop away, the eyes cloud, the cheeks hollow, that look appearing. Mum had been so brave. When they discovered that it was hopeless to attempt treatment, that it was too far gone, that it had a hold on major organs, dad had seemed momentarily stunned and so she had taken charge, asking that mum should not be told. She wasn't sure now if it was the right decision but mum had played along with it and pretended she did not know. They had pretended they did not know either. The strain had been unbearable.

If she was honest, she was glad it was over too, but only for mum's sake. She looked peaceful now. "Morning, miss. Out for a stroll?" She turned in alarm to see a policeman on the beat, a rare sight indeed and without the protection of his panda car he seemed almost as vulnerable as she, just a lone rather large man. His uniform was damp with drizzle, his eyes alert as if he was well aware of her intentions and she wondered how long he had been there, if he had been watching her. "Not a day for sunning yourself on the sands is it?" he remarked, rubbing his hands together. "They don't put days like this in the tourist brochure." He grinned suddenly and she found herself smiling back.

"I like it best like this," she told him, instantly womanly aware as she felt his eyes on her that she must look a fright, her short hair plastered like a black swimcap about her head, a few strands across her face, her eyes still bubbling with more tears, her cheeks red and raw from the cold sea air. She had cried enough. It was time now for composure. For a moment, looking at the policeman's sympathetic fatherly face, she felt a need to tell him. She knew what the response would be and she really needed a good old-fashioned shoulder to cry on. Someone to tell her that it would be all right, that in time this huge block of solid grief would begin to melt. Even if they were empty words, she needed someone to say it. It didn't seem fair to inflict her feelings on this man, not on a grey day like this, so she said nothing, smiling her goodbye instead.

She decided she would handle the funeral with adult composure. Dad would too, of course, although he had probably not worked out his strategy yet. Should he break down or would that be too obvious? Stiff upper lip, fighting off emotion, that's how he would play it. They would all marvel at how well he was bearing up and afterwards, back at the house, he would be in his element. The party . . . not exactly a party . . . but it would turn into one with some of the friends her father possessed. He would excuse it by saying it was a celebration of Ruth's life. Ruth, he would say, as he knocked back the whisky, Ruth would not want them to grieve. More to the point, mum would not want half that crowd in her home, toasting her demise, flicking ash on the carpet, messing up the kitchen. Annie looked forward to it with trepidation.

She returned to her car and sat a moment, steaming up, allowing her eyes to mist too for the last time. She wiped them with a tissue, blew her nose, and took a deep steadying breath. She had meant what she said to the policeman about liking the town on drizzly days like today. She liked the out of season time. Visitors were welcome, the very soul of the town in fact, but days like this were special when even the Tower was partially hidden in a grey swirling sea fog, when everything was shimmering like a still-damp watercolour. When she was a little girl they had played a game of who would catch sight of the Tower first as they returned home from visits to her grandparents in Harrogate. She had usually won, or mum had let her win, and she could hear her own childish voice calling out excitedly, "Mummy, there it is, there it is, did you see it?"

She sighed at the memory, started the engine, demisted the screen, and set off, driving down the road beside the promenade. They could scoff at it all they would but they didn't know it, they had never seen it like this with the Irish Sea pounding against its beaches, the salt wind blowing frantically round every sandy corner. Salt. Sand. It was in the very air she breathed. Fish and chip flavoured ozone.

She peered determinedly through the windscreen knowing she had to concentrate because this was no ordinary road and there was so much going on to hinder her concentration. To her right, trams clattering along on their track beside the prom and the central pier and on her left, the hotchpotch of brightly coloured vulgarity that was the Golden Mile. Bingo halls. Amusement arcades. Her dad's world. All so wonderfully, joyously tacky. She absolutely loved it. All of it. She managed a smile as she finally reached south shore and the pleasure beach, where the Big Dipper, the Big One, loomed beside the road. She shuddered even as she dared to take her eyes off the road to glance up. No thank you. She preferred to keep her feet firmly on the ground. One of them had to and dad lived on a different planet, constantly coming up with hare-brained schemes of the make-money variety. Mum used to listen to them, make encouraging noises and then smile and shake her head when he had gone. Sure enough, one by one, they all fell beside the wayside.

Blackpool . . . she was used to springing to its defence, used to the look that appeared on strangers' faces when she told them where she came from. It labelled her. Sometimes they went so far as to say "you don't look like you come from Blackpool". She didn't know whether to laugh or cry at that one.

Carefully, she negotiated the traffic, fearful as she passed a horse-drawn landau, very mindful that she was a new driver, guilty even because dad had forked out for the car, a fairly new red Mini, without a single grumble. He was like that, generous with money as if that somehow made up for it all, all the emotional neglect. She'd far rather he'd been like some of her friends' dads. Tight-fisted with pocket money and treats but real dads. Proud dads.

She drove to just beyond St Annes, to the house they'd only moved into a few months ago, the house mother had hated, the house that did not feel like home. Home was the house they lived in when she was little. Mum had preferred the greener suburban landscape rather than this outlook of grassy mounds atop the soft, shifting sand dunes that hemmed the beach. You got used to the layer of sand eventually. Mum had opposed the move but she hadn't the strength to argue, struggling with the onset of her illness, so move they had. Dad had designed it himself, with the help of one of his dubious friends who fancied himself as an architect. It was surprisingly old-fashioned with huge picture windows and mum said she felt she was living in a goldfish bowl, had not relished the prospect of summer visitors staring in as they trekked by on their way to a sandy picnic. There was no privacy and he would not allow blinds or nets. Let the sods see in . . . he said, puffing on his cigarette, cocking a finger towards the window . . . I've worked hard for all this and I'm proud of it. What wouldn't they give to live here?

It was a burglar's paradise. If they ever got in past the security alarms, they wouldn't know where to start. Trash and the real thing mingled uneasily, dad's taste such that you could be forgiven for mixing them up. Beautiful Chinese rugs in shades of pink and silver on top of polished floor. Original very modern paintings, bought with appreciation in mind and because dad liked to pretend he knew what they were supposed to represent. Crystal. Chandeliers. Garish leather seating and piled-up cushions. Glass-topped coffee tables with carefully selected books lying on them when he only ever read cheap newspapers. Let's put the notice in the *Telegraph* he said when mum died. As if it mattered. Which of their friends read the *Telegraph*? An expensive chess set when he didn't play chess. An enormous-screened television. A shiny chrome bar in the corner with more than enough bottles of gin and whisky. Huge mirrors doubling the size of the room and reflecting the naffness of it all. His silver cups. His prized dancing cups. Pictures of him in his ballroom dancing days, accompanied usually by a lovely dark-haired lady rather than mum.

Annie stood stock-still in the doorway and surveyed it all. Somehow there was nothing of mum any more, never had been really, for she had been too ill to cope with the decoration. Everything was dad.

The house was silent. Quickly, she went into her bedroom. It was her own little world and he had not interfered with her choice of colour scheme so that it was calm and restful in lilac and cream. She actually liked the view from her window of the dunes and distant sea, although just now it looked damp and uninviting. Childhood memorabilia were all around, her teddies sitting nicely on the pillows. Transition time, and suddenly, she felt very grown-up. One of them had to play at being grown-up and her father was unlikely to change from being the permanent overgrown schoolboy. Naughty and outrageous. It was up to her now to take over the running of the house, to do all the things her mother had done. Mum had been obsessed with not bothering dad with trivia. What he would do when she went off to college, she had no idea. She worried about that. Mum had worried about that, at the last. He would probably get someone in to do the work, a housekeeper, although he did not like strangers in his home, picking amongst his things. He locked the drawers in his desk in his private study and always pocketed the key. One would almost think he had something to hide.

She sat down heavily on the bed and picked up one of the teddies, cuddling it close. Perhaps it would be best if she did not go to college. She could get a job so that she could stay here and look after him. Iron his shirts and things. Mum used to lay his following day's clothes out for him. Annie smiled a little. Fool that mum was.

She felt a bit better. Going for a walk had cheered her up and she was more settled now she knew that she would not kill herself. It was a sobering thought to realise she had even considered it. It was just that there was nobody to talk to now that mum was gone and seventeen was a terrible age to be when there was nobody to talk to. Her girlfriends were no help, crying more than she, struck dumb at the news. She'd never had any really close friends in any case, preferring mostly to be on her own. She recognised now that it was a mistake, now that it was too late.

Mum had been her one best friend with dad the butt of their feminine mutterings. A sob caught at her and she stifled it at once. No more of that. She would go to school today. Nobody expected her to but she wanted to. She had to face up to the tearful embarrassment of her classmates sooner or later and the sooner the better. She would feel heaps better when the funeral was over. Only then would she be able to get on with things and make plans.

She was dressed in her school uniform, dark blue knee-length skirt, blue blouse, navy sweater, when he came in. She was sitting warming herself by the flickering flames of the gas fire, drinking a cup of coffee. "What time do you call this?" she called out brightly before she could stop herself.

"Half past eight sweetheart." He glanced in the room, smiling, "Role reversal? Aren't I supposed to be the one who says that about you? Not that you would dream of staying out all night, eh? What's the Mini doing in the drive?"

"I've been out. I got up at six and took the car into town. Had a long walk along the north shore."

"A walk? In this? You must be mad." He flopped down opposite. He was casually clad in tight jeans and his beloved suede jacket which he now heaved over the arm of the chair. His shirt was dark blue silk, the neck unbuttoned to reveal the hair of his chest, although how much longer would he be doing that now that it was beginning to grey. He no longer wore the gold medallion having decided it was passé. His hair was long on his collar. "Is *that* your father?" the girls at school said the first time they saw him. Their own dads looked like dads ought to look. Fattish and baldish and ordinary. Her dad had to look like a male model or a film star. A very good-looking man and, at this moment, he was auditioning for the understanding father part. Was there no limit to his acting abilities? "Annie, sweetheart . . . I know it's hard for you," he said, running fingers through his hair, one of those supposedly unconscious gestures of his that was unbelievably sexy or so the girls at school said. "You and I have got to help each other through this. Your mother's best out of it, isn't she? There was nothing anyone could do for her. I still can't believe it. Why her? She wouldn't have hurt a fly, your mother. Why did she have to suffer like that? Bloody terrifying how quick it got her."

She swallowed, looking hard at him. For a second, she thought she detected genuine emotion but she was not sure. She couldn't trust him. He had cheated mum and her much too often. She had seen the disappointment and grief in her mother's eyes, had watched the silly little efforts mum made to get him to notice her, the new dresses, the perfume. Annie hardened her heart. Brilliant performance, she wanted to say. Instead she rose in a single graceful movement, a slight boyish figure barely five feet tall who would never ever run to fat and smiled sweetly at him. Two could play at that game. "Cup of tea or coffee, daddy?" she enquired. "You look quite exhausted. What have you been doing?"

David watched as she drove back into Blackpool to school. He wished she didn't wear her hair so short, shorn almost and unattractively spiky. Or those clumsy looking shoes. The overall effect was much too butch for him. Why the hell hadn't he got a feminine type daughter instead of this aggressive sulky one? She'd never get herself a boyfriend unless she prettied herself up a bit, wore a nice short skirt when she went out at the weekend instead of those jeans. A short sexy skirt. He was worried that she was going back to school so soon but had been unable to persuade her not to. It was her decision. Tough cookie, Annie. Just for a moment, as she'd got her things together before she set off, he'd wanted to hold her to him, say something, but he'd seen the set of her jaw, the expression, and hadn't bothered.

She was taking it hard. He had not seen her cry but he supposed she must have because he noticed her eyes, red-rimmed. She and Ruth had been close, friends he supposed, and they had succeeded in shutting him out of a whole lot of things. He had not minded knowing it was the same for most dads but, now that it was too late, he wished he'd done it differently, talked to her more when she was a little girl, done father-daughter things, become more of an influence. The . . . God, it was almost contempt . . . the way she looked at him was a kick in the teeth.

He was not going to let it upset him too much. No woman and that included his daughter would ever really succeed in upsetting his drift. He would have coped much better with a son, he felt, all that man to man stuff, giving him the benefit of his considerable experience, but they'd never had the son they wanted. Ruth had been a bit of a loser where having kids was concerned. Delicate, that was Ruth. Two false goes and then a nail-biting pregnancy with Annie who managed to be pale and intense and miserable even when a baby. Too serious by half. Dour, wasn't that the word for it? No sense of humour. Just like her mother.

Perhaps he should go to work too. He controlled the whole rigmarole from a suite of offices of a building overlooking the prom. Some po-faced accountancy firm on the floor below and insurance agents on the floor above. Ambrose Entertainments was the interesting bit sandwiched in the middle.

On balance, he decided against putting in an appearance yet because it would look bad, it wasn't the right thing to do. They could cope a while, that shower of his, although not for long. If he left them too long, one or other of them would make a bloody cock-up. That was the trouble when you steered the ship, you couldn't stay below deck too long or you would end up on the rocks. He never bothered with holidays because he was scared of leaving them, scared of the potential high-risk botch-ups. They didn't know everything and they could accidentally land him in a load of trouble. He chose not to tell them everything so he had to live with that. Surround yourself with incompetents and, by God, did you stand out.

He strode into the kitchen that was now Annie spick and span, and made himself a cup of instant coffee, carrying it back into the sitting room and reaching for his silver cigarette case. He took out a cigarette and lit it. Nobody now to mutter and sniff their irritation at the habit for Annie was a bit more relaxed about it than Ruth. Funny but the smoke, with the under-the-counter, behind-the-bikeshed feel gone, was not that enjoyable. He squashed it out and sat quietly, going through the funeral arrangements in his mind. There would be a good turn-out although Linda was not coming thank God. Until she mentioned it, he'd never given it a thought, never meant her to come, but for some reason she'd got it into her pretty dim head that he was about to issue a black-edged invitation. Like hell! How could he explain her away if anybody asked? They mostly knew, he supposed, but he liked to keep up some pretence. Oh, by the way, this is Linda. This ageing blonde tart is Linda. This is the woman I went to when Ruth was ill. This is the woman I went to long before Ruth became ill. Ten years give or take. He'd even been unfaithful to Linda.

Put like that, he sounded a right sod. He was one. It wasn't his fault. Women were to blame. Too damned complex. He would never understand them, starting with Barbara Anderson all those years ago and ending now with Ruth. Linda was not worth considering. Her sheer stupidity annoyed him, her glaring lack of intelligence, her wide-eyed innocence. It might have worked if she'd been young but she wasn't. Not anymore. She was ageing fast, too many vodkas and late nights and, in her line of business, it mattered. It mattered a helluva lot.

She danced too but with nowhere near as much finesse as Barbara. Barbara Anderson was sexier with her clothes on than dear Linda was with them off. Linda was only fit to be a stripper or exotic dancer as she preferred her job description to be but she had once entertained big ideas and he had managed, years ago, to get her into the chorus on one of the summer pier shows. She had been pitifully grateful, but she had made such a mess of the dancing that she hadn't survived a week. Standards were high. Top notch for Blackpool shows. Second-rate dancers like Linda didn't stand a hope in hell. The audience, TV trained to a man, could spot amateurs a mile off.

Now she was expecting great things again. Of him. She was expecting to be centre stage in his life now that Ruth was gone, expecting to move in with him maybe. Some hope. He was planning to ditch her but it was just a matter of picking the right moment and he would wait until after the funeral. Just now, he was enjoying the response all this was creating in her. She was being the soothing little woman, inviting him to cry on her bosom, cooing soft words of comfort, crying herself even. The stupid bitch.

On floor to ceiling glass-fronted shelves beside the fireplace stood his trophies. He had talent. Dancing feet. A rare thing, talent like his, and it was a constant irritation that it had never come to anything. He reckoned, given the right opportunity, he could have gone far. If Barbara had stuck with him, they could have gone far together, a partnership made in heaven. They had such charisma they could have done for ballroom dancing what Torvill and Dean had done for ice dancing. He could turn his hand to solo dancing too but it was a struggle because not that many solo dancers made it. God, you could count them on your fingers. Fred Astaire, Gene Kelly, Wayne Sleep.

David Ambrose! His name had a nice ring to it, would have looked great in lights. What he wouldn't have given for that chance. It wasn't as if he didn't have the looks. The clean-cut boyish looks that women went for. He enjoyed a stab at choreography too, anything to stretch his rhythmic talent. As ballroom dancing went, Latin American was his strength. He and Ruth had had a bash at it once, in competition, but she had let him down, not sexy enough. He missed Barbara. For the Latin American rhythms, you needed swaying hips and come-on eyes. Without the right partner, it was a lost cause.

It was all innocence with Barbara. A kiss, a fluff of a kiss and a gentle sort of commitment. She was a striking girl, dark almost black hair, and a very straight way of looking at you with those blue eyes. And wow, could she dance. She followed. She moved. Even the dancing apart was sensuous, the coming together a catch-the-breath situation. The audience loved it. He never worried that she would miss a step as he worried about Ruth. One missed step with Ruth and the rest of the dance was a fiasco. Barbara had possessed a natural grace, sexy with it, that made the men in the audience sit up and take notice. Damn it, he'd missed out where Barbara was concerned. He knew he was her first love and he'd been trying to play it cool, trying to be patient. A fragile thing first love, not to be rushed. Not so for him for he was already, at twenty, ridiculously experienced in romancing the girls. Nothing to it as long as you didn't allow yourself to become emotionally entangled. Nothing to it as long as you remembered that women liked little presents, little surprise gifts, and, if he couldn't afford a bunch of flowers, a single flower came out, thank God, as a special gesture. It was all in the manner of the giving.

She was in her teens when he first knew her. Gangly and giggly. Legs that went on forever. Before his eyes, she'd become a woman, filling out in all the right places thank God, her features softening, her eyes wiser but ever wary. They'd been pushed together as partners at the dancing classes years before when they were only kids by a bossy woman who turned out to have an eye for a brilliant combination. They just went together. They were already becoming known in ballroom dancing circles, surely destined to be leaders in the field when wham! . . . a bust-up. A bust-up in the middle of the dance floor when she stormed off, leaving him stranded partnerless, expecting him no doubt to run after her. Sod that. Shocked to the core for she had never given a hint that she would explode with a passion like that, he had let her go, intending to sort it out later, but instead she'd waltzed past with Guy Shawcross, boring git that he was, danced smoochily past him and Ruth whom he'd yanked onto the floor simply because even he couldn't do a waltz on his own. That was a mistake that had repercussions beyond the call of duty, whisking Ruth round the floor as he had in a fit of pique. How the hell he'd come to marry her, he had no idea to this day. He had never intended it. It had just happened. He'd never been in love with her but she was crafty was Ruth and wide-eyed with it, invisible claws sinking painlessly into him so that, once the ball was rolling, that was it. Sunday tea, her parents, best behaviour, and bingo! Before he knew what had hit him, she was proudly showing off an engagement ring and he was walking up the aisle.

Barbara, recently married herself, had the bloody cheek to accept the wedding invitation and had turned up with Guy in tow. She was dressed in pink, pink-hatted and prettily pink-faced. Clinging onto him. Guy. Guy, who had managed to be mountainously boring at twenty, so what the hell would he be like now? Serve her right. If she'd married him, she wouldn't be bored. He'd seen through the wedding fiasco, seen through the romantic glow she was trying to exude. She was jealous as hell. Livid. However, she and Ruth had been remarkably civilised and every year Christmas cards were exchanged. Tasteful printed cards from her, Seasons Greetings from Guy and Barbara Shawcross. Didn't she have a daughter too, a bit older than Annie? With a sigh he reached for one of his photographs, of him and Barbara, looking at himself first with a frown. He was still handsome, wasn't he? Approaching fifty, he could still win the ladies, couldn't he? Of course he could and he'd proved that time and again recently. Some men had it, that elusive it, and some men, Guy Shawcross included, did not.

He stood before the mirror and checked his appearance. He was still in shape, despite the booze and the cigarettes. He jogged as far as the car. He grinned suddenly. It wasn't fair, was it, that he could abuse his body and still have a headstart. His hair was his own, showing no sign of thinning although he used a colouring now. Maybe he would begin to let the grey show. Some women went for the mature look. He was after all a widower and good-looking widowers were thin on the ground. He could have his pick and the Rolls might swing it. The Rolls was burgundy with a rich cream leather interior. Ruth hadn't wanted him to buy it, had worried that it was too ostentatious, worried that people would think them show-offs. She used to sit beside him with a look on her face more appropriate to a beat-up Morris Minor, scurrying out and slamming the door before anyone noticed.

Ruth was like that. He had given her the cash to get herself nice clothes and she had bought her stuff from chain stores. Safe. She never had style. Show-off? So what. He liked the look on people's face when they saw him drive up in it. The car lifted him several notches up the ladder. Effortlessly. It was worth every penny and it wasn't as if he bothered with a chauffeur. Nobody else was getting to drive it. Let them debate as to where the money came from. His books were clean, all business dealings legitimate. More or less. Ambrose Entertainments at your service, a nightclub, amusement arcades, bingo halls, and a bowling alley on the cards because he judged that was in for a revival. The disco was profitable but a bloody pain in the neck because you had to be bang up to date or you were off the map. The guy who managed it was young and keen, knew precisely where he stood, knew that David liked to be kept informed about all the current trends. One of these days, they'd turn full circle and be ballroom dancing again.

He shivered, despite the fire. He no longer liked it here in this house. It was an expensive mistake and he needed to get out of it. There was a muffled silence about the place that worried him. The sand dunes opposite were getting on his nerves. The neighbours weren't exactly a bundle of laughs either. He would put it on the market and move back into Blackpool proper, maybe get a flat. Of course, he still had to provide a home for Annie so he'd have to discuss it with her, go through the motions anyway. When it came to the crunch, however, he would do what he wanted.

Miss Boyd called her into her office before she left school. For yet more sympathy? "How are you feeling, Annie?" she said kindly, "We didn't expect you back yet."

"I'm okay, thanks." Annie perched on the chair and smiled across the desk at her headmistress. "People have been nice, Miss Boyd. The girls and everybody."

"Of course. We're all sad for you." She glanced at her watch. "I won't keep you but I didn't want you to go without saying personally how sorry I am. If there's anything you want to talk about, please talk to me." She bit her lip, looked suddenly very unheadmistressy, "I didn't know your mother very well, Annie, but what I saw I liked very much. I mean that. I'm not just saying it. She was a very nice lady and she loved you. She was very proud of your achievements. I'm sure I don't need to tell you that the best thing you can do is to get good grades in your exams. It would really please her."

"I know. Thank you."

Her mother had liked Miss Boyd too, Annie thought, as she drove home. As far as she knew, all dealings with school, all her school-life, had been done through her mother. Dad never went near. Some of the teachers thought mum was a single parent. He never came to concerts, parents' evenings, sports days, anything. Mum did, smiling brightly as if she was trying to make up for it.

She realised, with a vague surprise, that the car had taken her, not home, but here, to a sidestreet in central Blackpool. The street where Linda lived. Dad paid the rent and she'd once seen a receipt, noted the address, once seen his Rolls outside the door. Conducting a clandestine affair and using a Rolls was a bit of a nonsense. He had no conscience, her dad.

Before she could change her mind, still not sure what she would say, she tugged her bag across the seat, climbed out and locked the Mini. A couple of youths eyed her coldly from their slouching position against a neighbouring door, deciding she wasn't worth a wolf whistle. The first knock produced no reaction and she felt her face flame as the boys stared at her. "She's in, darling," one of them called, just as the door opened and Linda Ridgeley stood there.

"Annie . . .?" She said wonderingly, "What are you doing here?" She looked horrorstruck. She was wearing a tracksuit . . . well, hardly that . . . shocking pink with outrageous padded shoulders, zip well down to show off a black lace bra. Red backless sandals on small feet. The hand that gripped the doorpost had chipped red nail varnish. It stood to reason it would be chipped. Annie wondered why she'd come. She rarely visited this part of town. Candy floss and hot dogs. Tolerable in high season when the little gift shops and ice cream parlours opened, it was at its worst just now, in this grey drizzle. Depressing.

"Can I come in, please?" she asked, hitching her bag onto her shoulder. "I need to talk."

Linda nodded. "Does he know you've come?" she asked, closing the door on them once they were in a narrow red-carpeted hall. Everything clashed. Far too many different shades of red. Annie did her best to keep a polite smile on her face, the sort of smile reserved for the moment you enter a stranger's home, very nearly knocking over a vase of artificial roses as she laid her school bag down beside a small half-moon table. "Come through to the lounge, love," Linda said and, as she turned to show her the way, Annie noted that the tracksuit zip was now well zipped up. The same dark red multi-patterned nylon carpet was in the lounge which had comparably awful embossed wallpaper and pictures of the Lake District in cheap frames. A stale perfume mingled with an undertone of bacon and eggs. "I'm so surprised to see you I don't know what to say," Linda muttered, closing the door behind them. She had a nice smile and, in fact, underneath the layers of thickly applied tan make-up there lurked a suggestion of prettiness. Tired now. Her grey eyes were highlighted with blue shadow and the blue mascara that Annie had always disliked. Badly bleached blonde hair, thin and out of condition, hung straight from a centre parting to lie just on her shoulders.

Annie held out her hand. "It's nice to meet you at last, Linda," she said calmly.

"Pleased to meet you," Linda replied, looking so nonplussed that for a dreadful moment Annie thought she was about to curtsey. "How did you know I lived here?" she asked, wary. "It seems a bit peculiar, you coming to see me."

"I wanted to see you," Annie said with a smile, "In any case, how did you know who I was?" she countered, determined to keep the initiative. "We've never met before."

"I've seen photos of you and your mum." She flushed. "I'm sorry about that. Nobody deserves that to happen. Rotten it is, cancer. I never thought it would be as quick as that. Horrified he was, your dad. And the worst thing was I had to be the one to break the news. I felt really terrible about that."

Annie nodded briefly, having taken all the sympathy she could for one day. She sat down as Linda motioned that she should, choosing an armchair near the fireplace. Incredibly, an old-lady type lace chairback lay on it. The fire was not lit, the dead coals just set with sticks of newspaper. A few dried flowers stuck up rigidly in a vase to one side. In front of the fireplace, a moulting sheepskin rug lay crookedly at her feet. Annie resisted an urge to straighten it. "You've known dad a long time, haven't you Linda?" she asked instead. She couldn't quite meet her eyes. She felt sorry for her and was amazed that she should. Of all the emotions she had expected to feel, that was not on the list. The poor misled woman probably expected dad to marry her now that there was no obstacle.

"Ten years. Ten years in May. I'd been trying to get into club work for ages." She sighed and pushed wearily at her hair. "I'd just come back from London when I met up with your dad. I'd been trying to get work on the stage down there. Dead loss really," she said flatly, "You'd think they'd have been glad to get somebody who could sing as well as dance. I mean . . . I wasn't expecting the star role, just chorus stuff but . . ." her shrug told it all. "So I came back home. Didn't like it much down there anyway. I was born in Blackpool, love. You should never leave your roots because you never fit in anywhere else." She pulled a tatty cigarette packet out of her pocket and struck a match. "Do you smoke?" she asked, dropping the packet on the table when Annie shook her head. "Do you want a coffee?" she asked awkwardly, "Have you come straight from school? Then you won't have had anything to eat? Do you want a sandwich?" The sudden maternal fluster seemed to startle her as much as Annie.

"No thank you." Annie wondered how old Linda was, probably not that much younger than mum. She felt older herself, in control. "I expect dad will want to move from St Annes," she said quietly, as Linda subsided into the chair again, "That house has only bad memories. I don't think I want to stay in it either." She stole a glance across. "Has he mentioned anything about it?"

"No." She was astonished and she was no actress. "He loves that house," she said fiercely, "Designed it himself didn't he? I think you're mistaken. Yes, I'm sure you're mistaken. I've never seen it but he's told me all about it. It sounds lovely," she added wistfully. "I like the sand dunes. Lovely they are. In summer, if it's really hot then your feet burn on them but just a few inches down, it's dead cold. Have you noticed? Funny isn't it? I always meant to ask somebody why that was."

Annie smiled gently. "So . . . you work in the club?" she asked, through a hard silence. "That must be interesting."

"It is." Linda brightened. "Although I don't really care for the dancing I do there. It's . . . well . . ." she puffed on the cigarette, flushed again, "Exotic stuff, you know a bit of titillation for the customers. The men. Tasteful though, don't get me wrong. I don't strip completely. Sometimes in the season I can get work in a show. Once I was in the central pier show. Ken Dodd was in it. What a laugh he is! I was in the chorus."

"Really? You must have enjoyed that." Annie was aware that she was in danger of sounding patronising and she did not mean to. Fortunately, it was lost on Linda.

"I loved it. Then they cut down the number in the chorus and, as I was last in, I was first out. That was the only reason, it wasn't that I couldn't do the work." She laughed, a nice open laugh, "It was a proper chorus. Good routines. Old-fashioned maybe but the audience like to see a chorus line." She eyed Annie shrewdly, "You don't know what I'm talking about, do you? I forget you're so young." She sprinkled ash into a pot dish. "Your dad can still dance a bit when he's a mind to. He does demonstrations sometimes. You know the ones I mean? At the Tower in the afternoon?"

"I know. He likes to remind everyone that he won cups for dancing. He'll have told you of course that he once featured on 'Come Dancing'?"

Linda nodded enthusiastically. "He does the choreography at the club."

"Does he? That must stretch him." Again, Annie regretted the sharp note in her voice, the sarcasm evident when she talked about her father but Linda seemed blissfully unaware.

"He loves it. He has a real gift. He can listen to the music and know what moves to make to it. That's not as easy as it sounds. All the girls think he's absolutely wonderful. They've all got crushes on him." She couldn't stop her pride surfacing. The other girls might have crushes on him but she was the one he loved. "Look, love . . . I'm going to make us a coffee. I want one if you don't. You just sit here. Want something to read?" she asked, hovering over Annie with hairdresser attentiveness.

Annie let her make the coffee, suspecting she needed time to think, time to ponder why David's daughter should have come here. She looked round the room finding its sheer exuberance oddly comforting. Every surface was crowded with cheap little pot ornaments. For the first time, she noticed a cat curled up on a chair beside the door, a black and white cat sitting plumb on a cushion. Sensing her watching it, it raised its head and stared at her disconcertingly with one green and one yellow eye. Annie smiled at it. She liked cats. She'd always wanted a cat of her own but mum had an allergy and dad didn't like them. He didn't like animals. "What's your cat called?" she asked as Linda came back, cigarette wedged in her mouth, carrying a circular tin tray, two Blackpool Tower mugs and a plate of custard creams.

Deftly, Linda juggled with cigarette, mugs and the plate before replying. "He's Blackbeard. Aren't you, precious?" She purred herself as she looked at him, "Isn't he beautiful? Different eyes, see? If you look, you'll see he has a black patch over the green eye. Unusual, isn't it? He's a stray. I found him at one o'clock in the morning, on the prom, soaking wet. Some unfeeling sod must have dumped him. He could have got knocked down by a tram."

"Poor thing." She exchanged a sad smile with Linda. "Lucky you found him," she added, meaning it. She sipped the coffee, strong and good, and wanted to ask why Linda had wasted ten years of her life on a man who would now drop her like a ton of bricks. She could not. There was a hope in the other woman's eyes that she did not want to be responsible for destroying. Dad would do it soon enough. She just knew it.

"What is it you've come for then?" Linda perched beside the cat, her hand absently stroking the fur and causing a loud purring to develop from the now slit-eyed feline. "Look . . . this is really embarrassing. I'm sorry if I've hurt you, love. I never meant to do that."

The decision leapt at her. "If you want to come to the funeral, please do," she said, feeling herself flush with embarrassment. Dad would kill her for suggesting it but it was something that had been worrying her. Mum knew about Linda. Mum probably had a sneaking sympathy for her. "We can say you're a distant cousin. Nobody ever knows who people are at funerals and all sorts of weird people are coming." She smiled, her embarrassment fading, "I don't blame you, Linda. It's him. He's like that. He thinks he's irresistible."

"He's not keen on me coming. I did say myself that I'd quite like to but it was a daft idea, wasn't it? And I've nothing suitable to wear. Nothing black. I would like to look nice if I did come. A black dress and some black shoes and a bag. I don't go for black normally."

"You needn't wear black. I'm not. I'm going to wear something bright, as a sort of statement. Mum would like that."

"It's good of you, love. Isn't it nice of her, Blackbeard?" she said, picking him up and sitting him on her lap. "But he'd go daft. He doesn't want me there. I suppose he's ashamed of me, deep down. Oh . . . I'm all right in . . . the thing is, we've been friends a long time, me and your dad. You mustn't think that . . ." she struggled gamely for the right words, "I always felt badly about it, about you and your mum and everything but . . ." her eyes were luminous now. "Sorry. These things just happen, love. You never mean them to. You'll see as you get older, when you get a boyfriend. I love him you see . . ." She tried a smile, lip trembling slightly and looked suddenly much older, a little scared, "I fell for him in a big way the first moment I saw him.

He says the sweetest things does your dad. Nice things. He has a lovely way with words. You know."

"I'm seventeen, Linda," Annie said quietly, "I think I understand. But you should forget him. Honestly you should."

She shook her head. "You don't understand, Annie," she said, the use of Annie's name springing out for the first time, "I can't help it."

Exasperation caught at Annie. "It'll end in tears," she prophesied, realising it was one of mum's expressions, that for a moment she sounded just like her, "He's not going to do me any good either but I'm stuck with him. You can walk away but I can't. He's my dad. Where can I go?"

"You can come here." The offer was immediate, impulsive and ill-advised. "I've got a spare room so if you're really stuck . . ." she looked worried, sorry to have said it.

"I'll probably be going to college in October. Or . . . if I get a job, I'll be able to get myself a place of my own. Either way, dad won't have to worry too much about me. Thanks for the offer," she added, knowing she would never ever take it up.

She was subdued as she drove home. All in all, she was glad she had done it. It changed her opinion. It was a mistake to judge people without actually talking face to face with them. Just as well perhaps that Linda had declined to come to the funeral. Linda was right. It was a daft idea. She was full of daft ideas. For instance, she was no longer sure she would bother to go to university. What possible use would a French degree be? She wanted to work with people. Social work maybe.

She'd like that. She'd like to help people like Linda, worn out, hopeless people like her. Thoughtfully, she considered the options. Either a course at university, more thought provoking, or an immediate job. Everyone would go bananas if she did that but it was time she made her own decisions. There was nobody to discuss it with now so she had to make her own decision. There was that job application at home, still waiting to be filled in. Should she?

The Rolls was in the drive and he was in the sitting room, working on some papers. He did not question her lateness, did not even seem to notice. Annie went to make tea, sniffing her irritation at the heaps of dirty coffee cups and cigarette butts his day had produced. When tea was nearly ready, she peered in at him, his papers now discarded, sprawled on the sofa, mouth open, a little grumpy snore coming from him. Sometimes, off guard like now, he didn't look quite so wonderfully handsome. There were times when, on the contrary, he looked quite ordinary. "Ham salad, dad?" she queried, enjoying his start of surprise.

He looked round, frowning. "Must've dropped off," he said with a yawn, "Where the hell did you get to after school? Ham salad? If that's all we've got, it'll have to do." He swung his legs round and stretched. As he did so, he smiled at her, immediately running fingers through his ruffled hair, tucking his shirt into his jeans.

Annie smiled back. She would not let him abandon Linda. She hoped, for Linda's sake, she was wrong but she had the feeling that he would want rid of Linda now. He would throw her to the sharks without a second glance.

4

Leila put the ten twenty-pound notes in the envelope and sealed it. She had a vague notion that you weren't supposed to send cash through the post but it would be easier for Daisy and she had never cared much for rules and regulations. She preferred not to use a cheque because now and again Guy went through her bank statements with her, quite ridiculously intense, complete with calculator, just making sure, he said, that the bank was not fiddling her.

She let him do it because it pleased him to act the dutiful son but he need not worry. Nobody, institution or individual, would ever fiddle her. She had never parted with anything that was to her financial gain and that had included dear Charles. She had made it impossible for Charles to divorce her without incurring an enormous financial loss, as a considerable portion of her own money was tied up in the business. It had made him hate her the more, of course, but hate was hate, varying levels hardly mattered. It had given her a perverse pleasure to put the squeeze on him. Serve him right for all the lying and the cheating. Serve him right especially for going from her bed to that of a *plain* woman.

Guy had thankfully inherited none of Charles's nasty ways but none of his charm either. He was a good considerate son but had no panache. How it had escaped him, she had no idea. He was also far too preoccupied with the business and did not look after Barbara as a wife should be looked after. He took the poor girl for granted and it was beginning to tell on Barbara. She was looking more and more put upon with each passing day. Their marriage looked shaky although Barbara would not give up easily for Barbara enjoyed the luxuries of life, had developed a sense of style that belied her humble background. Reluctantly, Leila had to concede that she quite liked her daughter-in-law.

Barbara had been a compromise initially. Guy was painfully shy when young, still was in an irritating way, and it had looked so unlikely that he would have the gumption to find his own partner that she had been forced to try to do it for him. At that time, the girls of the county set, the ones with excellent pedigrees, were particularly unattractive. It was looking very much as if she might have to resign herself to putting up with a large, cheerful, ruddy-faced girl who was more at home mucking out the stables than wearing a hat for Ladies' Day when, much to her surprise, Guy turned up with Barbara in tow, his face an absolute picture of delight. There was never any doubt that he loved her. As for Barbara . . . Leila had never been sure about that. When there was money on one side only, one never could be quite sure.

She ought to have realised that the relationship was unlikely to succeed long-term for compromises never did. Coming up soon for their silver wedding anniversary and she wondered how much longer it would last. A steady drifting apart, that's what Leila perceived, with not even the passionate anger that she and Charles had had. Once apart, it would be like wading through water to make it work again.

She returned her thoughts to her granddaughter. The child had phoned in a panic. It would seem she had spent nearly all her own money on furniture for the love nest and she was desperate. Two hundred pounds would mean so much to her just as it meant little to Leila. The boyfriend sounded shiftless. Daisy had sounded just a mite fed up with him and that was a wonderful sign. Love in the attic was wearing thin and obviously dearest Daisy was finding it hard to cope now that the blanket of cossetting had been whipped from under her.

Daisy who had everything she wanted when she was a child. An excellent school. Quality friends. Horse-riding. Ballet, although that had fizzled out fast as it had been very much her mother's idea. Daisy, bless her, had inherited Guy's clumsiness when it came to tripping the light fantastic.

And look where it had all got her. To a dubious liaison with a very dubious young man. However, all was not lost but she had to work fast. The liaison had to be seen to be the act of a girl in love who was therefore temporarily unhinged. Leila intended to make sure that Daisy's reputation was unsullied. What Daisy needed was a good marriage.

Yes. She needed a good marriage to someone with class and money and she knew a good many very good families who might have a son of the right age. It was simply a matter of picking through them, although Barbara had gone huffy at the suggestion saying that marriages were not arranged nowadays. Daisy must make up her own mind.

What piffle. The child did not know her own mind at a mere twenty. She needed guidance and she, Leila, was the one to give it. What she did not know about the workings of a man's mind was not worth knowing. The secret of a happy marriage was getting the better of the battle of the minds. She had left it too late with Charles and, instead of stopping him in his tracks she had allowed the fellow to get off his mark and down the home stretch. She would not make that mistake again. She could sum up a man now from across a room and she vowed that it was going to be the last really useful thing she did with her life, to find a suitable match for Daisy. She planned a wedding in autumn, without doubt her favourite time of year. In Harrogate of course. She could see the whole scene so clearly and that would keep her going, although she knew it would be no easy matter to persuade dear Daisy where her duty lay. Of course there was still the unfortunate problem of the boyfriend but she would get round that. Being eighty had its compensations. People, most people, thought you utterly ga-ga. They did not realise that, behind the rotting facade, there might lurk a brain every bit as sharp as it ever was and just as devious. She exercised her brain daily for she was determined to go out of this world with her senses intact. She had to, if she was to meet up with Charles again in the next one.

The boyfriend could be bribed. It was not the first time she had used money to get her way and it would not be the last. She would have to get him on his own without Daisy hanging onto him. She picked up her letter and frowned. She would drive over instead to see Daisy. Durham, wasn't it? Leila hadn't the faintest idea why the child was in Durham but that's where she was. Such a nuisance because it meant an unfamiliar drive and the car really only liked to go places it knew. It was apt to wander erratically otherwise, up dead ends and the wrong way down one-way streets. Street signs these days were so very confusing and other drivers so impatient. Let's see . . . it would take several hours but she could do it in the one day if she set off now.

That decided, she moved fast or as fast as her eighty-year-old body would allow. First, she had to change and she wondered what to wear for a trip to Durham. She had never been there but she decided it warranted formal attire. Not that her entire wardrobe was not formal, but there were variations within it. The Jaeger wool and angora brown suit and her fur coat in case it was cold up there. The mink Charles had bought her once to assuage his conscience. Fur coats were under threat but she did not let it worry her. She refused to be intimidated.

Carefully, she dressed, studying herself in the mirror when she was ready. The whole world's disintegration could be traced to the moment women had taken to wearing trousers. She wished she could wear ankle length skirts that swished as she moved. So graceful and elegant. The suit was however beautiful and it fitted her slim body perfectly. She smiled at her reflection. Not too close. The encouraging thing was that, once you were over seventy five, the ageing process slowed. After all, there was a limit to how incredibly ancient you could look. Wrinkles ran out when there was no more room for them.

She applied lipstick, the familiar plum red, rouge and powder, and a splash of her perfume, the one Guy and Barbara had bought her for Christmas. Sweet of them. She was so glad they had not yet resorted to old-lady presents, bedjackets, lavender water and the like. Impatiently she sifted through her wardrobe. A hat? She considered and thought not. She wore her silver hair swept into an elegant chignon, the same style for years past, and was expert at pinning it up. She reckoned she could pass for early seventies and, as long as she remembered to take her time when walking, she was fine. The high heels made sure she walked with neat steps. With a final satisfied glance in the mirror, she picked up gloves and handbag and went to get the car.

It was a crisp clear morning, a hint of winter still around but a vague promise of spring also in the air. The extensive lawns were still very green and moist after their recent covering of snow, and on the hilltops a dusting was still visible. The last of the winter snow. The drive curved through clumps of rhododendrons towards the garage, discreetly off to one side. As she approached it, Leila sighed, aware that her neighbour was at work beside the tall hedge. He at once leaned on his spade. "Off out, Mrs Shawcross?"

"Yes. To Durham." She smiled at him, the silly old fool. Of course she was off out. "Henry, you will keep an eye on the house, won't you? I've just remembered that I've left the jewels out and I'm not going all the way back. They're just tipped out on the dressing table."

He looked at her oddly and then smiled too. "Always one for a joke, Mrs Shawcross. Don't you worry. You enjoy your day out. I'll keep an eye on things for you."

He would too. Wasn't he a retired chief inspector? She was not joking, incidentally. The jewels were indeed in a glittery heap as carelessly as if they were the costume variety and Leila knew that's where they would be on her return. People were neurotic these days about robbery. However, Barbara would be furious if she knew. Barbara thought they ought to be in a safe deposit box but what was the use of that? What was the point of owning them if you couldn't get them out, as she frequently did, just to sit and look at them. Touch them. They fascinated her. She adored diamonds most of all, adored the way they flashed in a myriad of colours as they caught the sunlight. In addition to her large ruby engagement ring, she always wore at least one of her pieces, one fabulous piece, so that people would look and wonder. Today she was wearing a brooch, sapphire surrounded by tiny diamonds, given to her by Charles for her fortieth birthday. It had to be said that, for a cheat, he was generous. She had never had the slightest qualms about accepting his gifts.

How did one get to Durham? Head towards Guy and Barbara's to begin with but turn north at some point. Something like that and she was determined not to ask Henry for directions as that would mean a detailed map and much pontificating. She started the car and drove sturdily out of the garage, deciding she had better get out and shut the garage doors as Henry was watching her every move. She waved to him as she set off, driving towards Blubberhouses initially then Ripon. She tried to concentrate, as she really ought when driving, but she found her mind wandering, letting the car go its own sweet way.

How would she handle this today? A delicate business and she must try not to upset or offend as she was sometimes apt to. Daisy and she were close which was precisely why Daisy had chosen to reveal her whereabouts to her rather than her parents. They had been so very parent-like, handling it in a way that guaranteed Daisy's fiery departure. Of course Daisy had rebelled. Leila recognised in her granddaughter the young girl she had once been herself. People forgot. They looked at an old woman and saw an old woman. They forgot that, years ago, she had been young, skin clear, eyes shining, body tempting. Like Daisy, Leila as a young miss had been pretty rather than beautiful, effervescent, intelligent and well connected, all qualities that had attracted the dashing Charles Shawcross, although it was still a sadness that it was perhaps the well connected that had attracted the most. Charles never did anything without a purpose.

Daisy, therefore, was a bubbly bright child and this boyfriend was her first, the first man who had ever paid her any real attention. She wondered just how much it would take to pay the tiresome boy off. She could offer to set him up in a business of his choice at the cost of selling off a couple of pieces of Charles's stuff. It was most appropriate that she should use his gifts for such a wonderfully peculiar purpose.

She turned off the road leading down into Harrogate in the direction of Ripon, negotiating its tortuous one-way system before winding northwards. Once out of Ripon, it was straight up the A1 to Durham, wasn't it? Sitting very firmly in the inner lane, nudging fifty m.p.h., she urged the car on its way. She could stop somewhere, she supposed, and ring Daisy to let her know she was coming but she decided against it. She loathed these cafés that were at the side of roads these days, both the food and people distinctly unappetising. Daisy would be delighted to see her. Surprised but delighted.

*   *   *

They'd had another row last night. About money. Alan was so laid back about it and it annoyed Daisy. It was she who stood at the check-out at the supermarket in a panic, trying to do sums in her head, wondering if she had enough cash. They had decided on a cash only policy as a means of controlling their spending. What they didn't have, they couldn't spend. Daisy was a mite put out. After all, it was mainly her money. She had, after some thought, cancelled her credit card knowing it was the only sensible thing to do but nearly breaking her heart in the process. Cutting it up had seemed so final. Trying to make do with such a pitiful amount each week for the housekeeping was really getting her down. She needed at least fifty pounds extra for food alone but Alan didn't see that. And there was no way she was going into a butcher's shop and asking for scrag end. She was a vegetarian in spirit anyway.

It was fizzling out and they both knew it but were not quite ready to admit it. Daisy was fed up to the teeth with the job, could have cheerfully flung food in the face of some of the guests who treated her like dirt. Some were nice, of course, gave her a good tip and a smile but she was more used to being on the other side of the fence and she couldn't stand it much longer.

Alan was painting but not selling. In other words, contributing nothing, except the dole cheque. If he showed some concern it might help but he had that peculiar lack of interest about money that some people from his background exhibit, and seemed not to believe her even when she flashed her bank statements at him. All her Micawber-like predictions of gloom wafted over him and he just grinned, which was infuriating, and said that it would be all right and that she shouldn't worry.

She was on late shift tonight but there was no way she was spending the morning in bed making up after their quarrel which was what he wanted. He thought making love solved everything. She was up early, having her morning cup of coffee alone in the living room of the flat, sitting in one of the new chairs, imagining she was back home in Harrogate. On spring and summer mornings, they would often have breakfast in the conservatory, overlooking the garden. Some of mum's homemade marmalade. Hot rolls. A pot of fresh coffee. Oh how she missed it.

It was difficult to admit that mum and dad might have been right. She was indeed stupid to throw away the chance of going to university and getting a degree. Taking time out had proved to be the waste they said it would be. And now she was reduced to this. Waitressing for fun in the holidays was okay but not as a permanent job. Now it was just a hard slog to nowhere.

"Alan . . ." She took her coffee, or what passed for coffee, through to the bedroom, standing in the doorway, deliberately out of reach. "We have to talk."

He couldn't have been asleep because he sat up in an instant, the new patchwork duvet wrapped round him. Wary. Eyes a little sad. "I know that," he said quietly. "Sorry about some of the things I said. I know you're trying your best but you're just not used to economizing."

"Neither are you," she said, infuriated at the casual remark. "Didn't I sell the car on Friday?"

"Yes you did. I know that hurt, Daisy. And I honestly don't mind you buying the desk. And the chair . . ."

"Alan . . ." she warned, sensing a new row brewing. "It was my car. I could do what I liked with the money." She wished she hadn't said that. It sounded childish.

"Well . . . yes . . . in theory." He smiled but she could not. "You're not enjoying this much anymore, are you?" he said, running a hand through his already ruffled hair. "Look Daisy . . . this is supposed to be fun. You and me. We shouldn't be arguing like this. If you want to go back home, then it's okay with me. I understand. I really do."

She shot him an irritated look. Oh great . . . shove the responsibility onto her. "You'd better get yourself out of bed," she said, going out and somehow managing to avoid slamming the door.

Durham was much smaller than she had imagined. Hardly big enough surely to call itself a city. The massive stone cathedral dominated the town, the tight hilly streets all around giving a cosy feel, the river twisting below. The sun was out but it didn't have a great deal of warmth in it yet and Leila did not feel too hot in the mink. She had to stop and ask three people before she found someone who knew where Daisy lived. She set off walking, silently cursing the cobbles, leaving the car parked on a double yellow line, half on the pavement, in a narrow side street beside one of the university halls of residence. If she was given a parking ticket, she would plead extreme old age and fragile state owing to the number of pills she was obliged to take for her heart condition. Growing old had to have some advantages. She didn't have a heart condition, not so far as she knew, but she had used that one on more than one occasion. People rarely checked. People did not dare to check when she spoke with such authority. It was amazing how trusting people were. An old lady with a heart condition was certain to bring a look of concern and sympathy.

She had intended to work out what she was going to say on the journey but, in the event, she did not seem to have done that. But no matter. She was here and business had to be done. She would take them out to lunch. A splendid lunch somewhere expensive. They would like that because they probably lived on beans and toast and a sprinkling of love. Piffle to all that. Love in the attic, love on a shoestring, whatever . . . it was all very well short term but to be avoided at all costs as a permanent situation. She couldn't think of anyone she knew whose love would survive under conditions of poverty. Guy and Barbara would be daggers drawn in a week if there was suddenly no money. It was a fact of life and it was no earthly use taking a high and mighty stance. Money mattered. Status mattered.

She had never met the boyfriend and, accordingly, she would form her own opinion. Barbara and Guy had only met him the once apparently and had been quick to make assumptions. Leila was determined to give him a fair chance. She would try not to be fazed if he turned out to be a clone of Charles, charm oozing out of every hot manly pore. Charles had possessed enough charm for three men, dispensing it all his life with devastating effect. For God's sake, he was still dispensing it to the nurses on his death bed. They had all thought him utterly charming just as they had thought her cold and detached because she had been most unobliging and been unable to drum up any tears.

Charles had set her pulses racing at eighteen when she first met him. One smile. One so romantic kiss on the hand. One deep look from those eyes of his. That had been that and it was funny that not one ounce of that formidable charm had gravitated towards his son. Where Guy had inherited his shyness from, Leila was at a loss to understand. He had gone to a good school, achieved suitably impressive grades, but the polish that it should have provided in tandem seemed to have escaped him. He was competent, that went without saying for wasn't the business doing well at a difficult time, but he lacked presence. He had no fire. He wasn't even devious either. Guy was open and trusting and the trouble about people like him was that they showed every emotion on their faces. Lately, she detected a look on his face that perplexed her. She so wished Guy would do something outrageous once in a while, even have an affair. Something unexpected. Show them all that he wasn't as overwhelmingly dull as he made out. Plodding and predictable. Who would have thought she would produce a son like that?

Daisy's flat was over a shop, with a separate entrance. She rang the bell and waited. It was a secondhand bookshop and the owner sat reading his paper and watching her through the window. She had been in to enquire and she had seen his greedy eyes on the large rings on her finger, seen those eyes glitter as he stared hard at the skins of her softly silky coat. Yes, everything's real, she nearly said, refraining from opening her coat to show off the brooch too.

She was just about to ring a second time when the door opened, a tiny bit, and Daisy peeped out. Pretty, blushing as soon as she saw her. "What are you doing here?" she demanded, opening the door wider so that Leila glimpsed steep stairs and a threadbare carpet. "I told you not to come, gran. I hope you've not told mum where I am?"

"I most certainly have not." Leila smiled, leaning forward to peck her cheek, "How are you, darling? May I come in? I have driven goodness knows how far on that dreadfully busy road and I am very tired."

Daisy let her pass into the hall, annoyed eyes on the mink, "Really, I wish you'd give that awful thing to Oxfam. Dead animals!" She shuddered, taking it from her, distastefully draping it over her arm as if it were skunk. "Come on up to the flat, gran. I warn you, it's all a bit down market for you."

"I didn't expect the Ritz." Leila managed a short, unconvincing laugh. The hall was clean if uninspiring. She thought of the house in Harrogate with its beautiful spacious rooms, its gentle colours, its lovely antique furniture, its flowers, its expensive linens. Oh dear. That poor Daisy should be reduced to this. However, it might make it easier. What Daisy needed was a new relationship so that she could quickly forget all this nonsense. She needed a marriage, no less, to a man with good connections and she was beginning to think of some possibilities, all with wonderfully snobby mothers who would be delighted to be associated with the Shawcrosses of Harrogate. Charles, despite his failings, had been gloriously powerful, ruthless and arrogant, with leanings to being a nineteeth-century sort of benefactor, bestowing gifts on deserving causes when it suited him. Charles was almost the inventor of positive public relations. The Shawcross name was spoken of in hushed tones, a name to be treasured.

Matchmaking was such a delicate matter. As Barbara could not be guaranteed to help she would have to do it alone, but she did not anticipate too many problems for wasn't Daisy a pretty, intelligent girl? Not too intelligent, for girls like that were off-putting, but intelligent enough. An old-fashioned girl at heart despite the stab at this modern liberation stuff. The liberation stuff was all right in principle and Leila was firmly for putting men in their right place but there was no point in having to work yourself to a shred to prove a point. Feminine wiles were a joy and these feminists had done themselves a great disservice when they tried to dispense with them. Leila felt sure she could teach them a thing or two. Hadn't she made Charles's last years sheer hell?

Added to Daisy's delightful physical attributes, there would be a handsome settlement so what could the objections be? The young men would fall over themselves to marry her, gently prompted by their mothers. First thing then was to establish contact with the mothers. She wanted to inspect all aspects of them, before deciding which family to honour with her granddaughter's hand. Oh dear, these stairs went on forever. Leila took her time. One careful step at a time. Time to recover her breath. Daisy, bless her, did not barge on but waited patiently, one step ahead.

"Here we are, gran." The steep stairs turned sharply and came to an end. "Would you like a cup of tea? Sorry we don't have Earl Grey. Will Co-op Dividend do? It was on special offer this week." A quick unrepentant grin accompanied this remark. Leila looked at her granddaughter with a sigh. She looked about fifteen, her face clean and free of make-up. Her hair was caught up in a ponytail with a ribbon, just as she had worn it when she was a little girl. Leila sighed, remembering. Co-op Dividend? How quaint. She couldn't recall ever having drunk that.

"This is . . . sweet," she murmured, taking in every detail of the room where Daisy lived in a single sweeping glance. Cheap and cheerful she believed the catchphrase to be. A bright sofa. Pine table and chairs. Thin rugs on bare floorboards. Flimsy gingham curtains at the window. The boy, rather to Leila's surprise, sprang up at once and came to greet her, holding out his hand. His jeans, identical to Daisy's, were paint-stained, as was his tee-shirt. A few canvasses were propped nearby, scenes of Durham. Oh . . . she hadn't realised he was a painter. Barbara had not mentioned that, which was just as well. Painting as a living was hardly likely to bring in a decent workable salary.

Leila took his hand, smiling briefly. She felt a great relief for, had he been a presentable type, she might have started to worry whether she was doing the right thing. As it was, there was no doubt, reinforced now with the knowledge that he dabbled. This young man was dispensable. "How very nice to meet you, Alan," Leila said, wondering if his hand was paint-stained too and glancing at her own just to make sure. "I'm glad you're here too because I shall need to speak with you before I leave."

"Will you?" He shot her a defiant glance out of wicked slate-grey eyes. His eyelashes were long and black, far too luxurious and wasted on a man, eyebrows brooding. Deep-set eyes, high cheekbones, firm mouth, strong nose, and a mop of dark curly hair. A period face, a rogue without doubt. His ancestors were very likely highwaymen. "You'll be wasting your time," he said quietly, "Daisy's parents rejected me simply because they thought I wasn't good enough. They never gave me a chance." A thin smile appeared and as promptly vanished. "Are you a snob too, Mrs Shawcross?"

"Yes I am and proud of it," she said, as Daisy giggled.

"How many people would change places with me given the opportunity? I might as well enjoy life. I own several houses, jewels, shares. I never have had to worry about where the next penny is coming from. Budgeting I'm told is such a bore. As you no doubt know," she added with a smile. "How do you two manage by the way?" She waited, noticing the sudden silence.

"We manage," he said at last, sullenly. "Daisy has a job, waitressing. It'll do until she gets something better. I'm trying to find a market for my paintings." He had a dark complexion, the sort of man who needs to shave twice a day, a thing he did not bother with too much for he had . . . what was it called . . . designer stubble? Knowing eyes like Charles. Oh yes, Leila could see perfectly well the kind of man he was and dear Daisy was making the same mistake she had made with Charles. Of course it was slightly different. Charles had had money and power and this boy had neither but they both possessed a sexual quality that was hard to define. It oozed from them both and Leila could see, to her dismay, that it had quite poleaxed dear fragile gullible Daisy.

"So you don't have an actual job that brings in money?" Leila enquired, wondering who would employ him, an aspiring painter. "Have you tried to get a job, dear?"

He was saved the embarrassment of an answer by the arrival of Daisy with a tray. Proudly, Daisy laid it on the table. Leila was pleased to see the china matched although it was that thick sort of pottery ware she disliked. "I can't remember if you take sugar in tea, gran," Daisy said, flushing, "If you do, I'll have to see if I can find some."

"No thank you. Alan and I were talking, darling," Leila told her, "And if you don't mind, we would like to continue our conversation later. Alone."

"Oh no you don't," Daisy said at once, flashing a warning glance towards him, "You can say what you have to say in front of me."

"Very well." Leila subsided into a huffy silence, not too concerned. She knew how to deal with Daisy. "I shall take you both out to lunch," she said, sipping the awful tea. "Have you something to wear for lunch?" she directed the question to

Alan, knowing that Daisy had brought her collection of clothes with her.

"I've got something in for us," Daisy said tightly, "Thank you for the offer, gran, but no thank you. You can eat with us if you like," she added as an afterthought, "We're having cheese omelettes for lunch. And a bread and butter pudding I've made myself from some leftover bread." Her defiant glance towards Alan was not lost on Leila.

"It sounds . . . delightful," Leila said carefully, marvelling at the child's ingenuity. "However I do not wish to impose myself on you." She returned her cup to the tray. "Perhaps while you prepare your meal, Alan can show me round the cathedral? I find churches depressing but I do feel I ought to visit it. Churches remind me of funerals these days," she said, "At my age, you can't keep up with the funerals. And why are churches so very cold? I'm sure God never intended us to suffer from chills in the bone whenever we visit His house. I see you've drawn a picture of it," she remarked, indicating one of the canvasses.

"Yes. I've drawn a picture," he said drily and, for a moment, Leila was taken aback. What was it about this young man? Something, and to her irritation she did not know what, something was bothering her. He spoke with an ordinary everyday accent, well modulated, not particularly Northern thank goodness, quite a passable manner of speaking in fact. "I'd be delighted to show you the cathedral," he said, unwinding from his chair.

"I'm coming with you," Daisy said, that little stubborn streak still with her, "I know what you're up to, gran, so don't look so innocent. I know you've been sent by mum to get me to go home."

"And you've no intention of doing that. Have you?" Alan said, a slight smile surfacing. "We're happy as we are, Mrs Shawcross."

Leila nodded. What were these two playing at? "You're absolutely wrong about your mother, Daisy," she said firmly. "She just sits anxiously by the telephone waiting for you to call. Please ring her, darling. You're being very unkind putting her through all this. Be that as it may . . ." she said quickly, as Daisy frowned, "I am here simply because I wanted to make sure you were all right. I haven't been able to sleep worrying about you." She thought of the two hundred pounds in her bag but she could not hand the money over to Daisy whilst he was in the room. One had to allow him some self respect in front of his sweetheart. She would slip it into Daisy's hand as they left.

"My daughter-in-law says that she knows precious little about you, Alan," Leila remarked chattily as they set off for the cathedral. "You rather upset them I'm afraid by being so secretive. Have you something to hide?" She gave him a moment to consider. "Perhaps you'd like to talk to me about yourself. And your family?"

"Not particularly." He smiled, a little smile. "Are you sure you haven't been sent by Daisy's parents? As a not very subtle ambassador?"

She glanced sharply at him. He was brighter than she first thought. Considerably so. "I most certainly have not," she said. "People do not push me around, Alan. I do precisely what I want. I always have."

"Okay. So why shouldn't Daisy do what she wants?"

She ignored that. Feigning extreme tiredness, she struggled towards a nearby bench. "May we rest? I realise it's a bore but I'm eighty and I have to pace myself these days."

They sat beside the river, the dark water quite still. The sun broke fitfully through the clouds and suddenly the scene before them was softly aglow. At her side, she heard Alan's sigh of contentment as his eyes scanned the river and the bank opposite. Artist's eyes of course. They tended to see things differently. "Of course Daisy must do what she wants," Leila said irritably, "Have I ever said otherwise? Please don't confuse me with her parents. They're a little old-fashioned I'm afraid."

"And you're not?" He laughed at that. "Leave us alone, please. We'll survive. I admit, it's not easy but we're determined to muddle through together."

He no longer looked quite so bribable. Stay out of my granddaughter's life suddenly sounded not only melodramatic but out of the question too. He would very likely bite her head off at the suggestion. However . . . everyone had their price and what wouldn't he give for the opportunity to exhibit his paintings. Yes . . . she would work on that line.

"I'm only asking for time," she began slowly, putting a restraining hand on his arm as he made to leave. "Breathing space. Give Daisy a little breathing space. She's very young, far too young to be thinking of marriage. Stay out of her life for a while, it needn't be long. And then, if she and you still feel the same way, then . . ." she took a deep breath, "So be it."

"We weren't exactly thinking of marriage," he mused, picking up on her point. "But . . . what's it worth . . . this breathing space?"

Ah . . . she had him. "If we must talk money," she said with a sniff, "Then I suppose it's worth a considerable amount."

"How much?"

"Shall we carry on now?" Leila let him help her to her feet and they walked to the bridge and weaved their way across through the pedestrian traffic. The hill up to the cathedral was steep and she found it hard work, no conversation possible. That did not matter because she preferred to let him mull it over. They were after all on the same wavelength although it was something of a surprise that he seemed to be agreeable in principle to a bribe with so little effort on her part. A measure perhaps of his true feelings for Daisy. Daisy would be well rid of him.

They wound their way up and up, ever up. At last they arrived at the green in front of the cathedral and he stopped, seeming to realise that she would want to catch her breath and also take a moment to gaze at her first sight of it. "Most impressive," she murmured, meaning it. "Thank you, Alan," as he took her arm to escort her inside.

She glanced at him, pleasantly surprised at his natural politeness, wondering with a twinge of guilt, if he really did love Daisy. If he did then she was sorry. Sort of sorry. The sunlight blitzed through the stained glass window and they stood silent. In awe. Leila bit her lip, the guilt swelling. Oh dear, God had this ability to make her feel extremely anxious and it got worse as she grew older. When she eventually met up with Him, she was going to have to do an awful lot of explaining. She glanced up, dizzy, telling Him silently that she was only doing this for Daisy's sake. Someone had to guide her through this awkward time and nobody else had the gumption to do it.

"Do you want to . . . pray or anything?" He looked embarrassed and, despite herself, she warmed momentarily to him. She wanted to say she was sorry but it was impossible. There was no way he could become part of the family. One simply had to draw the line somewhere and, even though his background was a mystery, it was sure to be unexceptional and he fell far short of her expectations for Daisy.

"I'd just like to sit quietly a moment if I may?" She slipped into a pew and closed her eyes, shutting him out, feeling the silence echo all around. Church silence. She did not pray as such. She just talked to herself and if God happened to be listening then she did not mind. She reiterated that she was doing this for Daisy and Daisy alone. Well . . . perhaps a little for herself too but surely at her age she could be granted a little late happiness. Seeing her granddaughter married, suitably married, would give her great happiness. She wanted someone with a nice pedigree so that the announcement would sound suitably grand. A tall handsome man, probably some years older than Daisy. In his early thirties therefore, ready to settle down, ready to start a family, established in his chosen career. She sighed, opened her eyes and blinked. She could see Daisy, beautiful in white lace, carrying a bouquet of tiny pink roses. The vision evaporated as Alan, whom she suddenly realised was sitting squashed beside her, coughed to attract her attention.

"Amen," she said, frowning at him.

"Thought you'd dropped off," he said cheekily. "Shall we have a tour around?"

"I've seen enough thank you." She followed him, her heels making an unwelcome clicking sound on the aged stones. At the door, she reached into her handbag for a sizeable cash donation to deposit in the box. She fluttered in a banknote, waiting whilst Alan was shamed into fishing in his jeans for a coin.

"I'm willing to give you two thousand pounds," she told him, pausing outside to slip on her gloves. "For that, you must go away soon. I'll leave you to think of an excuse for poor Daisy.

As I have already said, if you both feel the same way after . . . say, two years . . . then so be it. I shan't want the money back. Look on it as a gift."

"But you expect Daisy to be married to someone else by then? In two years time?" he asked matter of factly. "Or one of us to be married to someone else?"

"Two years is both a long time and a short time," Leila said. "A short time if you consider your whole life together. On the other hand, two years is a long time for me. I may not be around in two years. Even if I'm not, I would like to think that you would honour our little arrangement."

He nodded. "I don't mind admitting I'm short of cash. I've had the opportunity to arrange an exhibition but I need money. I'd like to specialise in northern scenes, some oils but mainly watercolours. I'm beginning to feel more at ease with watercolours. I know it's not easy to be successful but a lot of it is luck too. I just need a lucky break."

"And this could be it," Leila jumped in at once. "A proper exhibition. An article in the paper. A few people interested. I have quite a few paintings myself," she added, "My late husband was a keen collector."

"Really?" He glanced at her, sensing that she was a little weary. "Would you care to rest again?" he offered, "There's another bench over there."

She shook her head. "I would prefer that we conclude our business. I can let you have a cheque now for two thousand pounds. I would then expect Daisy to tell me shortly that the affair is also concluded. Is that clear?"

"It is. However . . . two thousand is not enough. I don't want to hurt her. I love her you see."

What price that? Leila clicked her tongue. Damn the boy, he was going to be awkward. "I'll double it," she said helplessly. "Four thousand. There . . . you can really get yourself started for that. Organise any number of exhibitions."

"It's chicken feed," he said quietly. "What I really need is a year off to paint and market my work. A year when I don't need to worry about money. A year when I don't need to scratch about looking for temporary work, that sort of thing. A year when I can just relax and enjoy the painting."

She saw clearly that it meant a lot to him. "Four thousand," she repeated. "That's my final offer."

"Ten thousand."

She sniffed and stared hard at him. "Eight."

His eyes glittered. "Done," he said.

5

David loved the bustle of Blackpool. It had life, damn it, vitality and it was too carefree to worry about what people might think. True, he had chosen to move out to St Annes and he now wondered why. He needed to be at the heart of things, in Blackpool itself. Years ago, he had promised himself he would set up shop here and, by God, he had.

The first million's the hardest don't they say. The first few thousand were the hardest as far as he was concerned and getting the money together for that first venture, the renovation of the nightclub, had been the hardest for him. The trouble was that the consortium who loaned the money still thought they could dance in the wings and have a say in the running of the place when the debt was long since paid off. Or at least, that particular debt.

It was a good investment but then he reckoned he had a nose for a winner. He didn't do too badly on the horses and the dogs either and, over the years, they'd earned him a tidy sum. It wasn't a surprise to him therefore that it turned out to be a goldmine, that first club. Grotty and run-down but in a good spot and he had tarted it up to just the right degree, put a doorman outside, charged the earth to get in, membership fiddles included, and soon it was earning enough in the summer and through the illuminations for it to tolerate the slack period in the winter months which he spent re-tarting it up, adding a layer of glitter, booking in some speciality acts for the season. The disco, a few streets away, came later, for the kids, a seething hotbed for holiday romances. A manic disc jockey, splinteringly decibelled top-of-the-minute noise, a million flavours of crisps, flashing hypnotic lights, the crazed body movements that passed for dancing and he had it made. He called it "Ambrosia". Fitting he thought although some clowns thought he meant the rice pudding.

When they first married, he and Ruth had a flat near the railway station. Flashing lights from the gaudy illuminated guest house opposite and noise all day and all night. Ruth spent her days working as a hardware assistant in Lewis's department store and her nights, or rather some of them, trying earnestly to get pregnant. She'd wanted a baby straight off but she was a slow starter in that department. It wasn't his fault. Christ, no. He knew at least a couple of girls whose offspring might be his so there was nothing wrong with him. That's when the extra-marital affairs started. When you had to think about a baby every time you made love, it was a bit of a turn-off and it wasn't as if Ruth was that enthusiastic or energetic in the first place. Persevering would be a better word.

She was happier when they could afford to move, having worried constantly that a flat over a tatty joke shop was no place to bring up a baby, if there was ever a baby to bring up. The flat was too down-market, a bad address on the business cards he had printed. He made a move as soon as was possible. No half measures. He skipped the terraced house, the semi, and went straight for a big red-brick detached near Stanley Park, a bit suburban for his taste but the move was calculated and he had to make some concessions to his wife, although at the time he could barely afford it. She loved it there. She made it a proper home, doing housewifely things like making up the curtains herself and it soon filled with an endless supply of crochet mats and cushions, as well as discounted hardware from Lewis's. She also did suburban things like gardening and chatting to the neighbours which was more than he ever did. When Annie was born, it put the icing on Ruth's cake, and he realised now what a good mother Ruth had been. She gave up work cheerfully as soon as her pregnancy was confirmed. At his suggestion, because having a wife who worked in hardware took some explaining amongst the people he was trying to impress. She was at her happiest just spending time with Annie when she was a baby and toddler, talking to her, reading to her, taking her for walks in the park. The nearby park featured a lot in her early life, that and the sea, for nobody could live in Blackpool and not be acutely aware of the sea. They hadn't managed to get out together much as a complete family. Pressure of work and all that.

Looking back, he saw that the female conspiracy had begun when Annie was in her cradle and had never let up.

How could he get Annie to like him more? It wasn't too late, was it? Lying on the sofa in the house opposite the sand dunes, David tried to figure it out. Thank God the winter was nearly over. He hated the cold. He hated the stormclouds bombing in from the sea. He hated the emptiness.

Blackpool though was his town, pure and simple, a dream fulfilled and, in her own quiet way, Ruth had liked it too. She'd never told him otherwise but then she wouldn't. She wasn't the sort. She kept herself firmly in check did Ruth. She had existed on a low simmer whereas he liked to live life on full scorching red heat. Why not? When you saw how life could deal a blow, switch you off, it wasn't worth playing safe. Look where playing safe had got Ruth.

The glitter and glamour and gutsy enthusiasm of this town had overwhelmed him from the first moment he had seen it. It was everything he hoped it would be. They had come for a competitive dance, launched rather abruptly into it. Barbara had been damned nervous, face pale, eyes wide with astonishment, looking like an angel in softest blue, a very waltzy dress with a billowing skirt over a multitude of creamy petticoats, tiny straps slinking over her powdered shoulders, her dark hair tumbling in waves about her face. Pale blue satin shoes and pale silk stockings to complete the ensemble. They were easily the best-looking couple there and whether that had any bearing on the result he had never been sure. They had been competent in the waltz. No more. In the Latin American section, with Barbara brilliant in red, sizzlingly sultry, silky, sexy, they were superlative. Unbeatable combination.

Seeing her picture, looking at it rather for the first time in years, had brought it all painfully back, and last night he'd decided to try to contact her to tell her about Ruth although he didn't know why. He didn't want sympathy but he felt she ought to know about Ruth for hadn't they been friends? Sort of. He couldn't find the address list anyway for Ruth dealt with things like that nor could he find a phone number. She was still living somewhere in Harrogate, he thought, but it was evidently ex-directory. There was a number for Shawcross Enterprises and that was probably her husband but he had no wish whatsoever to speak to him. Big, boring Guy. How the hell Barbara had found it in her heart to prefer him was incredible. He'd been quick off the mark, too, obviously waiting his chance, devious bugger, pushing himself in where he wasn't wanted. Their little crowd had never wanted Guy as part of it, toffee-nosed they called him and that's exactly what he was. Private school. High-class parents. Always got money in his pocket. That had hurt. Turning up one night in a car, a brand-new Triumph Spitfire of all things, a bit flash for Guy, twin carbs and the bloody lot. He'd been almost shamefaced at the extravagance, insisting that he'd saved up for it himself out of a holiday job. Balls! Nobody saved nearly five hundred quid from a holiday job. They all knew his mother had bought it for him for his 21st. All he'd got for *his* was a new suit from Burtons. He'd looked good in it, he recalled, but then he'd always been a snappy dresser.

Barbara hadn't been particularly impressed, either by Guy's car or by his suit, but then that was Barbara. She liked to pretend that things like that did not matter. She always thought she was a touch above the rest of them and he felt sure, well almost sure, that she'd married Guy for the money and one thing money could not buy was dancing feet. Serve her right therefore that he was so clumsy and uncoordinated. Big broad chaps like him often were. Dancing with him must be hell. Once Guy Shawcross had got Barbara on the dance floor that first time that was it. Bound together as if they were glued. For ever. Ruth would have made Guy a good wife. They would have made a truly wonderfully boring pair. They'd married the wrong people and there was no point in denying it.

He shifted on the sofa, reached over and lit a cigarette. He was bored at home and he really needed to get back to work, into the swing of things, but it was too early. Things ran okay, the club, disco and amusement arcades ticking over under their personal managers, really ticking over at this slack time of year, but that didn't mean that he trusted any of his staff. His number one assistant was a sly devil and David knew he fancied his chances of taking over when David retired. Sod him. He had no intention of retiring. Nevertheless, it meant that he had to keep his senses on alert for any attempted coup. His assistant was the sort who would drop him in it from a great height. He knew he walked a tightrope but, in over twenty years, he had never fallen off. Some swaying but he had kept upright. He still had the contacts, the greasy-handed variety, and he had no need to humiliate himself in front of bank managers to raise ready cash.

He would be glad when the funeral was over. That was really bugging him, the funeral. He didn't know what he was supposed to feel . . . what did he feel? . . . pissed off he supposed but that didn't seem the right emotion. He had never loved Ruth as he might have loved Barbara. Snooty bitch. Life with old Guy would suit her down to the Harrogate ground but with him, she could have had real passion, the hot pounding variety. Love in the afternoon, for God's sake. Love in the middle of the morning if it took his fancy. He bet Guy Shawcross had never made love in the afternoon under the pier or in the sand dunes at midnight. Neither had Ruth.

Poor old Barbara. She didn't know what she was missing. Love when you might get caught out at any second was bloody exciting. Barbara as he remembered her was coolish about sex but he felt that something lurked in her very deep down and it was worth the researching. Barbara, he realised now, was a very good tease just like that blonde with the green eyes, eyes that had promised the earth, body that always pulled back.

Women were the bane of his life but he couldn't damn well do without them. Linda was beyond a joke now. Ten years or so, on and off, and he couldn't understand for the life of him why it had dragged on so long. It was like having all the disadvantages of marriage without any of the perks. Linda nagged him now for Christ's sake. She was on at him to take her out in the Rolls. She didn't like the thought of being hidden away now. She wanted to go away after the funeral for a few days now that their relationship was legitimate. He knew damned well what she was hoping for and she could forget it. Marriage to

Linda was not on the cards. Not in the past. Not now. Not in the future.

As soon as the funeral was over, he would call it off. Strangely, it worried him, the calling it off. He had had enough practice at doing just that with other women, other times, but Linda was so trusting with the brains of a wide-eyed hen. He supposed she must love him or think she did to have stuck it out like this and he was sorry therefore to hurt her. He hoped she wouldn't do anything stupid like throw herself under a tram. No. She wouldn't do that. She was soft as jelly was Linda . . .

Annie peeped in the room, saw him stretched out on the sofa, his eyes closed. "Dad . . .?" she said quietly. "Are you awake?"

"Course I'm awake." He moved slightly, and opened his eyes, took stock of her. "Is that one of your mother's pendants?"

"Yes." Annie guiltily fingered the pendant at her neck. "She said she wanted me to have it."

He waved his hand irritably. "I know. I didn't mean anything. Of course you should have it. Who else? It just looks different on you, that's all."

Annie smiled a little. For a brief moment, a little nugget of warmth and understanding passed between them. She didn't know if dad was aware of it but she certainly was. She didn't want to spoil things by discussing the funeral but needs must. "I just wanted you to know that everything's organised for the . . . what do you call it? . . . the refreshments after the funeral," she said, "Mrs Summers next door has offered to come in and help but I told her we had hired caterers. Did I do the right thing? She seemed a bit upset. Perhaps I should have accepted? She liked Mum."

"Sod Mrs Summers. If she's angling for an invitation, she can forget it." He sprang instantly to his feet, going to pour himself a drink. "It's called a wake. I thought you'd know that. Don't they teach you anything at that school of yours?"

"Sorry. I know it's called that. I just forgot."

"Sorry too. I'm a bit on edge." He smiled. "Thanks for arranging things, love. You've been wonderful."

"I invited Linda to the funeral. Miss Ridgeley." She spoke calmly, even though the unexpected praise had startled her.

"She said no. I went round to see her the other day and asked her. I thought it only fair to ask her seeing that she's such a friend of yours."

"You did what?" The drink slopped as he spun round, "What the hell were you thinking of going to see her? You had no business, young lady. In future, you can keep well out of my affairs."

"Affairs?" Annie felt her heart pound. She couldn't let it pass, she couldn't. She owed it to mum. "How long did you cheat on Mum?" she asked softly, feeling her cheeks burn, seeing his astonishment. "When did it start? When I was a baby or before that? Did you imagine that she never knew? Even I knew for heaven's sake as soon as I was old enough to know about these things. You broke Mum's heart."

"Watch it, madam." He looked at her, holding her gaze, his own eyes shocked, before downing his whisky in a single gulp. "I'd keep quiet if I were you, Annie, before you say something you regret."

It was too late. She couldn't stop herself now. "Didn't you think she knew about the number of times people saw you dancing at the Tower with other women," she said, unable to stop her voice from rising or worse, shaking. "And what I can't forgive you for is that you carried on doing it even when Mum was ill. You shouldn't have done that, Dad. You shouldn't have done it."

He did not flinch. "That's business, dancing at the Tower," he said quietly, "You know I like to keep my hand in, teaching. There's nothing else to it. It's still bloody useful to know how to do a waltz. I'd teach *you* if you'd let me. Look . . ." his smile was brief, odd. "Let's not quarrel. We've just got each other now, Annie, you and me. Your mother wouldn't want us to quarrel." He raised his eyes heavenward as if she was already up there, watching them, before the absurdity of the gesture struck him and he looked down, embarrassed.

Annie laughed. "What play are those lines from? Honestly, do you expect me to believe all this grief you're supposed to be suffering? It's *me* who's suffering. I loved her." She bit her lip to stop the trembling, determined not to break down into tears.

"So did I." There was a short miserable silence as Annie

struggled with her composure, already regretting all this. "You don't know the half of it. I could have walked out, any time, but I didn't. I didn't want to leave your mother stranded. She was never short of money, you had everything you wanted."

"Thanks a lot." She tried to smile but she knew it would come out twisted, angry. "Admit it. You're glad. Going to see her at the hospital was a real chore, wasn't it? Sitting there with nothing to say." Her voice caught and she turned away, rubbing at her face with her sleeve.

Silence again. Years of frustration. Misunderstanding. "Don't you ever speak to me like that again," he said finally, dangerously subdued. "I'll put this down to your being upset," he said, picking up his car keys. "I'm going to Linda's. And I don't know when I'll be back so you needn't wait up for me."

The door slammed behind him.

Annie was shaken by the row. She shouldn't have said those things to him. She remembered suddenly the way the spring in his step was missing on those visits to the hospital. There hadn't been much to say sitting there beside the high hospital bed, mother propped against pillows, face drawn and pale. The flowers and the useless Get Well cards on the locker beside her. It had been difficult to think of anything positive but he might have made some effort.

Pity about the row. It had upset her just when she was coping a bit better. She was glad she'd got over the ordeal of returning to school, at least that made things fractionally easier. Miss Boyd had spoken to her again, happening to run into her in the corridor, her manner sympathetic without being too mushy. Annie appreciated her doing that. She so admired her and worried a bit about Miss Boyd's reaction and that of her other teachers if she decided to get a job. They would not be pleased and that was putting it mildly.

According to school gossip, Miss Boyd lived alone in Lytham and there didn't seem to be any men in her life. Annie and her friends decided that it must be of her own choosing for she was attractive if not exactly young. Beautifully neat. Someone had once seen her at the theatre with a man but he had been incredibly old so maybe he had been her father or an uncle.

Annie liked to think that Miss Boyd was perfectly capable of conducting her life happily without the need for a man to prop her up.

She would probably be much the same. After dad, Annie wasn't sure she would ever be able to find a man for herself that she could trust. Really trust. Dad had been spinning yarns for so long, he probably didn't know what was true and what wasn't. Miss Boyd would sort *him* out. She smiled at the very idea. Miss Boyd would have him sussed out in two seconds flat.

The house was quiet with him gone and she picked up her own car keys, needing a spot of fresh air. She would take a run to the green in Lytham, she decided, as she backed out of the drive. Mum had particularly liked it there. She had once told Annie that dad had promised her they would retire there and she was delighted at the prospect. Annie had played along with it but she suspected that it was just another of those things he said. His promises were like sticks of rock. Meant to be broken. He would never move to Lytham. It was hardly his scene. Deadsville, he'd once called it.

It was growing dark, the sea brown and sludgy in the Ribble estuary, the mudflats moist, the headland opposite a faint blur. A dull day had produced a dull evening and the late clouds hung aimlessly in the tired sky, a pale white sliver of a moon peeping out from time to time. Annie stopped the car on the coast road and stared out at the indistinct view, at the green and the windmill. She stepped out and walked towards the sea, feeling suddenly close to her mother, as if she was at her side. In a way it was comforting. If she wanted, her mother could always be there for her, at her side.

It wasn't fair. Life just wasn't fair. She could do without all this, just before her exams. Most evenings, she sat with her books on her desk and thought about other things. About mum mainly and what might have been. Dad had never been around when she was little. Never once helped out. She'd once heard him boast that he'd never changed a nappy in his entire life. Although, according to mum, he'd been quite moved on the day she started school, rushing to get his camera before she and mum set off. The photograph was the proof of the pudding. A tiny little Annie in a tiny little uniform, rather forlornly clutching a little bag, trying to be brave but the lower lip trembling. Maybe he'd realised then just what he'd missed. Of course it was already too late for the damage was done and he was not far short of a stranger in her eyes. He was still a stranger. She had no idea what he thought about, deep down. Now that mum had gone, he could have his freedom again, were it not for her. She hated to think she might cramp his style.

With a sigh, feeling the weight of the world on her slim shoulders, Annie strolled on. The clouds passed over and the moon perked up and sent silvery shadows across the shallows. Sounds of the evening settling in. Softly moving, plopping water. The smell of wet sand. Her senses on alert, she closed her eyes and listened. Breathed deeply. And slowly relaxed.

Walking back later towards the row of big houses fronting the green, she wondered whereabouts in Lytham Miss Boyd lived. Somehow, her living here was exactly right. Exactly the sort of place she would expect her to live. Annie wouldn't be surprised if she saw her this very minute, walking crisply towards her. She hoped not. With her exams looming, she ought not to be wasting time on late evening strolls like this.

She wondered what traumatic event would happen next. She recognised her father's restlessness. If, or rather when, he moved to a bachelor flat, where would that leave her? She was not going to play gooseberry to his ladies. A memory of Linda surfaced and she smiled. Poor Linda. She was pretty certain Linda would not feature in his future plans. But the question was, would she?

He drove too quickly, rather stupidly taking his anger out on the beautiful car. Annie's harsh words rung in his head, refusing to go away. How dare she? Accusing him of not caring? What the hell did she know about adult feelings? She was only a kid.

His breathing calmed as he neared Linda's and he slowed to a more respectable speed, stroking the steering wheel, his way of apologising. The normally garish street looked pretty dismal in the evening gloom with most of the summer shops temporarily boarded up. The street was in direct line for the beach, the packed central beach, the thoroughfare in season for the little troops of donkeys, its tallish buildings forming a wind tunnel. The sand blew in constantly and he frowned as usual as he saw the thin layer on the bonnet of the car. It looked out of place here, in this street, a street of beat-up Minis and failed MOT rejects. He caught a few sly glances from some kids as he clicked the door shut, locked it and walked over to Linda's. He gave them a warning look. If one of those kids so much as leaned on that car, he'd have them. It was no longer new, far from it, it hadn't been new when he bought it for even he hadn't been able to afford a new Rolls but a Rolls was a Rolls was a Rolls. Age did not matter. If anything, it added to the touch of class, gave it that interesting pedigree. Pity it wasn't the same for humans. He sighed as that thought hit him. Once you touched forty, you were on the slippery slope. The thought of growing really, pathetically old appalled him. He'd walk into the sea first. For God's sake, buck up, he told himself, wallowing in self-pity won't get you anywhere. There had to be a bright spark somewhere on the bloody horizon but, at this moment, with Ruth's funeral looming, he couldn't find one.

He had forgotten his key so he knocked on the door, ignoring the titters of the kids as he did so. She was not home. Stupid of him to have expected her to be in on a weekday but it did not help somehow and he felt ridiculously disappointed. He contemplated going to the club and watching her act. Act! . . . that was a laugh. She fancied she could dance, pink feathers to go with the flushed face and fishnet tights. She had no style. After doing it for the last ten years, she still hadn't got the hang of it. Nobody bothered to turn round from the barstool and look. Most of the regulars used her spot to go and order extra drinks. The opening bars of her music, Linda one-tune, was the signal for a mass evacuation. She looked as if she was going to run off stage halfway through and the relief in her face when it was over was transparent, her grateful smile the best part of the act. A coy stripper, that was a good one.

He scribbled a note and pushed it through the door, hearing a plaintive miaow from behind the letter box. Why she bothered to feed that smelly cat he had no idea. She could come to the funeral if she wanted and, if anyone asked, she could be some distant cousin, one of the unmentionable wings of the family. It would show Annie that she didn't have a monopoly of delicate feelings although he still wondered at the wisdom of it. Ruth would have had a blue fit.

When he got home, Annie's light was still on and he contemplated knocking on her door and asking if she wanted a cocoa or something. He had no idea what she drank at bedtime. He was actually standing outside her door trying to work out what to say before he decided against it. Tomorrow, he would give her a cheque and tell her to get herself some nice clothes. Women liked that.

He poured himself a drink and sat awhile unwilling to go to the bedroom he had shared, albeit briefly, with Ruth. Everything of hers had been cleared out but something of her lingered and it haunted that room more than anywhere else. The faintest sniff of the perfume she had used. It disturbed him, that smell. Tongue-clicking, head-shaking Ruth, smiling that mummy-understands sort of smile. She'd always treated him like a child, a naughty child who needed to be fussed over occasionally. He stubbed out his cigarette and promptly lit another, pushing two fingers into the air as if he heard her annoyed exclamation. Sod it Ruth. What does it matter now? You're the one who got cancer, not me.

Shame hit him hard and knocked him back. He wished he could send that thought back to where it came from. He squashed out the newly lit cigarette and dropped his head into his hands. For the first time since Ruth died, grief pierced him. A sound escaped him. On the last few visits to the hospital, conscience pricking sorely, feeling a real swine because he'd just come from Linda, he had fought against the dreaded silence of the visit, the staring at her pale pained face and started to chat, promising her a holiday, a really great holiday, when she was better. Where would she like to go he had asked? The Caribbean? Italy? Or somewhere even more exotic, the Far East maybe? He would take her wherever she wanted to go, money no object. She had looked at him and smiled. I wouldn't mind a trip to Scotland she had said, seeming to give the matter a great deal of thought, the western islands.

Typical. She'd turned her nose up at the exotic life even then, even when they both knew it was all a sham. They both knew she was dying. Bloody hell, Ruth, he found himself thinking, why did you have to go and spoil it? We were used to each other and we would have carried on forever and a day the way we were. You wouldn't have minded me growing old, losing my looks. You knew I was a bastard and you didn't care because you loved me.

Her photograph with her accusing eyes stared solemnly at him from the mantelpiece and he reached up and held it close a moment. Too late. Annie was right. Going to the hospital had been a chore but he could have made it easier for Ruth. If the positions had been reversed, she would have done that for him. He could have helped her on her way, said he loved her, couldn't he? He could have held that skeletony hand, looked deep into those shadowy eyes and let rip. He had an actor's gift, didn't he? Positions reversed, he could have done a great deathbed scene. Ruth would have stayed with him, he just knew it, stayed and talked him through it and out of it. He'd not wanted to be there because he was scared. Scared to see her like that.

As it was, Ruth departed life quietly, alone, at precisely ten thirty-three, in the few moments it took the nurse to go out of the room and get something. He was sorry for that. Bloody hard luck that. Everybody needs a hand to hold just then.

So what was left for him now that she was gone? Success mattered. Not the small-time success he enjoyed but something much more. He wasn't satisfied with what he had. He wanted to expand, try something new maybe, so that he wasn't so dependent on tricky deals that could go either way, not so beholden to the men from his past who were a tram's ride away from being crooks. He needed to get into something that wasn't quite so tied up with the summer trade, for all it needed was a lousy English summer and they were on a slide. Lousy summers made people think of abroad. Lousy summers made them flock to hot Mediterranean beaches.

He had a vision. He might be small-time but Blackpool was not. How could it be with the Tower and the Pleasure Beach, biggest and best. He had a vision of something spectacular. An enormous indoor complex kept at a constant sweating temperature where the visitors could wander around semi-naked. The theme was the problem. There had to be a theme these days. The only ones he could come up with already existed elsewhere. If he could only think of something different, something original, he would get that nervous accountant of his to work out a business plan. God, it would make him a bomb and that's what he dreamed of. He wanted people to have all the advantages of the Med without the downside. Foreign money was inconvenient, foreign languages were a bore and foreign food was crap.

He needed to drum up finance but it would be a winner when he had thought it through. The weather would become irrelevant. It could be pissing with rain outside and it would matter not a damn. The Ambrose All-weather Fun City? David sighed, not wanting to listen to the little voice that warned him it was all make-believe. If Ruth were here, she would listen sympathetically to his plans. He could always count on her to listen when everyone else turned aside. She was the only person who ever knew about his ambitions, the only person he could trust not to laugh at them. Why shouldn't he have a vision? Everybody had dreams but some people did something about them, made them happen.

Ruth had faith in him for what it was worth. She was surprised at some of the ventures, disapproving naturally of the nightclub and refusing to set foot in it. She worried about the amusement arcades, said it was too tempting for the kids. Ditto the bingo halls for the pensioners. She would have preferred it frankly if he had turned out to be a nine-to-fiver with a packed lunch in his briefcase and a pension, old Guy Shawcross to the hilt.

Totally depressed, he went finally to bed. They were going to give Ruth a decent send-off and that would please her. Top-notch arrangements were in hand, only the best for her. Top of the range coffin. A nice service at the Methodist Church she had occasionally attended. A single rose for the coffin from him. He liked that touch and it would appeal to Ruth. Women liked touches like that. Romantic touches.

Alone in the bed, he lay quietly, not sprawled out but lying comically neat in his half. Outside, he could just about hear the sea if he strained his ears. He listened. A clock ticked. Ruth's perfume, damn it to hell, lay in the air, more obvious in the dark. After all this sodding time! Absently, half asleep, he turned and automatically felt the other side of the bed. Nothing but a cold sheet and even Linda was better than a cold empty sheet.

He would get married again. It had to be marriage with him. Why marriage and not living together he had no idea for he never considered himself conventional. Far from it. Annie would be awkward about him remarrying but Annie would have to learn to live with it. Annie would regard it as a betrayal but Annie was not his keeper. She was his daughter and the trouble was he couldn't find it in his heart to love her any more than he had loved her mother. Irritation was the emotion he suffered where Annie was concerned. And it was doubly irritating that his daughter could read him like a book. It would be better when she was away at college for he was sure he would not be alone for long. After a suitable period of mourning, he would be well and truly back in business.

6 ∫

"He's in a meeting, Mrs Shawcross," Gladys said with a welcoming smile, "I can disturb him if you like."

Barbara returned the smile and sat down. "No, no, don't do that." She glanced at her watch. "I'll just wait if he won't be too long."

"Of course. Will you excuse me while I . . .?"

"Oh please, carry on, forget I'm here," Barbara said, wishing now that she'd never come. Stupid idea. She hoped it would not be too obvious to everyone why she was here. She had never done this before. Checked up on him. She had no idea what she had expected to find. It wasn't as if she had hoped to catch him out, find him and Gladys sprawled naked on the desk. She was being perfectly ridiculous about this. For heaven's sake, she had been a secretary herself, years ago before she married Guy, and there had never once been any funny business. Guy would treat Gladys Ward precisely how she had been treated by her boss, old Mr . . . goodness, the name escaped her. Such an age ago.

"Would you like a coffee or cup of tea, Mrs Shawcross?" Gladys asked. She was wearing a bright green suit that looked good on her, although the cheap scarf spoilt the effect. Barbara, accepting the offer of coffee, did a comparison between that and her own. No comparison really in the cut or style or the cost. However, would Guy notice such things? Gladys was younger than she, quite pretty, and supremely efficient judging by the manner she briskly conducted the phone calls that kept coming her way. Somehow, she managed to conjure up two cups of coffee as well.

"Such a nuisance, isn't it?" Gladys said, handing her one with another pleasant smile.

"What is?" Barbara asked stupidly, feeling less and less in control of this ridiculous urge to pop in unexpectedly.

"Locking yourself out of the house," Gladys said. "I used to do it all the time. Now of course, I have to make sure I remember. When you live on your own, you have nobody to fall back on as it were."

"You live alone?" Barbara sipped the hot coffee, helpless in the role of interrogator. "I hope my husband doesn't make you work too hard," she added with a forced laugh. "Work, work, work, it's all he seems to think about."

"Not quite . . . he . . . " For a moment, to Barbara's surprise, she seemed a little flustered. She also blushed. "He's a very nice man to work for, Mrs Shawcross. All the staff think so."

Barbara clinked her cup into the saucer. Well . . . well . . . Why did a woman blush when she talked about a man? She scrutinised Gladys as she worked at her desk. Mrs Ward was an attractive lady in that extraordinary way of some oversized women. She dressed carefully and Guy particularly liked that in a woman. She also had the most marvellous pale complexion to complement her reddish colouring and lovely brown eyes. There was also a sympathetic gentle air about her and you didn't remember afterwards that she was overweight for she did not seem so as she floated about on her high heels. Perhaps it was not such a strange idea after all and Guy spent a lot of time with her, working time certainly but how could you work with someone for so long and not be a little curious as to their private life. She and Guy must often talk over their coffee as she and Gladys were doing now.

But what would Gladys think of him? Barbara saw that Guy might well appear charming with that ridiculous tendency of his to shyness. Shyness in a grown man was appealing, even more ridiculous because of the power Guy wielded as head of the organisation, power that Gladys would be all too aware of. His vulnerability, and Barbara recognised this as dangerous, would bring out the mothering instincts in any woman including Gladys who looked to be very much the mothering sort with that big friendly bosom of hers. She hoped that Guy had not been spinning her the tale about his wife not understanding him. The thought of them discussing her at all was appalling and unnerving.

"It is a nuisance, Gladys," she said now, remembering her excuse for being here in the first place. "Very silly of me but, to be honest . . . " she felt herself grow hot with embarrassment, "I'm shopping today for an outfit for a funeral and, as you can imagine, it's upset me a bit. I'm not quite myself. My mind must have been on the funeral when I left the house key inside."

"Oh dear, a funeral? I am sorry." She smiled with sympathy before resuming her work.

The door to Guy's office opened at that moment and a group of people filed out looking rather pleased with themselves. Guy was the last to appear, talking even as he came through the door. "Gladys . . . can I have a word about this evening? Whenever you're ready . . ." He stopped dead when he saw Barbara. "What are you doing here?" he said, the smile a touch late. "Something wrong?"

"No . . . well, yes." She rhymed off her excuse, not sure if he believed her or not. Frankly, she was past caring. What was he up to this evening? With Gladys? Wasn't this evening one of those that was supposedly reserved for the architect? The architect that probably did not exist.

Dazed with suspicion, she pocketed the spare key he gave her, said a quick goodbye and drove to the shops. At least the doubts in some strange way helped her decision to attend Ruth's funeral. Guy seemed unconcerned, giving his total support to her going along, but she still felt guilty mainly because she didn't feel an ounce of compassion for poor Ruth and it seemed awful to go to a funeral without feeling that. Worse than that, she knew she was only going so that she would see David again. The funeral gave her the excuse she needed and she wondered if the dreams had been some sort of premonition, if they had been preparing her for this, if indeed she had not willed it to happen.

Flashing her credit cards helped lighten Barbara's mood considerably. She liked spending money. She did not spend it with quite the same aplomb as Leila but she was a close second. In disgustingly rapid time she spent several hundred pounds on clothes for the funeral, before popping into her hairdresser to book an appointment for a restyle, shorter with a fringe perhaps and some highlights. Odd really but she felt she ought to present some sort of new image for David even though he hadn't seen her for years. She hoped that David would like her hair now it was no longer the very dark brown he would remember. Her eyes were just the same though and David had said something wonderfully poetic about them. She smiled at the absurd memory. Guy would go puce before he would utter such things.

Laden with up-market carrier bags, she dropped into the charity shop to check the rota, not entirely surprised to find Meg there, a disgruntled Meg holding the fort alone because her rota companion had failed to arrive. However, Meg was delighted to see her, even more delighted to see she had been shopping and insisted on having an immediate fashion parade, putting up the closed notice on the shop door so that they would not be disturbed. As she frequently donated a generous cheque to supplement the shop funds, Meg treated the whole thing in a distinctly cavalier way.

The outfit, a dress and wrap, was much admired. When Barbara explained it was for a funeral, Meg agreed it was sober but smart. Very suitable. As Barbara re-folded the new clothes, Meg made coffee, in no hurry to reopen the shop. For her stint as shop assistant, she was wearing one of her boutique casual outfits. "Have you heard from that daughter of yours?" she asked, pulling up a chair beside Barbara.

"Daisy?" Barbara enquired foolishly, as if she had a dozen daughters. Damn Meg. "Not recently," she said, realising that Meg had got wind of the little problem with Daisy. It was unfortunate but it wasn't something you could keep a secret for long. Now that Meg knew, that was very much that. How she came to be married to such a nice unassuming man like Howard never ceased to surprise Barbara. Howard was a bluff cheerful hospital consultant. He didn't deserve such a coldly calculating wife who pulled all the strings she could to get what she wanted, often for charitable causes so it was impossible to complain without sounding mean. They had no children, from choice or otherwise had never been made clear, but Meg did seem to take a morbid delight in the trials and tribulations of parenthood amongst her circle. She lived on the outskirts of town, in a very beautiful old house, drove a white Saab, and led a very ordered life.

"She needs a good talking to," she said now, casting an annoyed glance at some ladies who were peering through the window in some puzzlement. "Oh God, I'll have to open up for them I suppose," she said, going to do just that before coming to sit beside Barbara again, leaving the ladies to browse.

Meg was tall and sharp featured with tiny black eyes, her glossy jet-black hair worn in a severe ballerina style, beautifully manicured hands that never went near a dishwasher let alone a sink. An enormous diamond glittered on her finger. "How you came to allow her to walk out is a mystery, Barbara," Meg went on in a low voice, unperturbed by Barbara's silence. "Leila tells me the boyfriend is unsuitable. Unemployed? Is that correct?"

Barbara bit back a retort. There was no point in antagonising Meg and it was mainly Leila's fault for discussing private family business with a stranger. Leila knew nothing about it. Leila had never met Alan. If only they had had the chance to get to know him a little before Daisy had told them she was moving in with him. They surely deserved some warning. They weren't prudes, she and Guy, but they had been upset that it had all seemed a *fait accompli*. They had no time to form an impression, any lasting impression of him, and that hurt. Could they trust him to look after Daisy? Daisy, for all her high-flown ideas, was basically a child still. She needed someone to look after her.

A sudden flurry of buying activity caused a welcome diversion and directly the ladies had left, Barbara stood up to leave too. "Must go," she said with a smile. "Lovely to have had a chat, Meg."

"You didn't tell me where this funeral is," Meg said, thankfully seeming to have forgotten about Daisy and the boyfriend. "Which church?"

"It's not here. It's in Blackpool actually."

"Blackpool?" Meg was aghast. "How do you come to know someone who lives there?"

"David . . . he's the husband of the lady who's died . . . David and I used to dance together and he always said he wanted to live there eventually. You've seen the photographs of me and David," she said quietly, not wishing to elaborate. It was something she wasn't keen on discussing but Leila, in one of her wicked moods, had once announced to a crammed coffee morning that Barbara had been a ballroom dancer, specialising in Latin American of all things, dragging out the photographs and passing them round amongst much hilarity. Just occasionally, Leila liked to remind Barbara of her roots, her plain roots, doing it in the most embarrassing way possible.

"Oh him. I'd forgotten." Meg gave a thin smile. "Personally I think that kind of dancing's a bit risqué. Those dreadful dresses. They're appalling. Did you really wear such things? I really can't imagine you doing so, Barbara."

"You've seen the photographs," Barbara reminded her calmly, "It was different then. David said . . ." she let it go seeing she was losing Meg's fickle attention. Her dresses had been beautiful. Of necessity, her favourite dress was sexy showing a lot of leg but in no other way revealing. She felt too much flesh detracted from the dance itself and the dance was everything. In the Latin American section, the dances were sexy. The movement. The music. The mingling of hot scarlet satin and David's figure-hugging black. Making love set to music.

"Do you know, I do believe I've never seen you dance," Meg said, "Isn't that odd? You and Guy don't seem to dance together." She frowned as more people entered the shop.

"He can't dance," Barbara said flatly, dismissing it, glancing pointedly at her watch, picking up her shopping.

"Do you fancy afternoon tea? I'm shutting up shop now," Meg said quite loudly so that the new browsers looked round awkwardly and began to disperse, "I'm utterly exhausted."

"Sorry. I don't have time." Barbara's attention was caught by a harassed young mum trying to control an impish toddler whilst pushing a pram, looking as if she would give her all for a few hours' freedom and all she and Meg could do was debate whether or not they had time for afternoon tea. Damn it, Barbara, she told herself firmly, what's the point in feeling guilty just because you have what you have. You give to good causes. What more can you do? However, the pinched face of the woman, echoed in the child, pinched her conscience too and suddenly dulled her post-shopping thrill. Sighing, she turned her attention back to Meg, who had not given the woman a passing glance.

Outside, walking back to their cars, Meg reflected that there was a touch of spring in the air or was it her imagination? Surprised, for it had not occurred to her, Barbara sniffed the weak sunshine. Meg was right. Snowdrops were through in the beds, mingled with orange and purple crocus, opening out to drink in the pitiful warmth. The daffodils and tulips were beginning to sprout, not long now. Yes . . . Spring was in the air. She and Guy were married in late spring. She wore a simple high-necked white dress and a long train, carried a bouquet of freesia. The gown was her choice and she had to fight for it. Leila had wanted frills and lace and fuss and, if Barbara hadn't put her foot down, Leila would have completely taken over. Leila had set her heart on an autumn wedding for them, for some reason, but Guy had overruled her in a rare touch of obstinacy.

It was very much a spring wedding. The bridesmaids wore pale green and carried bunches of fresh flowers. Too late she learned that green was an unlucky choice for a wedding. Ridiculous, of course, but she was superstitious and if only she had known that . . .

It was really too bad of Daisy to deprive them of a daughter's wedding. Modern of her but nonetheless disappointing. With Leila constantly harping on about weddings, Guy had better not forget that their silver wedding was coming up soon. She was damned if she was going to remind him.

Sitting in his office, Guy put down his pen and frowned. Barbara's surprise visit was worrying him. She'd never, as far as he could recall, locked herself out of the house before so why now? She was definitely not herself these days and he guessed it must be Daisy. He hoped to God she would get in touch with them soon. Time to forgive whatever had happened. Barbara must be worrying about her and to top that Ruth Earnshaw dying seemed to have upset her too. He supposed that happened when someone died young and Ruth had only been Barbara's age but he couldn't for the life of him understand why she was bothering to upset herself further by going to the funeral. Her absence would not be a problem and, indeed, would David seriously expect her to attend? Of course not. Funerals in his opinion were best avoided although it had to be faced that soon enough he would have to attend his mother's. She couldn't go on forever although he sometimes wondered. She might just be the sort who would toddle along high-handedly until she was a hundred. God . . . his mother at a hundred still shouting the odds . . . it didn't bear thinking about.

Once you were turned eighty however, it could happen at any time and nobody would express any surprise. He hoped it would not happen yet awhile because, difficult as she might be, he loved the old so-and-so. She was some character, his mother. She had only to snap her fingers and people sat up. Her attitude had always had the peculiar dual effect of both embarrassing and pleasing him. At school, she had caused such a furore arriving for sports day clad in some designer ensemble, spiking the sports field ingloriously with her heels, holding onto a large hat, bedecked with jewels, his father sauntering along behind.

She had that elusive something . . . presence. Star quality. Put her on a stage with a dozen others, and she would be the one you would notice. Whatever the elusive something was, he hadn't got it. If he snapped his fingers, people tended not to notice. He was intelligent enough to realise that his mother's influence might well have ground him down if he had allowed it to but he refused to let it. He refused to dwell on the serious down-effect she might have had, concentrating rather on the amusing side to it all. Hadn't he found his own bride after all when he knew perfectly well his mother was beavering about behind the scenes making the most indelicate noises in the direction of suitable families. Damn her, she was doing exactly the same thing again with Daisy, but Daisy was like him and would find her own partner. According to her, she had done that already although he was prepared to bet that wouldn't last. First love rarely did.

His mother was startled all those years ago when he produced Barbara but had welcomed her into the family, more or less. Frankly, it wouldn't have mattered what the hell she thought about Barbara because his mind was made up. He had fallen for Barbara in a big way, knowing almost from the first moment he saw her that he had to have her. David was an obstacle but he never really doubted that he would overcome that. It tickled him that other men couldn't quite grasp how the hell he had managed it. He saw the question in the eyes and manner of the males of their acquaintance and it meant frequent candid looks in his direction. He knew what they were thinking. Barbara didn't realise the effect she had on men. Or maybe she did. He wouldn't know.

It was a waste of time and effort trying to analyse why she had married him. She loved him of course. He hoped to God she loved him. He knew she enjoyed the money and the power of his business success. When it came to business, he was totally confident. There was no place in business for a fumbling approach and he had been fed the company's ideas along with his baby milk. His father had been pure business.

His mother and father had been an odd couple. Two dominant types neither giving an inch. It made for an uncomfortable relationship and Guy supposed he had, not unnaturally, leaned towards his father. As he'd grown older, his father had casually tossed business problems his way, inviting comments, sometimes even acting on them and discussing the result. Very clever. By the time he took over, a little prematurely due to his father's unexpected death, it was ingrained in his pores, swimming purposefully in his veins. The newest building project they were engaged in was a small executive development, only at the pre-planning stage as yet, but he anticipated no great problems. Top quality of course, Swedish design, a natural woodland setting. Ten only where the site would happily take fifteen and that's why he was successful. He was not greedy, neither was he stupid, and already he had sounded out potential buyers so there was no danger of being landed with empty shells. He envisaged a difficult few years ahead with the market generally in such a sludge but they would come through it intact. As well as the holiday lets, he had one or two other irons in the fire, building related, all making a steady if unexceptional profit. Shawcross Enterprises would not go under. He felt very strongly that he owed his father that much.

He sighed and pushed disconsolately at papers on the desk. Tonight was the night. He was now racked with doubts. Gladys had said yes, pleased even that he had asked her but it worried him nonetheless. He wasn't one for the sentimental gesture and he wondered how his wife would react. You never knew how women were going to react. Sometimes it seemed such a pink misty romantic idea, the sort that should appeal to her. Sometimes not. Sometimes it seemed plain daft. He might have been wiser to play it safe, present her with a huge bunch of flowers, take her out for dinner, buy her something nice.

The idea, romantic or ridiculous depending on his mood, had come out of the blue when he'd been driving home listening to a new Frank Sinatra tape. His tapes were his own affair for Barbara preferred the radio when she was in the car with him, preferred her own choice of instrumental music when she was in her own car. He recognised he was something of an oddball where music was concerned. Always had been. He'd hardly dared admit in the old days that he preferred the old-style crooners like Sinatra and Nat King Cole to the Beatles or some of the other groups. This particular tape was a nice mix of swing and sentiment, gorgeous tunes, beautiful soul-searching words. Smoochy tunes they used to call them, last waltz sort of tunes when you were finally with the girl you hoped to take home. Alone in the car, rain persistent against the screen, he sang along in a bathroom baritone, completely uninhibited because nobody was listening, enjoying himself. Sinatra finished singing about April in Paris, paused, and started on the next. And that was when the idea hit him, like a bolt from the blue.

He buzzed Gladys and she came through, carrying her notebook. The green suit was nice and he liked the brightly coloured scarf. She seemed to prefer red lipstick and it was such a contrast against her very pale skin, skin that was freckled lightly as in the way of redheads. "Shut the door, Gladys," he muttered, feeling instantly and overwhelmingly guilty. "Have we a minute now?" He smiled, "What a day eh? About this evening," he went on as she returned to face the desk. "It's only just occurred to me that we won't have much time. Shall we stop off somewhere for a quick bite?"

She shook her head, sitting down abruptly and smiling at him. "I've brought sandwiches," she said, "Enough for both of us. It occurred to me too that we were going to be pushed for time and we don't know for sure if we'll find a nice café that's not too busy so sandwiches seemed best. A packed tea," she added as though he wouldn't know what sandwiches represented. "We can eat them here if you like, say we're working late, or we can eat them on the way. Pull off somewhere and eat them. That might be best don't you think?"

He nodded, pleased at the thought she'd put into it. A packed tea eh? He couldn't recall eating a packed tea or lunch for years. His mother's picnics had been up-market affairs with gigantic hampers, paté and champagne and fancy nibbles. Open air summer events. Classy dos. "Thank you, Gladys," he said briskly, "Nice idea that." His brief nod was his usual dismissal and she stood and turned to go at once, collecting her notebook and pen. "Oh, by the way, will you be changing?" he enquired, astonishing himself at his audacity, "I mean . . . that's very elegant but . . ."

"I've brought a longish skirt and top along," she said, a splash of colour unexpectedly flooding her face, "I hope there'll be somewhere to change."

"There is," he said swiftly, "Or so I've been informed. A lot of people come straight from work like us so they've made allowance for that, although it's mainly for you ladies," he added, "We gentlemen are required to wear a suit."

She nodded, the red lips curving in a smile, a nice smile. "I'm quite excited," she said happily, "You couldn't have possibly have known but it's something I've been toying with doing for ages. I've just never got round to it and like you, it put me off that I didn't have a partner. Funny how things work out, isn't it, Mr Shawcross?"

"Ah . . . well actually Gladys . . . could you call me Guy this evening?" He did not meet her eye, fussing with papers on his desk. "It's just that it might seem odd to the others if you address me so formally. Not that we're trying to hide anything," he added, wishing he hadn't as he looked up and caught her undisguised amusement.

"That's going to be difficult," she murmured. "After all, I've never called you anything other than Mr Shawcross but I do see your point. It will look funny, won't it, we'll have to be on first name terms. I might forget though," she said with a worried smile.

He tried to concentrate on his work when she had gone but it was an uphill struggle. Lies. Lies. The white variety of course but he hated to lie to Barbara although he was sure she was blissfully unaware of it. She seemed to shut off when business was mentioned. To console himself, he went through the arrangements in his mind again. Tickets already booked. Dates fixed. All he had to do was to get Barbara along without her knowing the reason. Simple. Well . . . simpleish. Tonight was the more immediate worry and he hoped to God that he would not meet anyone he knew. The Sherwood School of Ballroom Dancing. Oh hell! He had picked it at random so it was chancey but it was extremely unlikely that any of the people he knew would be there. He had deliberately chosen to drive to Darlington of all places just so they would go undetected. He knew not a soul in Darlington although he had omitted to ask Gladys if she did. What if she did? What if there were a whole gang of her relatives or friends up there? Oh God, he wasn't cut out for this hole in the corner stuff and it would show.

He would be utterly hopeless at this dancing lark, an embarrassment to his partner, and a joke to the rest of the class. Already, just thinking about it, he was beginning to feel hot and bothered, sweaty. God, what would Gladys think? He had an awful feeling she might turn out to be a natural. Smooth and sophisticated in her dancing, everything that he was not.

Pull yourself together. Here he was, head of the organisation, sifting through contracts, employing people, making decisions, and a little thing like this was threatening to swamp him. There would be nothing to it. Mind over matter that was it, although he couldn't stop the worrying thought that he would spend the entire evening looking over his shoulder.

7

Eight thousand. In the end, Leila reckoned she was lucky to get off so lightly. He had a business head on his shoulders, the dear Alan, and, for a moment, as they had bargained she had felt a grudging respect for him. Not for long, however, for no man worth his salt would accept a mere eight thousand pounds in lieu of Daisy's everlasting love. She was best rid of him. It would be difficult for the poor girl, betrayals were notoriously difficult, but she would get over it. Something about Alan worried her for there was about him a sharpness, a feeling that there was more to that young man than met the eye and she was rarely wrong in such matters. Still . . . she dismissed her anxieties and looked forward to Daisy arriving back in Harrogate before long for she would certainly not stay alone in a love nest. Guy and Barbara would of course be thrilled but she would have to remember to be careful and not give any hint that she had had a part in it. Eight thousand pounds. Rather a blow that! She had made a mistake, offered far too much as the starting price. She ought to have started off offering a paltry two hundred and then she might have got away with less than a thousand. The boy had taken her for a soft touch, damn him.

The deal was that the boy would wait a while, for discretion's sake, and then make his excuses and disappear off the face of Daisy's earth. Leila cared not a fig about his proposed exhibition, nor about his enthusiasm. His paintings were largely insipid watercolours, not her favourite medium, and, although she knew absolutely nothing about painting she guessed that they were very ordinary. He would have no talent. However, the money was his to waste as he saw fit, although, as a final act of foolishness and purely for dear Daisy's benefit, she had bought one of the wretched things at a grossly overrated price. Fifty pounds cash she had handed over for a singularly washed-out view of the cathedral itself. She would stick it on a wall somewhere unobtrusive. Either that or give it to Oxfam.

Arriving home, she drove the car into the garage, closed the garage door but did not lock it. The car was temperamental, thirsty too with only an eggcupful of petrol in it and would probably choose not to start if someone had a notion to kidnap it. Dropping the keys into her bag, she walked up the drive to the house, admiring it from afar as always, the stone acquiring a pinky hue as the sun lowered in the sky. Dark evening clouds were edged in pink too and the air was sweet and warmish. Spring. Yes . . . definitely spring.

Her house was beautiful and Leila loved it. She had fallen in love with it some years before she had actually been able to buy it, as it was then in the ownership of a couple of elderly sisters. Charles had not been interested, not in a house here in Skipton and that was probably the key to her obsession with it. She simply had to have it one day. She took the ages of the elderly sisters into account and vowed that she would pounce directly it went onto the market. One simply had to be realistic about these things. She ascertained that one had a heart condition and the other was chronically ailing. She kept her eye on it, passing it occasionally, irritated as she watched the garden growing ever wilder around them. Why on earth didn't they employ a gardener? It was so frustrating but, short of poisoning the pair of them, there was nothing she could do but wait.

At last, not before time, the sisters obligingly died, managing it quite neatly within a mere few weeks of each other and their executors, vague cousins, immediately put the house up for sale at a staggering price considering the state it was in. Apart from anything else, it smelt overwhelmingly of cat pee. Undeterred, Leila did indeed pounce, not prepared to risk losing it, and by that time there was no Charles to hinder and click his annoyance at the purchase for Charles had managed to die himself in the meantime. There was only Guy to hinder and click his annoyance instead but on a reduced irritation ladder. Guy was appalled at the state it was in, the interior dark and dismal, sadly so, but Leila delighted in returning it to its former grandeur. Solid and uncompromising in its dolls' house squareness, it had gracious rooms that she decorated in shades of yellow and cream. Warm sunny yellows in the rooms at the rear overlooking the rose garden and cooler lemons in the south-facing rooms. What nonsense people talked about it being too large for her living here as she did all alone. She liked a big house and had no intention of ending her days crammed into a bedsit with her prized possessions squashed in like sardines in a tin.

From the windows of the small study at the rear, her favourite room, she could see the broad paved terrace leading down to the formal rose garden, at its best of course later in the year. Despite the late hour, she strolled a moment outside feeling the comforting presence of the surrounding hills as they settled to slumber. Gently, she breathed in the cool country air. Barbara was quite right of course. She did love it here. Next to Harrogate, Skipton was her very favourite place on earth.

Guy and Barbara really ought to get themselves a place in the country where they could unwind. God in heaven, the man knew everything there was to know about the housing market so surely he could come up with something. Leila sighed, returning indoors and drawing the curtains. This would have been a splendid house to entertain in and she missed that these days. She entertained occasionally but her guest list had suffered of late and so many of her friends were gone. Dead. They had been such a jolly set in the old days, jolly well knowing how to party. Hunting parties. Shooting parties. Country weekends. A game of cards. Drink. Cigarettes. All the things Daisy frowned upon. The younger generation were singularly lacking in humour, full of pious ideas and environmental twaddle. Why should she have to worry about things like the ozone layer and recycling at her advanced age? One of these fine days they would be recycling human beings. There would be no such thing as a magnificent funeral. She intended her own to be truly wonderful, a day to remember. She reckoned, with her connections and her lifelong devotion to Harrogate and lately Skipton, coupled with her generous donations to so many charitable causes, she would merit a full page in the local papers. She'd already chosen a flattering photograph to accompany the article. Even when she was dead, that was no excuse for dropping standards.

It wasn't just Daisy who was fun-less, Barbara herself was weighed down with social problems, never wearing her silver fox stole these days because someone had passed a comment on it. Piffle to all that. One had to take a stand.

Sitting down at the antique writing desk beside the window, Leila took out pen and paper to compose a list. The paper was cream and heavy. She smoothed the surface, loving the feel of it, and uncapped her pen. A proper pen, of course. People who used biros were the scum of the earth.

She adored lists. Lists were terribly important and all things in life began with a list. A list of suitable names for the new baby. Of suitable schools. Suitable suitors. Now . . . let's see . . . the real possibilities. Serious stuff now. Pros and cons. Using a ruler, Leila neatly divided the page into columns. Families first then a check on whether or not they possessed a son of the right age. It was so easy to lose track these days and she must remember that small boys at prep school turned very quickly into eligible young men. The years flew so. She was fairly flexible about age. Anyone between twenty two and thirty five. Either side of that line was debatable.

She would start off with three possibles. Any more than that and it would become too complicated and she might get mixed up. She reached for her address diary and consulted her Christmas card list. Horrific some of these people, some of them long since crossed off, bankrupt or what have you, deceased. However . . . the Pattersons might be worth a try. Major Roy and his wife, Penelope. Since retiring from the army, he'd made his money latterly from frozen food or something equally dreadful but he had a nice home in the country and Penelope had big ideas. Little woman with a passion for cartwheel hats. They had a son, Piers. She hadn't seen Piers for simply years and, the unfortunate impression that stuck was of a small knock-kneed child. Still . . . he would wear long trousers now. Stock exchange wasn't it and that worried Leila for she disapproved of financial careers as a rule, much preferring the civil service or law or medicine. A career diplomat or medical consultant would be ideal. Perhaps she should sound out Meg Fairley on that one, for Meg knew everything about medical people and would know if there were any up and coming youngish consultants on the look-out for a wife. Meg Fairley whose airs and graces had never fooled Leila. She kept discreetly quiet about her previous life but Leila had her suspicions.

She jotted the Pattersons on the list. Alas, they weren't a particularly good-looking pair she recalled, Roy and Penelope, so it was unlikely that they would have produced a handsome son. Still . . . it was worth a try. If the Pattersons failed to come up trumps, the Findlay-Smith's were another possibility, Leonard and Irene. Leonard, one-time solicitor, was an almighty crushing bore but Irene was moderately pretty if a little dim, one of the last debutantes surely? Very well connected in her own right. They had a large spread-out family. Five or six wasn't it? Leila struggled to remember the name of the eldest boy, Michael she thought. Michael Findlay-Smith. Pale and asthmatic when she had last seen him but he had been only twelve or so at the time. Hopefully, he would have grown out of it. Sickly children sometimes made very interesting adults. He had gone to a very good school, that went without saying. She had no idea what Michael did now so that would need looking into.

Who else? She needed three families to start with, out of which there was bound to be one suitable. It wasn't asking much. One out of three. Ah yes . . . Charles Langstaffe with whose widowed mother she was vaguely acquainted. Tiresome woman. Pity too about the name Charles but it couldn't be helped and he couldn't be discounted until she had checked. Miriam Langstaffe lived in isolated splendour somewhere near Ripon, bit of an odd woman, strangely clad in mysterious layers, Isadora Duncanish, and that would not go down well at the wedding. Still . . . she might be persuaded to take some advice on suitable wedding apparel and Leila would be delighted to give that advice. She would take the dear lady shopping in Harrogate. She talked of Charles as if the sun shone out of him but that meant nothing. She herself talked about Guy as if he were the most dynamic man alive. Mothers were either notorious ill judges of their offspring or superb liars.

As the carriage clock chimed its delicate pings, she looked up and saw that it was eleven o'clock. My goodness. She must have sat here longer than she had intended. Worried a little that sometimes minutes even hours passed her by unnoticed, Leila capped her pen, blotted the page, and returned the notebook to the drawer, locking it. Today had been wearisome and at her age, you could not tolerate too many wearisome days. Tomorrow, she would rest. She would rise late, have a leisurely breakfast, and then put her feet up, relax and do some telephoning. Yes . . . she would spend the entire day on the phone. What absolute bliss!

She hoped the boy Alan would be discreet. Daisy must not link his decision to walk out in any way with her visit. She felt no guilt now it was done. One day Daisy would thank her. Perhaps one day she would tell Daisy but certainly not before the wedding. The wedding to dear Piers. Or Michael or Charles. A wonderful wedding with Daisy feminine in frills and lace, the guests elegant, the reception lavish. She would hold the reception here of course and the guests could wander in the garden. She would buy Daisy and whoever the groom turned out to be something splendid and the fact that she had been instrumental in arranging the wedding would remain a secret. The mothers of the prospective grooms would have to be handled with kid gloves but she knew they were her type and that she could count on their discretion.

The phone rang just as she was going up to bed. Annoyed, she picked it up, "Yes?" she snapped. "It's extremely late whoever you are."

"It's me, mother." Guy sounded harassed. "Where have you been? Barbara and I were getting worried about you. We've been ringing on the hour since five o'clock. If you hadn't answered now, I was going to drive over."

"I've been in longer than an hour," Leila said with a frown, "I can't have heard you. You fuss so, Guy."

"Where have you been?"

"Out, dear."

"Yes I know that. But where? We were wondering if we should call the police."

"Really, Guy, what on earth for? I'm quite capable of looking after myself. We've been for a drive."

"We?"

"The car and I of course. And I have no intention of telling you where. I do have a private life, Guy. Now . . . if you'll excuse me, I'm off to bed."

He tut-tutted his irritation. "We were worried, mother. You mustn't just drive off and not say where you're going. Suppose something happened to you? We'd feel such fools if we didn't know where you were."

"I'm sorry. I was not aware that I have to account for my every movement," Leila said tightly. Guy was impossible. Such a huffer-puffer. She was damned therefore if she was going to remind him this time about his anniversary. He should be worrying about his wife instead of her. If he didn't he would lose her.

At last, after promising Guy she would never do such a thing again, a promise she had no intention of keeping, she went up to bed. Excitement caught at her as she sipped her hot milk liberally laced with rum. She would start the process of elimination soon by inviting the Pattersons round. Afternoon tea. Such a genteel meal. She hadn't seen them for some considerable time but she would be excused the time lapse because of her advanced age. Wasn't Penny on some charity committee or other? In that case, the woman would jump at the chance of afternoon tea suspecting that a large donation was about to come her way.

Leila would of course write her a cheque for a few hundred but not immediately. A little gentle probing first.

Alan was quiet when he returned from the walk with her grandmother. Wisely, Daisy said nothing until gran was finally gone. "Well . . ." she then demanded of him, "What do you make of that? What trick did she have up her sleeve?"

"Nothing," he said with that smile of his, "I liked the old so-and-so actually. She was fearfully impressed with the Cathedral. Yes . . ." he added thoughtfully, "She's a determined lady, your gran. Speaks her mind."

"She's an absolute tartar," Daisy said with a sigh, "She scares everybody rigid in Harrogate. And I honestly don't believe that she didn't try to persuade you to leave me alone. She doesn't approve of you, Alan. Just like mum and dad. It's so silly. Just because you're a touch unconventional."

"She thinks I'm utterly charming," he told her, coming closer and holding out his arms. "Come here and stop fussing."

Daisy relaxed against him. She loved him. Damn it to heaven, she loved him and she wanted to be with him but not here, not in this flat. No matter how hard she tried, it would always be just a grotty flat. She wanted a proper home for them but she didn't see a way out of their predicament. It was living in a fool's paradise to assume that Alan's paintings would suddenly be spotted and sought after and worth a fortune. She thought they were beautiful but that was because she saw the amount of love and care he put into them. He breathed life into them.

"I want us to try again," she said, pulling away from him, needing to talk about this sensibly without the distraction of his nearness. "Start afresh. Think things through a bit. I think I'll look for another job, something that pays more. Then, as soon as we can, we can move into something a bit nicer." She looked at him, waiting for a response but nothing was forthcoming, "And perhaps you could get a job, too. Purely temporary," she added hastily, "You'll still have lots of time to paint in the evenings. As a matter of fact . . ." she paused, wondering if she should tell him, "One of the girls at work has an uncle and he's on the look-out for someone to help him."

"Doing what?"

"Something to do with shop fitting," Daisy told him, realising it was all pretty vague. "The job's not advertised yet. I'll find out more about it if you're interested."

"Why not?"

She watched as he returned to his painting. Another of the cathedral. She had hidden the two hundred pounds in her underwear drawer. She wasn't sure quite what she would spend it on. She ought to save it of course for a rainy day.

The trouble was the rainy days were coming thick and fast. Still . . . she would start applying for other jobs and Alan seemed willing to start earning too. He seemed different tonight, ever so slightly withdrawn. It was probably something her grandmother had said to him when they were alone. She had expected a blow by blow account when he returned. Had looked for something in both their expressions but gran looked just the same as usual.

She always looked as if she was up to something.

8

It was over. There was something poignant about the newly dug grave, Ruth's body now buried within it, a mass of floral tributes piled high above it. There followed those awkward few moments when everyone present struggled with their personal feelings and even Barbara, who had not known Ruth very well of late, felt a sadness as she stood a little back from the proceedings, not wanting to intrude on the family grief. Someone wept. Quietly.

The chill northern sea wind whipped round them and she shivered, huddling deeper into her wrap. Why was it that cold bleak days seemed so very appropriate for an occasion like this just as a sunny day was so welcome for a wedding. Thick clouds blocked out the sun and kept the temperature firmly down.

Barbara seemed to have spent the entire day keeping discreetly to one side, doing so before and during the church service, before tucking her little white car, the wrong colour for a funeral, at the rear of the sober procession of cars from the church to the place where Ruth was to be buried.

Her first sight of David in years had caused her heart to flutter. She knew him instantly. She knew him by his walk, seeing him from her position in a side pew as he entered the church. It was, of necessity, a sad walk, a little bowed, slow, but it was unmistakably him. It was as if he hadn't changed at all. He seemed not to have aged, having kept his hair and his slim dancer's figure, and he looked strikingly handsome in the dark clothes he was wearing.

He was busy now, now that it was over, ushering people

once more into cars, organising, and the young woman who hovered near him, reminding her of Ruth, was of course his daughter. There had been no tears from either of them and now the daughter was very pale but composed, managing a smile, wearing a scarlet suit and no hat. A pang struck Barbara as she stood and watched. The scarlet suit jarred. She realised it was a little gesture on the girl's part but it still jarred, uncomfortable in its brilliance. She wondered how Daisy would react if it was one of them. Would she feel the need for a similar gesture? Would she be as composed? A need to do something, to offer comfort to the young woman hit hard and she was walking towards them before she realised, standing again off to one side, as he talked to someone else. Patiently, wearing the smile one wears at funerals, she waited. As he talked, she reflected that it was not too late, that she could turn away and go. Now. And he would never know. He finished his conversation, shook hands, leaned to kiss someone's cheek, accepted yet another comforting handshake, before turning casually to face her. Too late.

"David . . ." her smile faltered and she saw his start of surprise. Recognition it seemed was immediate.

"Barbara . . . I didn't know you were coming." He stopped, lost for words, and she saw for the first time the signs of ageing, the slight loss of weight in his face, a few lines round his eyes and of course the sadness in them. He must be devastated. Utterly so. He gave her a quick but thorough glance that took her in very competently from top to toe. Foolish as it was, her clothes helped. She had taken special care with her appearance today and her make-up was, as suited the occasion, discreet. After consideration, hatless. Her hair, shorter, fringed, one shade lighter than normal. "How odd!" he murmured, "I was just looking at a photograph of us the other day." A smile flitted briefly and was gone. "How very nice to see you." He leaned towards her and kissed her cheek as he had kissed other cheeks today. She recalled he had told everyone how nice it was to see them.

"I felt I had to come. It's good to see you again," she said, her mouth dry with something approaching shock, "Although I wouldn't have wished to meet under these circumstances. I'm . . . Guy and I are very sorry," she finished quietly, offering a sympathetic grimace to the girl at his side. "This must be Annie?"

He nodded. "Annie, darling, this is Barbara Anderson . . ."

"Barbara Shawcross," she said quickly, smiling to indicate she understood the little slip.

"Sorry . . . We used to dance together in the good old days." For a moment, there was a trace of animation in his face, a loosening of the sadness.

"Of course. I've seen your photograph." Annie shook hands, a tiny girl who looked younger than her years. "Come back to the house, Mrs Shawcross," she said, remembering her duties, "We're having ham sandwiches and things."

"Hardly." David looked pained. "A small buffet, Barbara, and we would indeed be pleased to see you. Have you transport?"

"Yes. I'll follow you."

As they drove, in a less funereal mood now that the hearse had gone, Barbara could see the sea. It was angry, rolling in, crashing to shore, under a sodden sky. It disappeared from view as they neared David's house which was on the windswept road beside the dunes, brand new and looking it, characterless. By the time Barbara arrived, people were warming up, physically and mentally. A few careful laughs could be detected as they milled around the buffet. Not even remotely hungry, too nervous, Barbara found herself chatting to people she did not know about Ruth. Expensively clad people but hardly Harrogate people. Goodness . . . she was getting as bad as Leila, she would be comparing jewellery next. The consensus seemed to be that Ruth had been a wonderful woman, a marvellous wife and mother, and to be struck down at her age was nothing short of a tragedy and wasn't David bearing up well? Annie too? Feeling a little out on a limb but expert, from years of coffee mornings and cocktail parties, at small talk of the non-controversial variety, Barbara got through it somehow and one or two people made the connection between herself and David pointing to the photographs on display. As people drifted out, she stayed put. She wanted a private word.

The final guests departed, sadness again draining their faces, as they made their goodbyes and then Annie herself, with a vague smile in Barbara's direction, went out too so that they were alone. At last. Barbara gripped her glass tightly and felt panic rising like a sharp stone. What a fool to have come and she was even more of a fool to have stayed behind like this.

"I'm sorry, David," she said, rising awkwardly to her feet, "I must go. I have a long drive." She glanced at the debris on the table. "Do you want any help with that?"

"God no. The caterers will be back later to deal with that. I want you to stay," he instructed, pouring her another mineral water, adding ice and lemon, "Here . . ." he handed it to her, "Stay and talk. Please. Everyone assumed I wanted to be left alone, Annie included, but I don't. I want to talk about Ruth. I'm glad it's over, the funeral. You don't realise, you know, until you bury someone close to you, what an important thing a funeral is. You don't feel they've really gone until the funeral's over."

She murmured agreeably, not fully understanding what he meant.

"We were married a helluva long time . . ." he laughed, "Of course you know that. We had our ups and downs but it was okay. Not bad that eh? Twenty five years almost and it was okay. Bloody hard luck we missed our Silver. Ruth had plans for that. I was going to buy her this beautiful silver locket, something she always wanted. A surprise." He choked, disguising it with a cough.

Barbara looked away. "I didn't know her at all," she said after a moment, a moment for him to compose himself, "She was a private person, always was. I'm sorry about the silver locket," she said, "Twenty five years is a very long time to be with someone, isn't it? If nothing else, you get used to each other." She took a sip of water, anxious to say the right thing, scared of saying the wrong thing. "I can't begin to understand how you must feel." He did not say a word but she felt his response and for the first time she began to feel a genuine regret at his loss, began even to feel the pricking of tears behind her lids. "Can I just say again how sorry Guy and I were. It was such a shock seeing it in the paper like that." She turned, not wanting him to see the brightness in her eyes.

"Sorry. I ought to have let you know personally. I tried to but Ruth had the number. She would have known the number."

Restless, he sat down on the sofa opposite her, stretching out his legs and smiling. Twenty five years on and it was the same smile. The careless way with which he loosened his black tie and undid the top button of the crisp white shirt tore at her heart. David had a way with simple everyday gestures. "How is he? Old Guy?" he asked, "Property, house-building wasn't it? The recession must have hit hard."

"It's difficult," Barbara admitted, "But Guy anticipated it and started up several sidelines. We run a holiday let business as well. He's very careful, business-wise." She found she was sitting stiffly, not comfortable on the low squashy sofa. She was finding it difficult to keep her eyes off him. Flirting at funerals was forbidden. David was regrettably the sort of man who begged to be flirted with. "Guy's work is probably very boring compared with what you do," she said desperately, casting glances around, anywhere but at him.

"Very boring," he agreed and the smile remained, sizing her up, making her a little uncomfortable in its intensity. "You know me, Barbara, I never wanted my life to be routine. I wanted an element of chance to exist. Your Guy would have a heart attack if he knew some of the risks I've taken. Nearly ended up in jail once," he said quietly, "Escaped by a whisker. Ruth never knew anything about that. We didn't discuss the business much. She didn't approve of the nature of it."

Barbara raised her eyebrows. "Were you guilty?" she enquired, moved that he should tell her something that he had never told his wife. "Or was it one of those misunderstandings you used to get involved with?"

He laughed. "A misunderstanding of course. In my game, the entertainment game, in case you didn't know, you've got people hiding round every corner ready to stick knives in you. But . . . and this is the nice bit, Barbara . . . you can make a fortune out of it. Not just a steady income but a fortune. I own a nightclub, a disco, amusement arcades, bingo halls, that sort of thing. You've got to be constantly one step ahead, ditch things as soon as they've passed their peak and go all out for the new stuff. The holiday public have only got a short attention span so there's no time for nostalgia. Not a lot anyway."

"I'm pleased you seem to have done well." She glanced round

the room. It wasn't to her taste of course but some of the things in it were expensive. "You were always very sure of yourself, David, even in the old days."

"I'm not satisfied yet, sweetheart. I've got plans, big plans. Someday I might tell you about them."

She stared. The sweetheart hurt because he didn't mean it. It was almost his standard way of addressing women. She had heard it several times today already. "Guy always mistrusts people who claim to be able to make a fortune," she said tightly, irritated as soon as she said it because it sounded so po-faced, made Guy sound virtuous. "Money has to be earned, Guy says," she added, making it worse.

"Does he now? And what makes you think I don't earn mine?" He was not offended, amused rather. "I've never had a holiday in years. Spend every minute of the day at work, work all hours. Sometimes Ruth never saw me one week to the next."

"I'm sorry." Barbara sighed, remembering that the man was grieving. "I didn't mean to imply . . ."

"Do you always listen to what Guy says?" he asked and the sneer was there. Hidden but there. "Ruth used to listen to me and then do precisely what she wanted. She thought I didn't know that." He took a cigarette from a case, silently asked her permission before lighting it, "She was a good wife and I still can't take it in. I'm really cut up about it. Six months ago she was fit as a fiddle. Well . . . as fit as she was. She was always a bit frail." He smoked furiously and she suspected he was fighting his emotions, as he had been doing all day long. She wanted to console, to comfort, to simply hold him but she did not. "I'm bloody cut up," he repeated quietly, "I try not to show it. Stiff upper lip, you know the score? But I honestly don't know how I'm going to manage without her. She's not here anymore." For a moment, he looked lost, very alone, and Barbara felt her resolve weakening. All she had to do was to go across to him and put her arms round him. That was all. "She managed the house," he went on, "We never had anyone in to help. Ruth said she didn't want another woman flitting about the place so she did the lot. Know something?" He smiled a bit, flicking ash into the ashtray balanced on the arm of the sofa, "The other day we got a gas bill and I realised I'd never seen one before. Ruth used to deal with things like that."

Is that what Guy would miss if she were to drop dead or walk out on him? Her paying the gas bill? The little boy look David shot her was not lost on her. "If there's anything I can do to help," she offered. "Anything. You only have to ask. We . . . we should never have lost touch, should we?"

"We had to, Barbara." He was suddenly very serious. "I realised that when I saw you at the wedding, my wedding for Christ's sake. When you can't take your eyes off another woman on your wedding day, it's time to call a halt. I didn't want to see you again. I was frightened of what I might do. And I definitely didn't want to see old Guy again."

"I see." She tried a smile, difficult as her insides trembled. This was getting too deep, and, although she didn't mind him being reflective, it was also getting dangerous. One or other of them might say something they regretted. Perhaps David already had. She smiled again into the difficult silence. "It's not easy to remain friends, not when you've almost been . . ." she couldn't say it and didn't attempt to, shrugging the meaning instead.

"We should make up for lost time," he said abruptly. "We can't hurt Ruth anymore, can we?" He bounced up and went to the window, the one that looked onto the distant dunes and the pounding sea. "Poor Ruthie. She never liked this house by the way but it was what I wanted so . . . she was such an agreeable person, Barbara. Never argued. Always backed down even if she was right." His laugh was short, "Tell you something, it was no fun having an argument because she never stood her corner."

"You have a lovely daughter," Barbara said, trying to lighten his mood, "She'll be a great help to you. Daughters are so special, aren't they?" Before she could help herself, she was telling him about Daisy, unburdening herself on him, telling him all about Daisy and the boyfriend. "Sorry," she finished, suddenly realising that it was hardly a tactful thing to do, not to someone who was grieving. "I shouldn't be telling you my troubles. How thoughtless."

"It's okay," he said, returning to his former seat and lighting another cigarette, "Although I can't offer any advice. Annie isn't even at the boyfriend stage yet. Should she be?" He frowned towards her. "You don't think there's anything wrong with her, do you? We were at it at her age, weren't we, you and me?" He grinned, the suddenness of it startling her.

She did not return the smile, tugging at her skirt, fiddling with her belt, knowing he was damned well aware of her awkwardness.

"There's nothing wrong with Annie," she said firmly, "Girls develop differently and she'll have a boyfriend soon enough. Then you'll be wishing she hadn't," she added drily, "Remember what I've just been telling you about Daisy." She frowned at him, the grin replaced now by a very lazy look, one she knew well, one she had frankly forgotten about. "Nor were we at it, David, as you so crudely put it," she said, "Ours was a very . . ." she struggled to explain, "Innocent, wasn't it? So innocent."

"You and I came *that* close, darling," he said, indicating the minutest gap with his fingers, "You can't deny it. What the hell did we quarrel about? What was so important that you walked out on me forever?"

"I forget." She had forgotten, too, until that moment, "Something to do with the routine I think," she went on, trying to bring it back, "You had the damned cheek to criticise my technique. It was the first time you ever did that."

"And the last," he said with a short laugh, "I ought to have known you wouldn't be able to accept criticism. Did I tell you you'd been like a block of ice in the rumba?"

"Something like that." She tried to speak lightly because it was all so very long ago and best forgotten but it came back, the hurtful words. "And so I told you if that was the case, you'd better find yourself another partner. Something like that. I never for a moment thought you'd let me walk out like that." Unbidden, her eyes filled with tears and she blinked them hastily away, not daring to rub at her eyes. "I thought you'd come after me."

"I thought you'd come back," David said thoughtfully and the shake of his head said it all. For the briefest moment, they were young again, young and fiery, and angry. "Look . . ." he broke the mood with an effort, "Why don't you stay over tonight? You said yourself it's a long drive and you look tired. Annie will be back soon so we'll have a chaperone."

"Chaperone?" Barbara raised her eyebrows, "Surely we don't need one? I'm a married lady, David."

"Quite." He stared at her a moment. "I was only joking, for Christ's sake. You don't expect me to drag you into my bed, do you? Bloody hell, Barbara, Ruth's only just buried."

"No I didn't expect that. For goodness sake . . . but my being here wouldn't look right, would it? Of course I didn't expect that," she added, feeling her face flame because in some ridiculous way she had. "Thanks for the offer anyway but I will drive home. We must talk again sometime."

"Why don't we arrange to meet later? At a less harrowing moment? I need to get away and it would be nice to spend some time together, purely for old time's sake of course. Old Guy won't object to that, will he?"

"It doesn't matter what he thinks," she said quickly, determined to show that she was her own woman. She didn't need to ask Guy's permission to do things although she often did out of politeness. "I shouldn't have come today," she said, "It was a mistake. I thought we would be older and wiser and well . . . we may be older but I'm not so sure about the wiser bit."

"You do things to me, Barbara," he said, coming over to stand only inches away. A smile accompanied the remark and she made no protest as he drew her to her feet and closed the distance between them so that her head rested on his shoulder. It felt good. Different from Guy's shoulder but good. With a little sigh, he traced his finger along her cheek, "Oh, sweetheart, I've missed you," he whispered, breathing lightly against her ear, moving the gold drop earring aside as he dropped a little kiss there. "I've missed you so much and you are still my beautiful Barbara. Dance with me. A waltz eh?" Gently he moved his feet and his body and it was impossible not to move with him, step by step, impossible not to hear in her head the beat of the music.

They never heard the door so caught up were they so that Annie's voice shocked them and caused them to draw apart, instantly, guiltily. "Sorry daddy," she said, her smile thin, the red suit replaced by black leggings and black top. Funereal clothes now that it was over. "I didn't mean to intrude."

"You're not." Barbara pulled herself together quickly. "I was just leaving," she said, snatching up her bag and gloves, smiling at them both, catching the amusement in his eyes, the knowing look.

"You sure? In that case, I'll show you out," David said, accompanying her to the car. "Give me your phone number," he said as she eased herself in. "I'll call you soon. We're going to have that chat about old times, you and me."

Against her better judgement, she gave him her number, her heart thudding at her near escape as she drove away, watching him in the mirror until he was out of sight. If he rang, she would put him off. Dreams were dreams but reality was different and frightening in its intensity. She had expected her reaction to be dulled by the years. She had expected to be able to cope and she had expected that she would be returning home secure in the knowledge that she had killed the ghost.

She wouldn't have the guts to go through with it. David was willing and that niggled. She did not like to think she was being used as a sort of instant Ruth replacement therapy. Pity about the daughter and she hoped her witnessing their little dance together had not clouded her judgement. What must it have looked like to the child?

Thinking about Annie reminded her of course about Daisy, and that was enough to make the remainder of the journey home miserable.

Annie couldn't quite believe it of him, not at mum's funeral. No, that wasn't true. She could believe it. The two of them had looked very comfortable and she had been most embarrassed catching them together like that, holding each other close, although not so embarrassed as the lady had been. Mrs Shawcross. How elegant she was and so nicely and quietly spoken.

Now and again, she remembered her mother talking about her although there'd always been a touch of irritation in her voice, the faintest twinge of what Annie recognised as jealousy. Mum hadn't liked her. Reading between the lines, Annie realised that it was something to do with dad and the dancing. Mrs Shawcross had been a wonderful dancer and even the photographs showed that. No movement in photographs, just one moment caught in time, but you just knew looking at them that she and dad would indeed possess the electric rhythm he was always on about. He used to take a sort of morbid delight in telling her mother just how good a combination he and Barbara had been. Apparently mum had never quite lived up to his expectations as a dancer.

Why had she come? Annie mused on that, deciding that she was entitled to do so if she wanted as she was a long lost friend. Sort of. However, she wished she hadn't because it must have dug up memories for dad that perhaps he didn't wish to be unearthed. Despite everything, she'd worried about him today but he seemed to have coped well and the funeral tea had failed to degenerate, thank goodness, into a drunken party. For once, his friends had been remarkably circumspect. She'd caught Mrs Shawcross looking at him once or twice with an odd look on her face, a sort of wistful look. It made Annie wonder just how friendly they had been . . .

Not more complications. Annie sighed, feeling the release of the afternoon's tensions. It was over and she was glad of that. Now she could get on with things and she really had to stop dwelling on her father's love life. Let him get on with it too.

"Where the hell are those caterers?" He peeped in at her, as she washed up, "They should be doing that not you." He came to stand beside her, not moving a muscle to help but lighting up instead. "Went well eh?" Awkwardly he touched her shoulder. So lightly that for a moment she thought she imagined it. She turned quickly but he avoided her look, concentrating on his cigarette. "Surprised to see Barbara. She married into money, lives in Harrogate."

Annie nodded. "Mum told me. Nice of her to come, wasn't it?" She dried her hands. Smiled. The angry words of the other evening seemed to have been forgotten. There was no reason why she and dad shouldn't try to make a new start. This was how it would be from now on. Just the two of them. "I don't know about you, dad," she said, "But I didn't eat much from the buffet. Do you fancy something special for supper?"

"Couldn't eat a thing," he said, "I'll have to love you and leave you, Annie. I said I'd go to Linda's."

"Oh . . . I expect she'll want to know how things went." Annie tried to control her disappointment.

When he had gone, she went into the sitting room and

removed all the cards. The Sympathy cards. Masses of them. She knew there was one from Miss Boyd somewhere but she couldn't look through them yet. Too soon. She might read them someday when she felt a bit better.

She stuffed them in a drawer, at the back, and tidied the room, picking up the black tie he had discarded along with the jacket of the dark suit, carrying them through to his bedroom. The room was a bit untidy and automatically she straightened and smoothed and smartened it up. His expensive aftershave hung heavily about the room as if he'd been trying to get rid of the more subtle aroma of mum's scent.

Annie picked up a cushion on the sofa by the window and held it close, burying her head in it. Mum had often sat here, looking out at the sea. The cushion smelt vaguely of her, the familiar scent deeply ingrained.

Tears began to bubble somewhere deep down and she uttered a little sound, stifling them, tossing the cushion back as the doorbell rang. She looked out of the window and saw the caterers standing there. Smiling and chatting.

By the time she opened the door, they were suitably serious and sober. After all, it had been a wake.

"How did it go?" Linda was full of concern, and if she'd been a fetch-the-slippers-and-pipe sort of woman, God forbid, she'd have done just that. As it was, she tottered in holding a glass of whisky and water in one hand and a cigarette in the other. She was wearing very tight jeans and a low cut sweater, her hair pulled on top of her head in a style he liked with crinkly bits at the side and huge hooped earrings. David took the drink from her and raised it to his lips. He fancied getting her into bed tonight, probably for the last time, because he was going to have to put the brakes on this. Casting aside a notion that this was distasteful on the evening of his wife's funeral, he decided it was Barbara's fault. She had whet his appetite for it, slipping comfortably into his arms like she had, her body smelling of expensive perfume, her clothes sleekly expensive too.

"How do you think it went? It was a funeral, for God's sake," he said at last, as Linda sat in the chair opposite, the blasted cat instantly springing onto her lap. "We had a bloody knees-up, didn't we?" He gave a sigh, the vision of the grave and the graveyard causing a momentary shiver. It was dark now and Ruth was in there alone. Deep. Dark. Dead. "Things can settle down now," he said quietly, "Annie coped well. She didn't cry."

"Poor love. I'd like to help her if I can," Linda said, stroking the purring cat on her knee whilst she looked directly at David, "I feel so sorry for her and I feel like . . . well, I'm a sort of mother to her now, aren't I?"

"You . . . mother? Do me a favour, sweetheart." He laughed. Her indignation flared at once and she stiffened, accidentally sending the cat flying. It landed in an elegant heap and moved off, tail swishing. "What the hell can you do to help?"

"Women's things," she said mysteriously. "Shopping. Someone to talk to about boyfriends and things. Things she won't like to talk to you about. Does she have a boyfriend?"

He shook his head, "She's too uptight. I don't think boys interest her. A psychiatrist could go to town on her I bet. It'll be my fault of course. She hates me. I don't know what I've done to make her hate me." He remembered that line from a television play, adding his own version of a lop-sided smile to it, the one that melted Linda's heart. He saw her face soften and inwardly he let out a whoop. God, it worked every time. He didn't know a woman alive whom he fancied that it didn't work on. It had worked this afternoon with Barbara but that was a totally different set-up. He would have to be patient with Barbara Shawcross. She was something to linger over, to anticipate. Although he had been genuinely pleased to see her, surprised that she'd bothered to come, he had not felt much else for her. Time had mellowed his feelings and, if he'd perhaps been in love with her once or thought he had been, it was past. He had merely seen her for what she was, a still attractive middleaged lady with money who still had a bit of a thing for him. Could you credit his luck? It made him smile and only underlined this magical quality of his where the ladies were concerned. He didn't have to work at it. He wished he knew what it was exactly because if he could bottle it, his sex appeal, he would make a bomb. Barbara was his to dally with and he was in no desperate hurry.

"Annie doesn't hate you," Linda said, coming to sit on the floor beside him, resting her head against his legs. From this angle, he could see the dark roots in her hair where the bleach had grown out. From so close, he could smell the perfume, the one he had bought her for Christmas, and wondered why expensive perfume could smell cheap on some women. Linda drenched herself in it. That was why. "It's hard for her losing her mum and she has to take it out on someone. You're the one she's bound to take it out on. People always do that to the ones closest to them. Don't you see? It doesn't mean anything."

He supposed he did see. In theory. But Linda was wrong again. Annie might not hate him but she didn't love him either and, if he allowed it to, it hurt. "How old are you?" he asked, reaching out to touch her hair.

She half turned. "What a question to ask a girl," she said lightly, "What brought that on? You know how old I am anyway," she added defensively but not before he had caught the sound of guilt amongst the surprise. "You asked me that when I first came for the job."

"I know I did. You said twenty five," he told her glibly, "So that makes you . . . let's see . . . how long have we known each other, darling?"

"Six or seven years," she volunteered, turning now so that he could not see her face, "I forget."

"I don't. I checked the files and it's nearly ten, my love, so that makes you thirty five now, assuming that is you were telling the truth."

"David . . ." she rocked to her feet, a faint flush on her face, "Why should I lie? And, even if I did, what difference does it make? I still look good, don't I?" She jutted out her breasts and adjusted the sweater to make damned sure they were being shown to their full advantage. "Don't I?" she asked again, aggressive now, hands on hips.

He ignored that. "The difference, sweetheart, is that I don't have strippers in my club over the age of forty. It doesn't fit the . . ."

"I'm not a stripper," she interrupted angrily, "I'm a dancer. An exotic dancer."

"So . . .? They want young girls not some over made-up tart.

There's nothing so pathetic as an old stripper or exotic bloody dancer. What's the difference? A few feathers?" There was no kind way of saying it. He could pussyfoot round in all directions but it amounted to the same thing in the end. She had to go. He wanted her out of his life and that included the job. He had no intention of continuing to employ her, no way was he going to put up with the injured look in those eyes. He should have got rid of her years ago. He should never have taken her on in the first place except that he had fancied her like crazy. On stage, she was stiff-legged, like a jerky puppet, not one ounce of rhythm.

There was a silence. She put a hand up to her face and a faint smile flew over her. "I see," she said, and her dignity surprised him.

"I don't want you working in the club again," he said, taking a swig of his drink, realising too late that the way he was playing this, he'd be sleeping alone tonight. "Is that understood, sweetheart?"

"Yes." She smiled now properly and he remembered what had first attracted him to her. She had a bloody lovely smile. "I understand and thanks David. I honestly don't know what I would have done if you'd wanted me to carry on working afterwards. I've had it up to here with that job. I've never really liked it. I feel sick before I go on stage. Every time. I'm ready for . . . well, you can't call it retiring, not at my age . . . a rest if you like. And, you're right, it wouldn't be appropriate for me to go on working. Not after we get married." Her face gentled. "You're a daftie," she said softly, "Why didn't you just say you don't want your wife dancing like that in front of other men? There was no need to start playing tough. Over made-up tart indeed. You cheeky sod!"

Wife? The silly bitch thought he was building up to a marriage proposal. True, he might have mentioned marriage, occasionally, at strategic moments in their love life but he had never meant it. He would be a laughing stock if he married her. They laughed at her at the club, at her awful dancing. For a moment, he stared at her, stuck for words as she chatted cheerfully on.

"Annie was saying you might want to move from the bungalow," she said, "You're probably right. It'll have too many bad memories for you and, to be honest darling, it's not really my thing. Not a bungalow. It'll be best if we have a new start, you and me. We'll need to get back into town. How about north shore? I've always liked north shore best, up towards Bispham. In fact, David, I've been looking at some particulars of houses." She flushed. "Sorry . . . I hope you don't think it's too soon and everything, not with Ruth . . ." she paused, "Anyway, I've seen some that sound really nice. Semis. What do you think? I don't want anything too elaborate. Just a nice semi with a bay window, a little garden and a conservatory. I've always wanted that. Plants and things. And the garden will be nice for Blackbeard, won't it precious?" She tried to touch the cat but it slid by, still in a huff. "If we get three bedrooms, then there'll be a room for Annie as well as a spare in case we have visitors. You don't mind, do you? I haven't rushed you?"

A nice semi in Bispham? She must be joking. The woman was unhinged. She didn't seriously expect him to marry her, did she? He looked at her and saw she did.

9

"Alan . . . I'm back," Daisy said, depositing the groceries in the kitchen and putting the kettle on. First things first. She was absolutely whacked. Lunchtime had been really hectic. Something was happening at the university and they'd overspilled into the hotel. Academics, she decided, had loud voices and hearty appetites.

Having no car was worse than she'd imagined. At least it made her think a little more carefully about the groceries. They weighed so much. She was, she thought, rather getting the hang of it at last. The cookbook was a boon and it really was satisfying to think how much money she was saving.

She had asked discreetly about the job for Alan and the girl's uncle was willing to see him. No promises of course. She wished Alan was more enthusiastic but things were tough and it was only fair he pulled his weight. Something other than the painting.

"You out, Alan? . . ." she called, suddenly noticing the silence. He must be. Probably got his easel propped somewhere outdoors, taking advantage of the sunshine today. Daisy made herself a cup of coffee and carried it through to the living room. Five minutes with her feet up before she started. Goodness . . . she frowned at the notion. Had it come to that? She was beginning to behave like a housewife.

She would get in touch soon with mother. Gran had touched a nerve there. She was right of course. It wasn't fair. Mum and dad might have been over-hasty in their dismissal of Alan but she hadn't given them much chance. They needed to talk. Perhaps if she and Alan went to see them. Explained things a bit. Perhaps then . . .

She yawned. Realised her feet were throbbing. On them all day, up and down the dining room, fetching, carrying, catching snatches of conversation, smiling, smiling . . .

The five minutes stretched to fifteen and she finally made a move. Now . . . tonight she was cooking fish. Not frozen. Proper fish, real fish, from a slab. A little anxiously, she unwrapped the soft paper and looked at it. She preferred the packaged kind. This looked and felt very real. She consulted her cookbook and frowned. Damn. She had forgotten the ingredients for the sauce. Still . . . she would improvise.

Where was he? Hadn't mother once said you should never overcook fish? She would lay the table nicely first. She was getting to be rather good at this. Candles. Wine. Well . . . a bottle of wine occasionally was okay. A little treat. It was cooling in the fridge.

She smiled. Last night had been a bit special. To be honest, their relationship was volatile. And when they argued, it was always about money. She loved him and she was determined to try her best to make it work. She loved him so much but until last night, she hadn't been absolutely sure about his feelings. They would laugh in the future about when they were slumming it. Daisy glanced at the clock on the mantelpiece and, for the first time, saw the white envelope propped against it. Wiping fishy hands on her jeans, she moved towards it. Picked it up. It said simply "Daisy".

There really was no need to read it. She took it into the kitchen, left it unopened on the worktop. The fish looked enormous. Just for her. Furiously, she flooded it with lemon juice, pips and all, sprinkled it with pepper, wrapped it in foil, popped it in the oven. The lemony peppery fishy smell on her hands made her eyes water.

Or at least, she blamed it on that.

A quick look round confirmed he was gone. He'd taken everything of his and more. Helplessly, Daisy considered what to do. What could she do? He hadn't even had the courage to tell her to her face.

Just a letter . . . She picked it up again and finally read it before tearing it to pieces. At the weekend, Daisy decided, stuffing herself with bread and butter as she waited for the fish to bake, she would go to see gran. Gran always knew what to do.

About once a month, it was a family ritual that Leila came for Sunday lunch. She usually arrived about eleven o'clock which unfortunately gave them plenty of time for a leisurely chat.

Barbara finished checking on the meal, glanced out of the window and saw Guy's car turning into the drive. Sometimes, even now, Leila was capable of surprising them. For goodness knows how long, Guy had always volunteered to go and collect her, take her home, when she came for Sunday lunch. But it's such a drag for you, darling, she always said.

On this occasion, though, she had agreed. The car was in one of its useless moods. Or was that the reason? Could it be that she was beginning to worry about driving at her age? She insisted her eyesight and hearing were still good but it did concern them. Barbara had warned Guy not to say anything about that and he obviously hadn't because Leila was in an exceptionally cheerful mood. Barbara fussed around her, taking her coat, hanging it up. "Sherry?" she asked.

Leila accepted with a smile. "What's this about a funeral?" she said, "Guy's been telling me about you going to a funeral."

Calmly, Barbara explained about David and Ruth. She was determined to ignore the faint disapproval that Leila was managing to convey even without words. "He owns a nightclub and amusement arcades, that sort of thing," she added mischievously, knowing that would really get up Leila's nose.

It did. "How very vulgar," she tutted. She was wearing red but she looked good in it, as opposed to poor brave Annie. A crimson dress and cape with a black fringed rim. With it, she wore her diamond pin and the diamond and ruby drop earrings.

"Why did you go?" Leila asked, "It wasn't as if you knew her very well, was it? Guy said you hadn't seen either of them in years. You should have simply sent a card and some flowers. Funerals are so depressing and I should know. I seem to attend one a week these days. Thank the Lord I shan't know anything about mine." She leaned forward conspiratorially after checking that Guy had left the room, "I hope I can rely on you, Barbara, to conduct mine tastefully. Guy will go to pieces. I've left complete detailed instructions and I do insist they be carried out to the letter. None of this no flowers business. I want absolutely masses of cut blooms. And I want only the briefest mention of Charles in the notice, wife of will suffice, no beloved please. You may say beloved mother of Guy and devoted proud grandmother to Daisy if you wish. And I've made a few notes for the local press."

"Leila, please . . . " To her surprise, she found it was distressing her, "Let's talk about something else. What have you been up to these last few days? You look very pleased with yourself."

"I've not been up to anything," she said quickly. Too quickly? Knowing her, Barbara glanced suspiciously at her, not convinced at all. "Apart from an alteration to my will, leaving more to Daisy. She needs it more than you do. Guy says he doesn't give a toss. In fact, I think he was quite pleased."

"I'm not sure I am," Barbara said stiffly, "Not that Guy and I want anything more, Leila, you've been generous enough as it is but I do feel that it isn't good for Daisy, for anyone, to have it too easy. She's never earned any money of her own."

"She has. As a waitress."

Barbara stared at her a full minute before it dawned. "You know where she is, don't you?" she said. "You know where she is and you weren't going to tell us."

Leila sipped her sherry, seeming unconcerned. "You make such a fuss, you and Guy. I did promise the child I wouldn't tell you. It's all too tiresome. I hate secrets."

"But I'm her mother," Barbara protested, hopes rising nonetheless despite her irritation at her mother-in-law. "You have to tell me."

"I really don't see why. A promise is a promise. Don't worry, I've organised things," she said with a smile. "Complicated, of course, for nothing that child does is simple but I've had a little chat with her and convinced her that it would be best for everyone if she comes home to reconsider."

"Guy . . ." Barbara turned as he came into the room, "Did you know that your mother knows where Daisy is?"

"No he does not," Leila answered irritably for him. "Be patient, both of you, and I can guarantee that she'll be back very soon. I can't say exactly when but it will be soon."

"What about the boyfriend?" Guy asked, looking as dazed as Barbara felt. "Will he be coming back with her?"

"I think not." Leila held out her sherry glass. "Are we having wine at lunch? In that case, I won't have another, thank you."

Barbara exchanged a bemused glance with her husband as they went through to the dining room. It was at the rear of the house, cream lace and floral curtains veiling the view of the small garden. Guy helped his mother to take her seat at the circular table, which Barbara had laid with a pale blue cloth and the blue china. A tiny vase of flowers adorned the centre and crystal glasses waited to receive the red burgundy they would enjoy with their meal. Cheese and biscuits and fruit awaited on the antique sideboard.

As she settled herself beside Leila, Barbara knew, just by looking at Guy, that he was feeling as relieved as she was. It occurred to her that he had done a good job of keeping his concerns about Daisy to himself and it warmed her heart that he really did care about her. She had mistaken his quiet resignation about the whole episode for indifference. Of course Guy loved his daughter and she felt momentarily ashamed that she should have ever doubted it.

However, this was assuming that Leila was right and that Daisy was indeed coming home soon. In her bad moments recently, she had thought that Daisy might never come back, that she might never get in touch again and that she would be forced to spend the rest of her life wondering about her, worrying about her, crying for her. If Guy had seemed distant it was only because he was that sort of man, that sort of father. He loved Daisy but she didn't know if he'd ever actually told Daisy as much. He loved her too, Barbara knew that, but even with her he held something back. Therefore so did she. Theirs had always been a gentle love and, like weak tea, it was pleasant enough but lacking something. David's lovemaking would be no doubt equivalent to a double whisky. She knew that from the aftermath of the funeral. She sensed that as he held her.

"Did you have to bribe Daisy, mother?" Guy asked, crumbling

a fresh roll to spread with butter, "Or did you appeal to her better nature?"

Leila said nothing, starting on her soup, one of Barbara's favourites, tomato and carrot flavoured with herbs and swirled with cream. Barbara did not think that she had bribed Daisy. Daisy, despite her youth and faults, was vehement about justice and truth. The boyfriend on the other hand . . . it was just possible that Leila might have bribed him. It was the sort of underhand thing Leila would do and she had the means of doing it at that. Oddly, it saddened Barbara that Daisy could have been so mistaken in her choice of man. A man who loved her would not have been bribed. She knew with absolute certainty that Guy would never have been bribed to give her up.

Poor Daisy. They had to handle this carefully and not gloat about it. They must be sympathetic and understanding and try to put the whole sorry mess behind them. Given time, Daisy would forget him. First loves were easily forgotten although even as she thought it, she remembered David. A quarter of a century and more and she still hadn't forgotten the dratted man.

"Delicious soup, Barbara. As always." Leila pushed her plate aside, "Now . . . where were we? Ah yes, we were discussing Daisy. I want to put a proposition to you both."

"I'll clear these before you do that," Barbara said, glancing irritably at her mother-in-law. She had her officious tone on and it didn't augur well for the remainder of the meal. She had made a rich beef stew to be followed by a lime and orange syllabub in chocolate cups. The pudding was a new addition to her repertoire. She really needed their undivided attention and that might be difficult with Leila adopting her boardroom expression.

Sure enough, Leila chose to wait until the pudding was on the table. She took one look at it and asked if she might have cheese and biscuits instead. Then, as soon as Barbara produced these, she started again. "As I was saying," she said, "We ought to discuss what we are going to do with Daisy. Suppose she were to meet another young man, a much more suitable man, would either of you be averse to her marrying so young? After all, you married young, I married young, so there are worse things to do."

"You are hardly a good advertisement for it, mother," Guy said with a small smile.

"That was not my fault," Leila said crossly, "Your father was very plausible when he was young. A charmer . . . " she shook her head towards Barbara, "Remember him, my dear, he was charming, wasn't he? Utterly ruthless but charming with it. However . . . leaving your father out of this . . . frankly, I would rather Daisy married than go traipsing off to some university or other. Universities are not the places they were in your day, darling . . . " She glanced at Guy who, true to form, was now enthusing about Barbara's dessert. "In your day, they were such upright places. Now, it's all drugs and sex."

Guy nearly choked on his syllabub. "You don't know the half of it, mother," he said. "Students today are a deadly serious lot."

"Really, Guy? You do surprise me. No matter." She shrugged off her misapprehension without a care, "In any case, Daisy is a girl. Why should she bother? She knows all there is to know for looking after a home, employing staff, entertaining and motherhood. You don't need a degree for that, just common sense."

"Never say that to Daisy," Guy warned, as Barbara laughed. "Or she'll have you shot, mother."

"And don't start matchmaking either," Barbara joined in, knowing full well what was in the old lady's mind. "We've already discussed that and you know my views on it."

"I agree with Barbara," Guy said, a glint in his eyes as he probably recalled her attempts on his behalf many years ago. "The idea's preposterous."

"Why? Why is it so preposterous?" Leila's attempt at innocence was lost on them both. "The young of whatever era always make a pickle of choosing a partner if left to their own devices. If I can return to the subject of that father of yours, Guy. I was in love with the man and look what good that did me. If I'd listened to my mother, I'd never have married him. She had a much more suitable match in mind but would I listen? Love, that kind of inexplicable kind, so-called romance, is irrelevant to a successful marriage. It is by no means the be-all and end-all." She looked from one to the other of them, seemed about to say something more but resisted, pausing to help herself to more cheese.

"You're wrong, mother," Guy said with a puzzled shake of his head. "Of course love is the most important thing in marriage. Isn't it, Barbara?" He looked at her, full face, and smiled.

She smiled too. She had to smile but she could have qualified that to say that equal distribution of love is the most important thing. If one person loves more than the other then . . .

"Very well," Leila conceded, "It does help I suppose but financial security and a certain standing in the community rate as much more important. In my opinion, arranged marriages are extremely civilised and there is no reason why they shouldn't be successful. After all, you only have to look at the ridiculous divorce figures to realise that choosing your own partner is a lottery. And why on earth shouldn't you fall in love with your husband when you've been married a while. Isn't that a charming notion?"

"Try telling that to Daisy." Barbara smiled, not taking Leila seriously. Some of the things she said had really to be taken with a huge pinch of salt and, of course, her age was an excuse for odd behaviour. "Daisy will want to choose for herself and, if she makes a mistake, then . . ." she avoided the thought that darted through her mind. She and Guy . . . you could say that she had made the wrong choice for the wrong reason and the result was this . . . a tolerably happy marriage but with a lot of doubts surrounding it.

"You're fine ones to talk," Leila said, in a huff, "You were very quick to point out that you thought the boyfriend was a mistake. If that's not interfering, I don't know what is."

"Point taken," Guy said with a small smile. "We're going to do better next time. Aren't we, darling? Here . . . let me clear these." He departed with a tray of dishes and Barbara and Leila were left alone.

"What's the matter with him?" Leila demanded, "He's got that look on his face."

"What do you mean?"

"That look. The sort of secret look he used to have as a child. As his mother, my dear, I tell you he's up to no good. Are you absolutely sure about the secretary? Guy said you popped in unexpectedly the other day. Locked yourself out?" She smiled conspiratorially.

"I did lock myself out." Barbara reached for the wine, thus averting her eyes. "Shall we finish this off?"

"What's she like?" Leila moved her glass nearer and lowered her voice, "I used to use that excuse, dear," she said, "When I checked up on Charles. The annoying thing was I never actually caught them."

"I wasn't checking up on him, Leila." Barbara laughed and sipped the wine, the liquid slithering down the wrong way and causing a momentary, very opportune, diversion.

Leila obligingly patted her back. "How did she react on seeing you? Did she seem at all uncomfortable?"

"Shush . . ." Barbara lowered her voice, "Forget it, Leila," she said, holding onto a sudden extreme anger, determined she would not reveal her considerable doubts to her mother-in-law. The almighty cheek of the woman! "He's far too busy to have an affair," she whispered, "And, in any case . . ." She stopped. She had been about to say that Guy's interest in sex was minimal but decided she must not divulge secrets of their married life, especially to Leila.

"Just watch for the signs then," Leila murmured as they heard the sound of his footsteps crossing the hall, "Just be on your guard that's all." She smiled brightly as Guy appeared. "We were talking about you," she said, "You look tired. Barbara thinks it's high time you took some time off. I agree with her. I think you should whisk her off to some remote island in the South Seas. It'll do you both the world of good and the business, my dear, will still be here when you get back."

"We will take a holiday but not just now," he replied, snatching an irritated glance at Barbara. "It's a bad time. How can I relax when I have important things on my mind, important contracts just about to come to fruition? It wouldn't be fair on Barbara."

"Actually I have been thinking recently . . . Would you mind, Guy, as you are so busy, if I took a holiday alone?" She glanced at Leila for support and instantly got it. "Or I could ring up an old girlfriend and have a few days away somewhere. I've got heaps of invitations pending. You wouldn't mind, would you

Guy?" she repeated softly. The question hung in the air and she felt herself flush. An old girlfriend indeed!

"Of course he doesn't mind," Leila said, "I think it's a marvellous idea. You look peaky, my dear, and it will recharge your batteries so to speak."

"How do you recharge your batteries, mother?" Guy said, seeming not entirely willing to give the go-ahead, "You never go away yourself these days."

"Simply because I can't bear the fuss," she said tartly. "Packing and suchlike. Too boring. Also the remainder of the world is grossly overrated. None of it compares to Harrogate. Charles used to drag me all over the blessed place and it was always such a relief to come home. Appalling tea everywhere." Travelling thus dismissed, she smiled at them. "Now that's settled, have we time for a game of cards before you take me home? Do you remember the Pattersons, Guy? Roy and Penelope. Well . . . I was looking through my address book recently and I've decided to look them up. They're awfully fond of playing cards as I recall so, if I'm to entertain them, I'll need to brush up."

Barbara eyed her with exasperation. Guy must have inherited the guilty look from his mother. Or was the sudden shiftiness the start of senility? Looking at her mother-in-law, at the bright eyes, at the beautifully made-up face, that seemed a very foolish notion.

"I won't come in, thank you, mother," Guy said as he helped her out of the car. "Are you all right on your own?"

"I'll have to be, won't I?" Leila walked a little stiffly to her front door. "Are you sure you won't have a cup of tea?"

"No. I have some paperwork to sort through for tomorrow."

"Really? Can't your secretary do that?" She glanced at him, seeing if there was the remotest flicker of guilt, "What's she like, your secretary?"

"What do you mean? What's she like?"

"What does the woman look like?" She clasped her key in her hand and inserted it into the door.

"All right," Guy said, "Reddish sort of hair. Nice telephone manner."

"Smartly dressed?"

"Yes. Not so smart as you of course, mother, but then not many women are."

Leila beamed. "For a moment, you sounded just like your father," she said sweetly. "I am totally immune to flattery, Guy, and I will not allow you to change the subject. We were talking about this secretary of yours. Is she efficient?"

"Of course. Super efficient."

"Barbara tells me she is called Gladys. My dear, with a dreadful name like that, the poor woman has to have some consolation. I suppose being efficient and reasonably smartly clad is better than nothing."

"She can't help her name," he said tightly. "Goodnight, mother. I'll phone you soon."

"Goodnight, darling." She waved as he drove off and trailed through the house to the kitchen, putting the kettle on for a cup of tea. The journey home tonight had seemed endless. The kitchen was clean and tidy, her housekeeper a wonderful woman. She no longer lived in but she was at the end of a telephone close by should Leila need her urgently. Frankly, Leila preferred to have the house to herself. There was far too much nonsense talked about muggings and burglaries and she put such depressing thoughts right out of her mind. It was all in the mind and such a thing would never happen to her. That's why she was careless with her valuable possessions. That's why she told anyone who cared to listen about her wealth, her antiques, her furs. It was a challenge, a double bluff.

Nevertheless, she paused in the middle of pouring the tea as she heard a noise outside. From the side garden, a rustling in the shrubbery. It could be a cat of course but she doubted it. Hearing it again, she contemplated ringing her neighbour but he would very likely thunder round in true constabulary fashion, and she did not wish to be seen as a nervous old dear. Oh dear, this was all too boring coming as it did at the end of a long day. Taking a knife, a breadknife, from the kitchen drawer, she advanced towards the side door. She had no qualms about using the knife. She was not going to end up battered and bruised and looking all of ninety in the newspaper photograph that would accompany the article on her beating up. Nor did she wish to be referred to as an old age pensioner or senior citizen. Time they came up with a new flattering term for ladies and gentlemen of a certain age.

There was a knock on the door before she reached it. "Gran . . . are you there?" Daisy's voice was nervous too. "Is that you, gran?"

Leila unlocked the door and Daisy practically fell in. "I've been hanging about waiting for you for ages. Where have you been? The car's still in the garage. You left the keys in the ignition by the way."

"You were unlucky, darling," Leila was still brandishing the knife, "I don't usually lock the house doors but your father insisted. You know what he's like. Didn't you hear the car a few minutes ago?"

"I dropped off," Daisy said with a huge yawn. "I've been sitting on that seat in the garden. I've been here hours. I got a lift from a friend this afternoon. I suppose I should have rung first. You've been over to Harrogate then?"

"Sunday lunch." Leila replaced the knife in the drawer before opening her arms to her granddaughter for a hug. "What do you look like?" she said softly, moving the hair from Daisy's face, "We're going to have to do something with you if we're to get you married off."

Daisy ignored that. She collapsed onto a kitchen chair and looked as if she was about to burst into tears. "Alan's left me," she said dramatically. "Walked out, gran. Go on, say it, I told you so."

Leila said nothing. So . . . he had kept his side of the bargain. Good. "Do you want to talk about it?" she asked after a moment, touching Daisy's heaving shoulder, "Don't cry, darling. It upsets me to see you cry. No man is worth it. Save your tears for babies and animals, so much more deserving."

Daisy pulled a tissue from her pocket, a damp tissue that was partially disintegrated, and stabbed at her eyes. Blew her nose. "He left me a note," she said, "Didn't even have the decency, gran, to tell me to my face. He was seeing someone else. All the time he was with me, he was seeing someone else. Can you seriously believe that?"

"Ah! A two-timer." Leila shook her head, heaping sugar into Daisy's cup. Sugar for shock. "I thought he was too attractive for his own good. The eyes were a giveaway, dear. Eyes always are. He reminded me, regrettably, of that swine of a grandfather of yours."

"I feel so humiliated." Daisy's beautiful eyes were still moist. "He must have been comparing the two of us and I obviously . . ." she shrugged and for a moment, her pain distressed Leila, particularly as she had caused it. "I thought he loved me. He told me he loved me. And worse, I told him I loved him too. Can you believe he would do such a thing, gran?"

"Quite easily." Leila patted her hand. "Drink your tea." The boy had been a little quick off the mark but discreet. She would have preferred him to wait a while longer so that the decision would not be linked in any way to her visit. "Men are like that," she said. "With the possible exception of your father . . ." she frowned as she remembered his evasiveness, "Men are pigs. We women are infinitely superior and that's why we have been charged with the task of bringing up children. That is the most important thing in life. Let the men amuse themselves with their petty boardroom squabbles, my dear, we ladies have more important things to occupy us."

"Gran . . ." Daisy managed a watery smile, "You say some daft things."

"Go and have a bath and then we'll talk some more," Leila said, "Go on, off you go, you know where everything is. Afterwards, pop into bed in the blue bedroom and I'll bring you up cocoa and biscuits. Bourbons still your favourites?"

"Please." Daisy nodded, looking about twelve. "Thanks gran," she said, giving her a kiss. "You are wonderful to me."

Guilt pressed briefly on her when Daisy had gone. Perhaps she had been a little naughty doing this but it really was for Daisy's good. She grimaced and looked heavenwards. God would understand her motives. Once again, the image formed of dearest Daisy in white, her dark hair a soft halo round her head. A flowing lacy dress, a billowing froth of a veil and the Bamber tiara, the one that she had worn at her own wedding, the one her mother had worn before her and her grandmother before that. It was a source of irritation that Barbara had refused to wear it at her wedding to Guy. When she got it into her head, Barbara could be so very stubborn. Instead, she had worn a cheap little pearl thing from her side of the family. Nice enough but nowhere near as grand as theirs. Daisy would wear it.

She herself would wear blue, one of her favourite colours, a silk dress and jacket and a wide-brimmed hat trimmed with flowers, the fur stole if needed. People would remark how wonderful she was for her age. She hoped to goodness she lasted until the wedding and that's why, of course, she had to hurry things along. At her age, one never knew from one day to the next. There were strokes and suchlike. All too boring. She wanted to go out with a bang, in her sleep, when she had accomplished all she set out to do. She had so many things she wanted to accomplish that she was on target for living until she was a hundred. She certainly did not intend to expire until Daisy was married off. Suitably married off. Guy and Barbara had better stay married too or it would be too awkward. What was wrong with those two? Something was. There was no sparkle left, just a fizzle of a damp squib, a tolerance that appalled. They were acting strangely, both of them, particularly Barbara. The woman needed a bit of romance in her life. She was bored. Unfortunately Guy would not have noticed. For all his charm, Charles had been thoughtful or at least used that as his excuse for his abominable behaviour. He had never forgotten her birthday or their anniversary or the anniversary of the first time they met. That sort of thing. Guy's silver wedding was coming up and he probably hadn't given it a single thought. She ought to remind him as usual but Barbara had said not to.

That sounded ominous. If he forgot, it would be the last straw. She wondered if her daughter-in-law had it in her to go storming off. She doubted it. That's what Guy needed of course if he did forget, a kick up the backside, but she didn't think Barbara had it in her. Barbara worried too much about what other people might think. Barbara was dreadfully conventional.

She made the cocoa and carried it up to Daisy. "I hope those sheets are aired . . ." she said, smiling at Daisy who was propped up in bed, face scrubbed, hair brushed.

"Don't fuss." Gratefully Daisy took the mug and cupped it in her hands, warming them. "What am I going to do, gran?" she asked. "I don't feel I can face mum and dad just yet. All that I told you so."

"They won't say that. They'll be much too relieved to see you. And I don't think they'll be pestering you as to what you do next. I'll make sure, dear, that what you choose to do is entirely your own concern."

"Will you, gran?" Daisy pushed at her hair, blue eyes tired and dull. "Can I stay with you a while?" she asked quietly. "I won't be a nuisance. I'll help round the house. I need to think and then I'll have to look for a job."

"No hurry. Of course you may stay. I was just about to suggest that," Leila said. How convenient. An on the spot Daisy was much more convenient especially with the Pattersons due to visit. "I'm having guests in a few days for afternoon tea and you can help me get ready for them. Can you bake?"

"No. Can you?" A smile blazed. "Haven't you got someone who comes in to do that sort of thing for you?"

"Yes but I thought it might be nice if you made something. Home-made biscuits or scones. Mrs Patterson will be delighted. It's such a rare accomplishment these days for a young lady to be able to make scones. Did you ever meet the Pattersons dear? They're fond of bridge."

Daisy laughed. "Haven't they got a son called Miles?"

"Piers actually." Leila stopped, realising her mistake or potential mistake. Daisy seemed not to have noticed. Instead, she rambled on between sips of her cocoa, coming to the conclusion that Piers Patterson was the clumsiest most repulsive boy she had ever met. At fifteen, he was spotty and dumpy and a bit thick.

"He's something in the city now," Leila said carefully, "And, after all, none of us are at our best at fifteen. Such an awkward age for us all. Even I, I am told, was rather gauche. And you were all legs and teeth, darling."

"He won't be coming along, will he? Piers?"

"Good lord, no. I haven't invited him. In any case, he sounds utterly frightful," Leila said with a short laugh. She dare not catch Daisy's look for she wasn't sure if Daisy was teasing or not.

However, it did not augur well. Still, there were other young men if Piers was as appalling at twenty seven as he had been at fifteen.

An autumn wedding she rather thought. There was no point in hanging about once the decision was made, no point in cumbersome frustrating engagements. Autumn weddings had always appealed to her. The bridesmaids could wear velvet maybe or carry velvet muffs. Golden autumn hues. Leaves on the ground. Her favourite time of year. Perhaps they might persuade Daisy to wear her hair up to show off her elegant neck and the splendid diamond drop earrings Leila was intending to lend. Something borrowed. That and the tiara. Perhaps Barbara could come up with the something blue in addition to her mood these days that seemed permanently that colour. Of course she had cheered up immensely once she heard the news about Daisy. It had been nice to see how it had cheered the pair of them.

She returned her attention to the matter of the autumn wedding. October probably, no later. Piers would be splendid too, top hat and tails, at Daisy's side . . . well, perhaps not Piers. Certainly not Piers if he turned out to be repulsive still. Daisy must have a handsome escort if it was to be wedding of the Harrogate year. A tall handsome fellow was an absolute necessity. Her thoughts flitted uncomfortably to Alan and his dark brooding eyes, passable certainly in the physical sense but the relationship had been doomed from the start. The boy was obviously from peasant stock and that would not mingle well with the Bamber-Shawcross blood. Barbara's humble origins had diluted things enough thank you.

Cheerfully debating what hymns to have and already starting on a formidable guest list, Leila retired to bed. What fun!

10

Funny how you forgot about voices. He'd remembered her face, as it was, the way she walked, the set of her jaw. Things like that. But he'd forgotten her voice. The accent had changed a little, becoming more polished like Guy's he supposed but the tone was as it used to be, lowish pitched, deeper than Ruth's and Linda's. The lowish pitch was sexy. Smooth as velvet. A silken sheen to it. Soft. Slightly husky. Over the telephone, where every nuance was emphasised, he knew that she was nervous, that he made her nervous. It was as if they were young again and he was ringing for a first date. Sweaty palms. Trying desperately to mask the anxiety. Sad maybe but he found it exciting and amusing. The woman had the hots for him. No doubt about it. All he had to do was click his fingers at the appropriate moment and . . .

"Have I rung at an inconvenient time?" he asked, cradling the receiver against his chin as he made the call from the office. "I thought during the day might be best. You did say you were a lady of leisure, didn't you?"

She tried to hide her surprise at his call but did not quite manage it. Her slight laugh was forced too. "A lady of leisure?" she echoed. "Not quite, David, you should see my diary. There's something happening this week every single day. I'm in the charity shop today and later in the week I have meetings of my charity committees, the trolley tray at the hospital, all sorts of things. I don't go out to work if that's what you mean."

"Your choice or Guy's?"

"Mine. Guy would have no objection if I wished to get a job."

"Ruth never had a job after Annie was born. She was the domestic sort too."

"I'm not the *domestic* sort," she said irritably.

"Sorry. I forget you women are touchy about things like that." He grinned into the phone. She was being cool, remarkably so, but she couldn't completely hide the tension, the surprise that he should have rung.

"How are you, David?" she asked, seeming to make a conscious effort to pull herself together. "It was so nice to see you again even though we were both of us sad. I know it's still early days but are you feeling any better?"

"A bit." He frowned into the phone, wondering how he did feel, staring at the rain as it lashed against the window of the office. "Missing her like hell of course." He realised he *was* missing her, in all sorts of funny little ways. She'd always been there, dammit, when he got home tired and fed up, Ruth was always there with the tea and sympathy. Something like that. Someone who didn't mind him taking out his frustration after a difficult day. The more he thought about it, the more he realised how she must have loved him to put up with it. He should have found time for a holiday. Taken her up to boring bloody Scotland.

"And how is Annie? It must be very hard for her, being so young. It's ironic, isn't it? Daisy's intent on giving me the cold shoulder and poor Annie . . . girls of her age really need their mothers."

"Thanks for that," he said drily.

"Oh, I'm sorry. How tactless. I felt we parted under somewhat strained circumstances and I hope she didn't get the wrong impression. However, I thought it best not to make too much of it." She laughed again, shortly. "That's why I left when I did, a bit abruptly I know, and I wish now I'd had a word with her before I went, on her own. I'm not sure what I would have said but I might have been able to help. Have you any friends who might talk to her? Wives of your colleagues? Aunts?"

"No." Impatiently, he waved his assistant aside as he poked his head round the door. "Look . . . I'll have to be brief, I'm due in a meeting but I've been thinking about it and I meant it when I said I want us to get together sometime. Can you persuade that husband of yours to let you have a weekend away? You can think of some excuse surely, unless you're confident enough to tell him the truth. Somehow, knowing old Guy, I don't think he'd be too thrilled if he knew you were meeting me. He never liked my guts. I didn't like his either. If you ask me, people who have it too easy in their early years suffer from a basic character fault."

There was the shortest pause and then her voice again, "I'd forgotten just how direct you are, David. You're wrong of course but I'm not going to argue now." She spoke quietly but he sensed her irritation. Damn. It was a mistake to have criticised old Guy. "As to the weekend . . . I'm not sure I follow. Are you suggesting a weekend away with you? Alone?"

"Yes. It's time we were honest with each other, you and me." He chuckled, enjoying her discomfiture. It was thrilling when there was a bit of resistance and he fancied there would be a helluva lot of that from Barbara. She was a loyal little wife and she would take some prising away from Guy. She wasn't cut out for an affair, too strait-laced, but, in the end, she would do it. There would be a lot of soul searching involved but she would do it because she wanted to. He could tell that from the response when he had held her in his arms after the funeral. It had been a womanly response, nothing to do with the little stab at dancing, although he really wanted to do that, too, to get her on the dance floor, to see if they had lost their special touch or not. He felt not. Their body chemistry was perfect. Even without practice, she would still be able to execute a very satisfactory dance, not like that little green-eyed blonde who had now cancelled her lessons, presumably getting cold as well as clumsy feet. Sod her. He hoped she made a real botch-up of the dancing at her wedding do.

He knew exactly what was wrong with Barbara. Physically, big awkward Guy was not satisfying her, probably never had, that much was obvious. "We've wasted enough time," he said into a silence, "We both know what's what now so we needn't act as if we were teenagers. It's just a pity that it had to take this to get us together again, to get us to admit our feelings. We've been fools, Barbara, you and me. Fools."

"You misunderstand, David . . ." Her laugh was forced, uneven, "My motives for coming to the funeral were simply to offer some comfort. I felt I owed it to Ruth to come. The reason I came alone was that Guy was just too busy. He sent his apologies by the way.

There was no ulterior motive on my part." She paused, letting it sink in, "Unfortunately, you seem to have got it wrong."

"Barbara . . . be honest please." He smiled, knowing it would transmit over the wire. "We made a mistake years ago, a stupid mistake. That row! Just because I criticised your dancing, we lost each other forever. I can't think what got into me. You never put a foot wrong when you were dancing. Hardly ever . . ."

She laughed, a little more easily, "There you go again. Nobody was perfect except you, David. Your dancing was always perfect."

"Okay. So maybe I'm a bit touchy about that but all professionals are. When you're aiming to be the best, you can't afford to pussyfoot around. You've got to work at it, Barbara, and sometimes . . . just sometimes . . . I used to think you were a bit carefree in the commitment department."

"How dare you say that," she spluttered. "I'll have you know, David, I put everything I had into my dancing. I couldn't have given more."

"Okay. Hell, okay." He sighed. She *still* couldn't take criticism, twenty five years on and she still couldn't take it. "I apologise but that was no excuse for us ending up married to the wrong people."

"No," she said quickly, "Don't say that. I love Guy."

"And I loved Ruth. In a way. But there was never the sparkle with us, not like there was with you and me, sweetheart. I knew the instant I saw you again. I knew the instant I looked into those fabulous eyes of yours. God, they've not changed. They're still like . . ."

"Stop it," she interrupted. "I'm sorry but we really shouldn't be talking like this."

"Why not? Is Guy listening in on the extension?"

"No. And don't be flippant." An irritation was creeping into her voice but he still held out some hope. Surely he hadn't completely misread the situation? He was usually right where female responses were concerned and Barbara had, after a very slight resistance, relaxed. Who knows what might have happened if Annie hadn't suddenly appeared? "I have no idea how you've reached this conclusion but I can only assume you're still upset by Ruth's death," she went on, taking on a stiff, formal tone, "It will take some time for you to recover, both you and Annie. At the moment, you're not thinking straight."

"Oh yes I am. I'm thinking about you, Barbara. I can't stop thinking about you. I think about you when I go to sleep at night, I keep thinking about you during the day, my work's beginning to suffer dammit, and I dream about you. You're the first thing I think about when I wake up in the morning. Do you ever dream about me?"

"I hardly ever dream." Again, the nervousness in the reply. "I'm sorry I came to the funeral now. I never would have, if I'd known it was going to cause all this fuss. I made a mistake, raking it all up again when you'd forgotten all about me. I should have left it at that. You can never go back, can you? It's always a mistake to try to go back, because it's never the same. You're thinking of me as I used to be, David, and I'm not that girl any more. I'm forty five and I'm married to Guy. You're forty eight . . ."

"Forty seven" he said quickly. "Christ, don't make me older than I am."

"Seven, eight, what difference does it make? The point I'm trying to make is this, we've changed, both of us. I honestly can't think now why I came. After all, it wasn't as if Ruth and I were that close, was it?"

"She didn't care much for you either. She thought you were snooty, toffee-nosed. She said Guy was just the right man for you. She always said you thought you were a touch better than the rest of us. Between you and me, she was just jealous. She damned well knew I couldn't get you out of my mind. I don't know why she kept sending you Christmas cards. Habit I suppose. We none of us liked Guy, none of the crowd. Bloody condescending if you ask me. Why did he latch on to us? He wasn't our kind. Offering to pay for the fish and chips when we couldn't scrape a couple of quid together between us? I could have punched him on the nose for that. Would have but I didn't want to cause a scene."

"You do have a long memory." Barbara said quietly, "Look, David, I really feel that you and I have said all we need to say. I'd rather you didn't say unpleasant things about Guy. That's twice you've had a go at him and it's totally unnecessary.

He's a very kind considerate man and a wonderful father to Daisy."

"Ever the loyal little wife eh?"

"Yes." Her voice rose and he panicked, thinking she was going to slam the phone down on him. "Something wrong with that?" she challenged, hard-edged.

"Sorry, sorry," he said hastily. "Can't you see why I say these things? Because *I'm* insanely jealous that's why. I can't bear to think of him loving you. On your wedding night, dammit, all I could think about was the two of you and what you were getting up to. Guy Shawcross and my girl. It's not something I'm proud of but it's the truth. I couldn't bear it, darling."

There was a disturbed silence from her end then an anguished "Oh David . . ."

He breathed a sigh of relief. "Have you mentioned to that husband of yours that we held each other after the funeral?" he asked. "Have you told him that?"

"No. Why should I? There was nothing to it." That defiance was still there, but cracked. She was still thinking about what he'd said about her wedding night. Touch of inspiration to say that. The woman was denying her own feelings. "It's what any friend would have done," she continued with a brave attempt at confidence. "You were very sad and I wanted to comfort you. You shouldn't have read anything more into it. Forget it, David." She sighed now and he wished she were here with him. If he could only touch her . . . one touch was worth a thousand words.

Eyes narrowed, he glanced round the office, out of the window. It was still lashing with rain, belting against the window. His office was across from the promenade and today a sea fog shrouded the ocean so that you could hear but not see it. Stormy. It matched his mood exactly. He could kick himself for this, the wrong approach. Attacking was not the way with Barbara. Damn the woman, she was going to be just as hard work now as she had been all those years ago. He was going to have to go through the whole red roses and romance bit again as if she was still a virgin. "Sorry, sweetheart." He put his heart into that one. "My mistake. You're probably right. Forgive me, I'm not coping as well as I thought. But I still love you, Barbara.

I always have and I always will. Remember that." He did not wait for her reply, replacing the phone with a gentle click.

He stared at it a moment and then he smiled. Women went for that, the romantic crap. With a bit of luck it should have done the trick.

David's phone call had shocked her. His sheer conceit and arrogance annoyed her beyond belief. How could he with his wife barely cold? However, she was helping Meg today at the charity shop and so she had to put him out of her mind. Or try to.

Meg did not help. She was in a strange, pensive mood, though still managing to scare off most potential customers with a single withering look. "I was just thinking . . ." she began as they drank coffee during a lull. "That girl coming in for that dress reminded me."

"Which girl? Oh . . . the evening dress?"

Meg nodded. "The blue one. Lovely wasn't it? And didn't she look good in it? Well . . . I don't know why but she reminded me of me. When I was young . . ."

Barbara smiled. "Do we need violins playing for this?" she asked, her smile widening at Meg's wistful expression.

Meg did not smile. "I did a similar thing I suppose. Bought a dress for a ball. Bought it at a jumble sale in fact. That was a beautiful blue dress, too, with sequins. And that night I met Howard."

"You were wearing a jumble sale dress?" Barbara laughed her astonishment, "I thought you were rolling in money, Meg, even when you were young?"

Meg raised her eyebrows. "I may have given that impression," she said, "But I clawed myself up, rags to riches. What a story I could tell."

Barbara said nothing, wondering what had brought this on. She had never thought of Meg and herself as close friends and they rarely discussed matters as personal as this. It was therefore a touch embarrassing and she was not sure what to say. Come to think of it, Meg had always been vague about her life before she married Howard. They, neither of them, came from the area so it was pretty much of a mystery. "So your story is much the same as mine then," she said after a moment, for her own humble beginnings were no secret, not with a mother-in-law like Leila.

"I was engaged at the time to this other boy," Meg said, adjusting the pleated skirt of her oyster dress. Rings glittered. Her long fingernails were frosty pink. "I dumped him. Dumped him for Howard."

"We've all of us done that," Barbara said. "I wasn't engaged but I did have one or two boyfriends before Guy. You mustn't feel badly about it," she added.

"I don':," Meg said with a smile. "I married Howard, Barbara, because he was an excellent doctor heading for a top job. That's why. I dumped Andrew. He was struggling to be an electrician by the way. As I saw it, Howard was not repulsive and he loved me. I made a choice." She laughed, "And I can't think why I'm telling you this."

"Sometimes you can't bottle up things any longer. You needn't worry, I shan't tell anyone."

"You'd better not." Meg seemed to have recovered her composure. She tidied up her hair. "I saw him this weekend actually and I suppose that's what brought it on. He lives near my mother in Nottingham. He's married with four children. A fully qualified electrician now. His own little business." The slightest smile passed her lips. "So just think, that could have been my fate. An electrician's wife with four kids, having to do a part-time job to afford the little luxuries of life. Can you imagine?"

"No." Barbara eyed her curiously. "Would you swap? Given the chance?"

Meg smiled. "You mean would I give all this up?" She gestured vaguely towards her clothes, her jewellery. "You must be joking, Barbara." Absently, she fussed with the articles on the counter top. "After all, I dare say you'd think twice about leaving Guy too."

Barbara stared at her. For a moment, it was as if Meg knew. This entire conversation had been concocted because Meg knew. Were she and Leila in collusion? It was just the sort of underhand thing Leila would do, to get a third party to plant ideas in Barbara's head or to extract information. The electrician in Nottingham was a mere romantic figment of their collective imagination. Looking at Meg, it was highly improbable. "Why should I leave Guy?" she said briskly. "I have no reason to leave him."

David Ambrose could take a running jump, she decided as she washed up their mugs whilst Meg deigned to serve a customer. Nothing had happened between them, not physically, and she was already acting like a guilty person. If she let it drop now, then Guy would be none the wiser.

And then she remembered the secretary.

The nights out together began to follow the pattern of the first night. Guy had thought it better if they did not leave together. He needn't have worried for Gladys was nothing if not a born organiser and she thought of everything, looking so normal and self-assured throughout the day that he marvelled at her. Meeting up with Barbara unexpectedly had not flustered her although it had surely flustered him.

In the afternoon, she sat in on an important meeting with a group of associates, taking notes as usual, typing them up fast and presenting the finished papers to him for signature together with other letters. The work was immaculate. He recalled that she had never presented a letter for signature that had a mistake in it, a mistake of hers that is. She was a very good secretary and he would miss her if she ever left.

Why should she leave? Perhaps she would, if this disintegrated into a fiasco, if, despite everything, word got round. Sick with guilt, he picked her up as arranged at the bus stop near the office and she slipped into the car, smiling at him, and assuring him that nobody was any the wiser and, even if anyone had seen them, he was merely offering her a lift home, wasn't he? After all, he had done it once before. Quite. Once being the operative word. Once only and that was for a reason.

Very aware of Gladys's presence beside him and her strong perfume, he forced himself to concentrate on the heavy traffic on the hill out of town, forgetting for a moment that he was not heading home and having to change lanes at a very awkward point. Gladys made no comment at the hooting behind them, did not even inhale with exasperation as Barbara would have done.

"As soon as we get out of town, pull into a lay-by and we'll eat," she said and he glanced at her with amusement, remembering that she was a touch bossy with her juniors. She fumbled at her feet for a large bag. "I wasn't sure what you would like," she said, "So I've brought a selection. There's cheese and pickle on wholemeal. Ham salad on white and cottage cheese and tomato on granary. Apples and some crisps. And a flask of coffee. Will that be all right, Mr Shawcross?"

"A feast," he said with admiration. As usual he'd only had time for a coffee and a chocolate bar at lunchtime and he was hungry. Nor could he do what he was going to do on an empty stomach. The last thing he wanted was to listen to his stomach rumbling. Oh God, he wished he'd never started this. Already he had the uncomfortable feeling that it was all getting a bit too cosy and perhaps they might have been better to look out for a café for their refreshment. In some ways, a café would be less conspicuous. If anyone were to spot them eating surreptitiously in a lay-by, it would surely alert suspicions for, after all, a boss simply did not do that with his secretary. This whole thing smacked of secret rendezvous stuff.

In addition to the food, she had brought linen napkins and proper plates. "I think it's so romantic . . ." she said when they were tucking into the sandwiches. She ate with a verve normally absent in the women he knew. He liked it. None of this anxious nibbling but a good old-fashioned enjoyment of her food. "Such a romantic surprise for your wife," she added casting a sly glance his way, "What wouldn't I give for a man to do that for me?"

"I just hope Barbara agrees," he said, not able to keep the worry out of his voice, "I've never done anything remotely like this before."

"I can tell that." She smiled broadly at him, a few crumbs sticking to her shiny red lips. She had the most gorgeous smile, warm and uninhibited. "Would you mind if I asked you something? Something rather personal?"

"Not at all." Guy felt a moment's unease, preferring not to discuss personal matters but having no option under these most alarming circumstances. On the road, a couple of cars drove by, followed by a break in the traffic. Sudden silence. The lay-by was beside a field and over the wall he could see black and white cows standing chewing in that utterly zombie-like way of theirs. Nearer, on the grass verge, dusty spiky grass and some feathery wild flowers. He couldn't think why he was noticing these things for he didn't usually. They were the only car when there was room for about six.

"Tell me, what do you think of my name?" Gladys looked at him earnestly. "My name ... Gladys ... and please be honest."

"What do I think of it?" He took an apple from the bag and bit into it. "Well ..." he tried to be careful, anxious not to offend. "Isn't it a bit old-fashioned? Not that I know a thing about names," he went on quickly, "It was Barbara's idea to call Daisy Daisy. I suppose you could say that's old-fashioned too."

She shook her head. "Not in the way that Gladys is. How many baby girls are christened Gladys these days?"

"Not many," he admitted, wondering where this odd conversation was leading. "I must say, it's for an older person than you."

"Exactly. I really hate it. I had two Aunt Gladyses you see and for some reason my mother wanted to call me after them. I suppose I could change it but you never feel quite right about that, do you, not when your parents made a decision on your behalf? I never think of myself as Gladys actually. I'm more a ..." she screwed up her face in concentration. "What do you think, Mr Shawcross?"

"Guy please this evening. Try to remember." He spoke a trifle sharply, wanting to change the direction of all this. Frankly, a name was a name. He didn't understand the significance. "I don't know why you ask me," he went on, watching as she ate her apple, leaving little traces of lipstick as she waved it casually about, "I really haven't the slightest idea. As I say, I'm no good with names."

"Oh come on, you must have some idea." She poured them each a cup of coffee and replaced the cap on the flask. She handed him a cup with a smile and he relaxed. It was stupid to think there was anything wrong with this. It was just his guilty conscience that was all and what had he to be guilty about? Absolutely nothing.

"All right." He thought hard. "How about Chloe? Now I come

to think about it, I always think of Chloes as . . ." he stopped, about to say large but lovely ladies and not knowing if she would be offended by that.

"Chloe? That's nice. I like it." If she noted his discomfiture, she pretended not to. "It's modern and yet unusual. I'll have to look it up in my name book and tell you what it means." She sipped her coffee which was piping hot. "Have you ever thought that, in some ways, we become the person we're named? Oh dear, it's so difficult to explain . . ." she frowned, trying hard, "What I mean is, suppose I had been christened Chloe, would that have made me a different person? Would I have been thinner for one?" A tiny smile flickered.

"But seriously, I wonder how it affects us, our name. For instance, suppose you, Mr Shawcross, had been christened . . . let's see . . . Albert or Herbert or Cyril . . . would such an ordinary little name have made you a weaker person? Would you have been less dynamic? Would you still have been so successful? In other words, would a name like that, a real handicap if you ask me, have swamped your style or would it have made absolutely no difference?" She giggled suddenly, nearing spilling her coffee. "Albert Shawcross . . ." she murmured.

Guy took a gulp of coffee and winced as the very hot liquid flew inside. Wow! Swamped his style eh? Is this the way Gladys saw him? Dynamic, successful, a strong character? Time to call a halt to this. She was a trifle odd, Gladys, out of context. Out of the office. Briskly, he wiped his hands on the cloth she passed to him, "We'd better get on or we'll be late."

"And we don't want that. Not on our very first date, do we Guy?" She chuckled her delight as she threw the remains of their picnic into the bag, adjusting her skirt before turning to smile at him.

He started the car and pulled out a little fiercely into incoming traffic, not concentrating. He knew he'd insisted she call him by his Christian name but somehow he wished she hadn't done so the first time with such ease, as if she'd been thinking about him as Guy in her heart for quite some time.

Barbara spent the entire day shopping, buying clothes for the weekend that was probably not going to happen. What was wrong with her? She was in such a hopeless dither about this. One minute, stone cold and the next, hot with anticipation. She had bought a couple of nightdresses. A new smart cocktail frock. Casual trousers and some tops. And, for good measure, perfume. It was easy to get into a rut where perfume was concerned and it suddenly occurred that she'd been wearing the same one for months. She had spent a disgracefully long time dizzily intoxicated with scents at the perfumery before reaching a decision. She sniffed her wrist again. Yes, she liked it.

Buying the clothes helped. Whether or not she went away with David was irrelevant, shopping was good therapy and oddly eased her conscience. There was nobody she could talk to about this, none of her friends were friends enough that she could ask their advice, not even Meg whose astounding revelation the other day still perplexed her. Sad really that there was no one she trusted enough. Some of the friends from the past had been true friends but they had lost touch. They probably knew she was still around. They probably all thought, like Ruth, that she was snooty and too good for them now. Again, that was sad and she had never meant that to happen.

She had tried for a while, immediately after her marriage, to keep in contact with friends of her youth but it had not worked. Dressing down to meet them had begun to pall and, in any case, that was vaguely insulting to them when they wore their very best to meet her. It was amazing how quickly you learnt to differentiate between a chainstore and designer garment. Leila helped. Leila could spot the difference at a hundred yards.

It was then, when she began to see Leila's point of view, that she realised it was too late. Her world had changed to Guy's world and she could never go back. The trouble was there were always people like Leila to remind her that she did not truly belong in his world either. In other words, she was not far off a social misfit, her access to money and her powerful position as Guy's wife and Leila's daughter-in-law swinging it. Whilst she had that, whilst she had them, she was okay. As soon as she lost that, them, she was out. And that's why she had nobody to talk to about David. Not a soul.

After the shopping, she was tired. She prepared herself a light tea and then settled to a quiet evening in. It was Tuesday.

Tonight, they ought to have been entertaining friends to dinner but instead Guy was at a business meeting. With a sigh, Barbara turned off the lights in the dining room that ought to have been full of bright chatter, food and wine, and carried a lone cup of coffee through to the sitting room. She had just sat down when she heard a car stop outside. Oh no, it wasn't, was it? Not Leila.

It was.

"Where is he this time?" she asked shrilly, not waiting for an answer, "It's too bad of him, Barbara. What did I tell you about working late with the secretary? You must insist he puts a stop to it. You're far too lackadaisical about this, dear, and he must not be allowed to get away with it. That's how I let Charles slip through my fingers."

Barbara said nothing, taking Leila's jacket and hanging it up before escorting her into the sitting room. "What are you doing here?" she asked, aware at once that it sounded aggressive and unwelcoming. "I'm sorry." She smiled her apology. "It's just that we don't normally see you at this time of night. I thought you didn't like to drive in the dark."

"I don't. I had business this afternoon with my solicitor and then I had tea at a friend's and the time simply flew. May I stay overnight?" She flashed a tired smile. "Sorry to be such a bore but I can't face the thought of driving over the moor and the car's in a bit of a mood again."

"Of course you must stay. Drink?" Barbara hovered as Leila debated before deciding on a large gin and tonic. Preparing it, Barbara asked, oh so casually, if she had heard from Daisy at all. Her nonchalance did not work and behind her, Leila laughed.

"She's staying with me for a while. In fact, I must telephone her presently to explain I won't be home tonight. And, before you take the huff, let me say that Daisy did not realise I was coming to Harrogate today or I'm certain she would have wished to come with me. The poor child is resting. Recovering. She is quite confused."

"What about the boyfriend?" Feeling hurt by what she felt was her daughter's rebuff, Barbara subsided onto a chair with her own drink, "Is that over?"

"Indeed it is." Leila did not elaborate. "She needs time, my dear, before she faces you and Guy. She's frightened you're going to say I told you so."

"We wouldn't dream of doing that," Barbara said, with a heartfelt sigh. "When will children realise that, everything you do, you do for them? You'd think we were out and out enemies for goodness sake. It's particularly hurtful that she doesn't seem to think she can come to me." She cast a glance at Leila, exasperated, "She has to come to you instead."

"I know." There was quite a lot of sympathy in the voice and Barbara was surprised. So . . . somewhere there was a heart. Leila looked tired tonight, under the dying remnants of her make-up, although her white hair was immaculate in its bun, her eyes clear, the peacock diamond brooch glittering against the navy of her dress. "Don't be upset, Barbara," she said, "Daisy loves you both but it's very hard for her to admit her mistake."

Barbara nodded, trying not to get this out of proportion. Daisy was safe. Daisy was rid of the boyfriend. She should be delighted but she was not quite that. Relieved but not delighted for that would be to gloat and she could not do that. "Very well, Leila," she said, the ice tinkling in her glass as she raised it to her lips. "Can you act as go-between then? Please tell her that we love her and she's very welcome to come home whenever she wants to. No pressure. No pressure to do anything. We just want her home." Her eyes filled with tears and she sniffed, hoping Leila did not notice for Leila gave short shrift to tears.

"What have you been doing today? Shopping?"

A measured guess. As Barbara showed Leila the items she had bought minus the nightgowns, she was reminded of the reason for buying the clothes and of David's call. A weekend away with another man. It was hilarious that she was even considering it. He was right of course about her response and she was infuriated that her body had betrayed her in that way. David Ambrose's touch was akin to a lighted match against her skin.

"You seem preoccupied, my dear. Something troubling you?" Leila asked, after she had dutifully and genuinely it seemed admired the new clothes. "Something other than Daisy that is?"

"No. Nothing. Nothing at all."

Leila's look was sharp. "Really? If I were you, Barbara, I would buy two tickets to wherever, book a double room at a five star hotel, and present him with a *fait accompli*. Knowing Guy, he'll not want to go to the trouble of cancelling and everything. He may grumble but he will go with you. And, once you get him on his own, away from work, away from that secretary . . ." she raised her eyebrows. "It will work wonders, my dear."

"I wish you'd stop making these suggestions," Barbara said crossly, "Guy wouldn't know what to do if a woman tried to seduce him."

"Wouldn't he? Oh dear." Leila smiled. "Take it from an old trooper that he would. Away from their wives, men can be quite different. Away from the home, business men can be very attractive— " She took a swig of her drink and crossed her elegant silk clad legs. "Where is he anyway? Is he at the office?"

"At a hotel. With a client or rather an architect," Barbara said quickly, realising how lame it sounded even as she said it. "Tuesdays and Thursdays for the next few weeks."

"Which hotel?"

"I really don't know," Barbara said tetchily. "I haven't both- ered to ask. I trust him, Leila, so I don't need him to account for his every movement."

"Don't you? Suppose there's a sudden emergency? Suppose I suddenly collapse? Suppose I die? What then? It would be most inconvenient if you didn't know where your husband, my son, was. The police would take a dim view of that, having to send out an SOS."

She was right of course but Barbara was damned if she was going to admit it. Guy had not volunteered the name of the hotel and she had therefore not asked. If she needed to get in touch urgently, then she supposed she could ring Gladys at her home to find out his whereabouts.

"Would you care for a bite to eat?" She refilled Leila's glass and finished her own drink, anxious to change the subject, although Leila had lapsed into a silence that was frankly more worrying than if she had let out a string of abuse towards Guy. "And then, if you don't mind, I'd quite like an early night. I've been with Meg all afternoon and she wears me out."

"That woman wears anyone out." Leila said with a sniff. "I'm never quite sure about her. She's not from Harrogate so it's difficult to check on her. Do you know anything about her family? Her roots."

"Nothing." Barbara gave her a sharp glance. Leila was either a good actress or innocent of any plotting with Meg. "She doesn't talk much about the past." She decided to let it go before she was indiscreet herself. "Do you want something to eat?" she asked again.

"I'd love some smoked salmon. Do you have any?" Leila brightened up at the thought, "Do you know, I have this sudden urge for it. If it wasn't absolutely impossible, I'd swear I was pregnant. Did I ever tell you that I ate heaps of the stuff when I was expecting Guy. Smoked salmon and French paté and strawberries. Our housekeeping budget was sky high. And gallons of gin. I smoked like a chimney too in those days. Of course, nowadays one reads that drinking and smoking are forbidden from day one. Still . . ." she cast amused eyes towards Barbara. "Guy seems to have turned out reasonably well under the circumstances. He seems remarkably fit for his age, my dear. You obviously look after him well."

Barbara retired thankfully into the kitchen, knowing Leila would not follow. She leaned a moment against the bench and gave a deep sigh. That woman! There were times when she could cheerfully strangle her. How had Guy, someone as nice and unpretentious as Guy, managed to have a mother like Leila. Smoked salmon indeed! She'd have to make do with something else. Trust her to have expensive fads when she was pregnant. When she was expecting Daisy, her fads had been more mundane. She recalled that she had fancied scrambled eggs day or night. In fact, talking of scrambled eggs, that's what she would do now for her and Leila. Lightly scrambled eggs on hot buttered toast. Toss of black pepper and herbs. A little tomato and fresh parsley to decorate. Little touches were important. She put the plates to warm and began to beat the eggs. She could knock up a plate of scrambled eggs with her eyes closed.

She felt a little better about Daisy. Things would turn out all right, she felt it in her bones. Once Daisy was home, they would have a lovely day out together. Mother and daughter day out.

Lunch somewhere nice. And, if Daisy would let her, she would buy her something new to wear.

If Daisy wanted to talk about him, the boyfriend, then she would listen but she must try not to push it, try not to poke her nose in. She had to remember that Daisy was a woman now, no longer her little girl. She felt a moment's anger towards the man who had upset Daisy so but what was the point of that. She had to be thankful that Daisy was still in one piece, emotionally torn of course, but in one piece. She hoped she was not pregnant. Leila had said nothing on that score and that would be something Leila would have noticed straightaway.

She piled the eggs onto the toast, placed the plates on a supper tray and carried it through. "Scrambled eggs," she announced brightly, "And a milky drink later. It will help you sleep, Leila."

"I sleep like a top," she said, "It's you who look as if you don't. Are you having trouble sleeping, Barbara?"

Barbara sank a fork into the eggs. Actually, she would have preferred to sink it into her mother-in-law's neck. She did not need Leila to tell her that all this Tuesday and Thursday stuff was a bit suspicious. Nor did she need Leila to state the obvious. When men of her husband's age started behaving oddly, it usually meant one thing.

Daisy replaced the telephone receiver with a sigh. So . . . that's where gran had got to. It was a relief as she had begun to worry when she had failed to return. Gran really oughtn't to be driving at her age. Mother and gran would be talking about her. Daisy knew that. She would go over to see mother soon now that things had calmed down a little. In the meantime, it hurt that they would be saying what a silly child she was to be taken in by someone like Alan.

The pain was still there. Rejection. God, she could have killed him. She now knew what was meant by a crime of passion. He had had the brass nerve to move in with her, make plans, worse . . . make love to her, when all the time there was another girl hovering in the background, innocently waiting for him to contact her again.

She was a fool, this other girl. She was welcome to him.

Daisy relaxed in her grandmother's elegant drawing room, looking round the room with some pleasure. She had no idea what she would do with the furniture at the flat. Sell it, she supposed. No way would she ever live with that again for it would always remind her of him. All memories of him had to be thrown out. She wasn't even sure she would ever be able to set foot in Durham again. It mattered not a fig that their affair had been growing lukewarm. *He* had rejected her.

She couldn't sponge off dear gran forever even though it was rather nice to be here for a while. She would have to make a move, it was either a job or college. She reached for the heap of college prospectuses. Time to give this some serious thought. She eased herself up and opened her notepad. She would make a list.

Mid morning and the tide was in, a gentle lapping tide, the green-grey water rippling languidly against the slime of the sea wall, each movement an effort, a breathing and a slow slurping as it slid in and a little up the wall, the wetness spreading and retreating with a sigh.

In the sheltered sunken gardens within sight of the north pier, Linda was oblivious to it, although she had noted in passing that it was in its tranquil mood. It was cool and she was the only person sitting on one of the benches that were packed out, bum to bum, in summer. The lowered location made it a pleasant place to be and the cold sea breeze wafted over her head. She had needed to get out of the place she had called home for the past few years. She hadn't even bothered with breakfast. She'd just stuck her coat on over an old blouse and skirt and come out. Now she was hungry. What she wouldn't give for bacon and eggs and fried bread. She'd left Blackbeard his breakfast, bless him, little cat biscuits and some milk.

David's betrayal hit hard. She had set her heart on that semi with the garden and the conservatory. A conservatory especially where she could have plants and cane chairs, where Blackbeard could sit and sun himself in comfort in his old age. He deserved that, poor little sod.

Stupid of her to have expected anything else of David but her stupidity only underlined the way her life went. Everything she ever wanted was always round the corner, just out of reach. She didn't want much. She didn't want to win the lottery and have loads of money. All she wanted was a bit of security, a man who would love her and look after her and care for her. All she wanted was to have a nice house she could look after herself, hoover and polish it knowing it was all hers, buy a few new knick-knacks, be able to afford fresh flowers all the time, and she wanted to be able to stay in at night if she felt like it, stay in and watch telly.

She had thought David was the man who mattered, who might be able to give her all that, and had been patient, at first expecting nothing, worried even that she might be in danger of breaking up his marriage, spoiling things for the child. She tried so hard to be discreet. She never went near their house . . . well, only once just for curiosity . . . and she'd stood over the road and seen his wife and the little girl, about seven or eight she was at the time, a tiny girl with a ponytail. She felt she knew Annie. He'd talked about Annie a bit. Then, as the years passed, and finally those few months when Ruth was ill . . . she bit her lip. This is what happened when you wished someone dead. Poor Ruth. Poor Annie. And poor her.

Tears were a waste of time and only buggered up her mascara. They were finished now, replaced by a steely determination to get even. He was not going to get away with it. She had no job and no home soon for she wouldn't be able to pay the rent without the money he sometimes slipped her way, conscience money she now realised. It wasn't fair that he should cast her aside so completely, not when he had said they would get married. It was all verbal, of course, in the heat of passion at that, no letters, no incriminating letters, when she could have had him for breach of promise. So, in the end, it boiled down to her word against his.

She was going to scupper him once and for all. Hit him where it hurt the most and that was in his pocket, the business, the crappy business. The trouble was she knew nothing about it, so how could she do that? She could claim unfair dismissal, she supposed, have him dragged through court but she knew it would end in a public humiliation. For her. She'd had enough of that in her time. The audience watching her with something approaching loathing, especially the few women. Some of the girls managed to make it look artistic but she never had and she was having to apply extra layers of make-up to disguise the wrinkles these days. Let's face it, David had done her a good turn in sacking her but it left her high and dry with no prospects of another job.

Where else was he vulnerable? There was always the ladies thing with him, Mr Wonderful himself. She bet he'd never been given the brush-off in his life, never been stood up, never had to swallow his pride like she had over and over again. She'd love to see his face if it ever happened. He was still hanging onto those good looks of his but by a thread that was getting thinner by the year. When he lost his looks, his charm, he'd be a dead duck would David.

She managed a rueful smile, snuggling deeper into the big old coat she was wearing, her hair loose about her shoulders, freshly washed but in need of some salon treatment. Idly, she watched a little bird scrabbling about in the bushes and overhead, the gulls circled and screamed, sweeping seawards. For no special reason, for he wasn't a hunter, they made her think of the cat, alone in the house, curled up in his chair. When she got in, he would rub himself round her leg and look up at her anxiously, miaowing, wanting some milk and his lunch. A bit of meat out of his tin or a few sardines. What about him? He was coming with her wherever she ended up. She couldn't abandon him again. She loved him.

"Linda . . . hello . . . I thought it was you."

She looked up, startled, for she had not heard the footsteps. Annie stood there, wearing jeans and a big sweater and a pair of those big clumsy shoes the young girls wore. She looked a lot like a boy, a slender young boy. "Annie," she smiled, pleased to see her, "Fancy seeing you here."

"I often come for a walk in the morning," Annie said, "I park the car and have a walk along the prom. Do you want to come with me?"

Linda didn't like to say no, although she was ill-equipped for walking in her three-inch heels. She rose, still smiling, and walked beside Annie to the steps that led them up to the sea walk. The breeze met them at once and ruffled Linda's hair. Annie hardly had enough hair to be ruffled. "Quite a nice morning," Linda remarked, not knowing what to say to David's daughter. "Look . . . the sky's clearing, it will be lovely later. The sea's calm, isn't it?"

Annie nodded. "I love it. The sea," she said, "After mum died, I . . ." she did not finish, sighing instead, and stuffing her hands in her pockets. "I could just sit and watch the sea forever. I suppose it's because mum used to bring me on walks here when I was a baby. You remember things like that. Just think of the millions and millions of drops of water that make up the ocean. From one day to the next, it's never the same."

Linda earnestly nodded her agreement, putting on a serious face, as if she'd ever had the time or inclination to consider such a thing. Who cared about the millions of drops of water? The sea was the sea. Simple as that. No big deal. "Were you looking for me this morning?" she asked, not quite convinced that it was a coincidence that they had met.

"No. How could I know you'd be here?" Annie said with a quick smile, "As I said, I like to come a walk in the morning and today, I'm not at school . . . it's a day off. I'm not playing truant . . . so I thought I might walk a bit further than usual." She glanced at the strappy shoes Linda was wearing. "You okay to walk?"

"These?" Linda looked down at her feet as if she'd never seen the shoes before. "Oh sure, these are worn in. I could do a marathon in these. If I had the energy," she added with a wry smile. "I'm knackered most of the time."

Annie slowed her pace without comment. "Dad's putting the house up for sale," she said, "He's not wasted much time, has he? Did you know?"

"No." Linda struggled for the right words. She wanted to tell Annie exactly what was what but she didn't want to upset the girl. "Your father and I . . ." she began stiffly, giggling at the sober sound of it, "Well . . . we've decided not to see each other anymore." There. Annie could make of that what she would.

Annie raised her eyebrows but did not offer sympathy. "So you won't be moving in with him then?"

"Where are you moving to?" Anxiously she waited for the answer. He had to stay around within spitting, scratching distance if she was to have any chance.

"He's buying a flat facing the sea on south shore. Luxury apartment. He's suddenly decided that south shore's the place to be. I think he's got ideas for some sort of flashy development near there."

"A new club?"

"Oh, bigger than that. A theme park if you can believe it." She laughed her own disbelief. "It's all pie in the sky, Linda. He thinks he's an entrepreneur . . . that's someone who manages something spectacular, maybe a bit risky."

"I know what it is," Linda said in a small voice, wishing the girl wouldn't talk down to her. People were always talking down to her, as if she knew nothing. She read the papers, didn't she? Listened to the news. Knew what was what.

"Anyway . . ." Annie had flushed at the reprimand, "He's just a small-time operator but try telling him that. I don't know how he's the cheek to call that place a nightclub when all it is is a tatty bar with a few dancing girls thrown in. No wonder mum never went near. She didn't like that sort of thing."

It was Linda's turn to be silent. Annie was upset, of course, but it wasn't far from the truth. "What are you going to do then?" she asked after a pause, "Are you moving with him to this flat?"

They stopped for a breather. The sea walk was almost deserted, the seats all the way along empty and they leaned against the wall almost at the very spot where Annie had leaned a little while ago, just before the funeral. The early morning fluffs of cloud were lifting, the sea was changing colour and spreading out like a shaken blue duvet before them, the horizon etched in deeper blue and pink. Way, way in the distance a ship looked like a toy, looked as if it was standing quite still. They watched its infinitesimal movement.

"Linda . . .?"

"What?" They were very close, almost touching, and impulsively, she wanted to offer the child comfort, this girl who had just lost her mother. The irony of the situation did not escape her so she resisted, moved fractionally away rather.

"Can I ask your advice?" Annie turned troubled eyes to her. She did not wear make-up and she had a rosy childlike complexion, no spots, the pink glow exaggerated by the cold sea spray. "Do you think mum would mind if I didn't go to university? I'm sure I'll be offered a place but I'm thinking of turning it down."

"Well . . ." Carefully, she considered the question. How the hell could she answer that? It was offensive to say the least to try and put herself in the late Ruth's position, to try to offer the advice that she would have offered. She'd never had a child of her own, for God's sake, and she didn't know how to cope with it. If Ruth was watching them now, she must be near to explosion. "Well . . ." she repeated uselessly, trying to think it through, "I don't know. Don't you want to go?" she asked. "I thought you were dead keen. He's always said you're very clever. He's always said you'd have no trouble getting your degree and everything." She hesitated, supposing she had to tell her, "He acts like he's proud of you, love. He wishes he'd gone to university."

"I never knew that." Annie sighed, tracing her fingers along the rough concrete. Below them, the tide was slipping back, shallowing, barely reaching the bottom of the wall, pulling away, the sun now streaking across it, glinting. "I do want to go, Linda, but I feel I ought to stay with him." She moved off and Linda followed at a trot, her tight skirt preventing long strides.

"What for?" she said, "What do you want to be near him for?" she could barely utter the word David aloud. Not yet. "He won't expect that. He won't even thank you for that. He'll want you to go."

"Yes but is he lonely? Will he be all right on his own?" Annie gave a short brittle laugh, "Oh, I know he doesn't give that impression but I do wonder sometimes. What does he really feel about mum dying? He keeps it bottled up, Linda. Mum used to say there was more to him than meets the eye. She said he was a bit insecure. I wondered what she was talking about but . . . I wish we could talk, dad and me, without getting on each other's nerves. It makes me feel guilty like I'm not trying. I'm always saying really mean things to him. Sometimes . . ." she paused and bit her lip, "I wish he'd give me a hug and tell me he loves me. Daft I know. But I wish he would."

"Don't you feel guilty." Linda was tempted to tell her that her father was a bastard, tell her that because of her father, she was out of a job, would shortly be out on the street too. After all the time she'd wasted on him. "I thought it was all organised. You're doing your exams for it, aren't you? If you don't go, then what else can you do?" she asked, her mind turning to practicalities. "Jobs aren't that easy to find. I should know, I went to the job centre yesterday and there was bugger all doing."

"I think I already have a job," Annie said, "A friend of mine told me about it. I don't know why I applied but they were asking for a school-leaver with A levels to start in September and I just wrote off. I've had the interview and, providing I pass my exams, it's mine. It won't pay much but I've got a bit of money of my own." Her cheeks flushed redder. "Mum saved a bit and she wanted me to have it. I'm thinking of getting a little place of my own to live. A bedsitter or something. I don't think dad will mind and I'll still be near him. I can always pop round to see he's all right. Dad doesn't know yet, about the job, and I've not told them at school either. My form teacher and my headmistress will go berserk. I feel a bit rotten about it because I know they want what's best for me. They've both been very kind, Linda. But they don't understand my circumstances."

How much further were they going to walk! Feeling her shoes pinch, Linda pulled on Annie's arm to slow her down, "You're very clever to have got yourself a job," she said in surprise, "Well . . . that is good news. But think about university, love. I wish I'd gone. Not that I ever had the brains to go. Or the chance. It seems such a shame to turn it down. I know it sounds stuffy but you might regret it later on. Bet that's what your mum would say," she finished triumphantly.

"Thanks Linda." Annie's face was shining, hair damp against her skull. "I'm not going to blame you if I don't go. It'll be my decision. Don't let's lose touch, you and me. Never mind about dad. I'll let you know if I move and you'll have to come and visit. You ring me sometime, okay?" She glanced at her watch, "I'll have to get back. I've got some revision to do. Can I give you a lift?" She looked at her enquiringly and just for a second, in the smile, the tilt of the head, there was something of David, enough to remind Linda that this bright, fresh girl was his daughter. He didn't deserve a pretty little daughter like Annie.

She declined the lift and watched until Annie disappeared. She was at a loose end for the rest of the day. A coffee first, she thought, she could still afford to have a coffee out. Sod the expense. She would go to a particularly nice café that David had once taken her to. Fancied itself as a country teashop with lace curtains at the window.

A bell jingled as she opened the door and inside there were round tables with cream tablecloths and a bunch of little flowers in the centre of each, the menu propped against it. They did lovely cream cakes and scones and home-made parkin, proper pots of tea or coffee. Willow pattern china. Genteel that was it. The waitress, wearing traditional garb of black dress with a white frilly pinafore, sussed her out before she was through the door and could hardly get out the polite greeting.

"Table for one?" she enquired through tight lips, taking in Linda's bedraggled seaswept appearance. Linda hastily discarded her old coat hanging it on a peg near the door and tugged at her skirt, pulled at her blouse, before following the woman to a table deep within the shop where they could keep her hidden. "No smoking. Please." The waitress pointed to a sign. "What can I get you?"

Furious with the woman and furious with herself that it should bother her what a snotty little waitress thought of her, she ordered a coffee and a cream cake. As she waited, she longed for a cigarette. Last time she was here in this dump with David, they had smoked. "Mind if we smoke?" David had asked, already getting out the silver case, flashing his smile at a different waitress. "Seeing as it's you and there's nobody else in," she had said, smiling too and giving him the nod. So much for bitchy little signs.

Not knowing therefore what to do with her hands with no cigarette between her fingers, she clasped them together. One torn fingernail, bugger it, but the others were nice, very long. There was a man at another table, reading a paper, who had given her a quick glance before resuming his read. There was a time, years ago, when she would have merited a second look. Now, she wasn't even sure she minded any more what a man thought about her. She hadn't met a decent man in her entire life. Not one. She cast an irritated look at the man behind his paper and suddenly wondered what she looked like.

She would visit the toilet whilst they got her coffee and freshen up her make-up, brush her hair. As she got to her feet, she saw to her horror that there was a bloody great hole in her tights. Black tights at that. Quickly, she picked up her bag and went through the door marked Ladies.

It was nice. That was one of the things she remembered about this café, the nice loo. They had a nice loo at the club too, for the lady guests. That was shiningly white but this one was palest pink. Pink tiles. Thick pink carpet. Little bars of pink soap. Smelt nice. Clean. Someone was in one of the cubicles and she tipped her make-up onto the counter and surveyed herself in the mirror. God, she looked a mess. She tidied herself up, pursing her lips as she applied another coating of the bright lipstick she liked. Blusher on her cheekbones and just a bit more blue mascara. And a big splash of scent. Liberally, she sprayed in all directions. Coughed. Then, lastly, she took out her hairbrush and set to work, trying to smooth out the corrugations in the sleek style she was aiming for. The salty breeze did her no favours at all.

She had not taken much notice of the woman who was now washing her hands but as she pulled the brush through her tangled salty hair, their eyes met in the mirror. There was that brief moment's surprise as recognition dawned.

"Linda . . ." the woman smiled. "How are you? Last I heard you were down in London."

"Hello." Linda smiled, suddenly shy. She knew, without bothering to check, that there would be no ladder in *her* tights. She wished she was wearing something nicer than the old blouse and skirt. The skirt was a bit short, even for her. "London?" she repeated with a little laugh. "You *are* behind the times."

13 ∫

Leila had a lot on her mind. Firstly there was the tricky business of sorting Daisy out with a husband and now there was also this business with Guy. She did not like the sound of it. Out of hours business meetings indeed. One would have thought he would have been a little more original. Barbara seemed to believe him or, if she didn't, she was not yet prepared to admit it.

It had been the same with Charles when she came to think about it. She hadn't believed it of him either, not that first time, especially not with that secretary of his, Miss Chapman. She never had found out the woman's first name. Thin and sparrow-like and totally, she would have imagined, undesirable. What had the man been thinking of? She had therefore, quite reasonably, refused to believe it, had accepted the excuses for the late nights as purely business and, by the time she did accept it, it was too late.

And so it would be with Barbara and Guy unless she did something herself about it. What she proposed to do seemed a bit drastic but she had been led to believe that private detectives were extremely discreet. She regretted having to do it but there was no other way and she was certainly not getting involved with shadowing him personally.

So . . . there was something after all of Charles in his make-up and the thought was unpleasant. To be candid, it had upset her a good deal. She did not want that. She might have sighed at her son's dull approach to life, his lack of *joie de vivre*, the lacklustre way he treated his wife but she did not want another philanderer in the family. If, as she strongly suspected, he was having an affair with the secretary, she intended to take him to one side, confront him with the evidence when she had acquired it, and ask what he meant to do about it. All that, before she mentioned anything to dear Barbara. The practicalities of the private detective thing foxed her. How did one go about it? She felt it unwise to seek a recommendation from anyone. The Yellow Pages then? One read about such unsavoury characters and it seemed a dreadful gamble to pick one at random. She would telephone and enquire. See what they sounded like. Westbury Investigations specialised, it would appear, in matrimonial surveillance and Guy messing about with his secretary would seem to fit neatly into that category.

Sitting at her desk, thoughtfully, notebook and pen in front of her, the wedding guest list already partly compiled, she did not hear Daisy come into the room. She jumped when she did realise and slid the paper to one side as it was carefully headed "Daisy's wedding" underlined in red ink. Every list had a heading.

"Daisy, dear, it's time you and I had a little talk about the future," she said, spinning the chair round and looking fondly at her. She was looking very pretty these days, a bloom again in her cheeks, less tired, less haunted by memories of Alan, and now seemed as good a time as any to broach the ticklish subject. After careful consideration, Leila had decided she ought to know for, with her co-operation, things would go so much more smoothly. Trying to coax Daisy into wearing a dress would be impossible unless the child knew the reason. Daisy had always been a very agreeable child if one bothered to discuss and consult with her. "We need to get you a husband," she said, "And, as your own effort has failed so miserably, I have taken it upon myself to do it for you. A man who will look after you and provide the good things in life. A lovely home. Your own generous allowance."

"A husband?" Daisy laughed. "Gran, you are priceless," she said. "I don't want a husband. And, even if I did, I could find my own, thank you."

"Of course you want a husband," Leila said. "It's not as if you're one of those infernal career women."

Predictably, it was the wrong thing to have said. Daisy's face tightened and she sniffed her annoyance. "But I intend to be," she said. "It's just that I can't seem to make up my mind exactly what I want to do. Possibly economics. Or chemistry perhaps?"

"Nonsense," Leila retorted. "Ridiculous subjects. What on earth put those in your head? The mothers I shall be dealing with do not want a daughter-in-law who is an economist or worse, a chemist."

"Economics or chemistry," Daisy repeated darkly. "I could do either. I do know that I want to earn my own living. I do not want to be dependent on a man. This might be hard for you to understand but it is how I feel, gran."

Leila sighed, replacing the cap on her pen. "You'll be telling me next that you enjoyed life in the gutter?" she said, "In that dingy little flat? Don't pretend that being a waitress was fulfilling?" She regretted the sneer but it slid out before she could stop it. The idea of her own granddaughter bowing and scraping to customers, accepting tips from them, was exasperating. "You've not been brought up to do that, Daisy. You went to a very good school and you have family connections."

"And what do you want me to do? You and mother? You want me to sit around twiddling my thumbs, arranging flowers and things, entertaining my husband's guests, handing children over to a nanny, that sort of thing. In other words, nothing of any importance. Just like mother. You want me to end up unfulfilled just like her. She's bored out of her mind, can't you see that? Dad doesn't seem to notice." She slumped angrily onto the sofa and kicked off her shoes, tucking jeaned legs underneath her. "I am not suffering the embarrassment of you trying to arrange a marriage for me. It's an awful outdated idea. I can imagine nothing worse." She shuddered and gave Leila a very fierce stare. "You're not serious, are you? Is this a joke?"

"I do not joke." Leila rose to her feet and went to sit nearer to Daisy. The morning sun flooded through the windows and the garden looked suddenly springlike as the light streaked across the lawn. Spring. Summer. And then the gold of autumn and the wedding. Hopes receded a little but she shrugged off the doubts. "I'm sorry, my dear, if I seem to have sprung this on you but, believe me, I love you too much to ever embarrass you. I am much too devious to embarrass you. Tell me, how did you meet this Alan young man?"

"Do you have to remind me about him?"

"I merely wish to know. At a dance?"

"No." Daisy smiled slightly. "We don't go to dances, not the sort you mean."

"Where then? Were you formally introduced?"

"Gran, honestly . . ." Daisy laughed. "If you must know, although I don't see what this has to do with anything, we met because of the car."

"That little car you used to drive? What happened to it?"

"I sold it." She shrugged. "We were short of cash. Anyway," she carried on hastily, "I broke down and he was passing and he helped me." She shrugged. "We chatted a bit and then I asked him out for a coffee as a sort of thank you and that was that."

"You asked him out?" Leila clicked her tongue, "How romantic! But, do you see the point I'm making . . . every couple has to meet somewhere and all I shall be doing is making sure that it appears to be an accidental meeting rather than a contrived one. Leave the details to me. All I require of you is that you be there and look your usual lovely self. Preferably wearing a dress. Any young man worth his salt will be utterly captivated by you. Thank goodness you are beautiful otherwise it would have been too awkward. It would really test my ingenuity if I had to pass off an ugly granddaughter."

"I don't believe it." Daisy's astonishment showed in her eyes, eyes very like Barbara, glowing greeny-blue now, as she gazed at Leila. "Haven't you listened to a word, gran? You're a terrible schemer and I'm not being part of it. Accidental meeting, my eye. I'm only twenty. If . . . and I mean if . . . I get married, I don't intend to do it until I'm thirty at least. I want to be well established in my career before I even consider it."

"Thirty?" Leila frowned. "Do you realise that I shall then be ninety? I shall very likely be dead."

"Gran . . ." Daisy's voice gentled. "I'm sorry. I know you want to see me married and I know that you would look absolutely wonderful at my wedding but that isn't a very good reason for me to get married is it? Is it, honestly? Can we please forget this?"

"It's too late. I've already issued an invitation to the Pattersons for Sunday tea and I did hope you might be here too. We can use your waitressing skills," she added with a smile.

"Oh Lord, it's Piers Patterson isn't it?" Daisy sighed in her exasperation. "I'm on show to his parents, aren't I? That's why you wanted me to bake scones, to show that I'm domesticated."

"Don't worry about the scones. I'll get Mrs Harris to bake some and we can always say you made them. Mothers are fearfully impressed by young ladies who can bake. It shows a return to traditional values. I wouldn't go on too much about the career thing either. The mothers I know are not keen on careers. Just follow my drift. Agree with everything I say."

"Gran . . ." Daisy nearly screamed at her. "How many times do I have to tell you? I do not want to meet him."

"He's an architect," Leila went on, unperturbed by the outburst, "I have it on good authority, not from his mother incidentally, that he is no longer spotty or thick but rather attractive. He is not without talent it appears and he is definitely on the way up. I'm told that he's not one of these concrete and glass people but that his designs have great beauty. Sounds promising, doesn't it? He lives in an apartment somewhere in Surrey but he is actively engaged in looking for a larger house, even considering building one himself. He is, therefore, reading between the lines, also looking for a wife. Bound to be."

"Oh, is he?" Daisy said, "He can count me out. I wouldn't touch him if he was the last man on earth. You get worse, gran, you really do. Mum would go spare if I told her what you'd been saying."

"You must not tell her. She worries too much and she has a tendency to think roses and romance." Leila dismissed Barbara with a casual wave of her hand. "With your looks and your connections, dear, Piers need look no further. Of course, if you find him obnoxious then we'll dump him. I shall respect your feelings, my dear. There are a couple more young men we can try before we need to scour further afield."

"I'm going to see mum," Daisy said, giving her a look and scrabbling about with her shoes. "Do you think I should telephone or shall I surprise her?" She paused in the act of fastening her laces, "I'm a bit nervous, isn't that silly? I've been terrible to her. Never ringing her or anything. She might not want to see me."

"She will. I should surprise her." Leila smiled. "Take her some flowers. She will be so pleased to see you Daisy. How are you going to get there?"

"I did hope I might borrow the car? Please."

"Have you ever driven my car?"

"No. But I promise I'll be very careful. It's the same as any other car, isn't it? It has gears and a brake etc."

"Don't be cheeky," Leila said, "What I meant was that it is inclined to be temperamental if it knows someone other than me is driving it. The handbrake sticks and it misbehaves in other ways. Suppose you break down on Blubberhouses? That will be most inconvenient."

"I might meet another young man." Daisy said with a bright smile. "That's how I met Alan, remember? If I do, I'll get him to fill in a questionnaire on his prospects before I ask him for coffee."

"Manners, Daisy. Don't forget whom you are talking to." Leila cast her a reproving glance before reluctantly handing over the car keys.

"Thanks." Daisy clutched them to her. "Don't worry. I will take care," she added, more seriously, "And one other thing . . . will you please cancel the Pattersons? I really can't face them. Knowing what I know, I shall burst into giggles as soon as I see them."

"I'm sorry, it's out of the question. I have already issued the invitation and I am of a generation where one does not issue invitations only to snatch them back. Penny has already telephoned to confirm so, short of me dropping suddenly dead, I am powerless to stop it. However, if it upsets you so much, I promise I will not make any attempt to matchmake. I will not mention his name once."

Daisy hesitated, still not sure. "I'd better be there just to make sure of that," she said. "Just for you, I shall try my best to be gracious." She whirled out of the room to reappear again a moment later. "Don't interfere, gran," she said earnestly. "Things have been difficult lately and I need to work it out for myself, what I'm going to do next. I don't want to make another mistake."

"Of course, dear. Hand on heart, I shall not interfere."

Leila kissed her, watching through the window as Daisy set

off. Bless the child. She had to say she admired the stubborn streak. That made two of them and it was suddenly interesting to be contemplating a battle of wills. Such a pity that she could not devote her wholehearted attention to it but Guy's affair had to be dealt with too. She sagged against the curtains a moment before she regained control. Damn the boy! What was he thinking of? Barbara was so calm and beautiful. For a girl from her background, she had merged well. People enthused about her culinary skills. Her elegance. And, it was very rare these days that there was any trace of the accent she was born with. Those things mattered and Guy was a fool to throw them aside for a trumped-up secretary with a name like Gladys.

Recovering her composure, she returned to her desk and the guest list, taking out pen and ruler. One hundred and twenty already and there were simply masses more. And that was just the Shawcross list. The Pattersons would provide an equal number. She felt a certain confidence about Piers. She liked the name. It had a ring to it.

Now . . . where was she?

Daisy couldn't help smiling as she drove to Harrogate. Honestly, gran was the absolute limit. Husband indeed! The way she felt about men in general and marriage in particular at the moment she doubted if her grandmother would live long enough to see the wedding she was planning so earnestly. Alan would take some getting over, damn him. She couldn't just switch her feelings to someone else, just like that. She needed time.

She was a touch nervous about seeing her mother again. Apologies all round no doubt and some explanations but she hoped mother wouldn't want to go into it too deeply. Enough said already. She would be much more careful next time, if there was a next time.

She was reminded of Alan by such little things. Silly things. Thank goodness there was nothing in this car to remind her. This car was pure gran. Comfortable and elegant even it was losing its touch a little.

Nearly there. She loved that first sight of Harrogate, that first snatch of it snuggled in its bowl in the distance. She knew every inch of this road and she expected a glimpse of the town after the next bend. A little unexpected lump appeared in her throat. She must stop off and buy mother some flowers to go with the apology.

14

The dozen red roses had a note pinned to the cellophane. Puzzled, Barbara read it and then stood stock-still in the hall, holding the flowers a little away from her body as if they were a time-bomb. In a way, they were.

Why on earth had he sent roses? What would Guy say? Even Guy might have something to say that another man should send his wife roses. She carried them into the kitchen, unpeeled the wrapping, and plunged them unceremoniously into the sink. What was she going to do with them? A smile threatened at the very nerve of the man. She supposed she should tell Guy everything but something held her back. David and her worryingly sexual feelings for him were her secret, a little guilty secret that would go no further than it already had.

David was her lifeline and she was going to keep it that way. If Leila was right, and she was indeed beginning to wonder, then she had to make some plans in case Guy suddenly upped and left her. Middleaged men had been known to do it, although usually with a beautiful young thing. Under those distressing circumstances, a woman scorned, ridiculed no doubt by her so-called friends, David was that someone else she could turn to. All she had to do was to say the word.

She would set Guy a little test. She would see if he even noticed the roses. He would probably think she had bought them herself although she normally drew the line at red roses. Carefully, leaving the card in a prominent position, she arranged the flowers a little more artistically in a pretty pot vase and put them on the coffee table in the sitting room where he would not fail to notice them. The card said "To Barbara. A very special lady. From David." She smiled at the "special lady". No kisses. No love. Just that, a "special lady".

She sat on the sofa and looked at the roses and thought of the man who had sent them. What was she waiting for? She could arrange a weekend away without it causing a major upset. Guy seemed reconciled to the idea, happy for her to have a break, and in a way, his very willingness rankled.

If he loved her, he must surely wonder where she was going, what she was up to and with whom? Sending flowers to her home like this was typical of David. It was deliberate baiting, a throwing-down the challenge, a duel no less.

Outside she heard the unmistakable sound of Leila's car, the engine expiring suddenly as only it could. Damn. Standing up, indecisive, she tore the card from the flowers and stuffed it in the pocket of her dress. She did not want Leila picking up on this, sharp-eyed Leila who would certainly read an attached card with interest.

But the quick steps that hurried from the car were not Leila's and Barbara was not aware, until the very second she opened the door, that it was Daisy. After an emotional reunion on the doorstep when neither of them could utter a coherent word, Barbara happily installed Daisy in the sitting room by the fire and went to make coffee and slice some of Daisy's favourite fruit cake. Daisy had brought flowers too, a bunch of carnations. Barbara put them aside to sort out later, anxious to be with her daughter. Quietly, they settled together on the sofa, side by side. "Red roses?" Daisy's eyes widened in surprise, "How lovely! From daddy?"

"No." Barbara smiled, not able to take her eyes off her daughter, delighted that she looked so well, "They're from a secret admirer."

Daisy laughed, dismissing the little joke. Barbara contemplated very briefly telling Daisy about David but Daisy launched instead into a description of life with her grandmother and the moment, perhaps luckily, was lost. They agreed, amidst fond smiles, that Leila was a dreadful old woman but that this time her efforts would come to nothing. "I'm going to marry for love, mum," Daisy told her earnestly, eyes serious, "Like you and dad. Look how long you two have been married. Twenty five years nearly. What are you doing by the way for your anniversary?"

"Ah that . . . I want a word about that," Barbara said, catching sight of the roses out of the corner of her eye. She remembered the single red rose David had placed on his wife's coffin, recalled how the gesture had torn at her own heart. Just how much or how little had he loved his wife? She ought to refuse to accept the flowers of course but it was too late now. She returned her attention to her daughter, leaning across to pat her hand. "I need to talk to you about our anniversary."

"What's the matter?" Daisy was perceptive as usual, "Don't you want a big celebration?"

"I don't want any celebration," Barbara said firmly. "I mean it. I shall be very angry if you arrange a surprise. I don't want you to mention it to your father either."

"But I usually remind him and help him choose a present for you."

Exactly. Barbara smiled with an effort and touched Daisy's hand. "Please, darling, promise me that you won't remind him this time."

There was a puzzled silence as Daisy struggled to comprehend. At last she shrugged, unwilling but apparently agreeable. "I promise. If you're quite sure . . .?"

It was much, much later that Barbara reluctantly let Daisy go back to Leila's without a word of dismay at the odd arrangement passing her lips. Careful does it. She was concerned, although she had tried to pass it off lightly, at Leila's obsession with finding a husband for Daisy. Leila was so used to getting her own way and she would take some stopping with this daft idea between her teeth. Still, Daisy was no fool and she would not be palmed off with a man she did not love, well connected or not.

The phone startled her and she hesitated before she picked it up, wondering if it was David. "Barbara Shawcross," she said cautiously.

"It's me." Meg's voice flooded her ear. "I hear Daisy's back."

"Yes." My . . . how quickly news travels. "Thank goodness, she seems all right, Meg, she's just been to see me. It seems the love affair's broken up, thank God, although we didn't talk about it. She's staying temporarily with Leila, looking after her you know, although I'm not sure who's looking after whom."

"I know. Leila rang me yesterday. She seemed very interested in medical matters or rather medical consultants. I'm not sure what was the matter? Is she ill? I imagined she would be having private treatment? I've asked her over sometime for coffee. Perhaps she's lonely."

Barbara sighed. If Meg was somehow trying to make her feel guilty, as if she neglected Leila . . . She couldn't think why Leila had rung Meg either but she had more important things on her mind than deciphering the workings of her mother-in-law's mind. "Did you want something, Meg, or have you just rung for a chat?" she asked, smiling with determination into the instrument.

"How did your funeral go?"

"All right. As all right as funerals do go that is."

"Good. Now, Barbara, I'm ringing to ask a favour of you. Charity matter."

"Go on." Barbara restrained her sigh. Meg was awfully good at delegating the more ordinary aspects of her charity work to others, things that did not involve direct hobnobbing with the bigwigs. She waited with resignation for the favour to be asked. They were actively involved with organisational work for several charities, local and national. It could be one of a variety of things, from animal welfare to hospice funding.

It proved to be their cancer charity of which Meg was the chairwoman, Barbara a mere committee member. "They're having a conference, Barbara, seminar or what have you, a sort of thank you affair for the local organisers. Don't you remember they once held it at The Old Swan and last year, at the Gosforth Park Hotel?"

"Yes I do remember. I went to The Old Swan with you. Actually, Meg . . ." Irritated, she ploughed on, "You know my feelings on this. I think it's a waste of valuable resources. If the organisers are the people they ought to be, they don't need an expensive meal at a good hotel to tell them that they're appreciated."

"You miss the point," Meg said, "We pay for our own meal and each branch makes a contribution to the cost of the hotel.

Not a penny comes out of funds. It's a morale booster, Barbara, and it's most interesting to meet people from the other branches and hear their ideas for fund raising. Don't forget either that we work tirelessly, year in year out, and that we're forever putting our hands in our pockets. We need that little boost of someone giving us a pat on the back, telling us what happens to the money we raise, giving us the run-down on the latest research."

"Telling us what good girls we are . . ."

"Really, Barbara, if I'd known you were going to be so awkward . . ."

Barbara pulled a face into the phone. "What do you want me to do?" she asked. They were probably cutting costs and holding this year's events in a Little Chef. Meg would not set foot in such a place. "My diary is pretty full," she added, picking it up and rustling through it ostentatiously.

"I want you to represent me. We have to be represented for heaven's sake or it will look as if we don't care. It's the one day I really cannot make it, with another engagement I can't possibly cancel."

"When is it? I hope it's not next week."

"No." Briskly, Meg gave her a date. "They're holding it at Lytham-St-Annes," she said, "A lovely hotel overlooking the green and the shore. If you like, they offer the option of you staying overnight or a couple of nights even. Special rates for delegates if you're interested."

Lytham-St-Annes. She'd been there with David, just the once. Relaxing before the competition, they lay on the green, the sun hot on their bodies, and it was there that he kissed her for the first time. She had been expecting it, waiting for it, willing and yet fearful of it. Surrounded by people, it had of necessity been discreet, gentle, very much an *hors d'oeuvre*.

"Barbara, are you there?" The enquiry was irritated, "I thought we were cut off, you went so quiet. Well?"

"Well what?" For a moment, she was disorientated. "Oh, can I let you know? I'm not sure I can make it."

"I hope you can. It will be such a nuisance if I have to ask Connie instead. You know how disastrously she dresses and it will give such an unfortunate impression of the Harrogate branch. Susan can't manage it either. I've already asked her."

Barbara smiled. So she wasn't exactly first choice. "I'll let you know as soon as I can," she said, replacing the receiver. She tapped it thoughtfully. This was heaven sent, a perfect excuse. Representing Meg at something like that was not without precedent and Guy would not be in the least concerned.

Panic set in as she heard his car door slam. Would she be able to bluff her way round the roses if he asked? She would pretend she had bought them herself. They sat there, a blot of bright colour in the gentle-hued room, and he would surely notice them. "You're early," she said, raising her face for his peck on the cheek.

"Not complaining I hope?" He held her a touch longer than usual, his hand moving against her back. "You okay? You seem tense."

"I'm fine. Guess who's been to see me? She's sorry she missed you. She'll catch up with you later she says." She smiled with him, taking the opportunity to slip out of his arms.

"Daisy? Thank God for that. We're forgiven then?" He sighed his relief. "This calls for a celebration. Did she bring you those?" He inclined his head towards the flowers. "She *must* be sorry."

She did not contradict his assumption, although Daisy's flowers were in her study. "Coffee?" she asked.

"I'll make it. You look tired. Go and sit down. Black or white?"

She sat down. In the kitchen, she heard cupboard doors opening and shutting. She smiled. He never knew where anything was. Good old reliable Guy.

They would continue like this, day in, day out, for goodness knows how many years. She would sit here and wonder why she didn't do it while she had the chance. In that moment, and she had no idea why, she made up her mind. She would ring David tomorrow.

15

"I think we're getting better, don't you, Guy?" Gladys said, as they followed the others off the floor. "You still have a terrible look of concentration on your face but you don't stand on my feet quite so often."

"Thank you," Guy said drily. He was sweating under his suit and shirt. Tonight they'd tried out a couple of new dances and, amazingly, he'd thought that he and Gladys hadn't been the worst of the bunch.

"I mean it. I'm not just saying it," Gladys went on firmly, casting a smile his way, "In fact, considering it was the first time we've done anything even vaguely exotic, I thought we made a good stab at it."

He laughed. He knew now when she was teasing him and she surely was. However, he did feel they were making progress. Gladys had a light touch, and she was a quick learner, quicker than he. The first few lessons had been close on torture. Now, it was less torturous but more a race against time. He didn't expect to be competition standard but he did hope that he would be tolerable, someone who could dance a bit. He hoped that Barbara would notice the difference and he certainly had to get past the stage of counting the damn steps.

He was trying to avoid getting too friendly with any of the other couples, as he did not want to have to explain who Gladys was and why they were here. He was sorry therefore if he might appear brusque to them but there was no alternative. If it bothered Gladys, she did not show it, although she was a more natural chatterer and inclined to dawdle when the lesson was over.

"Oh . . . it's raining." Gladys clicked up her umbrella as they stepped out into a darkish evening, the air still chill. "Here . . ." she motioned that he should join her under its shelter and he obliged even though their sudden nearness, outside the dance hall, was unexpected. Holding her close as they danced was not proving a particular problem, as the holding was not an embrace but incidental to the main object which was to learn to dance of course. Being close to her now, off the floor, was a bit different and he particularly noticed, as if for the first time, her distinctive scent.

Poor Gladys. It amused him that she was having some difficulty with the Guy and Mr Shawcross bit. The other day, at work, she had called him Guy in front of a couple of his senior assistants and instantly blushed beetroot, although he doubted if they had noticed or indeed if they cared.

The rain bounced off the pavement, increasing in intensity, "Look . . . we'll get soaked." He drew her into a doorway to shelter, taking a moment to realise it was a restaurant doorway and that the waiter was just inside, peering out at the rain, smiling at them. The restaurant was softly lit, a pink and gold sort of place, the tables inviting, and the thought of food tempting. They had had to dash tonight and there had been no time for the sandwiches, the delicious ever varied sandwiches, that Gladys prepared for him.

"You hungry?" he enquired, huddling deeper into his mackintosh and watching the rain.

"You bet. I could eat a horse," she said in that wonderfully pragmatic way of hers, "Don't let that worry you. Missing a meal won't do me any harm whatsoever. I could do to lose two stone."

"You're fine as you are," he muttered gallantly, and before he could stop himself, he opened the door so that she had no option but to follow. The waiter, flourishing menus, appeared promptly, took away the brolly and their damp coats before showing them to a non-smoking table in the corner where they could see but not be seen. Guy was still full of a terrible guilt that they might be spotted.

"I feel a bit awkward about this," Gladys whispered, directly they had ordered and were alone once more, "I know we're not doing anything wrong, Guy, but I just feel funny. Having a meal with you, in a restaurant, is a bit different from sandwiches in the car, isn't it?"

"Relax," he said easily, casting a quick glance round himself. He knew not a soul. Thank God!

"Yes but do you think anyone suspects at work? I could have bitten my tongue off when I called you Guy in front of Mr Parker and Mr Welsh."

"Gladys . . ." he said patiently, smiling her cares away, "This is the very least I can do. I can't expect you to give up your free time to help me out and to do without a meal too. I will explain everything to Barbara later but obviously I can't do that yet. Not a word of this must get back to her."

"Of course not." She reached across the table and lightly touched his hand. "She won't find out from me," she said quietly, "I haven't breathed a word to anyone." There was a pause as he recovered from the jolt of her hand on his, under these circumstances not quite innocent. Smiling now, Gladys removed her silk scarf from around her neck to reveal more fully the black frilly top. Beneath it, her curves fought hard to remain confined. Outside the office, her taste in clothes verged on the frivolous. He liked her taste in clothes, sufficiently different from Barbara, and he found himself wondering what she would look like in something very glamorous, something slinky that would mould itself against her.

The guilty thought jumped at him and he dismissed it. Guilt. Guilt. All this stupid fiasco was producing was guilt. All this hassle just because he wanted to do something to surprise his wife. For the first time in ages, he wanted to be unpredictable. What a stroke of luck he'd played that Frank Sinatra tape and been reminded of their first dance together. The music, the words, had been like a bullet in his heart, bringing it instantly, vividly, back. Their tune. He wondered if Barbara would remember. Sure to. The ladies were good at things like that. He'd surprised himself for if anyone had asked, he would never have been able to remember.

He watched Gladys as she heartily tucked into her meal. He was a bit hopeless where women were concerned but he wasn't a complete idiot and he knew that, for whatever reason, Gladys had a crush on him for want of a better word. If only he had known that, he would have asked one of the other ladies to help him out. Doing this, making it all more personal, was asking for trouble and he regretted the impulse.

"This is really good." Gladys smiled at him. "I might even manage a pudding, if that's all right? Something really naughty with loads of cream."

With some resignation, he began to eat his lasagne.

"There's cold beef and salad in the fridge," Barbara said, rising from the sofa where he could tell she had fallen asleep. She had that look about her, wearing her blue velvety housecoat and slippers.

"You're very late." She yawned, running a weary hand through her hair. "What time is it?"

"Late," he said apologetically. "Sorry. It went on and on," he said, so full of remorse at the lie that he jumped as he felt the touch of her arm on his.

"Good meeting?" The enquiry seemed innocent enough but he thought he detected a wariness in her awakening eyes. "Are you getting anywhere with this chap?"

"Hope so. Fingers crossed for a decision soon." A great wave of desire for her swept over him and he pulled her roughly into an embrace. "You smell nice," he murmured against her hair. "Been in the bath?"

She nodded, her little uncomfortable wriggle just enough to tell him that, if he had any ideas in that direction, he could forget them. He let her go at once, dropping a very light kiss on top of her head. God, he wanted her tonight. Gladys's little antics, amusing almost if they hadn't suddenly seemed so sad, had made him want Barbara. His lovely Barbara.

Once in bed, he lay quietly, knowing she was as awake as he. "I think I might go to that conference at Lytham," she said, her voice for some reason with that edge of nervousness she sometimes displayed, "I told you about it, didn't I? The one that Meg wants me to attend. Meg has a cheek, doesn't she, expecting me to drop everything and go?"

"Stay overnight if you do go," he said, wanting to cuddle close, for starters, but sensing the faintest resistance. What was wrong? She wasn't normally this unwilling? It was weeks since they had made love. "Stay overnight," he repeated softly, "I don't want you tiring yourself out, driving there and back in the one day."

"Don't you, Guy?" There was relief now. "Good. I was hoping you'd say that. I might even stay two nights if you don't mind. It'll make a little break for me. It'll be very boring I expect but I don't like to let Meg down."

He patted her hand, knowing that was as far as he would get. However, despite his frustration, he smiled as he settled down. It was just like her not to want to let someone as overbearing as Meg Fairley down. In the darkness, Barbara smiled too. For a different reason.

16

Leila checked the afternoon tea she had organised for the Pattersons. Dainty sandwiches. Scones. A coffee fudge cake she was particularly fond of. Shortbread. "Don't, darling," she said irritably to Daisy as she nibbled at a sandwich. "They'll be here any moment and you don't want to have crumbs sticking to you. And don't guzzle when they're here either. Guzzling in a young lady is so common." She sighed, "Don't you have a dress?" she asked. "A pretty dress and some high heels?"

"No." Daisy grinned cheerfully. "They'll have to put up with me in jeans. These are expensive jeans, gran," she added, looking down at the blue denims. "Cost the earth."

"That's as maybe." Leila, who had never worn jeans in her life and never intended to, sniffed. "All this mixing up of genders. A woman's bottom is not designed to be stuffed into trousers of any description. It's so much more flattering to have folds of material draped over it."

Daisy finished the sandwich and replaced the cover over the tray. "Remember what you promised," she reminded Leila, "I'm only staying because I want to make quite sure you don't mention the name of Piers."

"I've already said I won't." Leila glanced at the slim gold watch on her wrist. "Where are these people? It's unforgivable of them to be late." She craned her neck as there was a crunch of gravel and the sound of car doors slamming. "About time. Now, Daisy, off you go and show them in and don't forget to smile."

Pulling a face, Daisy did as she was bidden. The Pattersons were frightful people, Leila remembered, as soon as they came in. Major Roy was aggressively large, Penny equally aggressive but small, with loud voices as if they were deaf. Mrs Patterson was wearing a dark green tweed cape over a paler green suit, and a big-brimmed hat. Her husband was florid-faced, heart attack material, with a tendency to peer round in a short-sighted manner through thick glasses. He was in rough Harris tweeds, brogues, a check woollen shirt and mustard tie. Leila pinned a smile to her face as securely as the emerald brooch on her dress. So very predictable, the Pattersons, superbly cast as the country squire and his lady. They ought really to have a couple of drooling dogs in tow. Hearing a barking from without, she realised they did have but they had blessedly left them in the car. They were certainly not setting foot inside.

Pleasantries were exchanged and Leila was quick to catch the glance that Penny cast Daisy's way. The child looked lovely. At least the blue sweater was pretty, her colour. She intended to keep her promise to Daisy although if Penny herself mentioned the boy then there wasn't much she could do about that. She tried to stop giving Penny's husband an exasperated glance. He looked for all the world as if he were the murder suspect in an Agatha Christie play, that or the unfortunate victim. She hoped Piers had not inherited his clothes taste or that of his mother either. The suit she was wearing was fairly nice but she suspected of inferior quality to the ones in her own wardrobe. One had only to look at the cut.

"I think that went rather well," Leila said, turning inno-cent eyes to Daisy as the Patterson's dog-laden car disap-peared down the drive. "We now know where to concentrate our efforts. What was it? String quartet at the Hall on the 17th?"

Daisy was stuck for words. She couldn't believe her grand-mother had done it. It would be funny if it wasn't so serious. "You can forget that," Daisy said, flinching a bit as she caught the full force of her gran's suddenly icy look. "What did I tell you? I warned you not to say a word about Piers." She shook her head in disbelief, reaching for a piece of coffee cake. Anger always made her eat. The soft spongey mixture folded into her mouth and she spluttered through the crumbs. "You promised, gran."

"Don't speak with your mouth full." Leila still retained that air of innocence, "I didn't bring his name up, dear. His mother did. Mothers always want to talk about their offspring. Too boring I agree but that's what they do."

"And you knew that of course. You were relying on that." Daisy licked her fingers, wiped them on her jeans and started to clear away the best china in a very cavalier fashion. Serve gran right if she broke something.

"Control your temper, Daisy. It's most unladylike." Leila followed her into the kitchen. "You must admit, that photograph showed him to be quite presentable, didn't it? I thought he had a very attractive smile."

"I don't care what he looks like," Daisy said, taking another piece of cake. She looked with exasperation at her grandmother who was hovering in the doorway. "He sounds boring as hell."

"Daisy! I will not tolerate such gutter language." Leila sniffed. The look that followed made Daisy feel about ten years old again. "Piers sounds utterly charming. Not only is he an extraordinarily gifted architect . . ."

"According to his mother," Daisy pointed out drily.

"According to his mother," Leila conceded. "He is also a musician and I like that. It shows a sensitive streak. I admire artistic people."

Daisy let out a snort of derision. She wanted to ask what about Alan in that case but didn't want to drag all that up again. Yesterday, she'd managed to go almost to the end of the day before she thought about him. "I don't want to meet Piers," she said stubbornly. "You never listen, gran. I find the idea of matchmaking revolting and his mother's just as bad as you. All these cock-eyed schemes . . ."

"Daisy! What has got into you?" Leila clicked her tongue irritably. "I shall buy tickets for the charity recital. It will be most interesting to hear Piers play his . . . violin, is it? Or cello? And you shall have a new gown for the occasion. I want my granddaughter to look beautiful. Piers will be absolutely bowled over by you, darling."

Daisy sighed, suffering the embrace that followed. She loved her grandmother. Of course she did. And she would be truly devastated when she was no longer with them. But honestly . . .

"Something very feminine, dear, off the shoulder perhaps. Pale blue I think. Such a flattering colour for you." A little pat on the shoulder followed, presumably to say that she had forgiven Daisy her outburst.

Daisy gently pushed her away. "You can waste your money on tickets if you like," she said quietly, "But I'm not coming with you, gran."

"I might as well have a new gown, too, although, at my age, dear, it's so difficult to find something to flatter. You must help me, Daisy."

Daisy sighed.

Daisy was still in a huff at breakfast. Leila ignored her, glad when she finally went out. The child was being a bit of a pain about all this but no matter. A small battle of wills that was all, and one that she intended to win.

She had two telephone calls to make this morning. Firstly, the private detective to arrange a meeting. Under no circumstances was she demeaning herself by going to his seedy office. She assumed it would be seedy, private detecting being such a dubious profession. He must come to see her and she told him, over the phone, that she hoped he would take the necessary precautions and not turn up looking like a private detective. "My neighbour is a former policeman and he is forever snooping around," she confided. "Do not for goodness sake tell him who you are."

"Of course not, madam," he said, sounding peeved. "My business with clients is very confidential. I would not dream of discussing you with a neighbour. You need have no fears, Mrs Shawcross. The last thing I look like is a private eye. Dirty macks and sly fags are way off target."

Leila rang off, feeling unsure now she had set things in motion. Did she really wish to know if Guy was having an affair? It was one thing suspecting it and another to have it confirmed. If she discovered he was, what should she do then? Ah well, it was done now, wheels in motion, and the man was coming to see her tomorrow at eleven. She would offer him a cup of tea and a plain biscuit. And get Daisy out of the way.

Thoughtfully, she reached for the telephone once more. She patted her hair and rearranged her skirt before picking up the receiver. Now for a much more pleasant conversation. With Penny Patterson, Daisy's future mother-in-law.

17

He hadn't heard from her since he'd sent the roses. Suppose old Guy had got to them first. That would have cut him up but it was no more than he deserved for neglecting Barbara. With a bit of luck, it might have caused an almighty bust-up although old Guy didn't look the sort who had the passion in him for a bust-up, almighty or otherwise.

Women went for roses, red roses. Since the funeral, he'd thought about her a lot. Women had always succumbed to him eventually, all except Barbara Anderson. It was entirely a matter of time and judgement. She was frightened of her own feelings and it was quite exciting trying to guess her reactions to the various situations he could place her in. He expected that she would be shocked but thrilled to get the roses and he was going to wait awhile before phoning her again. He wanted to listen again to that lovely nervous voice as she made her excuses, pretended that everything was under control when it damned well wasn't. In the meantime, for the first time in God knows how long, he was without a woman and it was beginning to have an effect. He'd been over hasty in dispensing with Linda for she was better than nothing. He didn't expect to see her again. She had already left the club and he had filled her spot with a young long-legged brunette, who could dance in a fashion. She certainly made the customers sit up and take notice.

In the mood he was in, surfacing only slowly from the turmoil of the past few bloody awful weeks, he could have done without business problems and, at the moment, he had a few of the cashflow variety. People were leaning on him, he was leaning on other people and the whole lot of them would topple in a heap if they weren't careful. Somebody, somewhere, must have some ready cash.

Morosely, he stood at the window of his office and stared down and out. It wasn't a bad day, fresh looking with blue bits in the sky and he suddenly fancied skiving off. A blow in the fresh air would do him good and he was fed up of accounting problems, head spinning with figures. That accountant of his was a nervy sod. Making his mind up, he slipped his jacket on and strode out, not bothering to tell anyone where he was going. Downstairs, coming out of the lift, he nearly collided with a pretty redhead in a short leather skirt and they both said sorry, side-stepping and doing a little dance as a result.

"Do you come here often?" David asked with a grin, gently steadying her with his arm.

"Not often," she said and giggled. He recognised her as a girl who worked at the club, behind the bar he thought.

"Can we help you?" he asked, guessing she was probably on her way up to their floor. "Got a problem?"

"No, it's my day off," she said, fussing with the frilly edge of her blouse as she spoke. Her eyes were grey and alert and she was not in the least shy. He would put her in her early to middle twenties, quite a startling looking big-busted girl with a delicate splash of freckles on pale skin. A natural redhead then. The red was a burst of sunshine and gold dust, twisted and plaited, probably waist length. He imagined running his hands through that. Wild. Wonderful. "I was just going to see if Margaret was in," she said, "She's been off with a cold," she explained, standing close to him, very still. "I wondered if she was back because we usually have lunch together."

"She's not back yet," he said, not having a clue who Margaret was. "Look . . . " he glanced at his Rolex, "I'm just about to have a bite to eat. Want to join me? I hate dining alone and my business colleague's cancelled at the last minute."

She nodded. "All right, Mr Ambrose," she said, "But I'll have to pop to the Ladies first and freshen up."

"For God's sake, call me David." He smiled. "See you in a minute then, sweetheart?"

He hung about the corridor when she had gone, irritated at the clumsy way he'd tackled that one. A bit over hasty there.

However, she could have made an excuse and she had not, so presumably there was some hope. What the hell was her name? He struggled to remember and couldn't. He was hopeless with names. She knew him though. Mr Ambrose. Was there some promotion he could offer her? She was rather an appealing young thing, ridiculously young, not that much older than his own daughter. Hell's teeth, was he reduced to this? Cradle snatching. He didn't need to forage round for sex, for God's sake, he had more charm in his little finger than some guys had in their entire bodies.

He slipped round the corner to check his appearance in the mirror that was in the entrance lobby beside the potted plants. Not bad. Not bad at all. He had paid a fortune for the suit and the shirt and by God, it showed. He'd moved on a bit since that shiny number from Burtons. Those were the days eh! Checking that nobody was about, he took out a comb and did his hair, temporarily hidden from anyone in the corridor. It was then he heard her voice. The redhead's and another girl. "Where is he then?" the new voice said, quite low but loud enough. "Are you sure you're not having me on? You did say it was him, old hot-pants, didn't you?"

"It was definitely him. Call me David he said. I felt sorry for him." The redhead didn't sound sorry. "Hasn't he just lost his wife? Although they do say they weren't happy."

"Not surprising with all the carrying on he does. It's disgusting if you ask me. He must be fifty if he's a day. Fancy trying it on with you?" The tone mellowed and they were moving away, "I suppose he might have been attractive once. What are you going to do? Wait for him to come back?"

"No. I didn't fancy lunch with him anyway. I'd rather have fish and chips with you."

"Let's go to Harry Ramsden's. We can have steamed ginger pudding."

They gave a collective sigh. "Come on, then, I'm famished," the redhead said with a giggle.

Hardly daring to breathe, realising his chest was actually hurting from the effort of trying to hold his breath, David looked at himself in the mirror, his eyes shocked. He daren't go through the lobby because they were hanging about but there was an escape route through a nearby door. He couldn't hear what they were saying now but he could hear giggles and it was as if an ice-cold arrow pierced his heart. Old hot-pants? My God, they thought him a dirty old man.

Quickly and quietly, he stepped through a door and out. Bloody trollops. What did they know? He wouldn't have touched either of them with a bargepole. He shrugged off their comments briskly but that didn't stop him taking another frantic glance at himself directly he was back in his office. Attractive once? He'd show her. He snatched up the phone and dialled Barbara's number. This was a beautiful woman who desired him, a proper woman not a slip of a girl, and, as he waited for her to answer, he felt his confidence returning. He'd best forget girls of Annie's age. They were too juvenile for words and it was also distasteful. Barbara's unmistakable voice came on the line, "Hello sweetheart," he breathed. "Did you get the roses?"

"Hang on . . ." He could hear background noises and then, after a moment, as if a door closed, silence. Her voice again, breathless. "I have visitors," she said quickly, "So you'll have to excuse me."

"Did you get the roses?" he repeated softly. "And did you like them? Red roses for a very special lady."

"I got them." She did not say thank you. "I didn't tell Guy they were from you. I don't think he would have been too pleased."

"Doesn't he send you roses then?"

"Sometimes." She was being cagey, deliberately so. "They were lovely of course," she said quietly. "But you shouldn't have sent them, David."

"I know. They embarrassed you."

"I have to go. I'll call you."

One bloody rebuff a day was enough thank you. "I've heard that before," he said sharply, patience gone.

"No, I mean it, David." He sensed her urgency, as she rushed her words, "In fact, I may be coming over to Lytham on business soon. I still have to finalise the hotel booking but I'll probably be staying at least one night."

"Will you indeed?" Doubts disappeared. "Then we can get together?"

"Maybe."

He decided not to push his luck. "You'd better get back to your guests," he said, hoping he sounded as deep and soothing as he was trying his damndest to sound. "Let me know where you'll be staying and we'll fix something up. Dinner perhaps?"

"Perhaps. Goodbye then."

She was being cautious. Someone might be listening in. "Goodbye my darling," he said. "Don't forget I love you. Do you love me?" He grimaced, wishing he knew when to call it quits. He was rushing her, like a bull in a china shop.

There was no reply just the click as the phone was replaced.

The Rolls looked out of place in the school car park amongst the teaching staff's ageing Metros and the like. David cast an admiring glance at the only other classy car there, a red sports model of uncertain age, open topped. He'd often fancied a sporty car but he couldn't bear to part with the Rolls.

The school was red-brick and solid and Annie attended the sixth form here. She called it a sixth form college but it looked just like the old school to him. Just a separate wing as far as he could see. Still . . . he supposed it made her feel more grown-up although they were pretty strict insisting that the sixth formers wore a uniform. He was surprised there hadn't been a revolution about that but they seemed to be all like Annie, the terminally dull variety of adolescent. There had been a few grumbles apparently but that was all.

He'd received a message from the secretary, a summons to attend no less, and it was very inconvenient. He'd had to cancel a meeting to be here so it had better be important or else. Ruth always used to deal with things like this. When Annie was little, he'd never managed to get to parents' evening, concerts, sports days, always tied up with something but he never felt he'd missed anything because Ruth always gave him a very earnest blow by blow account when she got home. Annie was never a problem, buckling down and doing her homework, passing exams, being a star pupil in other words. She must get that from her mother, this anxiety to please. He'd not told Annie about this summons to see

Miss Boyd the headmistress or she'd have gone into a tizzy about what he should say and what he should wear. He'd decided against a suit, favouring smart casual, one of his pale blue sweaters with a toning shirt and navy trousers. He was wearing a discreet cologne, expensive stuff just to show this headmistress that he was not your common or garden workaday dad. He liked the length of his hair, the way it curled over his collar, probably just a bit long for a bloke his age. Ruth had tut-tutted about it frequently but that had made him like it the more. As he patrolled the corridors, he was not unaware of the looks he was attracting from passing members of staff.

Where did this woman hang out? This Boyd woman? He stopped a fluttery young girl and asked and she directed him to the door where he was then obliged to wait on a seat outside for what he considered to be too long. A light above the door announced that she was engaged but he knew better. He knew all about ploys like this, designed purely to unsettle him, to give her the initiative. He remained calm, refusing to be unsettled by a bitch of a headmistress. What had Annie been up to? The mind boggled for he couldn't imagine her getting into any kind of trouble. Suppose she was pregnant and scared to tell him? Christ, he'd never thought of that before but, even as the thought entered his head, he threw it out. Pure fancy. Just because, when he was her age, several girls of his acquaintance could have easily been pregnant by him, did not mean that Annie was promiscuous. Annie was Ruth's daughter for God's sake. She was built in her mother's mould and she was the sort who would save sex for her wedding night, for the poor sod who married her.

"Mr Ambrose . . . would you come in please?"

Feeling guilty, he followed her into the office. She was young. Young for a headmistress anyway and she looked like she was miscast too. Where was the steely quality, the powerful voice that cut through cement, the big feet, the permed hair, the sensible suit. All the things he remembered from his headmistress at his junior school in Harrogate. What a tartar she had been. This woman, in her late thirties or early forties, was wearing a crisp beige blouse with the top three buttons adrift, a short straight dark skirt and a slightly lighter very nicely cut jacket. She had ash-blonde hair cut into one of those very short challenging styles and bright blue eyes that now stared at him across the desk. She wore no jewellery and no discernible perfume. She sized him up and if his appearance surprised her, she did not show it.

"I'm pleased to meet you at last, Mr Ambrose," she said and her voice was well modulated, BBC general purpose but with a trace of northern roots if he wasn't mistaken. "And may I say first of all how very sorry I was to hear about your wife. Please accept my condolences and those of the staff."

"Thank you." He tried the lop-sided grin but it seemed to make little impression. In fact, she seemed preoccupied, confirmed as she opened a file, a slim file with Annie's name on the cover which he had read upside down. Anne Grace Ambrose, the full title no less. "Something the matter?" he asked, fed up suddenly, remembering that the guy he'd had to put off this morning was not the sort of man you put off for long. "Don't tell me Annie's been caught smoking in the lavatory?" He smiled full width now, wondering if he could risk her wrath by asking if he could smoke. A glance around confirmed there were no ashtrays. It figured.

"Goodness no." She did not smile. "Annie is an excellent pupil." She looked down at the sheet of paper in the file, slim well cared-for hands, the nails longish and surprisingly painted pink. Good God, what was the world coming to? "I did think that perhaps you and Annie might have discussed this before you came to see me."

"Discussed what?" He adjusted the double cuffs of the shirt. "I haven't seen much of her lately and she doesn't know about this . . . summons?" He chose the word carefully, watching her reaction.

"I'm sorry if it sounded terse but I did want to see you urgently. Annie wants to decline her place at university." She smiled briefly, "I do know she's been through a very difficult time but we can't allow her to waste herself like this. Not without a fight. She's a certain candidate as you know for university and she will get the grades they've specified. I hope you haven't been trying to dissuade her, Mr Ambrose?"

"I certainly have not." He was momentarily astonished, looking blankly at her. "But why?"

A certain relief spread across her features. She was an attractive woman, managing to carry off the strong patrician nose that added character to her face. "Then she hasn't discussed this with you?" she asked, not waiting for his reply. "Good. In that case, I think I know what's wrong and we're going to have to work together on this, Mr Ambrose."

"Too bloody right," he said, apologising with a wave of his hand. "She's going to university. I want her to go. Her mother wanted her to go. She wants to go herself. What's she playing at?"

"Annie is a sensitive girl as you will know . . ." She waited for him to agree although why he should be an authority on Annie was beyond him. "She and her mother were close and this has been a very unhappy time for her. She has managed not to let her personal sadness interfere with her school work and she is very much on target for A or B grades, Mr Ambrose."

He found himself unable to say a word. He felt a genuine sadness for his daughter. She was his daughter after all and she hadn't deserved to be landed with this, at this crucial time. "I'm doing my best," he said at last, pleased that Miss Boyd had given him a few moments to compose himself, "She needs a woman friend to talk to, I suppose. She won't talk to me. There's things girls of her age don't want to talk to a man about, especially her father."

"Quite. And I'd like to help there if I may." She smiled and he noticed she had no rings on her finger. Again, that figured. A career woman. He wondered if there was a relationship because she had a distinctly earthy quality that meant she was unlikely to lead a nun-like existence outside school. "I would very much like to talk to Annie on a more personal level. I've tried to talk to her here . . ." she spread her hands wide in a despairing gesture. "Not surprising, it's been a little stiff. I have gleaned from her, however, that she feels she'll be letting *you* down if she leaves you on your own."

He stared at her, aghast. "That's stupid," he said, "I . . ." he paused, about to say something on the lines that he was actually looking forward to her going away but stopping short as it occurred it might sound just the teeniest bit callous.

"We have to persuade her otherwise then, don't we? You and I. She's got herself a job, by the way, in an accounts office. Whilst it's commendable enough, in its way, she's worth so much more than that and I feel very strongly that we have to make her see sense before she throws her chances away. She'll love life at university . . ." A bright smile flashed and he noticed what lovely even teeth she had, "I certainly did."

He nodded his agreement, as if he'd gone to such a blessed institution himself. "What do we do then?"

"I have to have your support."

"You've got it, Miss Boyd. One hundred percent." He was appalled that this woman opposite should be under a misapprehension, should think that he was a man to be pitied, a lonely man for God's sake. He was not overly concerned about Annie. Silly bitch! He would sort Annie out and get her to go to university as planned. He owed Ruth that. "How about chatting to her in a more congenial setting?" he said with a brief, concerned fatherly, smile, "You're most welcome to come along to our home. Annie will rustle us up something to eat and we can talk and get her to see sense."

"I think not," she said. "If you're agreeable, I'll make my own arrangements about the venue. I just wanted to see you to confirm that we are united on this. I didn't want to jump in if you had also decided against her going. I would have been disappointed but, if that was your wish, as Annie's father, I would have accepted it. You'd be surprised, Mr Ambrose, how often that sort of thing happens. Parents, misguided indeed, manage to deprive their children of the chance."

He had to resist an impulse to ask her to call him David. He'd never been involved with a schoolteacher, a headmistress at that, and the idea impishly appealed. However, he'd have to take this very carefully. Miss Boyd would be as difficult as Barbara. Coupled with that, she would be the first woman he had ever dated who had real brains. His own brain, entirely full of devious ideas as it was, was dazzled at the prospect.

Annie was hot with embarrassment. How dare Miss Boyd do that to her? Send for her father as if she was a little five-year-old doing something naughty. One of her friends had seen his Rolls, told her about it, and she had seen him leave herself, seen him casually crossing the car park. Sauntering in that way of his. What had Miss Boyd said to him? Worse . . . what on earth had he said to her? And what if he'd tried it on with Miss Boyd . . . he couldn't look at an attractive woman without trying it on. His voice changed somehow. Lowered a notch.

She would say nothing. Pretend she didn't know about it and wait for him to make a move. The more she thought about the job, the nicer it seemed. It would be wonderful to earn money of her very own and, if she went to university, she would have to ask him for extra, still be dependent on him. He would hand it over as he always did without too many grumbles but that wasn't the point . . .

Miss Boyd might be her headmistress, a caring one at that, but that was all. She had no right to try to force things. It was no business of hers. If mum was here . . .

If mum was here, there would be no question. She would be going to university and that would be that. But mum wasn't here. And would mum seriously expect her to leave him on his own? He wasn't fit to look after himself. He'd go to pieces.

Annie spent the day on tenterhooks, expecting the summons to attend Miss Boyd's office. To her relief, it never came and she scuttled off home at four o'clock.

"We need to have a chat, you and me," he said as soon as she was through the door. "You'll never guess where I've been this morning. Inconvenient as hell."

Annie was prepared. "We can talk now if you like," she said heavily, "Before I start tea."

"I'm not in for tea," he said, "My day's been completely cocked up. Just stopped by to pick up some papers. Catch you later."

18

"I wish they wouldn't keep bombarding us with all these other dances," Guy grumbled as he and Gladys exited into a warmish evening. "It's the waltz I need to practice. How did I do tonight?"

"Very good," she said gravely. "I'm beginning to feel quite confident as I follow you. And you didn't step once on my feet not even in the quickstep. That was a laugh, wasn't it? I was nearly on my knees after that."

He smiled but he was still concerned about his lack of progress. He seemed to be going backwards, not so good now as he had been in the first few sessions, although maybe he was becoming more critical. Yes . . . that was it. The more you knew, the more technically adept you became, the more you picked at little faults. When he waltzed Barbara onto the floor on their anniversary, possibly with a roomful of people watching, it had to be done with aplomb.

They were early and, because it was such a pleasant softly scented evening, with spring fairly barging in now, they walked a longer way round to the car park. Guy was relaxed, no longer looking over his shoulder, confident that nobody was going to see them, not a word of this was going to get back to Barbara.

"I'm so glad Daisy came back home, or at least to her grand-mother's," Gladys said thoughtfully, stopping their progress a minute to step out of her shoe and flick an offending tiny stone onto the pavement. The awkward manoeuvre meant she had to hang onto his arm so that she did not overbalance. He laughed with her as she slipped her foot back into her shoe, readjusting her skirt and top too with a familiar rapid movement. "I told you not to worry, didn't I?" she continued cheerfully, "I knew she'd get fed up of the boyfriend. Girls rarely end up marrying their first love. What's happening now then? Is she going to college?"

"That's a bit of a sore point," Guy admitted, "We're not pushing her although I would like her to go. It seems to me essential to have a degree these days." He glanced cautiously at her, "What about you, Gladys? You're bright. Why didn't you . . .?" He realised the impertinence, "Sorry, you don't have to answer that."

"It's okay. It never occurred to me," she said, "I wanted to be a secretary so that's what I did. I left school at sixteen, did a year's secretarial course and bingo . . . got my first job straight off. Sometimes I wish I'd done something a bit more significant with my life but not often."

"Regrets? We all have regrets," Guy said quietly, "My wife used to be a secretary before we got married but she gave it up when Daisy arrived. I wonder sometimes if she ever regretted that. If she'd have liked to carry on, maybe do something else."

"Why don't you ask her?" The smile was cheeky but he did not mind, so much more at ease with her these days. He had to be careful however not to be indiscreet about his personal life for Barbara would not care for that. Some things slipped out unfortunately, notably matters concerning Daisy, but he was beginning to learn how to handle them. This time, he stayed silent. Glancing at Gladys, he saw that she was a touch flushed. Yes, she had got the message. Don't overstep the mark.

They paused as they passed the Civic Theatre, taking a moment to see what was on in the foreseeable future. Quite a few interesting sounding plays and he certainly wouldn't have minded seeing one or two of them, as would Gladys, but he had to dismiss the idea promptly. Remember . . . this togetherness was a sham. They were almost back at the car, walking down a pretty ordinary street, a street of neat terraced homes, a corner-shop street with a fish and chip shop at the very corner they were approaching. The smell drifted their way and Gladys wrinkled her nose, "Fancy some chips?" she said, "I shouldn't but it won't hurt once in a while. I'll get them, Guy, you got the meal last time." She was rummaging in her handbag for her purse and, although it was against his gentlemanly instincts, he let her. She peeped inside and declared that there were tables in the back if he wanted to sit down.

He had a sudden impulse to do just that. It was years since he'd sat down for a meal in a chippy. With Barbara and the old gang. He'd always been embarrassed by their lack of funds and they disliked it intensely if he offered to pay. So, after a few goofs, he'd played along with it, forking out the same contribution to the bill, to the penny, seriously joining in the debate as to whether or not they could afford mushy peas *en masse*. This was just Gladys's way of repaying him for the meal he had bought her and it would be silly to refuse. With a sigh, he looked into the steamy vinegary interior and followed her inside.

Opposite, some distance up the street, a man paused, checked his watch, and jotted something down in a small notebook. Not an easy place to loiter without suspicion, he thought irritably, as he walked briskly on past the chippy so that he could pick them up when they came out. The one-way system had nearly buggered him up tonight on the way in and Guy Shawcross was not a good driver, apt to do unexpected manoeuvres. Maybe he had his mind on other things, namely attending to the needs of the lady he was escorting.

It was easier now they were on foot. Strolling. Fish and chips! God, he was slumming it. He wasn't sure what the snotty old dear expected but it looked very much as if the son was running true to form. If those two weren't in the throes of a passionate affair, he was King Kong. You only had to look at the way she looked at him. Unmistakable. They made a nice couple. He'd always liked his women with a bit of meat on them.

"Thank you very much, Mr Westbury." Leila counted out the money. "I thought you would prefer cash," she said, not quite hiding her distaste as she looked at him. He was sprawled, no other word for it, on her sofa, wearing a hideous checked jacket over a checked shirt with a crumpled collar. His trousers were just that important fraction too short, showing off those disgusting white sports socks which he wore tucked into well worn shoes. All that walking about, Leila supposed.

"Do you require a receipt, madam?" He seemed to catch her

look and straightened up, "Everything goes through the proper channels, Mrs Shawcross, VAT included . . ."

"That is encouraging. I will not, however, require a receipt. Oh . . . how tiresome . . ." The outer door opened and Daisy made her usual clattering entrance into the hall. "You're to pretend to be someone else," Leila hissed at him. "She must not know who you are."

He nodded. "Do you have sufficient evidence or do you wish me to continue surveillance?" he whispered.

"No thank you. You have merely confirmed what I suspected already." She smiled, not wishing to discuss things further. His written report, smudged, written with a biro pen, lay unread on her desk and she intended to dispose of it directly. Such a nuisance for Guy to be playing around like this with Mrs Ward. She stood up and shook hands with Mr Westbury, not liking his eyes. As she escorted him out, they met Daisy in the hall, sorting out bags of shopping.

"Hello darling, I thought you weren't coming back until later," Leila said, "This is Mr Westbury, dear. And this is my granddaughter. Mr Westbury is . . ."

"In antiques," he said quickly, shaking Daisy's hand. "Your grandmother has some very valuable pieces." He stood shiftily a moment, his eyes alighting on the painting of Durham Cathedral that Leila had quite forgotten about. "Interesting," he murmured, peering at it as if he knew a Rembrandt from a Van Gogh. "This will be worth something one day. You mark my words."

Giving him an exasperated look, Leila got rid of him, hoping that Daisy believed him. Giving her a curious look in turn, Daisy made a pot of tea, coming to sit beside Leila. "You want to be careful with antiques people," she said with a worried smile, "Some of them are unscrupulous and I didn't like the look of him. Don't sell anything without asking another opinion, gran. I don't want people fiddling you. And he's quite right, you do have some valuable pieces. The grandfather clock alone must be worth a small fortune."

Damn the man. "Don't worry," she said, "I can handle the Mr Westburys of this world. Sorry about the painting," she added, as it occurred, "I'll dispose of it immediately.

I can't think why I hung it there in such a conspicuous position."

"Keep it," Daisy said, "Hang onto it. You never know. I used to think he had real talent but now I don't know. I suppose you have to admire him for trying to make it on his own without his family's support. They tried to make amends, offered to set him up in a gallery somewhere but he turned them down."

"Oh I see. I gather there's an estrangement then?" Leila enquired and, somewhere inside, a warning note sounded. She should have trusted her instincts. She knew there was something about the dratted boy. "People I know? His family? I didn't catch the surname."

"I didn't tell you." Daisy laughed. "And I don't intend to. His mother's Hungarian but he was educated entirely in this country. I think that's one of the things that attracted me. I've always been fascinated by Eastern European connections."

"Where? Where was he educated?"

"I have no idea," Daisy said, innocence hanging like a halo round her head. Leila did not believe her. "Forget him," she went on, "It's finished. Now, gran . . . you've been talking to Mrs Patterson, haven't you and don't deny it."

"I may have been." Her mind was still on Alan. Alan what? A family with connections? "The woman is lonely and rings me quite often. Why darling?"

"The two of you can forget that too." Daisy laughed. "And you can count me out of the musical soirée. Two tickets, gran? How could you? You promised."

"If you come to the musical evening, I promise I will not interfere. After all, you can give him the brush-off if you find him obnoxious. I would keep your options open, dear, if I were you. And I thought we'd agreed to go shopping for new dresses. I shall certainly need something new. Black? Do you think black will make me look too old? Pale blue for you as we agreed, it's your colour and you may borrow a piece of jewellery. Just the one piece. At your age, simplicity is best."

"And when we've crossed Piers off the list, who's next?" Her smile was defiant, "I shall work through your list and cross off every single one."

"List? What are you talking about?"

"I know you. You're always writing lists. Is this it?" She was over to the desk in a flash and waving aloft the Westbury written report.

"May I have that?" Leila asked coldly, retaining her seat. She held out her hand and stared hard at her granddaughter. Daisy knew just how far she could go and she had almost reached that limit. Leila would not tolerate cheek. "That paper you are brandishing is private. I do not wish you to read it. May I have it?"

The report was headed "Westbury Investigations" and included a damning list of times and places that Guy and Mrs Ward had visited. Leila had only glanced at it briefly but it seemed that Guy took the precaution of entertaining the lady to dinner many miles away. True, Westbury hadn't actually caught them at it but that was no matter. The intention was obvious. If they hadn't already, it was simply a matter of time.

Daisy's defiance was strong but her basic obedience stronger. To her credit, she did not so much as glance at it. She did as Leila asked.

19

The hotel was large and cumbersome, red bricked, multi-gabled with an astonishingly glitzy interior, an old-style seaside hotel reminiscent of Poirot mysteries with a faint sniff of sand and sea, but very pleasant for all that. In fact, Barbara preferred it to the modern five-star synthetics she and Guy usually frequented. She had spotted a grand piano in the dining room so at least she would be guaranteed a live pianist and splendid original food instead of piped music and standard pretentious buffet.

She squashed her guilt firmly but it threatened to billow up occasionally, particularly when she phoned Guy to tell him she had arrived safely. "Enjoy yourself, darling," he said, "Have yourself a lovely break. You deserve it." That hit hard.

Before she could change her mind, she telephoned David, his home number, but the answering machine was on, his voice brisk but still sexy, just as she remembered it. What was it about this man? She dialled his business number and was put through to him. "I've just arrived," she told him, trying to be light and relaxed, "I've booked in for a couple of nights. Alone. The conference is tomorrow, all day, but I think I might just attend the morning session and lunch. I don't know that I can face a whole day of medical lectures."

"Oh . . . you're at the cancer function then?"

"Yes." She winced as it occurred, too late. "They're going to tell us about the newest advances in research. Sorry . . . I didn't mean to remind you."

"That's okay." His laugh was slight though. "Is there anyone there that you know? Colleagues?"

"No, I told you, I'm on my own, the sole representative of

the Harrogate branch. I'm filling in for a friend who's tied up with something else this weekend."

"That's very public spirited of you," he said and this time the laugh was open, "Sure there isn't another reason?"

"David . . ." She sighed and flopped onto the bed. "Shall we stop beating about the bush? We've got to be honest."

"It's not me who's been beating about the bush, sweetheart. I knew the instant I saw you again that I wanted you. Oh never mind Ruth . . . we were married in name only for years. Of course I'm sorry about her, she was my wife, but, if we're being honest, then that's the truth."

She was shocked even though she had suspected it and it was not satisfying to hear, painful rather. Poor Ruth. "Guy and I . . ." she began, wondering how to say it without being mean to him, "We just sort of drift along these days. He's so terribly tied up in the business and well, things are a bit awkward just now."

"I understand. He wants shooting for neglecting you, Barbara." There was sympathy in his voice, "Would you ever leave him?"

She was reminded of Meg and the very same question. "Leave him? Of course not or at least . . . I don't know," she said miserably, "I'm used to him."

"Used to him? Good God, your marriage is in a rut, sweetheart. Why don't I come over to the hotel this evening and we can have dinner and that long long chat. Their dining room is excellent by the way. First class English nosh."

"Not tonight. I'm tired. Tomorrow if you like." She hesitated, not sure how to phrase it, "But it isn't an invitation to stay the night, David."

"Bloody hell, are you still at it? We're grownups, Barbara. Where's the harm in it? Will anyone know? And even if old Guy finds out, it serves him right for not looking after you properly."

Quickly, they arranged a time and left it at that. Barbara fingered the nightgowns that she had bought specially. Nightgowns that Guy had not seen. Nightgowns that he might never see. Holding the silky lilac material in her hand, she sighed. It was going a bit fast. She would have liked to get to know him again for, in many ways, she did not know him. She had never really known him, how his mind worked, what he thought, not like she knew Guy. She always knew precisely what Guy was thinking, more's the pity sometimes.

David was not far short of a stranger, a stranger who was about to become her lover.

20

"I want no excuses, Guy. I want the truth and I also want you to tell me what you intend to do about it," Leila said, as they settled at a table at The Crown for luncheon. She waved the menu aside and ordered soup and a plain omelette, waiting impatiently whilst Guy took an age to decide.

"I don't know what you're talking about, mother," he said, managing to look perfectly innocent. "I wondered what this invitation was about. You don't usually ask me out to lunch. Barbara's away for a few days so you could have come over to the house. Had you forgotten?"

"No. I called to wish her a pleasant weekend before she left," Leila said, not wishing to elaborate on that. Barbara had sounded strange, guilty if she wasn't mistaken and Leila did not understand why. "It's ages since we've dined out together, dear, so it seemed a good opportunity to do so." Leila glanced round the restaurant but they were unobserved in the quiet corner she had specified. "Now . . . I shall get straight to the point. Are you having an affair with your secretary, dear, this Gladys woman? The truth, please."

Guy stared at her a moment and then laughed. "No I am not having an affair," he said, "Shame on you, mother, for thinking it. Barbara and I are very happily married."

She sniffed, undaunted. "That's as maybe, but you have been seen with this woman, this Mrs Ward, out of office hours."

"I see. Gossip I suppose. What if Gladys and I *have* been together out of office hours. That doesn't mean an affair."

"Not necessarily but, in my experience, usually," Leila retorted. She was unwilling to tell him about the private detective, for she was loath for him to know that she had arranged to spy on him as that would cut their mother-son relationship to the core. "If you ask me, men and women cannot work together, at close quarters, without sex rearing its head. If you ask me, some of these young career ladies dress far too provocatively. Mind you, that didn't stop your father, dear. You should have seen his secretary. Brown frock and a cardigan. She rode a bicycle. The damned woman must have had hidden depths, very hidden. If you ask me . . ."

"Nobody's asking you, mother," he interrupted lightly. "It's lucky you're not running the business that's all I can say if you jump to conclusions like this."

"What are you talking about, Guy? We're not discussing business so don't change the subject. You haven't given me an answer."

"Yes I have," he said patiently, "Which you obviously do not believe. If you must know, mother, and I can see you won't let the matter drop until I tell you, I've been having dancing lessons," he said. "And Gladys very kindly volunteered to be my partner. You can't have dancing lessons without a partner you see."

"Dancing lessons? As in the waltz?" Leila felt her spirits lift. Relief ignited and the pain that she suddenly realised had been building up, the Charles-like pain, eased. Of course. She should have known better of him. Please God, let him remain faithful, solid and boring for all time. "But you can't dance," she protested. "You always refused point blank to learn. And you have no rhythm, darling. You're much too large."

"That's what you kept telling me," he said, "and I decided I'd find out for sure. It's been irritating me. Barbara just will not dance with me. She makes any excuse."

"I see. And have you? Any rhythm?"

"Not much," he admitted, "But I'm not bad now. It's been better than I thought. We've done all the dances you can think of, some speciality ones too I'd never heard of. But I need to concentrate on just the one, the waltz."

"Guy . . . you perplex me. What are you up to? You're obviously doing this for a reason other than just to please Barbara." Leila smiled gently, pausing as the waiter attended to them.

She reflected that today, goodness knows why particularly, he looked not far short of handsome, this big, broad-shouldered, fair-haired man who was her son. Dancing lessons? Who would have thought it? And it was very remiss of Mr Westbury not to have noticed that the establishment he had observed them coming out of was a dancing school instead of some tawdry hotel. "Would you care to enlighten me?" she asked.

"It all started when I was driving home listening to the radio," he said as they ate. "Frank Sinatra started singing 'Moonlight in Vermont'. Remember that?"

"Of course. Beautiful song." Leila looked at him thoughtfully, "These places always sound so wonderful, don't they? Faraway places. Often, when you actually visit them, they are such a disappointment."

"Not Vermont," Guy said promptly. "It's lovely. The last time I was in Boston on business, I managed to add on a little tour of New England. Of course it's probably at its best in autumn but nonetheless, I think even you might approve of it."

"I'm a little lost, Guy. Just what is the significance of this?"

"It's our song, 'Moonlight in Vermont'," he said, surprised, as if she should know. "It was the tune they were playing when Barbara and I first danced together. Blackpool. The Tower Ballroom. Remember the time we used to go around together in a crowd?"

"I do indeed." Leila shook her head and then smiled. "I was appalled. A most disreputable bunch as I recall. Why you had to abandon the friends from school I shall never know. Was it some form of protest, dear?"

"It was Barbara," he said with a quick grin. "I did a bit of detective work and found out who she went around with and pushed in. I don't know to this day how I had the nerve but I was determined to get to know her. The trouble was she was always hanging around with David Ambrose."

"Ah yes . . . the greasy-looking man in the photographs."

He smiled. "He irritated the hell out of me. He was always one of those super confident people so I couldn't believe my luck that night. They had a row and she walked off the floor. Just like that."

"And you seized your chance?" Leila watched him. She'd

never realised until this moment just how much he loved Barbara. The man was besotted still. In that case, what was the matter? Why was the marriage in trouble? If Guy still loved Barbara, then the problem must stem from her. There couldn't be another man. Barbara was not that sort. Not hot-blooded enough. No . . . Barbara would certainly not cheat on Guy.

Guy seemed oddly distant, his thoughts as far away as Vermont itself. "The band struck up a waltz," he continued, very quietly so that Leila had to concentrate. "It was late in the evening. Last waltz time. The lights lowered and the floor was empty. Glowing . . . I don't suppose you've ever been there but, as ballrooms go, it's pretty special."

Opposite him, Leila sat and listened, hardly daring to spoil the moment by asking a question. She'd never heard him talking like this before. Guy was so obviously back there in that sometimes vivid way of memory, back in the past, and it was a shame to remind him exactly where he was in reality. Lunching with his eighty-year-old mother was hardly the stuff of dreams, even if it was a superior restaurant and the company was most agreeable.

"We'd never danced before, not together, just the two of us. I made a hash of it. Kept standing on her feet. Kept apologising. She said it didn't matter. It didn't either because I was determined I'd not let her out of my sight again. I brought her home in the Triumph. My first car, remember that? And, after that, it was . . . well it . . . it all worked out for me."

But had it worked out for Barbara? Leila smiled at him, "And you're learning to dance as a nice surprise for her. I think that's wonderful, darling. She will be absolutely delighted. You must take her to a very grand ball. Will there be any on that day? I shall find out for you."

"She thinks I've forgotten our silver wedding," he said, "As if I would. She's told Daisy that on no account is she to remind me. Daisy did of course but she needn't have worried. I already knew."

Leila laughed. "Daisy is so like me," she said, flicking her fingers at the waiter and ordering a light wine to go with their meal. "This is such fun, Guy. I shan't breathe a word to Barbara."

"Keeping a secret is not one of your *fortes*, is it, mother?"

She dismissed his worries with a reassuring smile. "Not one word of this conversation will ever pass my lips," she said firmly, "Cross my heart and hope to die. Tempting fate rather at my age, dear."

21

David saw the redhead as he was on his way home, hurrying across the lobby. "Here again?" he enquired frostily, "Don't you have a home to go to?" He made no reference to the lunch date that had never materialised. He hoped she'd enjoyed her fish and chips and ginger pudding. Pity it hadn't choked her. Old hot-pants indeed!

"I'm waiting for a girlfriend," she said, not giving an inch. He could tell what was in her mind and he wasn't going to give her the satisfaction of seeing him remotely rattled. "It's my half day," she added, suddenly mindful that she was an employee and that he, ultimately, was the boss.

"And you choose to spend it hanging around here?" he asked lazily. "Good God, when I was your age, sweetheart, I had better things to do with my leisure time. Still do actually." He gave her a look, one of his well practised meaningful ones, and he saw her blush, cast her eyes down and look distinctly less sure of herself. Right, madam. That's what a mature man can do for you. Unsettle you. He glanced at his watch, "Got to dash. Interesting appointment this evening. Very interesting I hope." He winked and she blushed deeper. He just managed to refrain from patting her pert bottom as that sort of thing could cause havoc these days with all this bloody political correctness and walked out, hoping she was still watching as he climbed into the car. Thank God for the Rolls. The two-a-penny boyfriends she would have would be lucky to afford Annie's Mini let alone a Rolls.

Sod the redhead. Dinner with Barbara this evening. She was still playing hard to get but she was relenting a little. Worried but wavering. And, if nothing else, he was an expert at dealing with wavering women. A little gentle persuasion. If nothing happened this weekend, he was resigned to it. He'd worked out at last where he stood with her. She wanted him, for nostalgic reasons, rather more than he wanted her. She thought that she was in love with him. She was at that age when romance seemed to be passing her by. As for him . . . he might well have been in love once but not any more.

He needed to buy flowers and chocolates. She didn't look as if she was on a diet. A bit fuller figured perhaps but not much, not fat for God's sake. Fat women, fat people, left him cold. As far as the rest of her appearance went, the lovely dark hair had gone but she suited being a blonde. All in all, she was in pretty good shape. Aged nearly as well as he had himself.

He would wear a dark suit, white shirt and a plainish tie. Suitably sober as a recently widowed man should be. Some of the new aftershave. And, after dinner, they might take a walk along the shore. He would play it very quietly, gauge her reaction before making any move. Decide whether or not to kiss her. God, it was tiptoeing over coals time with Barbara. One false move and she would be scurrying off back to Guy in an outraged flurry.

When he arrived home, there was a car in the drive he did not recognise.

"Miss Boyd . . . oh . . . I thought you were the window cleaner come for his money." Annie crumpled the five pound note in her hand. The red sports car was parked beside her Mini in the drive. Following her gaze, Miss Boyd smiled.

"I hope you don't mind if I leave the car there. I like to keep an eye on it." She tipped car keys into her bag. And smiled again. "Sorry to stop by like this, Annie. I just happened to be passing and . . . well, I thought I might as well see if you were in. Are you alone?"

Annie nodded, remembering her manners suddenly and inviting her in. "Dad will be back soon," she said, tucking her blouse into her jeans, feeling the need to smarten up a bit in her headmistress's presence. Miss Boyd was immaculately clad as usual, although a bit different in casual clothes. She was wearing cream trousers and a black and cream low-cut sweater. Gold costume jewellery swung from her neck and ears and a number of gold bracelets jangled around her wrist.

"Do sit down." Annie took her into the sitting room, waiting for a moment for some sort of comment, ridiculously prepared to defend it if necessary. "I . . . would you like a cup of tea?" she asked nervously, as Miss Boyd settled herself on the sofa. She crossed her legs and Annie noted the high-heeled backless sandals and the red polish on her toenails.

"Later perhaps." Her mood was cautious and she seemed to be avoiding looking too closely round the room. "What's this I hear, Annie, about you getting a job? I must say you've sprung it on us rather."

"I haven't." Annie felt honour bound to point out. "I've discussed it with Mrs Bamber. I said I wasn't sure about university. So it stands to reason, I must be thinking about a job instead."

"I don't normally do this . . ." Miss Boyd leaned forward intently, "It's not very professional in fact but I feel so strongly that you're making the wrong decision, Annie, that I'm prepared to act unprofessionally for once. I want us to talk about it. Just the two of us. I feel I owe it to your mother to make you see sense. You're about to make such a huge mistake."

"I'm sorry, Miss Boyd, it will make no difference. My mind's made up." Annie perched on a chair, awkward in her own home. "I'm going to take the job. Of course I'm sorry about university but the way things are . . ." She shrugged, hoping she wouldn't have to go into detail. Surely Miss Boyd would understand her motives.

"Let me explain. I very much believe in doing things at the right time in your life," Miss Boyd said. "Putting things off has never been my philosophy. You see . . ." she paused as they heard a car's door slamming shut. "Oh . . . is that your father?"

"I expect so." Annie didn't know whether she should be pleased or not. She didn't want him butting in, putting on a show for Miss Boyd. They'd never got round to that chat yet because he was forever dashing off, using home more and more like a hotel. Perhaps it was his way of dealing with things.

What must Miss Boyd think of him? "Excuse me a moment." She left the room so that she could waylay him in the hall, warn him in case he came in cursing like a trooper about the traffic or the people he worked with or something.

"Whose is the car? Bloody beauty." He was through the door, doing what he always did first. Checking his appearance in the hall mirror. Smoothing down ruffled hair. Annie stood by and watched.

"Well . . . is it a boyfriend's?" he asked, adjusting the collar of his pink shirt. "Have you got somebody in there?" he cocked his head towards the sitting room and Annie shushed him with a look.

"It's Miss Boyd," she whispered, "She just happened to be passing and . . ."

"Did she now?" He raised his eyebrows. "Miss Boyd, eh! I'll deal with this, Annie. Off you go and make some coffee. Have you asked if she wants coffee?"

"She said later, dad." Annie hesitated. She didn't want to leave it to dad. He would say all the wrong things, show her up, make her out to be a little girl who didn't know her own mind.

It was already too late for he was opening the door, going through. Annie followed him as he crossed the room to shake Miss Boyd's hand. "Some car you've got," he said, "Midget, isn't it? You've got to hand it to them. That final version beat the earlier one all ends up. In my opinion of course."

"You're mistaken. It is the earlier version." Miss Boyd smiled a little and held out her hand, "Good afternoon, Mr Ambrose, it's nice to see you again."

"Annie . . ." He looked towards her, his manner concerned and fatherly, "Get us some coffee, there's a good girl."

Good girl! Annie retreated huffily into the kitchen. She waited for the coffee to percolate and leaned against the hatch to the dining area, trying to listen to what they were saying about her. The serving hatch was one of the old-fashioned features he had insisted on in the design, but it proved useful occasionally as now. If she left it slightly ajar, if they talked in normal voices, she could hear.

She heard Miss Boyd repeat that she was just passing and, on impulse, had decided to drop in for an informal chat. "I will get

Annie to university if I have to drag her there myself," she said, "I have a reputation as a fighter, Mr Ambrose, when it comes down to things I believe in. And I believe in Annie."

"Don't you worry about Annie. She's just after a spot of attention. She can be a bit stubborn sometimes. Just like her mother."

"A stubborn streak isn't necessarily a bad fault," Miss Boyd said and then her voice lowered and Annie could no longer hear distinctly. She heard her father laugh and heard a low chuckle in response. What were they talking about now?

She carried the coffee through when it was ready. They were sitting close together on the sofa and Miss Boyd looked just a touch flushed, not quite her usual composed self. "Thank you, Annie, that's very kind." She uncrossed her legs and moved a small table so that Annie could place the tray on it. "Biscuits too. How nice."

Dad never even looked at her, his eyes on Miss Boyd. Annie watched him carefully. She knew that concentrated look. He couldn't be thinking of Miss Boyd as the next conquest, could he? Surely not. They were miles apart. Intellectually and culturally. In every way. Although, at this moment, there was only a worryingly few cosy inches separating them and she mistrusted Dad's lazy smile, was suspicious of everything he did.

They sipped coffee for a moment in silence. Nibbled at biscuits. Annie searched her mind for something to say. Something sensible. Something self-assured. Something sophisticated.

Dad beat her to it, relaxed, arm resting along the top of the sofa. "Tell me, Miss Boyd . . ." he asked, "How did you get into teaching? It must be a wonderfully rewarding occupation. Something I might have done myself."

"You obviously know nothing about it, Mr Ambrose. You must ask Annie, she has an inkling I'm sure of what it must be like." She exchanged a quick knowing smile with Annie. "My career has followed a most interesting progression. I've had considerable experience in schools in various parts of the country but when this job came up, I did not hesitate. I was very pleased to get back to Blackpool. I lived here as a child," she said, "I always felt I would come home as it were one day. Now that I'm head, it's a little different. I

do very little teaching now. It's much more of an adminis-
trative post."

"Ah . . . management . . ."

Annie sighed. He'd better not start. He could be so embarrassing. Not daring to catch Miss Boyd's eye, she listened to
him going on about man management, team building, about
how he listened to the worries of his staff. He thrived on it,
on executive stress, he went on relentlessly, shamelessly, and
Annie had to fight a sudden urge to giggle. She knew exactly
what he was doing. Trying to make sure Miss Boyd got the
message that he was in a position of power, constantly making
decisions, dealing with huge sums of money. In other words,
trying somewhat pathetically to impress. Whatever for?

"Annie . . ." Miss Boyd broke in, interrupting him in full flow,
gloriously and probably mischievously ignoring him. "I'm not
going to insult you by insisting you stay at school. How can I
do that? You're grown-up now and you must make your own
decisions. Your father and I . . ." she glanced perfunctorily at
him and he smiled, having recovered swiftly from the rebuff.
"We're concerned about your motives and we would appreciate
it if you would at least discuss it with us first. Then . . . when
we hear all about it, we might well agree with your decision.
Tell us about the job." There was the slightest pause. "And the
prospects."

"It's in an accountant's. It's a junior job," Annie spluttered,
feeling embarrassed colour once more flooding her face, "It's
learning the job from the bottom up and I think that's the best
way. I shall have a day release for study and that could lead to
an additional qualification and, if I'm really keen, I could go
even further." She did not look at either of them. "I honestly
can't think why I wanted to study French. What good will that
be? I want to work with people."

"And you think you'll be doing that in a tinpot job like that?
A bent accountant's. Fat bloody chance, sweetheart."

"They're a reputable firm, dad." Annie frowned at him, looking
helplessly towards Miss Boyd for some support. She thought
she detected a trace of sympathy but she recognised that Miss
Boyd did not wish to overrule her father so there would be
nothing said.

"I don't know what the hell you wanted to do French for in the first place," he went on, his irritation now getting the better of him. "Each to his own language I say."

"The subject choice is no problem," Miss Boyd said calmly, taking the opportunity to step in, to control the conversation again. "We will have to reapply for courses but with the grades I expect you to get, Annie, it will be a foregone conclusion. You can aim for one of the courses that demand the highest grades and get them. Your father wants you to go to university, don't you, Mr Ambrose?"

"I do. And your mother would have wanted it too." He seemed to make a big effort, looked at Annie and smiled. Another scene out of his understanding father play. The pause was beautifully timed. He did indeed have an actor's skill. "Do it for her, Annie, if not for me. Don't worry about me. You know me, I muddle through."

"Thank you for that, Mr Ambrose." Miss Boyd said softly. "Annie can now make her decision, knowing that you will be perfectly all right without her."

"Of course I will." The indignation was strong, the implication being that Miss Boyd had misinterpreted his meaning.

They looked at her. It was all said. Now they awaited a decision. "Excuse me a moment." With what she hoped was a good deal of grace, Annie removed the tray and retreated into the kitchen, depositing the cups with a clatter onto the worktop. She gave a deep sigh. Her rebellion, she realised, had been short-lived. Never a rebellion as such for she had never seriously expected to go through with it. She had wasted everyone's time because she had always known, deep down, she would go to university. If she didn't, mum would find some way of expressing her disapproval. She had done it just to make them all sit up and think. Not take her for granted. Mum would have understood.

What were they saying about her now? She leaned closer to the hatch, screwing up her face in concentration. "She's got the message," she heard her father say. "Take it from me, she'll be off to university in autumn and, believe me, I really do appreciate your concern for her. I have an engagement for dinner this evening, long-standing one unfortunately with a business colleague, otherwise we might have enjoyed a meal together to celebrate. A small thank-you from me. Another time perhaps?"

Annie held her breath. He hadn't said that. She must surely have misheard. He hadn't asked Miss Boyd for a *date*? And then to her astonishment, she heard Miss Boyd, her voice a bit breathy, saying that she'd like that and giving him her phone number. And asking him to call her Felicity.

Aghast, Annie stood stockstill, not daring to move in case they somehow realised she was eavesdropping. She'd never live it down if any of the girls found out. Her father and Miss Boyd!

"Miss Boyd's leaving, Annie. Come and say goodbye."

She crept out of the kitchen, muttering her goodbye in some confusion, terrified of actually looking her in the eye, frightened of what she might see. Dad escorted her out and she could not hear what was said, heard the car start up after a few moments.

He came back in, humming a tune. "Nice woman that," he said easily. "You should take notice of what she says. She knows what's what."

"Dad, I . . ."

"What is it? Be quick, I've got to get ready for a business dinner." He was already tearing off his tie, unbuttoning the collar of the shirt.

"Nothing." She would tell him later what she had decided.

David could hardly believe it. Felicity Boyd had surely held his hand a fraction longer than necessary as he bade her goodbye. And the way she had slid into that car of hers . . . wow. The woman had class as well as brains and a touch of defiance too in the unexpected choice of car. Where had she been hiding? He watched fascinated as she waved, shot backwards down the drive and zoomed off with the panache of a racing driver at the starting grid.

He'd like to see Miss High and Mighty succumbing to him, pleading with him. What he'd give to see a woman's expression in those blue eyes, that special look he'd seen time and time again. After all, you couldn't fool him, and underneath that glossy slightly forbidding exterior there lurked a woman with a woman's body and a woman's needs. The thrill of the chase ignited in his heart. Damn it, he'd never been able to resist a challenge and Miss Felicity Boyd was issuing one, wasn't she? All that bullshit about just passing. She'd come to see him not Annie.

Something to look forward to there. But first, he was dining this evening with Barbara and you never knew your luck. He could dream about Miss Boyd at his leisure.

He heard the phone as he was in the shower. Hot jets of water powered down his body and he soaped himself lavishly. Not a spare ounce of fat. "There's someone on the phone for you," Annie shouted through the door. "Ringing from Lytham. Something about having to cancel your business meeting tonight. Shall I ask her to phone back?"

He stopped in mid lather and silently cursed. He might have known.

22 ∫

That morning, Barbara was up early, finding it strange to be alone in the big bed, and she had dressed casually, deciding on a walk before breakfast. It was spring, full and complete, and the air smelled so, the last of winter gone. She sniffed it appreciatively as she strolled in the early morning sunshine, the breeze gentle and loving against her face. She was thinking about David and tonight. Dinner. He would probably suggest another stroll out here, hand in hand. And then he would suggest he come back to her room with her and what would she say? What on earth would she say? She'd sounded like a silly little girl when she'd told him she wasn't inviting him to stay the night. It was time she grew up.

She stood and watched a few boats bobbing about on the estuary that was this morning a silvery glittery puddle, and it came to her that she did not want to hurt him. Guy. She did not want to leave him either. Leila was wrong of course, blissfully wrong, about him. Dearest Guy could no sooner have an affair than . . . well, the idea was preposterous. But this thing with David was something she had to rid herself of and perhaps the only way to do it, was to do it. Once and once only and she might tell Guy about it, sometime in the future. Knowing him, he would forgive her one little indiscretion. It was quite chic to have one indiscretion.

The lecture was to be held in the conference room and Barbara, changed into a smart suit, slipped into a seat at the back, smiling politely at the ladies already gathered. The lady on her right enquired as to where she was from and they had a brief chat about the respective merits of their home towns. The seat to her left was empty so Barbara deposited her bag and conference notes on it. She took out her little-used spectacles so that she might look more business-like and waited for the professor who was to address them.

Once this was over, this ridiculous thing with David, she would get herself back home and do something with her life. Daisy was quite right. She wasn't too old to start something new. Some sort of business. Fashion related as that would be tolerated by her friends. A little Nearly New perhaps, Designer Seconds. Yes, she liked the sound of that. Not in Harrogate but in one of the smaller market towns, maybe Skipton, although Leila may not approve. To hell with Leila! Guy wouldn't mind. Guy would be amused. The thought of his amusement tarred the dream. Let's face it, that's all it was, expensive ladies playing at expensive business games. If she was to do it at all, she would have to think it through, get a proper business plan proposed, make some financial provisions, make absolutely sure it succeeded. In other words, work at it.

"Thank goodness, Barbara . . ." Her thoughts were interrupted brusquely by the familiar all too bright voice, "I thought I'd be too late." Meg was standing there, pausing a moment before she sat down so that her splendid navy spot suit and white straw hat could be seen from all angles.

"What are you doing here?" Barbara said at once, "Did you think I wouldn't be able to cope?" Irritation made her frown. She had a notebook with her and she had intended to make copious notes on the proceedings so that she could report back at the next meeting. And now, here was Meg, every inch the chairwoman, determined to take over. Damn, she needn't have bothered coming.

"Of course you can cope, Barbara," Meg said, casting careful smiling glances around. "My other engagement was cancelled at the last minute and I made a spur of the moment decision. I didn't even have time to ring you. I did think you'd be glad of my company," she said huffily. "I'm booked in as well so we can have a lovely dinner together. It's always so boring dining alone, isn't it?" She ruffled through the papers they had been given, "I hope he's not going to talk down to us," she said, "There's no need for it. Nor is there a need for him to get too technical either. I should know, shouldn't I, although we're in orthopaedics."

Barbara smiled at the "we" as if Meg accompanied Howard into the operating theatre. Only then did it occur that Meg's unexpected arrival was going to put her in a very embarrassing position. She would have to telephone David to explain and she knew he would never believe this. A little disappointment nudged at her but she cast it aside, face flaming as she caught Meg's curious glance. "I must make a phone call," she said, fumbling with the stuff on her knee but it was too late as the doors slammed shut and the professor, bald but with a flourishing white moustache, dark-suited and bow-tied, strode onto the platform, smiling. A round of applause greeted him and Barbara hastily resumed her seat. She would ring at lunch time.

He wasn't in, the girl said, and she didn't know when he'd be back. Could she take a message? Barbara said no thank you and that she would ring him at home. The daughter answered at the second ring and, to her shame, Barbara replaced the receiver silently, not knowing what to say, not even having the nerve to say sorry wrong number.

The lecture had been frightening. All these damned case histories. But then, that's what she was in the group for, to raise money for research and she supposed she had to be content with that. What else could she do for heaven's sake? When you got down to it, thought about it, everyone knew someone who had died of cancer. She knew Ruth and a few others. That really put it in its frightening proportion. It gave an added urgency to their meagre fundraising and, despite what she'd said to Meg, she did feel pleased to be praised for her efforts. A young woman doctor took over from the professor and Barbara related more to her, admiring the confidence, the determination and bright shining hope the girl exuded. The lecture ended with Barbara feeling enormously guilty at what she had been contemplating. An affair would be a mistake, just an excuse for her current boredom and Meg, did she but know it, had put the stoppers on it in the nick of time.

"Did you get through?" Meg enquired, as they made their way to the luncheon buffet and conversation. She did not wait for Barbara to answer, making a beeline for the professor who was standing momentarily alone, looking bemused, holding a plate and glass. Less enthusiastically, Barbara followed, waiting patiently for Meg to finish giving him her own potted history before thanking him for his most illuminating talk.

His sharp eyes sized her up. "Is your husband in the medical profession too, Mrs Shawcross?"

"No. He's in business," she said feeling his attention dwindling. Not surprising, for Meg was in full enthusiastic flow, on about the newest advances in orthopaedic surgery now.

In the afternoon, they split into smaller discussion groups, listening to other people's fund-raising ideas, some of which were breathtakingly adventurous, compared to their own interminable coffee mornings, flag days and table tops. "I must say I think the idea of a formal dance is wonderful," Meg said as they disbanded. "A charity dance costing a fortune. Let's aim high. You'd be amazed at the people who would fork out for it, just to be seen most of them but who are we to query their motives. As long as they put their hands in their pockets, who cares? We could raise thousands in a single evening and we can't sniff at that, Barbara? Everyone would have a lovely time too. What's your opinion?"

"Yes, I like the sound of that. We could pick a date in summer, a Rose Ball, something like that. It's a wonderful time for a spectacular buffet. Strawberries and cream, salmon, masses of salads, iced tea and we could do lots of different ice-creams and summer fruit terrine . . ." She sighed, seeing it spread before her.

"I wasn't thinking so much of the food," Meg said, "We can leave that to caterers, Barbara . . . I'm thinking of possible venues. One of the hotels of course. We'll need to come up with a few ideas that we can present to the other girls but I'm sure it will be a winner."

They discussed it a little further then, making her excuses and arranging to meet Meg later for dinner, Barbara retired to her room. It was getting late and very remiss of her to cancel an engagement at such short notice, but she had no alternative.

Annie answered again and this time Barbara gave her the message, making some ridiculous attempt to disguise her voice. If she noticed, Annie did not comment. She merely said she would pass the message on.

23

It was the last of the dance classes. As part of his special thank you to Gladys and an alternative to an extra monetary payment which was inappropriate and even insulting, Guy booked a table for two at a country hotel near Darlington. He would break the news over dinner about the rest of his plans, the little surprise he had in store.

Was it his imagination or had she lost weight over the last few weeks? One or two people had mentioned it at work and she certainly was slimmer faced and it suited her. In fact, this evening, she seemed to have made a special effort and the dress was very pretty, a silky material, in lemon and white. She had done something to her hair, too. It was softer looking, gently waved. He thought they had all excelled themselves tonight, the entire class, not only that but they had enjoyed it. Actually enjoyed the dancing. They had changed partners just to prove that they could dance with anyone. It had been fun and funny and he was only sorry that he would not take up the casual "keep in touch" offers of various couples.

Feeling very pleased with himself, he smiled at her as she sat in a scented haze beside him in the car. "So, all in all, Gladys, and be honest, how do you think I'll fare?"

"With the dancing?" She laughed shortly. "You'll be fine, Guy. Your wife will be most impressed." Her voice had a sudden flat edge to it and he glanced sharply at her, very aware of it, wondering what had caused it.

"That was the idea, that she be impressed," he said, turning the car into the winding drive of the hotel, helping her out, looking with her at the old building, a former manor house, that nestled amongst trees, its stone softly grey in the approaching twilight.

"This looks impressive too, doesn't it?" he murmured, escorting her into the warm and welcoming reception hall. They had pre-dinner drinks in the drawing room whose stone fireplace contained an elaborate dried flower arrangement in the hearth. Brass and copper, old paintings, slightly worn carpets, creaking leather chairs abounded. And a lovely smell drifted their way as people at a nearby small table enjoyed their after dinner coffee, liqueurs and mints. From the heavily draped windows, they could see a wide terrace leading to the very large lawns. All the trees were budded now, some already leafed, bucketfuls of daffodils and tulips bloomed in the beds and there was a further enchanting display of spring blues and yellows nearer the house. In the mellow light, the old garden's glow was subdued but still beautiful.

"I hope all this hasn't been a major inconvenience to you, Gladys," he said at last, watching the departing guests with a polite smile on his face for them. He returned his full attention to his dinner companion. "When I think about it now, I had a helluva cheek to ask. You could have said no. I hope you didn't feel you had to say yes. I wouldn't have borne a grudge." He smiled at her, "I don't work like that."

"I know you don't," she said with dignity, "And it's been most enjoyable, Guy . . . I suppose now that it's over I'll have to get used to calling you Mr Shawcross again."

"In public I think it's best but in private it's quite all right for you to call me Guy."

"Thank you." He detected, or was he being over-sensitive this evening, a touch of sarcasm in the reply. "I shall miss these nights out," she went on with a little sigh, "I haven't enjoyed anything so much in a long time. I don't get out much as a rule."

"Why don't you? You should. You're still young. You should get out and meet people. You never know, you could get married again, assuming you want to, of course."

She shrugged. "Only if I met Mr Right. Corny, isn't it?" Her eyes twinkled and the bright red lips parted in amusement. "Seriously though, the trouble is that in real life the Mr Rights are in short supply. By the time you reach my age, the men I meet are either gay or married." She shot him a disturbing look.

He was struggling rather for an answer when the waiter arrived to tell them their table was ready. Following her into the dining room, he found, to his irritation, he felt a sudden need to check on the other diners. Fine. Nobody that he knew. He had better stay well clear of the subject of marriage and men. He hadn't meant to upset her, on the contrary he wanted to tell her that there must be a lot of men out there who would go for her in a big way, a warm, intelligent, nice woman like her. She had a very pleasing feminine way of looking at you and she was doing it now, making him feel strong and masculine, all very politically incorrect he supposed.

"Will used to wine and dine me," she said, "In the early days before it all went sour. I loved him then." She grimaced and fiddled with her cutlery, "Wouldn't it be great, Guy, if we could look into a crystal ball and see if marriage is going to work out or not before we go through the whole palaver. We were together four years before we realised it was hopeless. I suppose I just have to be thankful I didn't have a child. Life's complicated enough as it is. He has a child now," she added, her smile not coming off, "His new wife had a little boy." She sighed and very purposefully straightened her shoulders, "You and your wife . . ." she rarely called her Barbara, "you're so lucky to have a happy marriage. Planning this lovely surprise for her. I hope she appreciates it, after all the effort you've put into it, that's all."

"She will." He was surprised at the sharpness of her tone. "I'm sure she will."

"Now that you can dance, she'll probably want you to take her to all those dinner dances you've been avoiding," she said, her good humour resurfacing. "You'll not get out of it now."

He laughed. "I'll have to show off my new-found skills. She must have missed it, the dancing . . ." he said, trying to cope with the feeling that Gladys was in some oblique way, perhaps without realising it, criticising Barbara. "She could have carried on with it, got herself another dancing partner, gone in for competitions and what have you, but she wouldn't hear of it once we were married. She just seemed to turn her back on it."

"I wonder why."

He shook his head, slowing down with his soup as Gladys, unusually for her, nibbled absently at her avocado mousse. "Something to do with the dancing. She and her partner were very good. Barbara said that another partnership just wouldn't have worked for either of them. For her or David."

"Were they in love?" Gladys coloured, "Sorry. They both married other people so of course they weren't. You wonder though, dancing like that. You always want people like that to be lovers too. Dancing with someone, doing a waltz for instance, is bound to have some sort of effect." A smile played round her lips and he caught the meaning, only too well. "The relationship must have been purely platonic, like ours, Guy."

She had a spot of cream on her lips and he must have been subconsciously staring so that she became aware of it and licked it away, before wiping her mouth with her napkin. The ordinary little innocent gesture appealed. Her hand with silvery pink fingernails trailed the table towards his, stopping just short, that important bit short. She no longer wore her wedding band, just a pearl dress ring.

"My mother's been listening to some gossip unfortunately," he said, taking a deep breath, "Sorry about this and I wondered if I should bother to tell you but it would seem that people have been talking. About us. I put her straight of course but it's a bit worrying that rumours are circulating. Now that it's over, we'll have to play it down." He remembered worryingly what he still had in mind. Oh Lord, tongues would really wag then!

Disconcertingly, she smiled directly at him as the waiter cleared away their starters. Then . . . "Are you sure you're not enjoying this?" she said, "All this subterfuge? I'm not so sure I like being cast in the role of scarlet woman, not when I'm entirely innocent." The smile remained and he caught the flirtatious eye glance.

"Thank you for everything anyway," he said, formality prevailing, "I'd like you to come and meet Barbara properly sometime. Come for dinner perhaps. She's a superb cook."

"That would be lovely." Again, in an instant, her mood dulled.

Guy wanted to know what was wrong, wanted to make her

smile again but he sensed the danger. Gladys was a woman whom he liked very much, liked being the operative word. Barbara was the woman he loved. He kept his sexual energy on a permanent low, had to these days, but he was realistic enough to accept that he was only human and that he might not be able to resist the charms of a woman he liked who wanted *him*. And he had the feeling she did.

Across the table, Gladys was looking very pretty tonight, blooming in fact, eyes sparkling, skin glowing, occasionally subdued true but there was even an attraction in that. In other words . . . there was no other way of putting it, she was sexually inviting.

He still had another favour to ask of her. "Leading on from our dancing classes . . ." he began, realising at once as she smiled that he was being pompous. "May I just explain what is going to happen?" He had an impulse to pick up a knife, fiddle with the napkin, do anything that would involve delaying the inevitable. "Remember that seminar over in the States? The one we were sent details of?"

"The one we threw out. You said you couldn't justify the expense again, Guy."

"Yes I know I did." He looked carefully at her. There were times when being decisive was the only way forward. "I'm going to go anyway and you're coming too."

If he'd invited her to go to bed with him, she couldn't have looked more astonished.

24 ♪

Piers Patterson was a great disappointment. Not only was he an average violinist in an average quartet, he was also several inches shorter than Daisy. What a waste of a new dress and, for once, dear Daisy had been quite co-operative, not only coming along to the soirée with only a few grumbles, but also accepting the gift of the lovely blue strapless gown and looking an absolute angel wearing it. The pearl and diamond choker looked gorgeous round her slim neck.

"Serve you right, gran," Daisy said with a laugh, on the way home. "Oh . . . careful, do you want me to drive?"

"No, I do not," Leila said crossly, still profoundly irritated at the way the evening had gone. It wasn't as if they had played any tune she liked, just a selection of terrible screeching high-pitched music. She might have known, that was par for the course with violins, not her favourite instrument even if played with any degree of competence. She was annoyed with Penny. The woman might have said that the boy was only five foot six. She had seen Daisy for heaven's sake. She knew that Daisy was tall for a girl. Bound to be with her mother being tall and Guy, of course . . .

Next on the list. Who was it? Michael Findlay-Smith. Hadn't Leonard, the father, been in the navy? Oh dear, she hoped the eldest son had not followed in his footsteps. She didn't want dear Daisy hanging about on shore waiting for his ship to return to port. Distressing. She would give Irene a ring tomorrow. What was her charity? Save the Children? This business was already costing a small fortune, what with a hefty donation to Penny's charity, all to no avail. Guiltily, Leila retracted that thought as she noisily changed gear on one of the hills across the moor.

"I forget . . . did you say what Alan's surname was, Daisy?" she asked, still trying to glean information about that young man. Daisy was being distinctly evasive. She had spoken as if there was a rift between him and his parents, as if the family had money, and she had definitely said that the mother was Hungarian which added a bit of interest, a foreign connection. She had already gone through Daisy's diary when she was out but there was nothing, no address, no name. Without his surname, how could she find out anything about him? It was so exasperating.

"Gran . . . watch it," Daisy said, hanging onto her seat as Leila went a little too fast round a bend. "Won't you let me drive? Please."

"There's nowhere to pull in," Leila said, smiling impishly at her, "Did I hear you answer my question, dear?"

"Will you forget Alan? After what he did to me, I never want to see him again. And will you please stop interfering." Daisy sighed. "There's something I have to speak to you about, gran. I feel dreadful because you've been wonderful letting me stay and everything even if you do keep doing these other things . . ."

"You want to go home? Is that it?" She felt her spirits flag, just a little bit. She had grown quite used to having the girl around. She was company and she would have to get used to being on her own once more. Such a nuisance. "It's not because you think I'm an interfering old bag, I hope?"

"No, gran. It's not that." Daisy leaned over and patted her leg. "It's not that at all. It's just that I've got some job interviews and it'll be more convenient if I'm at home."

"What sort of job?" Leila sighed. What was the point in the child getting a job when she would be resigning in autumn?

"I'm trying for various things. Although I may decide, if I don't get any of them, to go to university and read economics. I have the grades to reapply."

"Finance." Leila clicked her irritation. "Why not wait a while, dear? Don't rush into anything whatever you do."

"It's two years since I did my A levels," Daisy said at once,

"So you can't accuse me of rushing. It's high time I got on with my life."

Leila had heard that one before. Best to leave it. Driving up a dragging hill, in second gear already, in a steady stream of irritated traffic with a heavily laden lorry at the helm was not the right time to discuss this.

"Keep your distance," Daisy ordered briskly, "And be prepared to stop if necessary."

"You needn't tell me what to do, dear," Leila said, sighing as the lorry slowed even more, "I have been driving for years."

"Just be careful that's all," Daisy said, beginning to sound worryingly like her mother. "You will be all right on your own, won't you, gran?" she asked after a moment's contemplation. "That house is too isolated in my opinion and anything could happen. And you have such lovely jewels. People will know about that. You shouldn't let antiques dealers in, gran. You never know, they might be sussing out the joint."

"What an expression! I don't know what's brought this on, Daisy, I don't let antiques dealers in," Leila protested. "Can't stand them. I know precisely how much everything is worth thank you. I don't need to ask their opinion."

"Why did you ask him then? Mr Westbury? Why did you let him snoop around?"

"Oh . . . him." Leila slammed the brakes on as they came upon temporary traffic lights. "The engine's stalled," she said irritably to Daisy, "It hates me to stop suddenly like that. What were you saying, dear, about Mr Westbury?"

"Forget him. Concentrate, gran. Go on, they're moving."

Leila let the clutch out. If she had to contact Westbury again, she might be forced to meet him in his seedy little office. That was preferable to Daisy accidentally setting eyes on him again and jumping to all manner of wrong conclusions.

She decided she would do a reconnoitre first as there was no earthly point in dragging Daisy along unless the young man was at least five eleven. She was not going to have odd-looking wedding photographs. The phone call to Irene Findlay-Smith was excruciating because the woman seemed idiotically incapable of understanding the point of Leila's call.

At last, perhaps it dawned. Anyway, eventually an invitation was prised from her and Leila was to go over for coffee and yes, Michael was home, on leave. Leave?

It was like drawing teeth and she had had to listen to interminable accounts of the entire family before Michael was mentioned. He was in the Foreign Office, based abroad. Oh . . . that sounded interesting. And no he was not married or engaged even. A confirmed bachelor, his mother said with a laugh.

Confirmed bachelor? That could mean one of several things. Worriedly, Leila decided it was worth going over for coffee and finding out. One look should do it. She had always known these things. Of course if he was . . . of that persuasion . . . then she would beat a hasty retreat and have to look at the other name on her list.

The Findlay-Smiths lived near Harrogate so it might be an idea to do a quick detour and pop in on Miriam Langstaffe as well, find out about Charles. She would call on the off-chance, say she was just passing. Miriam was always in, not far short of a recluse, with a couple of hairy dogs as companions. That decided, Leila dressed in a rose-pink linen suit with cream accessories, her string of pearls, her stole about her shoulders, and prepared to set off.

Daisy was out. Job hunting. As she checked her appearance in the hall mirror, Leila saw that the painting of Durham Cathedral, the wishy-washy watercolour, was askew. If there was one thing she could not stand, it was paintings not quite straight. She straightened it carefully, standing back and checking. And then it occurred. Good heavens, she must be getting senile not to have thought of it before and it couldn't have occurred to Daisy either, for there, in the bottom right-hand corner was the signature.

She needed a magnifying glass to decipher it but it was there. Alan Sillers. Sillers? Did she know them? The Sillers? She checked the telephone directory but there were no Sillers listed, only three Sillars. Damn. She knew he would probably have an exhibition of his paintings somewhere so it was simply a matter of going round art galleries and finding him. Oh dear, this was too boring. She would have to enlist Westbury's help once more. She would do it when she got back from her trip to Irene and Miriam and, whilst she was so close to Harrogate, she would probably drop in on Barbara. She'd never enquired if she'd enjoyed her weekend away in Lytham. Charming place, Lytham, bracing air, and St Annes had some lovely shops. Barbara would probably have spent her spare time shopping. Dear Barbara, if she only knew what Guy was doing.

Dancing lessons! She hoped for his sake that the outcome was satisfactory. The secretary had turned out to be just a good sport after all. Very obliging of her to help out like that. She believed him implicitly. Nobody could have feigned surprise like that and not mean it. The man did not have one adulterous bone in his body. Truly virtuous that was Guy. She would try her best not to give the secret away for Guy was right, it would only spoil the surprise.

25 ∫

"Are we setting off directly after breakfast, Barbara?" Meg asked, winding a way to a table by the window so that they overlooked the green and the sea.

"We don't have to go in convoy," Barbara said irritably, refusing the cooked breakfast with a wave of her hand. She couldn't eat a thing. She hadn't slept a wink. Just imagine, she could have awakened this morning with David at her side. "You set off after breakfast if you like, I shall go later."

"As you like." Meg eyed her with exasperation. "What's the matter with you? Are you always like this first thing in the morning?"

Barbara nodded. Let Meg think that. She closed her eyes, hearing the subdued sounds of breakfast all around. She wished Meg would go. She might then have chance to drive over to see David, to explain properly. She owed him that much at least. A proper explanation. She sipped an orange juice and tried to pay attention to Meg who disposed of a huge breakfast, toast and marmalade and three cups of tea. Barbara glanced wryly at her. The sea air must be doing her good. She'd have to watch it or she might put on half an ounce.

Finishing, Meg frowned at her, "Seeing that you're in an absolutely foul mood, I think I will be off." She glanced at her watch. "I'll check out now and, if I don't see you again, I'll see you at the next meeting. If you like you can give the conference report? After all, you were our official nominee. All right, Barbara?"

"All right. Sorry I'm not feeling too bright this morning." Barbara raised her cheek as Meg kissed it, managed a goodbye smile, difficult because she had just seen the maroon Rolls parking in the guest car park in front of the hotel. Oh Lord, he was here. He had come to see her. Frantically, she watched as he stepped out, locked the door, glanced around. He had not seen her at the dining room window and she retreated further behind the folds of the curtains. He was wearing an open-necked shirt, a suede jacket, dark trousers and he looked pretty near perfect. David's looks had always got to her.

She flew up to her room, and waited. From her window, she watched Meg depart, backing her car out of the space beside David's, not knowing the significance of course, not even bothering to glance at the Rolls. Meg wouldn't, as casting envious glances at a Rolls was not her style. Barbara hoped she had not appeared too strange to Meg this weekend. Dinner had been a subdued affair with Meg doing most of the talking but then that was not unusual. She had let Meg's chat spill over her, harmless enough, her mind firmly on her own problems. She really would have to get a grip on herself.

With Meg gone, the coast was clear. She checked her appearance. A touch nautical. Navy trousers and striped short-sleeved top in navy and white with a red scarf knotted at the neck and dangly red earrings, meant as a little fun gesture. She did not feel the least fun-like. Not the least. She strolled down to the reception area, using the stairs rather than the lift, so that she could get a longer view of the sofas and chairs and see if he was sitting there. He was. Smoking a cigarette directly under a polite notice requesting guests not to smoke in reception.

"Hello David." She went up to him and sat beside him. "You did get the message? I'm so sorry I had to put you off at the last minute," she said, getting to the point immediately. "What can I say? Meg, a friend of mine, turned up unexpectedly and I had to dine with her. Such a shame."

He stubbed his cigarette out on a saucer. "Did she just leave? This Meg? I thought I heard Harrogate mentioned. Dark-haired woman in a green suit?"

"That's Meg, yes." She looked at him hopefully. So he did know she was telling the truth. "I'm sorry. I was looking forward to dinner together."

"Anything else, darling? Anything else you were looking

forward to?" His smile was gentle, and as calmly as if it were the most natural thing in the world he let his fingers drift to her arm. "When the hell will you and I get together, sweetheart?" he whispered. "You're driving me mad."

"Perhaps it's fate," she said unhappily, removing her arm from his touch. "I accused you of not thinking straight, well . . . I'm just as bad. I can't think what possessed me. Meg was meant to be. I'm convinced of it because it's given us both time to think. Old fools, don't you think? Romantic old fools."

"Less of the old." His eyes were sad. "I'm not giving up on you, Barbara, not yet but I can see you're not ready. Old Guy's really got a grip. What I would like to do very much is to dance with you again. Just that. Every other partner I've had has been worse than useless. It's been so frustrating. You and I were a team, sweetheart."

She nodded, ridiculously pleased. "I would like to dance too. Like you, I haven't had a decent dance since we parted. Guy and I don't."

"Don't what?" He grinned suddenly and reached for another cigarette.

"Don't dance," she said, managing a slight smile.

"I teach dancing in my spare time, what spare time I have which isn't much. Latin American is still pretty popular. Mind you, I haven't danced properly in years. The young girls I teach don't have a bloody clue. If they're sensuous they forget the steps and if they remember the steps, they look about as sensuous as a supermarket cashier."

"You teach dancing? I didn't know that." She smiled. At last, she was learning something about him. "I did consider something like that but I don't think I'd have made a very good teacher and the thought of teaching unwilling little girls how to dance did not appeal. Daisy never had any wish to learn. Funny isn't it?"

"They're always on the look out for dancers to do demonstrations. They go down a treat. Fancy us doing one? Probably at the Tower. I've got some influence there and I can fix something up." His eyes sparkled, "We'd knock 'em out, Barbara. We really would. Remember that applause?"

"Oh, I couldn't. I haven't danced in ages," she said, but inside her, hope bubbled as his enthusiasm caught at her. "I couldn't just do it cold. We'd have to practice first."

"Of course. I agree. I wouldn't dream of doing it cold either. We were great, me and you, Barbara, and we should be just as good once we've polished up. I'll be in touch. I'll book us a date and I'll be in touch. It'll be just like old times."

"Yes." They exchanged a smile, both remembering. "You're not too upset about last night, are you?" she asked.

"No. Disappointed sweetheart, but it's better that we get to know each other again first." He glanced at his watch, "I've got to go. I've got a business appointment."

"I have to go too. Guy's expecting me home around lunchtime."

"Will you tell him that we met up again?" He grinned. "Or is it our secret?"

Barbara laughed uneasily. "Don't send me roses."

"That sounds like a song title," he said easily, as he kissed her goodbye.

David didn't know why he'd said that about the dancing. Last night, after she cancelled, he'd made up his mind she wasn't worth the hassle. Then, this morning, he'd thought what the hell, she was worth a final little effort. On the drive over to Lytham, he'd made up his mind to play it cool. Barbara was his whenever he wanted but what he wanted just now was to save her for some future date.

What he did want most of all, funnily enough even more than sex, was to dance with her. He really did want to enjoy that experience again, and, just thinking about it started him humming. He drove the short distance to the golf club, checking the time so that he didn't arrive too early. He mustn't look too keen.

He might have known she'd play golf. Miss High and Mighty. Inspiration that, asking her if she fancied a game. He'd never expected her to agree not at such short notice but she had seemed delighted and also agreed that they should have lunch together afterwards. She wasn't much good, she assured him, and she hoped that wouldn't spoil his enjoyment of the game too much.

Who cared about the bloody game? Her car was already there and she was waiting, chatting to some other people he vaguely knew. He wondered how long she'd been a member here, not that he came very often for he could take or leave the game. It was damned useful for contacts though and essential for business to be a member. She looked lovely. Cream again. Long pleated skirt this time and very crisp blouse with a cream and brown waistcoaty thing. Flat shoes so that, thank God, she was level-eyed with him. "Good morning," she said, greeting him with a smile. "Perfect day for golf, isn't it? Not too crowded either so we should get a good game."

He nodded, suddenly inexplicably nervous. He hoped to hell she'd meant it when she said she wasn't too good because he wasn't too good either. Sports, this kind of sport, any kind of competitive sport, were not his *forte*. What if she was better than he? This had been a mistake. They should have just stuck to lunch. He could have invented a hamstring or something.

To his relief, she was every bit as bad a golfer as she had implied. Her putting was atrocious and his that important inch better. Deliberately, he kept the chat general, leaving the serious stuff for lunch. She was surprisingly chatty when she got going, telling him all about her various teaching jobs down south. She had missed the Fylde coast however during those years and always intended to come back. The head post at the school was a dream come true. It was a tremendous relief for him to discover that she genuinely liked Blackpool as he did. She lived, however, in a big old house at Lytham, an enormous old house she told him that she had inherited from her parents. Too big for her but she was loath to sell. Her parents would not want her to sell and she had the oddest feeling they were watching over her, making sure she didn't.

"I'm selling mine," he told her, "I should never have moved to St Annes. Annie doesn't like the house, neither did Ruth, so I'm getting a flat in town. You must come and see it when I get the keys."

"I will. And if you need any help with the decorating, let me know. I've quite an eye for colour even though I say it myself." She laughed and pushed at her short hair. The suddenly strong sunlight bathed her in a delicious pinky glow and he was momentarily startled by it. Something else too. He liked her. Actually liked her. He realised he wanted to woo this lady. He did not want to hop into bed today or tomorrow. He wanted to get to know her first, wine and dine her, anticipate ... he just knew that she would be absolutely fantastic. Already, he knew that. He wouldn't mind waking up every morning with Felicity draped around him. Creamy and golden.

He won the round. Only just and he was left with the slightest suspicion that she had let him win. If so, it was a very feminine thing for her to do but he wasn't completely happy about it. Still ... what was a game of golf? That was the first and only game of golf they would ever play. He would make damned sure of that.

He was happier relaxed over a splendid lunch and it went swimmingly. She was very interested in the dancing, disappointed that she had never had the time or the opportunity to learn. He'd teach her he said, deciding as he looked at her that she could be a good dancer with the natural grace that she possessed. "Funny, isn't it, that we never met before?" she said, over coffee, "I've been at the school for five years now but I've never seen you at a parents' evening or at any of the school events. Only your wife." She smiled sympathetically. "She was a very nice lady. She thought the world of Annie."

He nodded. "Every time there was something on at school, I'd be tied up with business. Every single time. It wasn't that I didn't want to go ..." he added hastily, "But Annie never seemed to have any problems and Ruth used to keep me up to date. Good school you run," he finished, "One of the best in the area."

"Thanks, David, but I can't take all the credit," she said, "As you well know, it's a combination of things that make a success. The staff are very good and the pupils too, believe it or not, are generally a good bunch. There's the usual one or two of course." She grimaced, and he smiled, his turn to be sympathetic. "This year we have a particularly good upper sixth. Annie is one of a very competitive group. They should all do very well."

"We chose the school originally because it had such a good reputation," he said, not bothering to mention that he had left it pretty much to Ruth to sort out. Frankly he really didn't know one school from another. He put on his earnest face, although, strange to say, he found he was enjoying the tack of the conversation, actually listening to what she had to say, admiring her more and more as time went on. She did an important job and she did it well. He admired that. This was some woman.

"I'm pleased our reputation has stood up," she said. "It means we can't let our standards slip one little bit. The only problem is that we suffer from an acute shortage of funds," she said, "And that really irritates me. Take the library for instance. I'd like to update it, keep the classics of course as essential reading but update the rest of it for the children, particularly the younger children whom we're trying to encourage to read all they can. We've still got things like *Dora Alarms the Fifth Form* and *Stella's First Term at Boarding School*, books that the children can't relate to at all. Our fiction stock is very old and very poor, I'm afraid." She sipped her coffee and smiled at him. His heart jolted. Her eyes were the most wonderful blue. Angel's eyes. Eyes like . . . let's see . . . a morning sky, a clear morning sky when there wasn't a single cloud to be seen. Blue.

"Has anyone ever told you . . .?" he began but she was not listening, her mind still obviously on the damned school library. He shared her concern, of course, although books had never featured strongly in his list of priorities.

"What we really need of course is someone to offer to pay for a complete new stock," she said, "I would try for something like sponsorship but of course that's frowned on. Oh the PTA do their best. They're a very keen bunch. It's a constant round of table tops, car boot sales, things like that, but that just pays for essentials. It shouldn't of course but it does. Sad, isn't it? We are grossly underfunded."

"It's a disgrace, Felicity," he said, aware that he had never been a member of this bloody marvellous sounding PTA. Had Ruth? He signalled for the bill and threw his napkin on the table. "Now . . . shall we take a stroll? Or have you had enough walking for one day?"

"A gentle stroll would be nice," she said, "Thanks for lunch, David. It was lovely."

He paid by credit card trying not to look too surprised at the amount, leaving a hefty cash tip. At that price, it *should* be lovely.

Daisy was beginning to realise, somewhat to her shame, that A levels in chemistry, statistics and history did not actually qualify her for very much. Not in the workplace anyway. There was a junior assistant post going in a laboratory but she was dismayed at the nature of the job, then immediately a little guilty because, after all, what did she have to offer? She had no experience of any of the secretarial skills that were still much in demand and precious little experience of anything else.

Other than being dumped by Alan Sillers. It was when she found herself seriously considering her grandmother's efforts at steering her towards matrimony that she decided something would have to be done. She was only putting off the inevitable. Had in fact been putting it off for the last two years. It was time she went to university. Gran's plans for her would have to be put on indefinite hold. Poor gran. She had already seen a dress and jacket in silky grey-green that she wanted for Daisy's wedding. She was even beginning to worry about her hat. Daisy smiled as she remembered their shopping trip prior to the disastrous musical soirée. She had allowed gran to buy her the blue gown because it was beautiful and she loved it but, unfortunately, the evening gowns were right beside the bridal department. Gran had had one of her little "dos", claiming complete exhaustion and had been forced to rest a moment outside, blue-gloved hand clutched dramatically to heart. Perhaps Daisy could ask for a glass of water for her? No . . . she would ask herself. With a surprising burst of speed, she was already halfway into the bridal room, an eager assistant, all smiles, sweeping towards them through the racks of billowing white satin and lace before

Daisy realised what was happening. In the event, gran had insisted on a preliminary "look" although Daisy, hammered from two directions, had refused to try anything on. Assuring the assistant that they would be returning nearer the time, gran managed a graceful exit, an embarrassed Daisy in her wake. On their way out to the street, Daisy's furious, frantic mutterings had fallen on conveniently deaf ears.

She was not going to be lulled into marriage, just because it would please gran. Gran had always got her own way but not this time.

The Findlay-Smiths were one of those sort of cheerfully infuriating well-off families who managed to look as if they didn't have two pennies to rub together. They dressed moderately well, true, but their belongings, furnishings and furniture, had certainly seen better days. The house, a wonderful sprawling affair in large grounds, was a mess and Irene didn't even bother to utter the usual apologies for the state the drawing room was in. "How is Barbara?" she asked with a smile, "I haven't seen her for such an age. The children take up so much of my time unfortunately . . ." She passed over a plate heaped with roughly shaped pieces of cake. "My daughter Jane made these," she said, "They're a bit sticky I'm afraid. Treacle's a devil to measure isn't it?"

"No thank you. I'm on a permanent diet," Leila said firmly, pleased that at least the coffee was good. Strong and black. "I've come about Save the Children," she began, "As I told you on the phone, I'm about to give a donation but, firstly, I wanted to hear a little more about the current situation. What they're actually doing in fact. One does like to know where the money's going and with you being the chairwoman, I hoped you would be able to fill me in."

"Oh, that's what you've come about." Her face cleared. "I have a leaflet somewhere with all the information on. I could have posted it, Leila, although it's lovely to see you again and we will be most grateful for your donation. You're looking very well." She beamed. "I must say when you rang I thought it was all a bit mysterious. I thought it was something connected with Michael but I couldn't think what."

Leila shook her head. She simply could not survive in the

pigsty that was this house. The room was cluttered. Books on chairs. Newspapers. Supplements. Last week's probably. Teenage paraphernalia. Muddy football boots lying on what had once been a beautiful pale pink floral carpet. Irene must have no help. She must do the whole lot herself, or rather, not do it.

The fireplace was magnificent, brought firmly down to size by a selection of children's mugs on it sitting side by side with rather good porcelains. And the painting over the fireplace was blatantly askew. She took another long look at it . . . a view of Durham surely. "Lovely picture," she murmured. "I have a similar one. Is it an Alan Sillers?"

"Why yes, I believe it is." Irene stood up and peered at it. "Leonard's the one who's keen on paintings. He's forever going round exhibitions picking up what he considers to be little gems. This one he was particularly keen on, it being Durham. Michael was at university there and we're rather fond of the place. Quaint isn't it?"

"How much did he pay for it?" Leila could hardly believe her luck. "If it's not a rude question," she added with a smile.

"£150 I think," Irene said, "That's the sort of figure he usually pays, although we do have others scattered about. Watercolours mainly. Why, Leila? I didn't know you were keen on art."

"Oh but I am. Fiercely keen," Leila lied with a big smile. "Where was the Sillers exhibition? I'd quite like to have a look myself."

"He was just about closing up. Richmond I think. Leonard will know where he's heading next. He's not in just now but I'll ask him if you like and get him to phone you. He may even have a business card. They usually dole them out, don't they, these aspiring artists?"

"Thank you." Leila smiled her acceptance as she was offered another coffee. "So Leonard thinks he's talented, does he? This Alan Sillers?"

Irene smiled. "Maybe but, knowing Leonard, he may have been simply doing the boy a favour. We are vaguely acquainted. Alan is Lord Slewsbury's second son you know? His father wanted him to go into the family firm but Alan refused and there was an almighty row. Usual thing. The boy said he could get by without any help. Between you and me, Leila, I think he's having a pretty rough time of it. The paintings are nice enough, not that I know anything about them, but I hardly think he'll make a living out of them, do you? Some young people have such dreams. Thank goodness, Michael has his feet firmly on the ground. He's going far I do believe."

Leila's cup rattled with her excitement. Irene faded into a sort of semi-dreamlike state. She could see her vaguely, hear her distantly, but in the forefront of her mind was the title. The dratted boy was titled. She might have known. Of course he had that carefree aristocratic air about him. At least she now knew where her priorities lay. She had to call on him and reverse the process. Difficult. Embarrassing. But the wonderful, wonderful thing was that Daisy still loved him. All the rest were piffling details.

"Mother . . . oh sorry, I didn't know you had visitors."

"Michael, do come and meet Leila Shawcross."

"Hello Mrs Shawcross. You're not Daisy's grandmother, are you?" He advanced with a smile and an outstretched hand. Charming young man. Six foot or possibly more. Dark hair. Brown eyes. Nice looking. Well dressed.

"You know my granddaughter?" she smiled. Second choice certainly. He would do if Alan failed to turn up trumps. "Your mother tells me, Michael, that you're in the Foreign Office? She also tells me that you're a confirmed bachelor." She smiled across at Irene. "Didn't you, Irene?"

"Yes but that was before I heard the news." Irene Findlay-Smith positively glowed. "Michael's engaged. To a lovely girl. The Barrington's youngest, Leila, do you know her. She's called Phillipa?"

"Indeed. Congratulations." She smiled thinly. Another wasted donation but not a completely wasted hour. She had learned valuable information about Alan. She would take her leave now, leave a cheque of course for Save the Children, and call very briefly on Miriam Langstaffe.

Two hours and a very peculiar lentil luncheon later, she waved goodbye to Miriam. She had parted with another cheque for some local stray dogs' home. She had decided not to pursue Charles further. It didn't matter what the young man looked like or what he did, she simply could not stomach having

Miriam at the wedding. One had to draw the line. The woman was outrageous with the fashion taste of a bag-lady, as well as being a vegetarian and drinking only bottled water. And it wasn't as if they could hide her away, not with her being the mother of the bridegroom. Leila sighed, resigning herself to having to take the pink suit to the dry cleaners. It was full of dog hairs from Miriam's drooling companions.

Three blanks out of three but never mind. Alan was the one who mattered. Leonard would call when he got home and tell her where the young man was heading for his next exhibition. Leila hoped it was not too far away. All this travelling about was most wearisome.

"You look tired, Leila. What have you been up to?" Barbara led her through to the sitting room. "Guy's not in."

To her surprise, Leila made no comment, making heavy weather rather of settling herself comfortably on the sofa. "May I have a gin and tonic?" she asked, "A small one as I shall be driving back later."

"Stay if you like," Barbara offered, "I don't like you driving when you're tired. You need all your wits about you to drive in the dark."

"Are you suggesting I'm witless." Leila yawned, reaching out for the glass. "Thank you, my dear. Did you enjoy your weekend in Lytham?"

"Lovely thank you, although part of it was working. The conference you know. We may be organising a summer ball, something really splendid. You must come along of course. You and Daisy if we can persuade her."

"Of course." Leila sipped her drink, fingering the pearls at her neck. Barbara joined her in a drink, hoping she wouldn't mention Lytham again. Best forgotten. She still felt hot when she thought about what might have been. What very nearly might have been but for the intervention of Meg. She must have been temporarily insane to have considered such a thing.

"Guy's off to America," she said with a smile. "Unfortunately it's business, a conference on architecture I think, otherwise I might have gone with him." She reached for a leaflet, showed it to Leila, "See . . . it's in Boston. He went to it once before. His secretary's going with him this time," she added quickly, before Leila started fishing. "Work, that's all it is."

"I don't doubt it." Leila looked troubled, trying to hide it but not succeeding. Barbara knew her too well.

"What is it?" Barbara looked at her fondly. "You can tell me." She sighed, thinking suddenly and worryingly that sometimes Leila could look very very old. "Guy and I worry about you living alone," she said quietly, knowing how touchy Leila was about her age and her independence. "Sorry, but it needs to be said and Guy won't say it . . . you could come to live with us but . . ."

"Exactly." Leila sniffed her thoughts on that. "And don't you dare put me in a Home. I'm perfectly all right as I am, thank you. You'll be exactly the same when you get to my age." She reached for her bag and opened it. "This is what's worrying me, dear." She handed over a letter. "Read it."

"It's from Canada." Barbara took the thin airmail sheet. "Is this your cousin Phoebe?"

"Correct, dear. We've corresponded for fifty years."

"Fifty years . . ." Barbara was reading the spidery handwriting. "Oh . . . oh dear . . ." she finished and looked up. "And you two haven't met in over thirty years? I find that extraordinary, Leila."

"She's dying, Barbara. Six months to live at the very most. Mind you, she is nearly as old as I am so it's hardly premature. Still . . ." Leila managed a small smile, "Do you realise what this means? I'm going to have to visit the dratted woman."

Barbara was not fooled. Leila was genuinely upset by this, trying to hide it by resorting to her usual dry humour. "And the sooner the better I suppose?" she said quietly.

"Of course the sooner the better. If I leave it, she might be dead. Or I might be dead. I could go at any minute. At my age, dear, you have to live with that thought. Every day may be your last."

Barbara hid a smile. Leila was totally un-put-downable, although at this moment she looked very tired, which even her neatly applied make-up failed to disguise. "Would you like me to come with you?" she asked gently. "I don't think it's a good idea for you to go alone."

"Why not?" Leila demanded, feathers ruffled. "I'm perfectly capable, thank you, of sitting in a seat in an aeroplane, eating those revolting plastic meals and being met at the other end. If I go at all, and I have not yet made up my mind to do so, then I shall go alone. Dr Evans doesn't know what he's talking about half the time. What is it about Welsh people? Dr Phillips did me a great disservice by dropping dead on me. I was used to him and he to me."

Barbara sighed. What on earth was the matter now? Leila was so devious. "I think you should go," she said, "And Guy will think that too. You can't not go, or poor Phoebe will think she's been abandoned. Does Dr Evans think you shouldn't travel alone? Is that it?"

"What are you talking about, Barbara? What's all this about Dr Evans? I don't recall mentioning him." She resumed rifling through her handbag. "Do you think you could book me a seat on an aeroplane for sometime late next week? I'll fly out to Toronto, it's only a shortish drive to Phoebe's from there. One ticket for the best seats please, at the front."

Barbara frowned. Of course she'd mentioned Dr Evans, a mere few minutes earlier. It wasn't like Leila to be absent-minded. They did say that that was the way it started, senile dementia. What a nuisance all this was. Their wedding anniversary was fast approaching. Guy would be back from his conference by then but now she would have to be away herself. With a bit of luck, she would be back by then too, although, the way things were going, it would not matter. She had pulled back just in time from a disastrous affair. Her marriage, thin-skinned or not, was her top priority.

If . . . and it was a big if . . . if she met David again, it would be with Guy's blessing purely on the dancing front. Why not stage a comeback or at least a one-off? A final dance, one to remember. One that she could take to her grave.

Death reminded her grimly of Phoebe and of Leila. On the Leila front, she had no alternative. She was not allowing Leila to traipse off across the Atlantic on her own. She would go with her.

27 ∫

"I thought I told you not to ring me again, David."

"You told me not to send you roses, sweetheart." His voice was low, slinky. "How are you? I was just ringing to tell you that I've fixed us up with a demonstration dance in August. Get yourself a nice little red number."

"August? That's way off."

"Of course. We need to practice. We'll be rusty, both of us. We'll treat it like a competition, hone up for the actual date so that we're at our peak. Remember?"

Barbara considered. "I'd love to do it," she said, as if to herself, "But I'll have to talk to Guy about it first."

"Why? I thought you were an independent woman?"

"It's common courtesy," she said stiffly, and, quite suddenly, she realised that she was emerging from this "David" thing. How stupid of her to have merged the dancing and the emotions, to have made the mistake of thinking they were in any way connected. For all his faults, she loved Guy, damn him. If she couldn't change him then so be it. "I will talk to him," she said, "I hope we can arrange something but it's strictly business from now on, David."

He laughed. "You were always one for changing your mind, sweetheart. As a matter of fact, I'm glad you feel that way because it's strictly business with me too. I'd like to tell you that I've met a very special lady. You're the first to know."

"Oh?" She did not say it was a little soon, nor did she remind him that he'd stroked his fingers up *her* arm and looked deeply into *her* eyes just a short while ago, or that he'd called her his special lady too. What a short memory he had. Inside her, deep down, something finally fizzled out as if ice had dropped onto fire. "That's nice for you," she said. "I want you to be happy, David. Like me . . ."

"You and Guy okay now? Little differences resolved?"

"We're fine." She smiled brightly into the phone. "He's off to America on a business trip but when he gets back we'll be celebrating our silver wedding."

"Congratulations. You never know, Barbara, I might be celebrating too shortly. You don't think it's too soon do you? To be thinking of getting married again. She's single, no strings attached and she's a very classy lady."

"If it's what you both want, then I don't think it's too soon," she told him. "What about Annie? What does she think about it?"

"She doesn't know yet but I think she'll approve." He chuckled but the deep throaty sound no longer made her knees shake. She could now see through David for precisely what he was.

"Keep in touch then," she said lightly, "And I hope we can get together for the dance. I would really like that."

The house was at the top of a tree-lined avenue, behind tall hedges. The neighbourhood was top class of course but chronically dull. He'd go spare living in this environment. Ruth would have loved it. The lawns of Felicity's house were close cut, weedless, edged, the early shrubs colourful, the big bold door with its brass knocker most impressive. It looked like it belonged to a headmistress or a retired bank manager. The MG was in the drive, angled in the turning circle as if she'd slewed to a halt. The car was a conundrum. They didn't go together somehow and it excited him. He'd always liked a woman with a touch of mystery and her choice of car hinted at that. Not sure if she was watching from within, seeing a curtain move in fact at one of the upper rooms, he walked confidently to the door and rang the bell.

"I have to warn you, David, that I'm not a very good cook," Felicity told him as she took his coat. "I did think of getting someone in to cook for me and saying that I'd done it myself but, in the end, I couldn't do that. It must be something to do with years of spouting about being honest to the children. I find it very difficult to lie. Anyway, enough of that . . ." she smiled, "Come on through."

He followed her. She was softly draped in peach silk, very nearly ankle length, a dress with a low neckline that moulded itself to her tall slim body, with matching shoes and the gold costume jewellery she was fond of. He wanted to kiss her, now, this very minute, but he was keeping himself in check. Careful now. She wasn't the sort you could pounce on even if he wanted to. He wasn't used to playing this game, most of the Lindas of this world would have had his shirt off his back by now. Conversation first. Conversation until he was blue in the face. Intelligent conversation at that. Not like Linda. Linda's ignorance of everyday facts amazed him. She must have never read a book in her life. She didn't know where places were, nothing about politics, nothing about the finer things of life. Before he'd got on at her, she'd serve you red wine with fish without batting an eye.

"Sit down and I'll get you a drink. What would you like?"

"Whisky if you have one. With water."

The interior of the house was very grand, the house itself worth a fortune on the current market, although he didn't care much for this type of thing. Give him a brand new one any day. Cream striped curtains at the window, cream upholstery, darker carpet, just a couple of prints on the walls. Plainish. Dullish. She certainly liked cream. If it was his room, he'd do it up a bit, put more stuff on show, have some books out. Where the hell were her books?

"I have a separate small library," she said, reading his mind. "There are so many rooms you see and I like to use all of them. So . . . I've put my books in the one room and I go in there when I want some peace and quiet. Would you like to see it later?"

"Thanks." He took the whisky from her. "You look absolutely gorgeous tonight," he said. "Has anyone ever told you that you have the most amazing eyes? My lovely blue-eyed lady."

"Please, David . . ." she turned away, and he suspected she didn't want him to see that she was blushing. "Dinner will be ready in ten minutes," she said, glancing at her watch. "I just hope it's okay that's all."

"Sod the dinner," he said, putting his glass down and going

over to her, touching her, pulling her towards him. "Hell . . . Felicity . . . don't you know what you're doing to me?" Silently, he cursed. What had happened to the slow patient courting? "I've never met anyone like you before. I've never met a woman who *thinks*, for God's sake. Ruth was only ever concerned with domestic stuff, the house, Annie . . ."

She looked at him. She was very close. Closer than she had ever been before. He looked at her mouth. Softly pink. Laughing, she dodged him as he was about to kiss her. "Dinner," she said, leading him by the hand through to the dining room.

Blue. With candles. Dark polished table. Pink carnations. A table set for two. Outside, he could see a narrow garden, very long, a lawn leading the eye to a distant blurry border. Old-fashioned sort of garden. He enjoyed her feminine anxiety as she served the meal. It was okay. Not brilliant but okay. Soup, home-made he guessed but too bland. Chicken in a spicy packety sauce. Something put him in mind of Linda and her cooking. Linda used to cook one-handedly, the other holding her cigarette. She wasn't that bad but her exceedingly small repertoire bored him after a while. She was just the same with her dancing. No bloody variety. "Piling me with cholesterol," he muttered as Felicity handed him his dessert, hot apple pie and thickly whipped cream.

"You don't have a weight problem," she said, weighing him up very effectively with her eyes, "In fact, may I say, David, that you are in great shape and no . . . I wasn't going to say for your age. Age doesn't concern me. Not one little bit."

"What's age?" he said. "A state of mind. If you act young, feel young, then you are young. Age has never mattered to me, sweetheart."

"Nor me . . . darling." She cast her eyes down at the endearment and his heart raced. Wow! Maybe he should reconsider his plans for wooing this lady. They couldn't be married for a while in any case as he would have to pay some heed to Annie's feelings and he didn't know how long he could last out without sex. Barbara Shawcross and her everlasting teasing was beginning to have an effect. It hadn't been her fault this time, admittedly, but he felt that there had been a certain relief there on her part. She was fighting her conscience was

Barbara and it was winning. One of these days, Barbara . . . one of these days.

"Cheese and biscuits?"

"No thanks." He finished off the wine and smiled. "Lovely meal," he said, "Thank you."

"You're welcome." She seemed distracted and he waited for her to compose herself. "I was just thinking . . . one or two of the parents . . . sorry to talk about school, do you mind? . . . well, one or two of the sixth form parents have donated prizes to be given out when their children have gone on to university. Prize for chemistry, history, that sort of thing. A book token usually. £25 or so. Something for the fifth form to try for. It's a nice thought, isn't it?"

"It is." He smiled his agreement. "Do you want me to do that? I'll give a prize for . . . what subjects does Annie do? . . ."

"History. English. And French."

"Right. Okay, I'll give an English Prize then."

"Oh no, goodness, you mustn't think I was asking you to," she said, looking very put out. "I haven't asked you over for dinner to bribe you, David." Her blue eyes twinkled. Gorgeous blue eyes. "I asked you because I wanted to."

"I know." He reached for his cheque book. "I know when I'm being bribed, darling," he said. "And you . . ." he reached over and touched her hand. "You wouldn't know how to, would you? Do the children know you're as innocent as this?"

"I'm not innocent." Tongue curled over her lips, eyes fluttered. "Whatever gave you that idea, David."

He felt a tightening inside. He knew that come-on when he saw it. "Felicity, I know we've not known each other very long but I feel as if I've known you forever. I can't get you out of my mind . . ." he frowned. God, was that a song? He battled on, seeing her watching him with a dreamy expression. "Those eyes. They're like the sky on a summer morning. Heavenly blue. I've never seen anyone with eyes that colour." He smiled, putting a whole lot of sincerity into that one.

"David . . ." she laughed. "You're incorrigible but you're right in one way. We haven't known each other very long and I'm sorry but I don't jump into bed until I really feel I know a man."

"Have there been many?"

She shook her head. "You know better than to ask that," she said with a little laugh. "If you've finished your coffee, shall we go through to the library? I'll show you the books. And, for goodness sake, put that cheque book away. I shall refuse to accept it."

"Sure." Bugger the books. He followed her into the deeply red room with its floor to ceiling shelves piled high with books. A couple of elderly easy chairs, a footstool. A place where he could see her sitting and reading on a winter evening. Proper books. Used books. Books that were thumbed through and read. The window looked out onto the quiet street. Somebody, somewhere, was mowing the lawn. Christ, excitement! Dead end alley. What a dump.

They might not see eye to eye on houses and decorating but they'd compromise. He'd never live here that was for sure. Not in Lytham. He saw no problems in persuading her to move to Blackpool. He had big plans. He intended to surprise her with a ring. Something very expensive. An engagement ring. That would do it. He hoped to God she wouldn't be like Ruth and want to wait until they were married. Miss High and Mighty was going to be very hard to resist. The peach dress looked like it would slide off very easily.

The idea came to him as she proudly showed him some of the old books. "About your school library?" he said, "Do you remember you were telling me how badly stocked it is? What would you say if, instead of a paltry book token, I give you a substantial private donation for some new books. We're talking a few thousand here, Miss Boyd," he said with a grin. "Not bloody buttons."

"David . . . I couldn't possibly let you do that," she said. "It would be marvellous of course, but impossible. You and I are personal friends, you see, and it would hardly be ethical. I'm sorry I can't accept."

"Of course you can." He couldn't stand it any longer. He drew her roughly towards him and kissed her, running his hands through her hair, down her back, squeezing her to him. "Marry me," he said, "I love you, Felicity. Marry me, please."

She wriggled in his arms. "David, I always thought you were

impulsive but honestly . . . we've only just met. First, a cheque for the library and now, marriage . . . you certainly know how to surprise a girl." Gently, with no malice, she pushed him away. Flushed. "You'll have to give me time to think."

"I'll write that cheque now," he said, reaching and finding his cheque book this time. "And you can have as much time as you like to think about the other thing. I don't want you to think I'm rushing you, sweetheart." He wrote the cheque and handed it to her. "Put it somewhere safe," he said with a smile.

"Thanks, darling." She slipped it down the front of her dress between her breasts, glancing shyly up at him through lowered lashes.

She thought she would never get rid of him. Felicity stood by the gate and waved as the Rolls disappeared down the avenue.

A proposal! She laughed quietly to herself as she went back indoors. Indelicately, she rummaged down the front of her dress in search of the cheque. It was a trifle damp. With a broad smile, she waved it aloft.

They had done it.

28 ∫

Leonard Findlay-Smith rang with the news that he was awfully sorry, Leila old thing, but he did not know where Alan Sillers was going next and he had lost the damned card that the boy had given him. There was no point either in contacting his father because he never heard a dicky bird from him these days either so ... it wasn't important, was it? Frankly, he thought the paintings were unlikely to take off. Pleasant enough but lacking that important something.

Leonard's information, or lack of rather, caused a minor headache and Leila grimaced as she replaced the receiver on the infernal man. What next? Westbury she supposed. It shouldn't be too difficult for him to locate Alan and, once he had done that, she could home in on him. She would say that she was doing it for Daisy. She would say that Daisy had begged her not to get in touch with him again. She would say that Daisy was very nearly pining away. She would say anything to get the two young things back together again. Lord Slewsbury! And Lady Slewsbury, she had ascertained, was indeed Hungarian, a charming lady, very nicely dressed from a photograph she had spotted in *Country Life*, although it would appear that Alan got his brooding good looks from his father. Alan was the second son, the first already spoken for. Well, that couldn't be helped and the wedding would still be jammed full of aristocratic guests, second son or not. Titles galore!

First she had to find the dratted boy. Oh dear, life was so complicated at the moment what with having to fly off to Canada next week. The boy would have to be found before then as she would like to finalise arrangements with him before she set off. She would ring Westbury and advise him of the problem. She assumed Westbury had nationwide contacts and it would therefore be a simple matter for him to locate the boy. All it entailed was scouring the various galleries and arty places where they held novice exhibitions. Westbury could do that standing on his head. One thing was certain. Westbury was not setting foot in the house again, not with shoes like that.

Oh well. Packing for Canada. She'd never had much affection for the place, too big and too cold, although they did wear their furs with panache, the only things that kept out the numbing winter wind. What a nuisance! What was the weather like over there at this time of year? Would they have thawed out yet?

Daisy was helping her mother to pack. It was not easy. They'd been at it all afternoon already. Items had been discarded then repacked only to be discarded once more. "You can always buy things when you get there," Daisy suggested at last, rehanging a cocktail frock for the umpteenth time. "Are you sure you don't want to take this with you?"

"I suppose not," her mother said doubtfully. "Really, Daisy, your father doesn't have the same problem. It's so simple for men."

Quite. And talking of men . . . she had not told her mother about Alan. He had contacted her. The secrecy and speed of the phone call had taken her completely by surprise and, only when the line was dead, did she think of the things she should have said.

If things had gone wrong with the other girl . . . if he thought he could just come back into her life just like that . . . he could think again. However, it took Daisy only about ten seconds to decide she would go to see him, find out what it was he wanted to talk to her about. She could handle him. She could handle him providing she kept him at arm's length. She hoped.

The little flutter of excitement, though, the dithering about what she would wear, said otherwise and she wondered if her senses were deserting her. She had said nothing about it either to her grandmother, who was, in any case, full of her plans to go to Canada. There was no point in bringing Alan back into their lives. Gran would steam ahead with the wedding plans and her mother would once again voice doubts.

"Daisy . . . don't just stand there, darling. We've got lots to do." Her mother was getting herself into a packing tizzy, piles of clothes everywhere, lightweight, heavyweight, middleweight, whatever. "How it's all going to fit into two suitcases, I shall never know."

"It won't," Daisy told her, literally rolling up her sleeves and starting afresh. "You're as bad as gran," she said with a smile, "She's got gloves and handbags and matching shoes and . . ." she stopped as her mother held out a small parcel wrapped in shiny silver paper.

"Put this somewhere safe, would you. It's for your father . . ." she smiled gently. "It's just a little something. I'm not dragging it all the way to Canada and back." She frowned as Daisy took the parcel and fingered the silver bow, "Such a nuisance, this thing with your grandmother. It's cutting it a bit fine. What if I don't get back in time?"

"Stop worrying. What is it? The present?"

"Oh. It's . . ." a smile hovered, "It's just a silver picture frame and I've put a photograph in it. One of our wedding pictures."

"How nice!" Daisy put it down carefully. "Quite romantic, mother."

The suitcases were filling rapidly, overfull, and her mother fussed with labels a moment, not looking at her. "You have his address in Boston if you need it. I might be a bit more difficult to locate as we shall be travelling."

"Enjoy yourself." Daisy impulsively went over to hug her. Had her mother ever felt about dad like she felt about Alan? She couldn't imagine it somehow. And yet . . . she knew about the surprise dad was planning. Extraordinary that he should go to such lengths. She hoped it would help smooth things over. In the meantime, her role was to make sure that mother took the flight to Canada with gran, that she didn't have second thoughts.

She seemed to be having them already. "I don't like leaving you, Daisy," she said with a worried smile, "What are you going to do with yourself whilst we're away? Are you sure you'll be all right on your own?"

"Yes, I'll be fine." Daisy said firmly. "I'm going to have all-night parties and fill the house with my friends and . . ." She stopped. Smiled.

"Are you getting over him? Alan?" The flippant remark was ignored, her mother looking at her seriously. "I'm so sorry. It'll take time, darling, but it will get better. Believe me, I know."

"I'm getting over him," Daisy said. "He shouldn't have walked out though, should he? That was a rotten thing to do."

"It happens." Her mother's smile was a touch crooked. "Once . . . years ago . . . I thought I was in love with David Ambrose. Then I met him again and realised I was not. Never had been really."

Daisy said nothing. It had taken her mother all of twenty five years to find that out.

She wondered how long it would take her.

Damn Alan Sillers. She loved him. She hated him.

Barbara was glad she'd arranged to accompany Leila on her mercy mission. Leila tried hard to give the impression she was still as active and confident as she ever was but Barbara knew better. The old car, with Leila at the wheel, was forever getting into scrapes these days. Leila was failing. Beginning to. It was faintly depressing but it had to be faced. Daisy had commented on it, too, for she had been worried at the presence of some suspicious-looking antiques dealer at Leila's home. They would have to watch her carefully. She was such a meddler, always had been, but now they would have to keep a close eye on her or goodness knows what she might get up to. On a whim, she might sell the entire houseful of antiques. Damn the woman! Barbara found herself thinking of her with affection. She hated to think of Leila not being around anymore.

The flight was uneventful with Leila mostly sleeping and, when she was not sleeping, eating or making fractious requests to the flight attendants. They did have time, however, during the long boring hours, for a little heartening heart-to-heart. "You know I thought that son of mine was having an affair . . ." Leila began, quite loudly so that Barbara had to shush her in consideration for the other passengers.

"You mean Guy?" she asked stupidly. She glanced out at the

clouds that lay in a fluffy feathery heap below them. "What about it, Leila?"

"I apologise, dear. I was wrong. I must confess the Tuesday and Thursday thing had me puzzled but I had it checked out and it was entirely innocent. The secretary is totally exonerated. The little thing with her was easily explained away so you can set your mind completely at rest."

"What little thing? And, what do you mean, you had it checked out?" Barbara stared at her in astonishment.

"I employed a private detective," Leila said as if it was the most natural thing in the world. "Westbury Investigations. I chose him from the Yellow Pages. In the event he turned out to be a tiresome man with shoddy shoes, but his conclusions, or to be more precise, later events were . . . well . . . conclusive. It's an enormous weight off my mind, Barbara. I was beginning to think like father, like son. You'll be delighted to know, my dear, that Guy is utterly faithful to you. Isn't that a relief?"

"I always knew that," Barbara said crisply, "It was you who doubted it." She wasn't sure if she was amused or annoyed at the old lady, "Does Guy know that you had a private detective trailing him? He would be absolutely furious. It's a bit much, Leila."

"Of course he doesn't know and you must promise, hand on heart, that you will not tell him." Leila shuddered, trying her favourite hand fluttering to her own heart gesture. "It's my advanced age, my dear, it makes you do the silliest things. Dearest Guy, if he ever thought that his own mother doubted him . . ."

Barbara smiled, picking up her paperback and putting an end to the conversation. Leila got worse. She was also up to no good where Daisy was concerned, apparently visiting various people doling out large sums of money to charity. Not that it wasn't commendable but Barbara suspected an ulterior motive, which must surely be linked to the fact that all the people possessed sons of a certain age. After all she'd said, she was still at it. Matchmaking. Daisy was aware of it but dismissive. Daisy's immediate plans were centred on a career, a university degree. Marriage, if she bothered, she had told Barbara, would come later. Barbara knew that Daisy was still a little in love with Alan.

You couldn't just switch feelings off like a tap. They trickled. Sometimes for as long as twenty five years.

Barbara considered that the little hiccough in her own marriage was over. She and Guy would continue to plod on for years to come and when she thought about it, it wasn't such a bad prospect. Before he left for America, she had come clean about David. Well . . . almost. What she had said was that David had been once more attracted to her and that she had had to put a stop to it. She had mentioned the demonstration dance, asking Guy's opinion, and he had said she must make up her mind. Do what she wanted. However, his face was tight as he said it and she knew his opinion. He was jealous. It was rather touching to see that he was jealous. After all these years. Love had bubbled up, at his outraged expression. Of course she loved this big daft hulk and what a fool she was to have ever doubted it. Not being able to resist being impish, she had asked with an indignant expression if he didn't trust her.

He trusted her, of course he trusted her but not David, he said. Wise man. It no longer mattered because she could cope with David now, now that he had got himself a new special lady.

As the plane sped her towards Canada, the paperback unread on her lap, she found she was wondering about the special lady. Another poor woman who'd been hooked very effectively by David's line. She felt a sneaking sympathy for her.

29

"I'm pleased you decided to go to university, love," Linda said, reaching for Annie's hand and squeezing it. "You've done the right thing."

Annie nodded. "I'm going to study marketing, Linda. That's something to do with business," she added, seeing the blank expression, wondering if she would ever get through a conversation with Linda without sounding condescending. "Then I can help dad," she explained, realising that's what she had meant to do all along. She would help him so that maybe eventually they would be able to consider some of his hare-brained schemes as proper business ventures.

"We must stop meeting here." Linda giggled, looking round the sunken gardens. "I like to come here. It's my place for thinking, Annie."

Annie nodded, understanding that. When she'd seen Linda sitting on the bench, she'd hesitated, not sure if she wanted to talk to her or not. In the event, Linda had looked up and seen her so that was that.

It was a nice day, warmish, bits of blue in the sea and the sky, the spring flowers now filling the beds in a burst of yellows and pinks. "How are you, Linda? I haven't seen you for ages," she said. "I've been busy at school."

"I've been busy too. I've got a new job. Looking after a house, cleaning and everything."

"Oh . . . and that's all right? It's what you want?" Annie asked, a mite discomfited that Linda was so easily satisfied.

"You should see the house. It's in this lovely quiet avenue . . . I love looking after it. It beats dancing." Linda looked quite cheerful. There was something different about her that Annie couldn't quite pinpoint.

"And how's Blackbeard? Mustn't forget him," Annie asked, "Has he moved with you?"

"You bet. Getting on a treat now that he has a garden to play in. Brought in a baby bird yesterday that he'd mangled . . . it didn't even have any feathers the poor little bugger," she said with a frown. "Bit of a shock him doing that but I still love him. He can't help it. It's in his blood."

They shuddered in silent sympathy for the baby bird and Annie shifted uncomfortably on the wooden seat. Above, a seagull, solitary, whirled and swooped. "Whereabouts are you then? Still in Blackpool?"

The smile flitted. Proud. "No. Lytham. Posh eh? Never thought I'd end up there."

"I'd better have your new address then," Annie said, not sure why. It wasn't as if they'd be corresponding. She sifted through her pockets for a piece of paper to write it down. Found a pencil too. Poised it. Looked at Linda enquiringly.

"Well . . . I . . ." She blushed and looked as if she wanted the ground to swallow her up.

Annie quickly stuffed the paper and pencil away. "That's all right," she said easily, regretting that she'd been a bit pushy. Why would Linda want to keep in contact with her either? "Sorry. I didn't mean to pry."

They sat in silence. Awkward. Annie glanced at her curiously. She wasn't drowned in scent today. Nor was she so tarty-looking. Yes, that was it! She was wearing pale pink lipstick and less makeup than usual. Her earrings were tiny pearl studs. Her hair was newly coloured surely for there were no dark roots showing and she wore it twisted up on top of her head. Quite sophisticated.

"I'm not being funny about the address, love," Linda went on, her face a picture of worry, "I'm not supposed to tell anyone really but . . . well, she doesn't know that you and me have got close. Like sisters, aren't we? Sort of. Although that doesn't sound quite right, does it, sisters . . . not when . . . well, the thing is . . ." she stopped, hesitated, "I don't know as I should be telling you really. She did say not to. Put the fear of God into me. As if I'd breathe a word . . . She said as if I told anyone and it got back, then I'd be out. And the cat too. Between you and me, she's not too sweet on him. But he's not going anywhere. Where he goes, I go."

"Linda . . . you're not making any sense." Annie smiled, hardly bothering to listen as Linda twittered on. A woman and a girl strolled towards them, arm in arm, so alike, so obviously mother and daughter that Annie felt a twinge of sadness. For mum. For herself. She forced her attention back to Linda as she felt her arm gripped.

"Promise you won't breathe a word to a soul."

"Linda . . ." Annie stopped herself from shouting her exasperation. "What is it? I promise I won't tell anyone. All right?"

"Well . . . no, I'd better not. I've said too much already." Linda stood up, fussed a moment with her hair. "Your dad said I never could keep a secret. Well, he was wrong, wasn't he? I never told your mother about us. Never breathed a word. Saw her once, years ago, with you. I could have walked up to her and told her but I didn't. No . . ." She sniffed and zipped up her handbag ferociously. "I promised her and I don't break promises. Don't think badly of her, Annie. She just wanted to help me, that's all. As soon as I told her about your dad, what he'd done to me, she said she'd think of something. Nice of her, wasn't it? We grew up together, you see, and we're family although her side were always a bit snooty and snotty. Still . . . family ties and all, they count for a helluva lot, don't they?"

"I suppose they do," Annie conceded reluctantly, the gist of the conversation lost on her. She was great at going off at a tangent, was Linda. The original butterfly mind.

"Goodbye then." She patted Annie's shoulder. "Look after yourself, won't you?" The hesitation was brief. "And him."

Annie nodded, unexpectedly moved. She watched, a smile beginning to form, as Linda walked away. Even with flattish shoes, the hip wiggle was still there.

Dad's car was in the drive. He had been very subdued of late and Annie wondered if it was delayed reaction to mum's death. The spark had gone from him and it worried her. He was drinking a lot of whisky and smoking even more cigarettes. People like him, effervescent, enthusiastic, had been known to sink rapidly into depression.

"Not going out tonight, dad?"

He shook his head. "Can't be bothered," he said, "Just fancied a quiet night in. Any objections? If you want the place to yourself, boyfriend or something, just say." He smiled, but it lacked his usual ease, was just a bit forced. "In case you're wondering . . ." he said, stopping her in her tracks before she started preparing their meal, "The reason I'm not going out is that there's nobody to go out with. Your Miss Boyd and I are no longer seeing each other. It didn't work out. We've called it a day."

"Oh, I see." It was hardly a secret. Annie knew about the golf, the lunches, the occasional dinners, although, with the exception of the golf, most of the meetings had been conducted discreetly out of town, almost as if Miss Boyd was anxious not to be seen with him. Annie had been keeping it to herself. She didn't think anyone else had seen them together. He had told her one evening that he was taking Miss Boyd to the opera in Manchester. He'd told her almost shyly, taking ages to get himself ready, asking her advice on what to wear and finally going out armed with a bunch of flowers and reeking of a different aftershave. Returning late. Alone.

"We decided we weren't compatible," he went on, "Ridiculous wasn't it? It would never have worked." He swung his legs round and sat up, reaching for the inevitable cigarette. "Just to show her there were no hard feelings, I gave her a bloody huge donation for the school library."

"A donation?" Annie stared. He never ever gave donations for anything unless there was something in it for him. Publicity. "Did Miss Boyd ask you for it?"

"No." He puffed on the cigarette. "It was my idea."

"How much was it for, dad?"

"None of your business. A few thousand . . ." he added reluctantly. "Should fill a few shelves. She was pleased as punch about that. She's keen on books. Got her own library at home. You should see that bloody huge house in Lytham. She rattles round it like a pea in a drum. Has somebody in to look after it. Doesn't look the sort to be handy with a duster, does she?"

Miss Boyd had got him to give her a few thousand. Suddenly, Annie saw Miss Boyd sitting here on the sofa beside him that day. Cosily. Behaving in a peculiarly fluttery way. It dawned. It dawned. What was it Linda had twittered on about? Linda . . . who now lived in *Lytham*. Kept house in Lytham. Kept house for whom? Linda's inane twitterings were beginning to make some sort of sense.

"She offered to give it back," he said quietly, "Can you credit that? Suggesting that I'd only given it in the first place because I was after something." He flushed, avoided Annie's eyes. "I told her to keep it." His shoulders straightened and he dared look up.

"You did the right thing, dad." Annie tried to smile even though her heart ached for him. He had salvaged something then. Got away with some of his pride intact. You had to hand it to her, though, she was cool as a cucumber. Offered it back indeed? A double bluff that.

No wonder he was deflated. Defeated. An uncomfortable thought intruded even as she tried to think of some words of comfort, came up with nothing. When you got down to it, Miss Boyd couldn't have been that concerned about her. She, Annie, wasn't special in any way. It had all been a means to an end. Linda and Miss Boyd were related somehow. Just how, she had no wish to know. She wondered if he knew. If he didn't, she certainly was not going to tell him. If he did, she would pretend she did not. They had pretended once before. They were good at it.

"I'm sorry, dad," she said at last, the best she could manage. "You're right. It wouldn't have worked. You didn't have the same interests, did you? Opera and books?"

He laughed before fiercely grounding out the cigarette. "And she couldn't cook for toffee either. It was as bad as Linda's. She's gone by the way. Don't know where the hell to but what do I care?"

Question answered. Poor dad.

Annie went for a walk before tea. Leaving him alone. She'd wanted to put her arms around him and cuddle him but he was so angry, stiff with it, that she thought better of it. She should be feeling delighted that he had finally got what he deserved but she did not. She just knew as she stared out at the sea, soft and gentle today, that mum would not feel delighted either. Despite it all, they both loved him. He'd lost mum. He'd lost Linda. And now he'd lost Miss Boyd. Miss Boyd had meant something to him at that.

Annie determined she would see some good come of it. If dad agreed, they might get a picture in the local paper of him presenting his magnificent cheque to Miss Boyd. As dad's future marketing advisor, Annie had to start somewhere.

30

Daisy listened. She had said her piece. Now she listened to him. It had better be good. When he had finished, there was silence.

Then a pleading, "Daisy, please . . . forgive me."

"I'm not sure I can ever forgive you," she said, but the relief in her eyes belied her words. "You should have told me the truth instead of letting me think there was somebody else. And just leaving me a note. Honestly . . . That was really mean, Alan."

"Oh hell . . . I must have been mad. Gutless. At the time it seemed the easiest way. That way I didn't have to face you," he said, "I thought it best if you got me out of your system once and for all and that seemed the best way to do it. I thought if I could get you to hate me . . ." He sighed. "Bad thinking eh? I'm sorry, Daisy. I shouldn't have done it."

She shrugged. "I can see your point," she said, looking as if the thought was surprising herself as well as him, "Vaguely. After all, we both of us knew it wasn't working out as we planned. We rushed into it, didn't we?"

"Exactly. We needed to step apart and review the situation so to speak. You tried, Daisy, harder than I did. But we neither of us are used to living like that." He smiled sadly, "You could say that your interfering old grandmother did us both a favour."

"It was still wicked of you, Alan," Daisy said, taking up a favourite position on the floor, nearer to him, cross-legged. "Taking money off an old lady like that."

"Why not? She offered it." He grinned. "I couldn't believe it when she started off with £2,000. I'd have settled for £200."

"Pig." She laughed with him. "Gran's got too much money

that's the problem. Even so, you should not have taken it. You should have told her the truth, that we were probably going to finish it anyway. That we kept changing our minds from one day to the next."

"Don't worry, I shall give it her back some day. With interest. And, didn't I keep my side of the bargain? Haven't I kept out of her granddaughter's life?" His smile was slight, "I only called you because I couldn't stand it any longer. I had to tell you the truth. There never was anyone else, Daisy. There's only ever been you."

Daisy ignored that. "How are things going? Seriously?" She looked round at the canvasses spread about, "They're really beginning to sell at last?"

"Don't sound so surprised." He came to sit beside her, putting his arm round her and giving her a brief brotherly hug. His face was very close, his adored face, his eyes warm and loving. She was so very glad that there was nobody else. "I am talented you know. I have to make it just to show them that I can do it."

"Gran's finally found out who you are so beware. I overheard her actually hiring a private eye to find you. Can you credit that?" Daisy said, shrugging his arm off lightly, "She was dancing on air. She kept asking me what your surname was and I wouldn't tell her. She was so frustrated and then it finally dawned on her that you'd signed your painting which, by the way, she now considers to be not far short of a masterpiece. She so wants us to get married and it's such a shame to disappoint her. Can you imagine gran having aristocratic connections? It would be all over town. Perhaps we should get married just to please her."

"No fear." He grimaced and Daisy laughed again, aiming a mock blow at him. "Sorry, I didn't mean that to sound as it did," he said. "If I wanted to marry anyone, Daisy, then it would be you. But . . ."

"I know. We've been through this time and time again," Daisy said with a little sigh. "We're both of us too young to take on the responsibility. I can't believe sometimes that we're being so sensible about it. I suppose it's because we've both of us seen all our friends' marriages disintegrating around them . . ." She bit her lip. "We are doing the right thing, Alan, I know we are. Marriage just gets to be a big bore. Take my mother and father for instance. They don't argue much, they never have, but it's all very ordinary. Domestic, you know. I don't know if they even make love any more." She blushed. "But I think they're happy. One kind of love I suppose."

"Same with my parents. All they ever seem to talk about is domestic stuff. There's no romance left." He exchanged a sad smile with her. "I think you'd better break the news to your gran," he said thoughtfully. "Save her the trouble of coming to see me. The private eye will find me. No doubt about that. And then what? I don't want her coming here armed with her cheque book. She has no shame, that woman."

"How much am I worth this time?" Daisy giggled. "You must pay her back, Alan, as soon as you can afford it. It's an awful lot of money."

"Will she even miss it?" He kissed her on the cheek. "Come on, I've got to get these packed and then I'm off. I've decided to concentrate on paintings of cathedrals and churches. An artist doesn't like to think of marketing but it makes a sort of sense, doesn't it? Becoming known as an expert in a certain field? I do believe I've found my niche at last. I love churches. I love the shape and the feel of them. I love being inside them. Not in a religious sense but . . . well, perhaps it is in a religious sense. Do you think I'm doing the right thing in specialising?"

"Wait and see. You're very good at them. No . . . I mean it, Alan." Daisy scrambled to her feet. "I'd better get home." She hooked her mother's car keys round her finger. "There's only me there just now. Everybody's in America or Canada."

"Everybody?"

She ticked them off on her fingers. "Gran's gone to visit an equally ancient relative and mum's gone with her to look after her and dad's gone to a conference in Boston. With his secretary."

"And your mother let him?"

Daisy laughed. "You don't understand, Alan. It's all a devious plot concerning their silver wedding. The secretary's in on it. Oh . . . I can't explain but you're quite wrong about him. Dad's not like that at all."

"Believe me, most men are," he said, starting to sort out his paintings. "Want to take one of these?" he asked, "A present for you."

She hesitated. "They cost £150, Alan. I can't take one without paying."

"Don't argue. I want you to have one. Which one will it be?"

She looked at them all, taking a moment to decide. She chose a misty morning, wintry view of Durham. The view from their flat. She'd watched him painting it. She'd worn an old robe and closed her arms around him as he worked, asking seductively if she was getting in his way. With a groan of frustration, he'd whipped round to kiss her, splodged her with paint and worse, smudged the painting. She could still see the smudge. Or was it wishful thinking?

"Thanks," she said awkwardly, watching as he wrapped it. "I'll hang it up in my room at home. It'll remind me of you." She was feeling choked, not knowing quite when she would see him again. They were being very adult, very sensible about all this, reviewing their feelings coolly and calmly before diving headstrong into what would surely be a too-early marriage.

"No hard feelings about this, Daisy?" he asked, not looking at her, still sorting paintings out. "We are agreed on it, aren't we? We neither of us want to get married for a long time, do we? We both of us need to pursue our own careers and being married and having a family will just get in the way. You go off to university and I'll get on with my painting. Now and again, we'll meet up. It's what we agreed, isn't it?"

Daisy was glad he was turned away from her so that she could not see his eyes nor he hers. She was not sure but she thought she detected a trace of desperation in his voice. But she was not sure. She was also not sure if she was looking at him for the last time. She touched his back gently. "No hard feelings," she said.

31

As Barbara arrived in Toronto, Guy's plane sped him to Boston. The business would take a few days and he found he was looking forward to it. Making overseas contacts was always good for business and it would be a hectic round of formal discussions and chat. From his experience, the leisurely chats produced the most lucrative results.

He had been happy to show Barbara the conference notes, where she had spotted his name amongst the participants. It made it only half a lie then. She had not queried Gladys coming with him, although he didn't normally bring her along on overseas trips.

It was no more than Gladys deserved though, helping him out like she had without complaint. After the first day, when her appearance at his side would be useful, she was free to do whatever she wanted leaving him free to while away his time in Boston before driving up to Vermont in time for his wedding anniversary.

The hotel they were booked into was situated beside a shopping mall and Gladys spent the afternoon shopping. Guy relaxed in his room, watching television, drinking iced tea, trying to fathom out the finer points of baseball. Tomorrow, when Gladys was gone . . . jetting off to the west coast . . . he would have the opportunity after the morning's meeting, to do some sightseeing in Boston.

Things could still go wrong. Timing wise. He was relying on his mother to get Barbara to the hotel by the lake in time for their anniversary. Anticipation of their reunion flooded him. He and Barbara had been going through a bit of a rough patch lately and this would be a turning point. A second honeymoon no less. A chance to relax and enjoy each other. Just the two of them.

He had another look at the silver bracelet he had bought for her. His beautiful Barbara . . .

He switched the television off, none the wiser about baseball, and lay down on the bed. Missing her. He was feeling a bit weary after the long flight, a bit confused with the time difference. The ringing of the phone startled him and he reached over and picked it up, "Hello?"

"Room 514 here . . ." A laugh then an unnecessary, "It's me. Are we dining out or what?"

"Oh hello, Gladys. What do you want to do?"

"Dine out," she said at once. "With so many delegates here, you'll never get a moment's peace, will you? You'll be talking business non-stop."

"Very well." It mattered little to him, although he realised he was hungry because he never enjoyed a meal on the plane. "Any ideas?"

"I've been talking to the girl on the desk and she recommends one or two restaurants in town."

"Fine. We'll do that. When will you be ready?"

"Twenty minutes."

As he got ready, showered and changed, Guy couldn't help thinking about what Meg had told him before he came away. She'd made damned sure she told him. What was wrong with the woman that she possessed such a destructive, vicious mind? Suspicious conniving Meg. He'd never liked her, thinking of her as chill and humourless but he'd never thought her quite so vindictive. She felt it her duty to tell him, because in her opinion Barbara was behaving disgracefully with David Ambrose. She'd known there was something wrong as soon as Barbara talked about going to the funeral, she told him, something in Barbara's attitude, something in her voice when she mentioned David. She had been a little naughty about the cancer seminar, she confessed, turning up unexpectedly like that. That had really swamped Barbara's style. Sure enough, she had spotted David coming to the hotel to see Barbara next day, knowing it was him because Barbara had mentioned in passing he had a Rolls and she'd recognised him from the photographs, not been at all surprised by the swagger. Meg had told Guy that her arrival had caused a great furore as they had obviously had to change their plans to meet. David Ambrose had been expected for dinner. A table for two. She regretted telling him this but she repeated that it was her duty to do so. Sorry, Guy. He could rely totally on her and Howard to give him their full support in whatever he decided to do.

Guy was furious with Meg for interfering and, even more, for the gleeful way she had thrown the facts at him. What right had she to delve into their private lives? It would appear, and he wasn't entirely surprised, that Meg Fairley had it in for Barbara. Maybe it was because Barbara was better looking although that notion seemed silly in the extreme. One thing emerged out of it. He felt damned sorry for Howard. No wonder the poor fellow went round looking as anaesthetized as his patients. Meg's mind was sharp enough to put the needle in anyone.

It hurt though. It hurt bitterly. But it sadly confirmed what he had always suspected. Barbara loved David more than she loved him. Fact of life. That's why this second chance had to be snatched. He had to win her back.

The knock at his room door after precisely twenty minutes announced Gladys's presence. She was wearing black. Slimming. Smelling of flowers. Carrying a lightweight stole. "You look nice," he said, smiling at her as he checked he had his room key.

"So do you," she said.

They polished off a bottle of wine with their meal and they'd already had some booze on the plane. It was a very good meal. Gladys was good company too, thrilled to be here in the States for the very first time, looking forward to her coming trip. She told him all about it, what seemed to Guy an action packed itinerary, starting off with a few days in San Francisco.

"You will be back here for the 14th won't you?" he asked, "There mustn't be any delays. I can't allow mother to travel back to England alone."

"Of course I will be back," she said. Their meal was over and they were relaxing a moment before making a move. "I will be there to escort her home. Don't worry, Guy. You and your wife can go off wherever you're going . . ." She shrugged but he did not offer any information about their own itinerary. It would be simply a leisurely drive to wherever took their fancy, stopping off at first class hotels, having a wonderfully relaxing time.

Gladys's cheerful conversation had flagged a little by the time they were back at the hotel. They took the lift to their floor and, in the lift, she sagged against him, saying she felt a touch whoozy. "I can't drink," she said, "Three glasses of wine is too much for me."

"Two and a bit," he corrected, holding onto her arm as they stepped out into the hush of the thickly carpeted corridor.

He realised the mistake later when it was nearly too late. But somehow, and he couldn't remember quite how, he found himself in her room, sitting in the armchair by the window looking onto the darkening city, watching as she rummaged through the drinks refrigerator.

"You said you'd had enough," he remarked with a smile.

"Yes I have. Of course I have." She closed it firmly and stepped out of her shoes. "Don't go yet. We could watch a movie together. It's not that late." She dropped her hooped earrings onto the little table beside him. "I'll just freshen up. Won't be a minute." Before he could argue, she was going through to her adjoining bathroom, gently closing the door.

He had to hang on until she came back out. Baseball was flickering on the television screen again. Frowning, Guy tried to concentrate, but, after a while, his eyes closed. He was tired. Not surprising because, taking the time difference into account, it was really about three o'clock in the morning. It *was* late. He wanted his bed. He needed all his wits about him for the rough and tumble of the business that beckoned in the morning.

"That's better." She was back, wearing a simple full length silky dress. Housecoat or something. Zipped to the neck anyway. It was a deep green, very flattering to her colouring, and she was barefoot. Little traces of talcum powder padded onto the plain dark carpet as she came over and sat in the other chair, switching on lamps as she did so, so that the light softened to a pinkish glow. Below and far beyond the window, the lights of the city blinked. She did not draw the curtains for there was nobody to see.

The chairs were a mere few inches away from her bed. Another colossal American bed. A little late in the day, it hit him and he rued his slowness. This was what was known as a compromising situation and he was a fool to have landed himself in it. Gladys had got it all wrong. Unfortunately, he had wined and dined her yet again and here he was in her room. She could be forgiven for getting it wrong.

"Switch that off, Guy," she said quietly, looking at him, any pretence there might have been evaporating with the look. "I can't stand baseball."

Perversely, he clicked the sound up a notch. He felt better with it on. The rapid excited commentary denied the cosiness she wanted. Nevertheless, he rose from the chair, feeling more comfortable on his feet. "Gladys . . . we'd better get one thing quite clear," he said, regretting the pompous note that had crept into his voice, wondering how to say this without causing her deep offence. "I'm a married man," he continued inanely, "I realise that all this . . . the dancing, the meals out . . . may have been a bit unusual but as far as I'm concerned, it's only been for one reason. And one reason only." He stopped. Stepped nearer the door.

She stood perfectly still, the sexy look in her eyes gone as swiftly as it had appeared. "Guy . . ." she said, her voice a whisper, her attempt at a smile not working, "You're not trying to tell me that I've misunderstood. Good heavens . . . you needn't have taken me out to dinner, you needn't have brought me here. I've had to put up with all sorts of coy remarks from the rest of the girls. What was I to think? I know you're a bit shy and I thought that . . ." her voice tailed off and she bit her lip.

"I'm sorry," he said unhappily, "If I've somehow given you the impression that . . ." he looked across at her. Her hair, freshly brushed, was beautiful. Gold bits. Red bits. Her eyes were deeply brown and thoughtful. He liked her very much. "I'm flattered," he said at last. "Some day, Gladys, some man's going to be very lucky."

Bad choice of words. She sniffed her contempt. The mood gone. "I probably won't see you in the morning," she said, no longer looking at him, "I have to be off early. I will make sure that nothing goes wrong with the other arrangements."

He understood her need to be alone. He didn't know what to say, what to do. A pat on the shoulder was insulting, a kiss on the cheek would be unthinkable. Anything he said could be misconstrued. He'd made a complete mess of it all. After all, he had suspected from the very beginning that she had a bit of a thing for him so this was hardly a complete surprise.

"Thank you again," he said, at the door. "I couldn't have done any of this without you."

"I'll look for another job when I get back," she said quietly, her voice steady and composed. "No . . . it's the only way. How can we work together now? How can I face them in the office?"

"Hell . . . if I'd known, Gladys, that this would happen . . ."

"You weren't to know." She looked at him, apparently resigned to it now. "I'm sorry. I feel a bit of a fool."

"You've no need to." Guy managed a rueful smile, "You're a very attractive woman, Gladys. Believe me, if it weren't for Barbara . . ."

She smiled too, although her eyes were sad. "I hope everything goes okay for you and your wife . . . she's lucky to have you, Mr Shawcross. I just hope she realises it, that's all."

The return to "Mr Shawcross" leapt out. He poured himself a stiff drink when he got back to his room. He'd never been seduced before. Well . . . nearly. For a moment there, it was tempting to give in. Nobody would have known. He didn't feel virtuous, however, not a bit. He felt as much of a fool as Gladys. More so. By his crass actions, he'd just managed to lose a bloody good secretary, he knew that much.

The glowing surprise he'd planned for Barbara suddenly seemed less wonderful. It had better work out, that's all, or it would have been all for nothing. Gladys loved him. He loved Barbara. And Barbara . . .? He shut his mind to what Meg had told him.

32

Ever since she arrived in Canada, it had been all systems go. Barbara was quite exhausted by the frenzied pace. The old ladies acted like there was no tomorrow, although, sadly for Phoebe, there weren't that many tomorrows. A few days relaxation at last was promised and from the inn overlooking the lake, Barbara stared out at the view. It was breathtaking, particularly so now in the early evening, the waters of the lake silent and shimmering, wonderfully peaceful and relaxing and she wished Guy was here to share it instead of Leila and Phoebe. Damn it all, she missed him. She was beginning to feel very much the odd woman out for the two old dears were constantly huddled together in a corner, talking about old times. Phoebe was worryingly like Leila, a Canadian version although she considered herself still to be English. Forty five years living in Canada did not make her a Canadian she was at pains to point out. You sound like one, you have an atrocious accent, Leila said to her, and what happened to your dress sense?

It was like that all the time. A fond sort of bickering and it was starting to get Barbara down. Since they'd arrived up in Toronto, Phoebe, or rather the man who drove her round, had dragged them onto trips here there and everywhere, places Phoebe had treasured memories of, places she wanted to see once more before she died. Barbara found it extraordinary. She wasn't entirely sure that, if she knew she was dying shortly, she would want to have a whistle-stop tour of places from her past. Whilst Barbara found it upsetting, the two of them talked about Phoebe's impending departure cheerfully and without embarrassment. Whilst Phoebe chatted incessantly about any subject under the sun, the more controversial the better, she refused to discuss her illness. Point blank.

Time dragged on, seeming to mean nothing to either of them, and a few days ago Barbara had reluctantly conceded that she wouldn't be home in time for their anniversary.

They were now in America, in Vermont, staying a few days at a lovely old inn overlooking Lake Champlain and today was her wedding anniversary. There were cards from Leila and Phoebe. Guy would be back in Harrogate by now and she had tried, time and time again, to phone home but there had been no reply. Where the hell were Daisy and Guy? It was quite ridiculous. Whoever heard of a couple actually being apart on such a day? The annoying thing was that he wouldn't know where on earth she was so she couldn't seriously expect a phone call from him either.

She felt an overwhelming irritation towards her mother-in-law for landing her in this situation, followed immediately by guilt because all this could not be helped and it was disgraceful of her to deprive the two old ladies of a little happiness together. Had the pair of them been as outrageous when they were young? Hearing the giggles in a corner, it was hard to remember sometimes that they had a combined age of well over a hundred and fifty.

There was a tap at the door and Leila popped round, "Aren't you ready?" she asked, coming in fully as she saw Barbara was. slumped in a chair by the balcony still in a towelling robe. "Phoebe and I are. We are also hungry. Or at least I am, you know poor Phoebe's appetite is gone."

"Then you go down," Barbara said shortly. "I don't know that I shall bother, Leila. Frankly, I'm sick of hotel food. What I wouldn't give for just a poached egg on toast. I may order something from room service."

"You'll do no such thing," Leila said, a choker sparkling at her throat, "Anyway, the food here is renowned. Phoebe says it has such a good reputation. We've booked a table by the window so that we can look out at the view and, after dinner, we shall dance. I thought you of all people would appreciate a dinner dance, my dear. They do say the band is very good."

Barbara grimaced. It looked as if Leila and Phoebe might

well have dancing partners as there were a couple of elderly gentlemen staying with whom they had struck up a friendship. She was damned if she was going to have Leila taking pity on her, alone, and suggesting they should dance together. There was no way she was going to accompany Leila on the floor. She would sit it out and watch and listen to the music. Why not?

She had a new dress with her, bought in Montreal. Shopping there had been the highlight of the trip and something she would not have missed. She'd foolishly not realised they would speak quite so much *French* there, but, fortunately for them, Phoebe rattled off the language with ease leaving her and Leila struggling gamely in her wake. Fortunately too, the French Canadians switched to English directly they knew whom they were chatting to, but it succeeded in making Barbara feel inadequate. Damn it, when she got home, she was going to brush up on it, make a determined effort.

Leila helped her choose the dress and it was green, a particular shade she had not worn for years. She had to admit she liked it. The dress was very plain with a deep vee neckline and she decided it needed no jewellery, just earrings, simple gold studs. Shooing Leila out, not forgetting to comment favourably on *her* new dress, she went to have a shower.

33 ∫

The shock of Guy's arrival, when she was sitting wallflower-like, watching the others dance, caused a tremor of indignation and anger. Speechless for a moment, she stared at him as he very politely asked for a dance. "What the hell are you doing here?" she asked as soon as they were on the little dance-floor. "You're supposed to be home. I've been trying to ring you, dammit. Do you realise it's our wedding anniversary?"

"Of course I do," he murmured, drawing her a little closer. "Happy anniversary, my love. This is my surprise to you."

"What is?" She leaned back and looked up at him. "You being here?"

He nodded. "That and the tune they're playing. Listen . . ." He smiled and she obliged and listened. " 'Moonlight in Vermont,' " he explained needlessly.

"So . . .?" she asked, puzzled. "It's lovely but they're always playing it. Somebody always requests it."

"Quite." A triumphant note in his voice. "Appropriate isn't it seeing that it happens to be our tune," he said, becoming a bit put out as Barbara remained impassive. "Surely you recognise it? It was the tune they were playing when we first danced together. At the Tower Ballroom, Blackpool. Don't tell me you've forgotten?"

Barbara grimaced as he stood on her foot, "I remember you couldn't dance," she said tartly, "Some things don't change."

"Hell . . . I've been taking lessons. I've got a certificate." He managed a smile, "Gladys was my partner in crime."

So that was it. "Tuesdays and Thursdays?"

He nodded. "Cost me a small fortune. I had to pay for her lessons too. And I had to buy her a few dinners."

"Where is she? Gladys?"

"California. All part of the plan," he said with a smile, "She's going to take mother home while you and me go off together. Wherever you want to go . . ."

She glanced at him sharply. Something in his voice. Gladys Ward was becoming something of a thorn in her flesh. "And I suppose Daisy knew all about it too." She laughed, finally accepting that she had been well and truly duped. Guy was suddenly concentrating too much to share her amusement, catching her foot again and apologising with a very irritated look on his face. Barbara glanced towards Leila who was sitting at the side of the room, engaged in earnest conversation with Phoebe. "And those two knew all about it, too. I might have known."

They paused, politely applauding with the other dancers as the music stopped, before changing to an up-beat number.

"Mother's extremely good at being devious," Guy said, brightening as he executed a clever little manoeuvre. "You were fooled, weren't you?" he said. "Come on, admit it, you never had the slightest idea? You thought I'd forgotten? As if I'd forget my own silver wedding anniversary." He did a few fancy steps, triumphant, and Barbara could hear him mentally counting. "I had to get you to Vermont just so we would be here when they played the tune. I asked them to play it by the way. I thought you'd be pleased . . ."

"Oh Guy . . . you are priceless." She pulled away, "Let's sit this one out."

She sensed his relief as she drew him off the floor. Then she told him.

"Are you sure?" He was horrorstruck.

"Absolutely." She felt a smile beginning. "My God, Guy, what an expensive mistake for you to make. We could have popped over to Paris for a whole lot less."

"April in Paris," he said tonelessly. "Chestnuts in blossom . . ."

"Etc." She felt a giggle beginning at the look on his face but managed to control it.

"I wasn't that far out," he said, slipping his arm round her waist. "Same sort of tunes, same sort of sentiments."

"Wrong continent." The giggle emerged and she felt him shake too. Sometimes, but not for some time now, they had silly little attacks of the giggles like this. In this decorous atmosphere, it was hardly welcome. But they couldn't stop themselves.

Barbara knew he was holding something back. She also knew that, if she asked, he would tell her. However, she was going to let it drift by, whatever it was. Some things were best left unsaid.

Guy could have kicked himself. Damn it, they *were* similar tunes so the confusion was understandable. He now knew he was not going to tell her about Gladys, about the way things might have turned out. What was the point of that? She would not tell him about David either, not the whole truth but he sensed whatever it was, it was over. And some things were best left unsaid.

34

They sat in a corner, the two old dears, crisply coiffeured and prettily perfumed, looking as if they were chatting about crochet patterns.

"Sex is overrated," Leila said as they knocked back the gin. "And talked about much too often these days. Sex, sex, sex."

"You and Charles always seemed so well suited in that way," Phoebe said brightly, smiling as someone frowned in their direction. Leila had a penetrating voice. "Do you mean to say it was never satisfactory?" she asked, lowering her own.

"I didn't say that," Leila said, "He was greedy. And devilishly attractive as you well know. Did he ever make a pass at you, dear?"

Phoebe shook her head and they smiled, watching as Guy and Barbara waltzed by to the tune of "Moonlight in Vermont". Leila looked across a little anxiously. "Oh dear, look at him, Phoebe, he's supposed to have had dancing lessons. He's no Fred Astaire, is he?"

Phoebe clicked her tongue, her attention diverted for a moment as the waiter brought more drinks. She was splendidly extravagant in purple, a dress that she too had bought on their shopping expedition in Montreal. "Never mind that," she said. "They look nice together."

"They always did." Leila regarded them with satisfaction. If you tried not to notice Guy's feet, they did look good together.

"I do so love this part of the country and I'm so happy to see it again," Phoebe went on. "Hugh and I spent some time together here before he passed on." She stopped, suddenly unable to continue.

Leila took her eyes off her son and daughter-in-law who were now off the floor and giggling in a corner and smiled at Phoebe. Phoebe looked very frail and old. They fell silent, both remembering Hugh.

"Drink up," Leila said at last, brightening with an effort. "I've never thanked you properly for what you did. I must say it was a stroke of genius you writing that you were dying. That did it, you know. It added the touch of urgency and Barbara simply had to agree to come with me. I also gave the impression that I was a touch forgetful which instantly got her worried. When I phoned you, I merely meant you to pen a general letter inviting me to visit sometime. There was no need for such drama." She smiled, "I might have known. You and I are a devious couple, are we not?"

"Oh Leila, it's true," Phoebe's voice was strangely flat even allowing for the nasal tones of her unfortunate accent. Leila glanced sharply at her. "When you rang, I thought we might as well use it to our advantage. There has to be some advantage."

"What do you mean?" Leila stared at her, horrified as Phoebe quite calmly sipped her gin. "You're joking. You can't be dying." Her voice had risen and she steadied it, holding her glass in both hands as she felt them tremble. "Everybody else dies but we keep going, you and me." She stopped for Phoebe was very quiet. "Why didn't you tell me sooner?" she asked. "I had no idea. I wouldn't have been so flippant if I had known."

"I like you to be flippant as you put it." Phoebe managed a slight smile. "Six months at the most, Leila. I don't know if I'll make it to that wedding you're planning for Daisy."

"Perhaps we can bring it forward . . ." Leila gulped, not able to carry on. How very stupid. She reached across the table and held Phoebe's hand. Their eyes glittered and neither of them could say another word.

Having raided the drinks cabinet in her room, Leila was now mildly inebriated. Well at least Guy and Barbara seemed happy, having gone off to bed rather early, full of smiles. Now . . . where was Daisy's letter? She found it and read it again slowly, focussing with some difficulty.

Daisy and Alan were back in touch, it would seem, and after careful consideration, for all sorts of wonderfully commendable reasons, they had decided not to pursue their relationship. Daisy was going to study economics and Alan was to continue to paint his rather wonderful wistful watercolours. They, neither of them, would marry for several years nor was there any commitment on either side. Incidentally gran, Daisy wrote, Alan offered his apologies for taking the money from her and promised to pay it back at the earliest possible opportunity.

Leila let the letter waft onto the desk. The pair of them did not know what they were talking about as it was perfectly obvious that they were head over heels in love. The whole business was a ridiculous misunderstanding. When she returned home, she would try once more with Alan, plead with him to follow his heart, plead also with Daisy. There simply had to be a wedding in autumn. She had set her heart on it.

Once Phoebe was gone, she would be alone. Nobody else of her generation left in the world, not one of the jolly old crowd. She had outlived the lot of them but it left only a hollow feeling. She shivered as she realised they all had a head start up there.

No matter. No time for self pity. She had things to do. Even though she was dreadfully tired, she unpinned her hair and brushed it free. She wondered if she could tolerate another gin and tonic but decided against it. Phoebe would very likely be a wet rag in the morning and one of them had to have her wits. With a sigh, she returned to the paper on the desk. She hoped she would not need to compose another list so this was merely a contingency plan. She needed three more candidates then for marriage to dearest Daisy.

Didn't Michael Findlay-Smith have a brother Andrew? Chartered something or other so he was worth a try. And what about the Rutherfords, dreadfully dull the parents but that did not mean that the son would be equally so. And of course James Parker whose family had suffered the most appalling mishaps over the years, forever poised on the brink of catastrophe, lurching from one calamity to another. Their bad luck couldn't last for much longer surely. She would leave him to the last for she refused to have tragic faces on the wedding photographs and James's mother Ellen was so mournful-looking. Poor woman. One of the others would surely come up trumps.

In the meantime, she would revise the guest list. One or two deletions and a couple of additions. She pulled paper towards her and began to write.

35

The cheque had been cashed so he could kiss goodbye to that. By God, was he angry. He didn't like being made a fool of and Miss High and Mighty had done that. The courtship had been going well, slowly does it, restaurant meals, even a trip to the opera in Manchester that had cost a fortune and bored him rigid. Just to please her. In other words a gentle getting to know each other. He'd sent her flowers, not roses, but a mixed bunch of blooms he had chosen himself that he thought she would particularly like, creams and whites. He had tried so hard. Tried not to swear so much, tried not to sound so uncouth, not to smoke so much. Tried, dammit.

And then she invited him again to her home for dinner and something in her expression had told him that this would be it, confessions of everlasting love time. His heart had pounded like a lovesick youth at the prospect. He hadn't known what the hell to wear. He'd bought a new, rather sober shirt. Striped tie. He'd even asked Annie's advice.

As he drove to Lytham, he went over what he would say, rehearsing it, rephrasing it when it seemed daft, trying not to be so bloody corny this time. He was going to be so gentle with her, so tender. He had even been fool enough to buy an engagement ring. She had waited until after their meal before she told him. Many regrets of course and he supposed you could say she'd let him down gently. He wouldn't know. He'd never been let down before, not properly. And yet, she somehow, bitch that she was, managed to convey very clearly the reasons why. He wasn't good enough. He had been fun for a while, her bit of rough maybe, but long-term it just wasn't on. That's when she had offered to give him his donation back. He'd had to grip his chair because his instant reaction had been to tell her to stuff the donation. He'd kept his cool. Told her, off-handedly, she could keep it. Insinuating there was plenty more where that came from.

Recalling the moment with a shudder, David stared out at the sea from the dunes. His house opposite now had a For Sale board hammered into the front lawn but he couldn't care a damn about that. The warm soft sand sifted over his shoes but he did not notice, staring out at the sludgy brown of the sea, seeing it rolling gently in. He pulled the jewellery box out of his pocket and opened it, staring at the solitary diamond as it glittered coldly at him. Nothing flashy because he thought she wouldn't like that. This had been for her. For Felicity. To be followed by a wide gold band. Felicity would have been a good second mum to Annie. Annie liked her. Annie wouldn't have minded.

He had nobody. Annie would be gone soon and he had nobody. Fifty was knocking at the door and he had nobody, not even little Ruthie. He sighed, controlling the stupid sob, feeling tears welling in his eyes. Thank Christ, there was nobody to see him. Come on, buck up. He could end it all now this minute, walk into the sea, let the water slip over him, welcome it. That way, old age would never catch up with him. He'd be remembered as he was now. In his prime. Just as Ruth would never grow old. He couldn't imagine what she would have looked like. Old.

He looked towards the water and wondered how far out he would have to go before it was deep enough to slip over his head. He knew he would not. He hadn't got the guts for that. He didn't want people wisely nodding their heads, saying they didn't think he was coping very well, saying that Linda had left him too, and wasn't his daughter going off to university so that he'd be on his own. No wonder he'd topped himself, poor soul! They'd end up feeling sorry for him and he wasn't having that. He needed to get back to work fast, get something moving, recoup some of the money that he'd squandered on library books.

He drove sedately to the office, still feeling shaky, and, almost to his surprise, everything at the office was normal, so very normal. It didn't seem right for things to be so normal, not after the humiliation he'd suffered.

Annie was right about the donation. Good PR that. She had all her wits about her, did his daughter, pity she'd not got some of his zest too. Still too po-faced for his liking. Still, he wouldn't mind her working for him when she finished university. Having a graduate on the books would stir some of that crowd up, raise the tone a little.

About the donation . . . Someone else would have to drop the news, of course, and he'd reluctantly own up to it, like Annie suggested. He could see the headline "Local Businessman Funds School Library". He'd better get some quotes ready for when they came to interview him and knock a few years off his age too.

He spent a full hard morning at his desk, organising, sorting out, telephoning, looking over some new contracts. The bowling alley was completed, finance and papers through, and he anticipated opening in summer. Get the show on the road eh? He saw it as a winner. With all the visitors this place had, quite a hefty number would end up ten-pinning and fast-fooding it. There'd be an adjacent café for that. Special discount offers too for the nightclub and disco. Bit of marketing linkage there.

He had a sandwich at lunchtime, rolled up his sleeves and worked on and gradually, oh so gradually, the pain eased, the shock diminished. He'd been a fool over Miss High and Mighty just as he'd been a fool over Barbara and Linda. The only trouble with Felicity was that she'd really conned him. He had genuinely begun to feel a real affection for her, began to think that this was a woman he could spend the rest of his life with. With her intellect, she could have pulled him up the social scale a bit more, made him a helluva lot more acceptable to the nobs, smoothed out the rough edges. He had fallen in love with her. Just as, years ago, years and years ago, he had fallen in love with Barbara. He had buggered that one up too.

Tired, he called it a day, snatching his jacket and briefcase and exiting via the stairs. Running down them. Keep fit that was the ticket. Maybe he'd take up some exercise, start jogging, join a gym, maybe even open a gym, a fitness centre, as a lot of people were keen on that sort of crap. Perhaps he'd even give up smoking. Or drinking. He couldn't give up both.

He crossed the lobby quickly, pulling the car keys from his pocket. The little redhead was there, trying to hide behind a potted palm when she saw him. "Not you again," he said irritably, as he passed. "You can't stay away, can you?"

"I'm waiting for . . ."

"Don't bother," he growled and then he stopped. Something in her expression. He pretended to be searching in his briefcase just to give himself a moment to think. She was very young. Far too young. However, a little harmless fun would not go amiss. He would not be contemplating marriage again for some time to come, not after this last fiasco.

He smiled and glanced at his watch. "We never did get that bite to eat," he said, "I know this very discreet restaurant. How about it, sweetheart?"

She nodded. And fluttered her eyelashes.

God . . . he'd give it one more time.

In the privacy of their hotel room, Barbara slipped the bracelet on, admired it. "Your present's at home," she told Guy, reaching up to kiss him. "All these convoluted arrangements of yours . . ."

"Want to dance?" He pulled her close, moved and she moved with him. "See . . . I'm fine if nobody's watching. As soon as I get an audience, I go to pieces."

"Is this a waltz, Guy?" Barbara asked mischievously.

"Of course," he said. "What else? You'll have to imagine the music."

She did. Dancing in the confined space of their room, the lake outside now darkly cool, she imagined more than the music. Remembered the ballroom that first night, the lights, the glitter. All the old crowd. David and Ruth. Poor Ruth. Poor David.

Here she was, still dancing with Guy, and it was much the same when you got down to it. Twenty five years give or take. But this time, she didn't feel the need to show off to David for she rather liked being here alone with Guy. She nestled against his shoulder, that same sturdy shoulder, and it was where she wanted to be. She listened to him, unmusically humming his version of their tune, and smiled.

Exclusive CDs to enhance your reading pleasure

There is nothing better than a relaxing read and nothing quite like your favourite music to compliment your mood.

Each of the CD compilations are performed by the world's top artists. The choice is yours, all you need to do is send £1.98*per CD to cover postage and handling and indicate which CDs you would like. Please allow up to 28 days for delivery.

HOW TO GET YOUR CDS:
Simply complete the coupon below with the quantity of each CD you wish to purchase and send with your cheque to Hodder Headline CD offer, P.O. Box 2000, Romford, RM3 8GP.

Hodder Headline CD offer
Please send me:
Qty.........HH01 Essential Opera @ £1.98 p&h each
Qty.........HH02 Classical Masterpieces @ £1.98 p&h each
Qty.........HH03 Rockin' n' Reading' Hits of the 60's @ £1.98 p&h each
Qty.........HH04 Unmistakably Jazz @ £1.98 p&h each
Qty.........HH05 Movie Sensations @ £1.98 p&h each
Qty.........HH06 Gregorian Chants @ £1.98 p&h each
*Please note these prices apply to the UK addresses only. Please see below for other areas.

Enclose a cheque/postal order payable to FM LTD. Please write your name and address on the back of your cheque/postal order.

Name & Address...

....

....Postcode ☐☐☐☐☐☐☐☐

POSTAGE AND HANDLING PAYMENT METHOD
UK & Ireland – Cheques or Postal Orders ONLY £1.98 per CD
Europe including Eire – Eurocheque in £Sterling ONLY or Visa/Mastercard Credit Cards £3.25 per CD
Rest of the World including USA and Canada – Eurocheque in £Sterling ONLY or Visa/Mastercard Credit Cards £4.25 per CD

Please debit £................ from my ☐ Visa ☐ Access

Card No ☐☐☐☐☐☐☐☐☐☐☐☐☐☐☐☐

Expiry Date ☐☐ Signature...

ENQUIRY HOTLINE: 01708 336888
If you do not wish to receive further mailings for products within the Hodder Headline Group or carefully selected companies please tick here. ☐ Offer subject to availability. Please allow up to 28 days for delivery.